Her body felt like a glass of bubbly champagne. Every nerve ending was sparkling, creating a satisfying buzz that ran from her lips to her toes. Granger's mouth was warm over hers, a welcome contrast to the biting cold around them.

They both pulled back at the same time, coming up for air.

"Don't tell me that was a mistake," she said softly. "We both wanted that kiss."

"It wasn't a mistake." Granger looked at her. The brown of his eyes seemed darker suddenly.

"So what do we do now?" Because she wanted to keep kissing him but she didn't want to mess up their friendship.

"I have no idea." He reached out and touched her arm. "We can't bring my daughters into…whatever this is. I don't want them getting confused or getting their hopes up about us."

Joy swallowed. She didn't need to get her hopes up either. "Not that we're dating," she said. "We just kissed. Two times."

"Let's make that three," Granger said, leaning in.

PRAISE FOR ANNIE RAINS AND HER SWEETWATER SPRINGS SERIES

Sunshine on Silver Lake

"Readers will have no trouble falling in love with Rains' realistically flawed hero and heroine as they do their best to overcome their pasts and embrace their futures. A strong cast of supporting characters—especially Emma's stepmother, Angel, and the many returning faces from earlier books— underpin Rains' engaging prose and perfectly paced plot. Lovers of small-town tales won't be able to resist."

—*Publishers Weekly*

Starting Over at Blueberry Creek

"This gentle love story, complete with cameos from fan-favorite characters, will enchant readers."

—*Publishers Weekly*

"A sweet, fun, and swoony romantic read that was both entertaining and heartfelt."　　　—TheGenreMinx.com

Snowfall on Cedar Trail

"Rains makes a delightful return to tiny Sweetwater Springs, N.C., in this sweet Christmas-themed contemporary. Rains highlights the happily-ever-afters of past books, making even new readers feel like residents catching up with the town gossip and giving romance fans plenty of sappy happiness."

—*Publishers Weekly*

"Over the past year I've become a huge Annie Rains fangirl with her Sweetwater Springs series. I'm (not so) patiently waiting for Netflix or Hallmark to just pick up this entire series and make all my dreams come true."

—CandiceZablan.com

Springtime at Hope Cottage

"A touching tale brimming with romance, drama, and feels! I really enjoyed what I found between the pages of this newest offering from Ms. Rains...Highly recommend!"

—RedsRomanceReviews.blogspot.com

"A wonderfully written romance that will make you wish you could visit this town."   —RomancingtheReaders.com

"Annie Rains puts her heart in every word!"
—Brenda Novak, *New York Times* bestselling author

"Annie Rains is a gifted storyteller, and I can't wait for my next visit to Sweetwater Springs!"
—RaeAnne Thayne, *New York Times* bestselling author

Christmas on Mistletoe Lane

"Top Pick! Five stars! Romance author Annie Rains was blessed with an empathetic voice that shines through each character she writes. *Christmas on Mistletoe Lane* is the latest example of that gift."

—NightOwlReviews.com

"The premise is entertaining, engaging and endearing; the characters are dynamic and lively...the romance is tender

and dramatic...A wonderful holiday read, *Christmas on Mistletoe Lane* is a great start to the holiday season."
—TheReadingCafe.com

"Settle in with a mug of hot chocolate and prepare to find holiday joy in a story you won't forget."
—RaeAnne Thayne, *New York Times* bestselling author

"Don't miss this sparkling debut full of heart and emotion!"
—Lori Wilde, *New York Times* bestselling author

"How does Annie Rains do it? This is a lovely book, perfect for warming your heart on a long winter night."
—Grace Burrowes, *New York Times* bestselling author

ALSO BY ANNIE RAINS

Christmas on Mistletoe Lane

A Wedding on Lavender Hill (novella)

Springtime at Hope Cottage

Kiss Me in Sweetwater Springs (novella)

Snowfall on Cedar Trail

Starting Over at Blueberry Creek

Sunshine on Silver Lake

SEASON OF JOY

ANNIE RAINS

FOREVER

NEW YORK BOSTON

Copyright © 2020 by Annie Rains

Cover design and illustration by Elizabeth Turner Stokes
Cover copyright © 2020 by Hachette Book Group, Inc.

Bonus novella *The Christmas Wish* by Melinda Curtis © 2019 by Melinda Wooten

Forever
Hachette Book Group
1290 Avenue of the Americas, New York, NY 10104
read-forever.com
twitter.com/readforeverpub

First Edition: October 2020

Forever is an imprint of Grand Central Publishing. The Forever name and logo are trademarks of Hachette Book Group, Inc.

The publisher is not responsible for websites (or their content) that are not owned by the publisher.

The Hachette Speakers Bureau provides a wide range of authors for speaking events. To find out more, go to www.hachettespeakersbureau.com or call (866) 376-6591.

ISBN: 978-1-5387-0092-1 (mass market), 978-1-5387-0091-4 (ebook)

Printed in the United States of America

OPM

10 9 8 7 6 5 4 3 2 1

ATTENTION CORPORATIONS AND ORGANIZATIONS:

Most Hachette Book Group books are available at quantity discounts with bulk purchase for educational, business, or sales promotional use. For information, please call or write:

Special Markets Department, Hachette Book Group
1290 Avenue of the Americas, New York, NY 10104
Telephone: 1-800-222-6747 Fax: 1-800-477-5925

*For David Hemby, my dad and
the greatest storyteller I know*

Acknowledgments

'Tis the season to make a list and check it twice. My list of those who've helped me with this book, and in my author career, is long. I'm so thankful to every person who has offered their time, knowledge, and support in bringing Joy and Granger's story to life.

First, I want to thank my family. With every book, I have a greater understanding of my family's own sacrifice to help me bring these books to the shelves. Thank you, Sonny, Ralphie, Doc, and Lydia, for making sure I have the time I need to get these stories written down. You are my personal heroes every day, and I love you all so much!

Secondly, my editor Alex Logan deserves an award greater than my thanks. I do believe I have the most amazing editor in the world (I might be biased), and I'm so lucky to have worked with you on this series. I'm also in awe of my publisher, Grand Central / Forever. Thanks to everyone who works so hard behind the scenes!

I also believe I have the most wonderful agent in the world in Sarah Younger (again, I could be biased). Thank you, Sarah, for your encouragement, advice, support, etc., etc., etc.! You are amazing!

Thank you to Rachel Lacey for always being my first reader—you make my stories so much better! Thank you to Tif Marcelo for your constant cheerleading in this author journey—some days that's the difference between putting words on paper or procrastinating because they won't come easy. Thank you (again) to my husband, Sonny, for helping me plot and develop the apple cider recipe in the back of this book. I also want to thank my mother-in-law, Annette Rains, for taking care of the kids while I plotted and drafted this book last summer. I'm not sure I could've written this story without that added time to focus.

This book is dedicated to my dad, David Hemby, who I also want to thank here in my acknowledgments. Mom often says, "I don't know where you got your writing talent." I do believe the answer is from you. You are a master storyteller. I learned from watching and listening to you over the years. Thank you for that, and for being an amazing father above all.

Last, but never least, I want to thank my readers for returning to Sweetwater Springs again and again, story after story. Your kind words, reviews, and support are such a gift. Thank you. I hope this holiday season is a merry one for all of you!

CHAPTER ONE

Joy Benson picked up her pace, walking faster as she burrowed into the depths of her lightweight jacket. Fall in Sweetwater Springs was as chilly as it was beautiful. As an artist, she could appreciate how the colors of the valley changed from varied golds and greens to deep crimsons. Try as she might, she'd never fully captured the magic of it on a canvas, but one day...

Her steps slowed as she approached an empty storefront in the downtown area. Wasn't this the old clockmaker's shop? Where had it gone? Joy guessed there wasn't a lot of need for handmade clocks anymore, but still, the shop had once been a living, breathing part of Main Street. Now it stood vacant—and a little sad.

Joy eyed the time on her cell phone. She was already running late but she couldn't help taking a moment to cup her hands over the glass and peer inside. She'd been looking for a place to open an art gallery. A place where she could display and sell her work along with other pieces from local potters, sculptors, and artists like her who dabbled in everything. For a while now, she'd run a successful Etsy store online. Her goal at the start of this year, however, was to find a physical location to work out of. A place where she could also teach her classes instead of doing so at the local library.

This place would be perfect.

Except for the tiny detail that this was Main Street, a location that was undoubtedly out of her price range. That was especially true now that her car had decided to die and she was using a chunk of her savings to fix it. Which was why she was walking to the library this afternoon. And if she didn't hustle, she'd be late for the class she was scheduled to teach there.

Reluctantly, Joy turned from the store window. It wouldn't hurt to call the real estate agent handling the property later and at least inquire about the details. Maybe by some miracle it wasn't out of her price range. The season of miracles was almost upon her after all. Not that Joy had ever experienced a Christmas miracle herself. In fact, she'd experienced the opposite last year around the holidays.

A chill ran down Joy's spine, and she quickened her steps as much to outrun the memory as to make good time. She walked another half mile away from the downtown area until she reached the Sweetwater Springs Library. Then she opened the door and stepped inside, standing in the entryway a moment to catch her breath. As she removed her jacket and repositioned her bag on her shoulder, the door opened again, and two little girls rushed in, nearly knocking her over.

"Whoa!" Joy's arms flew out to catch herself against the door to the main room of the library. Then her purse slipped off her shoulder and spilled out onto the floor.

She'd been meaning to clean out her bag, and the contents were now laid out before her. Gum wrappers galore. A comb. A notepad. And a business card that Aunt Darby seemed to have in endless supply for a local matchmaking service. Every time Joy saw her favorite aunt, Darby was handing her a card and urging Joy to "try again." Joy wasn't necessarily anti dating right now. She just didn't need a service to help. *Thank you very much, Aunt Darby.*

Joy knelt to collect the items.

"Are you okay? Willow doesn't know her own strength," a deep voice said.

Joy knew that voice. Something warm moved over her as she looked up and met Granger Fields's dark gaze. "Oh. Hi."

"Joy," he said, acknowledging her with a dimpled smile. "I didn't realize that was you down there. Do you need help?"

Before she could insist that she didn't, Granger knelt in front of her and grabbed the business card.

Mortification flooded Joy's system. "That's my aunt Darby's." She snatched the card, hoping he hadn't read the name. His grin told her he had though. *Great.* He was going to think his girls' art teacher was clumsy, gum smacking, and desperate.

"The contents of a woman's purse are supposed to be kept secret, right? Should I cover my eyes?" he teased.

Joy nodded seriously. "Yes, please."

Apparently, Granger was only joking, however, because he continued to grab her items one by one and toss them inside her bag. Then he stood and reached out a hand to help her up.

Joy stared at it for a moment, her brain misfiring right along with her heart. She had a teeny, tiny crush on Granger that she'd been actively ignoring for months. When he'd first started taking his girls to her art classes here, she'd promised herself that, despite being incredibly attracted to him, he was look-but-don't-touch where she was concerned. She had no intention of getting involved with a handsome single father. That was too complicated, and if and when she started dating again, she was keeping things simple.

Granger kept his hand outstretched. Reluctantly, she slid her palm against his calloused one, no doubt the result of chopping trees on his farm. As soon as she was on her feet, she pulled her hand away and took a tiny step backward, giving her attention to his two little girls who were now bopping up and down on each side of him.

"Hi, Abby. Hi, Willow," Joy said, smiling as she looked at them. Joy was a sucker for a cute kid. She'd spent a large part of her teens and twenties working in childcare. In fact, being a nanny was how she'd put herself through art school. Her parents had refused to pay when she'd dropped out of nursing to follow her passion but she'd taken out a loan and she'd persisted. People had told her that she'd never make it as a starving artist but she hadn't given up then either. And now, she fully supported herself with her art. Yeah, she'd walked here because her car was on its final miles. But she had a car and a nice town house. And she had more than enough food in her fridge.

Not a starving artist.

"Ladies first." Granger opened one of the double doors that led into the main room and looked at Joy. "I promise we won't try to bowl you over this time."

She glanced over her shoulder to catch him wink at her. It was an innocent wink but it still made her insides turn to something akin to Jell-O. Then she stepped into the room filled with quiet whispers and the smell of books, old and new.

"Hi, Joy!" Lacy Shaw, the librarian here, waved from behind the counter.

Joy waved back. Lacy was a good friend of hers. She'd always been quiet, but her new beau was bringing out a less introverted side of her these days. It showed in the way Lacy wore her hair down on her shoulders. Gone were her cardigans, replaced by cropped lightweight blazers.

"Miss Joy?" Willow tugged on Joy's arm as they continued walking to the far corner of the library. Willow was a tow-headed seven-year-old, a second grader by Joy's recollection and a ball of enthusiasm. This child would probably get excited over doing chores. "Can I be your special helper today?"

Joy chose one child at the start of every class to pass out supplies and collect them at the end. "Of course you can, sweetheart." Joy looked at Granger's older girl. Abigail was nine and the calmer of the two sisters. She had long, dark-blond hair that she wore in a low-hanging ponytail and pink-tinted glasses that she constantly pushed up on her nose. "Abigail, I have a job for you too," Joy said. "Follow me."

Joy led them to where she held classes and handed Willow some river stones to place on the table for the other students. Then she handed Abigail some paintbrushes to distribute. Joy handled putting out the palettes and a variety of paint. When they were done, Joy filled some cups with water, and Willow put one in front of each place setting.

Other children began to wander in as they prepared the space, hurrying to the table to get their preferred spot.

"What are we doing today?" Abigail asked once everyone was seated.

Joy clapped her hands together at her chest, eying the children and not the parents, who sat along the wall— Granger included. He usually sent the girls with their nanny, Mrs. Townsend. But lately, Mrs. Townsend had been under the weather, and he'd been coming more often with them. "Well, in honor of today being Halloween, we're painting pictures of candy on river rocks. You can sneak them in the trick-or-treat basket at your home tonight and that will be your trick instead of a treat."

The kids all giggled. She had to admit that she'd thought herself a genius when she'd concocted the idea in the middle of the night last week.

"You have to try to paint the candy as realistic as you can to trick the treaters tonight," she said with a wide grin. "That's why I brought the real thing for you to use as your model."

Willow's eyes went wide. "Can we eat it too?"

Joy laughed softly. "You'll have to ask your parents." Her gaze unwittingly met with Granger's, and if a heart could sigh, hers did at the sight of his overgrown chestnut-colored hair and tanned skin that acted like a canvas for his light brown eyes.

She reined her gaze back in and looked at the children. "All right. Let's get started."

Half an hour later, there were dozens of river stones on the paint-splattered table. They were painted with designs of Tootsie Rolls, M&M'S, Starbursts, and Skittles. And the kids were sugared up as well as high on the excitement of the adventure to come tonight as they went door to door.

Willow raised her hand and signaled to Joy to lean in for a secret. "I'm going to try to trick my dad with this stone," she whispered loudly. "He always tries to steal my candy after we go trick-or-treating."

Joy laughed and looked at Granger.

He shook his head and palmed his face adorably before standing. "All right, girls, tell Miss Joy thank you."

"Thank you!" Abby and Willow said in unison, throwing their arms around Joy's waist.

"You're welcome. Have fun tonight, okay? Halloween is one of my favorite holidays. After Thanksgiving and Christmas."

"Those are my favorites too," Willow said, bopping on the balls of her feet. She was much more talkative than her older sister, who typically didn't say much. Joy knew that the girls' mother wasn't in the picture anymore. That was a lot for two kids to deal with. Abigail had obviously taken some of the maternal responsibility on her shoulders.

And Granger bore the rest. Which was both honorable and another reason that Joy planned to keep her crush to herself. From the outside looking in, Granger's life was complicated. And Halloween or not, her heart didn't need any tricks or treats tonight or any other night.

* * *

There was nothing Granger would rather do than spend the afternoon with his girls but he had a lot of work to do right now. It was the last day of October, and tomorrow started Merry Mountain Farms' Christmas season. After the fire that had wiped out half the trees this spring, the farm was already operating at a deficit.

"Daddy?" Abby tapped his shoulder as she approached from behind. "Did you see the rocks I painted at the library?"

Granger was sitting at his desk, where he was supposed to be working. He had an open-door policy when he was in the house though, and not a lot of work ever got done here. He lifted his gaze to his oldest daughter, taken aback by how much she looked like her mother with her long, blond hair and freckled cheeks. "I did. You're an artist."

"Like Miss Joy," Abby said, a smile touching the corners of her mouth. His girls looked up to Joy Benson, especially Abby, who loved to draw and paint. Willow, on the other hand, had been missing having a mother like her friends lately, and any woman in the right age group who gave her the least bit of attention was her new best friend.

"Maybe so," Granger said.

"Why did you take us to the library again today instead of Mrs. Townsend?" Abby asked. "Where is she?"

Granger sighed and rubbed a hand on his forehead. The girls' nanny had called out again this morning. Lately, his girls were running circles around Mrs. Townsend. They lived in a house on the same property as his parents and the Christmas tree farm, so someone was always around to help if needed. Mrs. Townsend was only there to make sure the girls ate their after-school snacks and did their homework while he and his parents ran their homegrown business, which included caring for the evergreens, the apple orchards, and the strawberry fields. "Mrs. Townsend will be back tomorrow," he said. *Hopefully.*

Abby shrugged her tiny shoulders. "I like it when you take us instead."

He smiled. "I like it too. And tonight, I'm taking you and Willow trick-or-treating. Why aren't you putting on your costume?"

Abby's eyes lit up behind her thick glasses. "I'll go do that."

"Help your sister too?" Granger asked before he could think. Lately he'd been wondering if he'd been asking

Abby to help Willow too often. Abby deserved to be a kid and not be responsible for her younger sibling so much. Granger couldn't do everything on his own though. That was why he needed a nanny in the first place.

Abby headed toward the door. "Don't forget your costume, Dad," she called before disappearing. He heard the patter of her socked feet race down the hall and up the stairs toward her bedroom.

Granger chuckled and closed his laptop. He wasn't getting any more work done this afternoon anyway. He'd looked at the numbers. With the shipment of trees that he'd ordered from Virginia, they'd be able to satisfy customer demand this holiday and avoid losing their customers to the competition. The Virginia tree farm had to make a profit, though, which meant that Merry Mountain Farms wouldn't. These trees would be sold to Merry Mountain Farms' customers at the same cost as the other trees.

A sigh tumbled off his lips as he stood and headed into the kitchen. He dipped into the fridge and grabbed an apple, taking a huge bite. There was one solution to fix the decreased profits. He'd spoken to his father about bringing back the lighted hayrides they used to run.

There was a trail on their property that weaved through the woods. They used to drive Grandpa's tractor pulling a large trailer that could accommodate twenty or so guests, driving past lighted displays in the dark. It was magical, and Merry Mountain goers had adored the experience, making it part of their holiday traditions.

Five years ago, his father had shut down the ride after a little boy somehow climbed over the ride's guardrail and fell out, breaking his arm. The family had sued, and Granger's father had decided to put all the lighted displays and props in storage under proverbial lock and key.

The lawsuit hadn't gone anywhere, of course, because parents were supposed to watch their children. There were warning signs posted that read as much. The rides were safe, and they brought in customers and income, which was needed this year. His father didn't agree when Granger had brought it up last week but Granger planned to broach the subject again. They had to do something, and this would be easy. They already had everything they needed.

Someone knocked on the back door. Granger turned just as his mom stepped inside with a large basket of candy in her arms.

"Aren't you going to dress up?" she asked, laying the basket on the counter and giving him a hug.

"This is my costume." Granger pulled back and gestured at his long-sleeved T-shirt and jeans. "I'm going as a grumpy Christmas tree farmer." Which wasn't far from the truth right now.

His mother swatted him playfully. "Are you taking the girls downtown for trick-or-treating?"

Granger reached for a miniature candy bar in the basket. "They'd be pretty sad trick-or-treaters if we tried to go around here," he said. The farm was expansive, stretching all the way to the border of Evergreen State Park. It wasn't inside a neighborhood where door-to-door trick-or-treating made sense.

His mom's gaze landed on the painted river rocks on the counter. "Aren't those cute?" she said, picking one up. There was a Hershey's Kiss painted on the top. It wasn't good enough to trick anyone, but Willow had been proud of it nevertheless. "Is this what Joy taught the kids at the library this afternoon?"

"Yep." Granger unwrapped his piece of candy and popped it into his mouth.

"The girls just love her. I don't know why she's still single."

Granger avoided meeting his mom's gaze. He knew what she was thinking. His mom wasn't so subtle about making sure he knew exactly which females in town were available should he want to start dating again.

"Maybe that's what she wants," he said, thinking about that matchmaking business card that had fallen from her purse earlier today. She'd claimed it was her aunt's, and if Joy's aunt was anything like his own mother, then he understood perfectly.

"Nonsense. No woman wants to be alone," his mother said.

Granger bit his tongue. His ex-wife had. She'd wanted to be rid of her family so badly that she'd packed her bags soon after Willow was born. She'd been diagnosed with postpartum depression, which he'd vaguely understood at the time. What he didn't understand was why she never returned. Willow was seven years old now. Erin's PPD had passed, and she clearly wasn't coming back.

"No man wants to be alone either," his mom continued, oblivious to his inner thoughts.

Granger side-eyed her. "I don't have any inkling of an idea what alone feels like. Between you and the girls and Tin"—he gestured at the sleeping sheepdog blocking half the doorway—"I can't get a moment's peace."

Tin lifted her head at the mention. She'd been a Christmas present for the girls the year that Erin had left the family. Granger had brought her home as a sort of consolation prize. She'd been the size of a football back then and had an attraction to the silvery tinsel on the tree in their living room. Abigail had named her Tinsel but over the years that had shortened to Tin.

"Joy's a beautiful woman," his mom continued. "Caring too. Do you know she volunteers at Sugar Pines Community Center all the time?"

Granger attempted to grab another piece of candy from the basket but his mom blocked him.

"That's for the kids," she said. "She drives her aunt around town too because Darby can't drive anymore."

Granger looked up. "I didn't know that."

"Darby has epilepsy. Her sister, Joy's mother, should be giving her rides but she's too busy at the hospital to make time. Joy makes time though. That speaks volumes about her character. She's loyal."

Granger reached for a piece of candy again. This time his mom didn't stop him. "Enough matchmaking, okay? I need to be focused on the farm right now. At this rate, we're not going to make any profits this year unless we can get Dad to consider bringing back the lighted hayride."

His mom's smile wilted. "Good luck with that. I've never seen your dad so upset as when that kid got hurt on our property."

"It wasn't his fault," Granger said, unwrapping a Twizzler this time. He took a bite.

"Well, I know that. But it's not me you have to convince. I'd love to see the rides happen again. They were so special. It was one of the most anticipated holiday events around here."

Before Granger could say anything more, Willow barged into the room, dressed as a monkey wearing a pair of Minnie Mouse ears. "Nana!" she cheered. "Are you going with us?"

Granger's mom laughed. "No, no. I'm staying here, darling."

"Boo," Willow whined. Then she reached for her father's

hand. "I'm all ready to go! I want to leave now so I can get as much candy as possible."

Granger inspected the costume that his mom had helped put together. If it had been left to him, Willow would probably be wearing something store-bought. "I'm sure you'll get plenty of candy tonight, Monkey Mouse," he teased.

"Daddy, I'm dressed as Minnie Monkey," she corrected.

Abby entered the room as well. She was wearing an artist's smock, splattered with paint, with large brushes poking out of the front pockets. She had paint splattered on her cheeks and in her hair as well. "I'm an artist," she declared as if that weren't obvious. "Can we stop by Miss Joy's house so I can show her?"

Granger made the mistake of looking at his mom when Abby said this.

"Well, I am sure your father can arrange that. Can't you, son?" She patted his shoulder.

"Please, Daddy," Willow asked. "I want Miss Joy to see my costume too!"

Granger chuckled. He wasn't kidding about never getting a moment's peace. He had to admit there was some part of him that wanted to see Joy again tonight though. He'd always found her attractive. But the way she interacted with his girls and the contagious nature of her laugh reeled him in—even if he always managed to break the line. "I guess we can swing by Miss Joy's home," he relented. "But just for a couple minutes."

CHAPTER TWO

*J*oy felt like she was back in her college days. While in art school, there'd been all kinds of parties that had required her to dress up. Tonight, she was dressed as an artsy twist on a peacock. She wore royal blue from head to toe and had a headband that she'd decorated herself with a variety of brightly colored feathers, all fanned out over her dark hair. She'd done the same to the belt she was wearing around her waist. She'd gotten a little carried away with the face paint and jewels too, but this was much more toned down from those college days in her early twenties. She'd even used some hair chalk to color a few strands of her hair royal blue like her costume— and some part of her, the artist, wanted to keep the blue locks after tonight.

The doorbell rang.

Joy grabbed her nearly empty basket of treats and hurried to the glass door, her steps slowing when she saw the man and two little girls standing on her stoop with a large dog. Joy knew that man and those girls. She also recognized that lovable canine.

She smiled brightly and opened the door to the chorus of "Trick or treat!" Laughing, Joy held out her basket. "Wow. If not for your dad, I might not have been able to figure out who you were. Those costumes are amazing," she told Abby and Willow. "Minnie Monkey and a famous artist?" she asked.

Abby looked up. "I'm supposed to be you."

"Oh, wow. I see the resemblance," Joy said, glancing up at Granger. Then she reached over and patted Tin, who was also in costume tonight. The big, lovable dog wore a Wonder Woman cape draped over her back. It was tradition in the downtown area where Joy lived for trick-or-treaters to bring their dogs in tow and for those manning the doors with baskets of candy to have dog treats on hand as well.

"How many pieces can we have?" Willow asked, digging her small hand into the basket that Joy held out.

"Don't be greedy," Granger said.

"Oh, there's no such thing. Besides, I think the crowd is dwindling, and I don't want to be stuck with all this sugar later. I have a sweet tooth late at night," Joy confessed.

"I see the tricks in there." Willow offered Joy a wide gap-toothed grin. "You're good at drawing but I can tell which pieces are just rocks."

Joy laughed and looked up at Granger, meeting his eyes. She wasn't sure she'd ever stared into them at night. The colors were deeper, richer. They made her want to grab her oil paints and search for the ones that would re-create them.

"How do you like my costume?" Granger asked, his voice deeper than she recalled.

She lowered her gaze to scan his body—big mistake.

The man was all lean muscle, sculpted like a marble statue. "What costume?" *Handsome single dad? Hot Christmas tree farmer?*

Granger held open his arms. "I'm the Grinch."

Willow started giggling. "Daddy, the Grinch is green. You're not green."

Abby smiled too. "I have paint in the pockets of my apron. I can paint you green if you want," she offered with a mischievous grin.

Granger held up his hands. "I don't think so." His phone rang in his pocket. He pulled it out, checked the caller ID, and gave Joy an apologetic look. "Mind if I take this?"

Joy shook her head. "Not at all. The girls are fine with me. Tin too. I have a treat for her inside." Joy gestured the girls into her living room.

"Thanks." Granger lifted the phone to his ear and connected the call.

Joy exhaled softly as she turned to the girls. "So have you had fun so far tonight?"

"Yes!" Willow cheered. "I got so much candy. I can't wait to eat it all."

"Not in one sitting," Abby said. "Just a few pieces."

Joy smiled at the mother hen. "That's true. Your sister knows best." Joy reached inside a large Ziploc bag where she kept dog biscuits.

"Do you have a dog?" Willow asked.

"Me? No, I have a cat. Her name is Chelsea."

Abby looked around. "Where is she?"

Joy looked around as well. Chelsea only came out on her own terms though. "Well, when dogs come around, she usually hides. Cats and dogs don't always get along."

"We have barn cats," Willow said. "And they don't like Tin because she chases them."

Joy fed Tin a biscuit. "Well, we'll have to make sure to keep you away from my Chelsea, then. Chelsea fights back. You're big but she's tough," Joy told Tin, running her fingers through the dog's thick fur.

The doorbell rang, and Joy straightened and reached for the basket. "Wanna hand out the candy for me?" she asked Abby and Willow.

In lieu of an answer, they raced toward the door, looking disappointed when they saw that it was only their father standing on the other side. He didn't look quite as happy this time.

"Your impression of the Grinch is getting better," Joy commented, opening the door to him. "Was that phone call bad news?"

He nodded and stepped inside. His gaze dropped to the girls, and Joy saw his hesitation. The news was bad enough that he didn't want to discuss it in front of them right now.

"Hey, girls," Joy said, lowering her gaze, "I'll let you in on where Chelsea is hiding if you promise to be gentle with her. Can you do that?"

Willow looked like she was about to burst with excitement.

"I'll make sure she's gentle," Abby promised, pushing her glasses up on her nose.

Joy nodded. "Chelsea likes to hide in my closet with all my fancy shoes. She's a cat after my own heart...My room is all the way down the hall. Approach her slowly and let her come to you, okay?"

The girls nodded and then hurried away.

Then Joy turned back to Granger, her gut tightening. "Okay, what's going on?"

"It's Mrs. Townsend," Granger said grimly.

Joy's hands immediately flew to her mouth. "Oh no. Is she...dead?"

* * *

"Dead?" Granger shook his head. "No. But her physician is concerned about her continuing to work. Apparently, her blood pressure is elevated, and she's having dizzy spells. Her doctor warned her not to drive or watch small children right now."

"That's pretty difficult for a nanny," Joy pointed out.

"Exactly. Mrs. Townsend says she's worried that something bad could happen to the girls, and it would be all her fault."

Joy's brow furrowed. "She raises a good point. I mean, wasn't she with Willow when the farm caught fire this spring?"

Granger shook his head. "No, but she should have been. That was one of the days she'd called out. I hate to admit I've had the same concerns as the doctor. But I was hoping to wait until after the farm's busy season to figure out what I should do."

"When is she quitting?" Joy asked.

Granger frowned. "She just did. She's retiring, effective immediately."

Joy's hands dropped back to her sides but her mouth remained open. "What? But the girls need her."

Granger pulled a hand to his forehead. "I know." And he was worried about how the girls would react. Another female figure was leaving, without warning. Would they feel abandoned? Willow would for sure. She was still young, and lately she'd been asking a lot of questions about where her mother was.

Joy reached out to touch his arm. "I'm sorry, Granger."

He tried not to notice the decreasing space between them that buzzed with awareness. An awareness that he'd been actively ignoring for a long time now. "Mrs. Townsend has to take care of her health. I understand that." He sighed. "Tomorrow starts Merry Mountain Farms' busiest season though, and my dad can't do the job all by himself. Mom will help as much as she can, but she and my aunts run the cider house at Christmas…I'm not sure what I'm going to do."

Joy gestured to the couch. "How about I make you a cup of tea? I know it's not a solution but sometimes it helps to sit back and relax. That always helps me, at least."

"Tea sounds great, actually." Granger walked to the couch and plopped down. Tin immediately moved over to his knee, laying her large, furry head right on it. Granger wasn't sure if Tin was sensing his distress and trying to comfort him or if she was taking advantage of the opportunity to get a little scratch behind the ears.

"Sugar?" Joy called from the kitchen at his back.

"Yes, please. If the kids are getting sugared up tonight, I might as well too, right?"

Joy laughed and headed back to him a few minutes later with two mugs in her hand. She put his down on the coffee table in front of him and brought hers to her mouth. "I'm afraid the tea will counteract any sugaring up. It's chamomile. It'll soothe whatever ails you."

Granger side-eyed her. "I seriously doubt that. But if that's true, I'll be coming back to your place for more."

The air electrified between them.

Joy looked away and continued talking. "Well, your girls are the sweetest. I'm sure you can find someone else to watch them with no problem. I mean, it's just after school hours, right?"

Granger nodded. "Until mid-December when they get out for the holidays. Then I might need full days as well…Are you looking for a job by chance? The girls adore you. And it's just after school, like you said."

Joy reared back, her expression twisting. "I have a job. I'm a working artist. And I don't take care of kids anymore."

"But you could," Granger said. "It's starting to get cold outside, and I noticed you walked to the library earlier today. Your car is acting up again, I'm guessing. The money would help."

"My car is already in the shop. I pick it up on Monday." She stared at him for a long moment.

"I know it's a lot to ask. But this would be temporary. I just need to get through the season." Granger hadn't touched his herbal tea yet. He reached for it and took a sip, needing something to occupy his hands. If Joy turned him down, there'd be hours of interviews and decisions. And what if the girls didn't like who he picked? They already loved Joy. And more importantly, he trusted her.

Joy continued to stare at him, her expression unreadable. Not that he'd ever known what a woman was thinking. "I'm sorry, Granger. But I'm busy too. I run my Etsy store and teach classes at the library and the community center. And all my spare time goes to creating my own artwork. I would love to help you out but I'm afraid I can't."

Granger's disappointment came in as quickly as his excitement over the idea. Joy would have been the perfect solution. But now he had a big problem. Mrs. Townsend had retired the day before the tree farm officially opened for the year. And this season was especially important because it could very well make or break the family business.

He blew out a breath and sipped his tea. "I understand.

I'll figure something out. Maybe the girls could stay at the cider house with my mom during the hours they're home and while I'm working."

Joy nodded. "That sounds like a plan. It even sounds fun."

Granger lifted a brow. "I was a kid growing up on that farm once. It's not as fun as one might think."

The corners of Joy's mouth twitched in a smile. "I was the lonely latchkey kid because my parents were always working at the hospital. That's not much fun either."

Granger tried not to take offense. He'd never pegged himself as the kind of parent who hired a nanny but he'd never planned on the mother of his children bailing on him either. "I'm always around, and as soon as I step inside the house, my time is the girls'."

"Oh, I know you're a wonderful father. I wasn't trying to say that having a nanny was wrong. I'm just saying that whatever solution you find for the girls will be fine. No place or person is perfect."

But Joy would have been perfect, in his opinion.

"I'll ask around for you if you'd like," she offered.

He took another sip of his tea and then placed the cup on the coffee table in front of him before standing. "That would be great. Thank you."

Joy stood as well, her gaze fluttering to meet his as they stood face-to-face in her dimly lit living room. She tried to take a step backward but Tin had moved to stand behind her, blocking her path. Granger reached out to steady her.

"You've already fallen once today on my account," he said. "Let's not make it twice."

Joy laughed softly.

Then Granger took a step back, giving her the distance she seemed to be seeking. Giving himself the distance too. Increasing the space between them didn't lessen the charge in the air though. It only lessened the probability that he would act on it.

* * *

Joy walked over to the hallway to peer into the darkness. "Girls? Everything okay back there?" She wasn't too worried about that. She'd just needed some excuse to distance herself from Granger. For a moment, she could've sworn he was flirting with her.

She liked to be flirted with, she did. But Granger had been taking the girls to her classes off and on for months. And she loved the girls. Any kind of involvement between them would only make things weird. She didn't like the awkward tension that was always left behind after a failed romance.

Willow and Abby came out of her room with large smiles on their faces. "We found her!" Willow said.

"But don't worry, we were gentle with your cat," Abby added.

Joy nodded. "I'm sure you were. Your dad is off the phone. There might be a little more trick-or-treating to be had." She glanced over her shoulder to look at Granger. She suspected that he might be done with the Halloween festivities but the lure of candy would have the girls scampering to leave sooner.

"Yes!" Willow said. "There are a few more houses on this street that we haven't hit yet. Let's go, Daddy. Let's go!"

Granger sighed. "Okay, but only three more houses. You have more than enough candy, and it's getting late. We need to get back home."

"So we can eat all the candy!" Willow declared, running to the front door.

"Have fun, guys." Joy shared one last look with Granger that left her unsettled. She couldn't quite pinpoint the dominant emotion in the glance. Was it disappointment? Worry? Attraction?

She only knew what she felt at this moment. Relief . . . and maybe a little bit of regret too. She loved those girls, and caring for them would've been a great side job. But she'd started this year by promising herself that she would be a full-time working artist, supporting herself by only taking art-related jobs. And in doing so, she'd made a goal to open her own art gallery. Caring for Granger's girls would only distract her from her goals. And seeing Granger daily would be another unwanted distraction.

* * *

On Monday, Joy grabbed her belongings and headed out the door. Once again, she was walking to her destination but not for long. Today, she was getting her car back. Then she'd run some errands before heading over to Sugar Pines Community Center to teach an art class early this afternoon. They didn't pay her but Joy often got hired to do private lessons. She handed out business cards, and sometimes folks went to her website and purchased a piece of her art.

Joy walked fast as she made her way to the auto mechanic's shop. The temperature outside was frigid, and a body in motion was warm. She let her gaze wander over the distant tree lines and the mountains beyond. Living in Sweetwater Springs was an artist's dream. She could pull inspiration from everywhere she turned.

She reached the mechanic's shop and pulled open the door.

"Hey, Joy," Steve Capps said as she entered the shop. "I had a feeling you'd be in this morning."

"I miss driving," Joy said. And she was tired of walking. She stepped up to the counter and pulled her wallet out of her purse.

Steve rolled his chair up to the computer on the other side of the counter and tapped the keys. "Okay, let's see here. You needed new spark plugs, brake pads and fluids, and a new alternator. You were overdue for an oil change and tire rotation as well."

Joy nodded as he rattled off a half dozen more items. She'd agreed to all those things. The engine of her car was starting to protest even turning over because she'd neglected it for too long, and she knew it would have a harder time when the first big freeze arrived.

"So the total for all of that comes to two thousand three hundred and eighty-seven dollars."

Joy's knees nearly buckled. "What? That's more than you quoted."

Steve's brow furrowed as he looked at her. "The initial quote was just for the new alternator and spark plugs. Then we spoke on the phone again, and I told you about the other items that needed to be done. You agreed to everything."

Joy felt sick. She had agreed; she just hadn't realized exactly how much more it would cost her. This would wipe out every penny of what she'd been saving to open her art gallery.

"We can set up a twelve-month payment plan, if you need it," he said.

Even over twelve months, that was a large chunk of change. What choice did Joy have though? She couldn't make money without a vehicle to get her to her jobs. And in another month, there could be snow on the ground.

Walking in three to five inches of the white stuff wasn't practical.

Joy looked at Steve and forced a fleeting smile. "Thank you for working on my car. A payment plan would be great."

He nodded. "You got it."

She made the first of twelve payments, got her keys, and plopped down in the driver's seat a few minutes later, feeling deflated.

Then she drove toward Sugar Pines Community Center, taking the long way down Main Street so that she could drive by the empty storefront she'd spotted yesterday. A FOR LEASE sign was still in the window.

Joy swallowed. Then she pulled to the curb and jotted down the number on the lease sign. She'd call this evening and schedule a viewing. She'd never been one to give up on a dream. The bill for her vehicle was a little bump in the road but she would sell more of her art pieces and teach more classes. She would do whatever it took while also keeping to her resolution that she would only take art-related jobs.

Which was why she couldn't say yes to Granger's offer to nanny his girls. Even if some small part of her had wanted to.

CHAPTER THREE

Granger reached for a third bite-size piece of chocolate and peeled the wrapper off.

"Don't touch that." His mom walked into the kitchen and shook her head. "That's the girls' hard-earned candy."

Granger always obeyed his mom, always had, but she wasn't being serious, and he knew it. He popped the chocolate into his mouth and chewed. "I'm the one who took the girls out. Trick-or-treating isn't easy, you know. I earned it too. Besides, Willow spent the weekend bouncing off the walls. I'm doing her and her teacher a favor."

His mom laughed and turned on the stove's over-head light.

Granger watched her. "What are you doing?"

She glanced over her shoulder. "Making breakfast. The girls have school today, and they can't focus without a proper meal in their bellies."

"You don't think I'm capable?" Granger asked.

She turned to face him and put her hands on her hips.

"Of course I do. You've been providing for them on your own all these years."

"Not exactly on my own. I've had you and Dad. And Mrs. Townsend." He met his mom's gaze and sighed.

She walked to the fridge and grabbed a carton of eggs. "It was time for her to retire anyway. We all knew it."

"I just don't know what I'm going to do." He'd spent all Sunday mulling over his choices. He didn't have any. Everybody he knew had a job. And if they didn't, there was a good reason that would keep them from caring for his girls. He knew a lot of teenagers in the area but, call him overprotective, he wanted someone experienced. He didn't want to have to worry that Willow would wander off.

"You know I'll help as much as I can," his mom said, "but this is the time of year when the farm needs me most."

Granger nodded. "I know." His mom always turned a profit at the farm by selling cider from the orchards. She ran the books and tracked everything that went in and out. She was as integral to the farm as he and his dad were. "I just wish Mrs. Townsend could've waited to tell me she wasn't coming back until after the holidays."

Abby stepped into the room. "Mrs. Townsend is gone? What happened to her?"

Granger's heart plummeted into the bottom of his stomach as he turned to Abby. "She's fine. Nothing happened to her." He put on a smile, hoping to convince her. "She's focusing on her health and has decided to retire."

Abby stepped closer. "Just like that? She's not coming back?"

"I'm sure she'll come to visit." At least he hoped so for the girls' sakes. "But she won't be your nanny anymore," he said softly. "I was going to tell you later. Maybe after school."

As if understanding exactly what he meant, Abby

nodded. "I won't tell Willow. She'll be upset, and that's not good before school."

Granger swallowed. "It's not good for you either. I'm sorry, Abs."

She shrugged, the corners of her mouth lifting along with her tiny shoulders. "I'm older. I can handle it." He guessed this was nothing after having her mom turn her back on her, walk away, and never return.

"It's okay if you're sad. We can call Mrs. Townsend so you can talk to her." After what his children had been through, this would be tough for them. Maybe he needed to get them back in with the counselor Abby had seen when she'd realized that she was the only one of her friends that didn't have a mother around.

Granger turned as his mom put a hand on his shoulder. She must have sensed the heaviness of his thoughts.

She smiled at him and then looked at Abby. "I'm making scrambled eggs and bacon, your favorite. Do you mind telling Willow that it's breakfast time? We need to get you both fed and to the bus."

"Okay." Abby turned and dutifully walked back down the hall.

Granger exhaled. "Well, I blew that."

"You did no such thing," his mom said. "She'll be fine. She's young and resilient. It's you I'm worried about."

Granger looked up. "Me?"

She returned her attention to the stove. "You're old and not so resilient."

"Thirty-one isn't that old, Mom."

"When you have two children to care for, it is." She pointed her spatula at him. "I can see that guard of yours thickening. You're disappointed with the way Mrs. Townsend handled the situation. You feel let down."

"I know her health has to come first. And I'm happy for her. Mrs. Townsend deserves to retire and take care of herself... But yeah, I do feel a little let down."

"What you need to understand is that *everyone* will let you down. I'm your mother, and I've let you down a million times."

Granger watched her work at the stove. "I can't remember you ever letting me down."

"Because hopefully the times I've been there for you outweigh the times I wasn't. That's what matters." She scooped some eggs onto a plate and slid it in front of him. Then she prepared plates for Abby and Willow too.

The girls headed into the kitchen a moment later. As usual, Willow was excited about the day ahead. Granger met Abby's gaze across the table though. The light in her eyes was dim behind her pink-rimmed glasses. He hoped one day she could say the times he'd been there for her outweighed the times he'd royally screwed up too. Because she certainly wouldn't be able to say that about her mother.

Granger's cell phone rang in his pocket. He pulled it out quickly and checked the caller ID. "Mom, do you mind finishing up breakfast? I need to take this."

She shooed him away. Granger stepped outside and connected the call. "Hello."

"Granger. This is Bill Mack. I'm afraid I have bad news," Bill said, cutting to the chase.

Granger leaned against the side of the house. "Oh yeah?"

"We were hoping to be able to ship you those evergreens to help you out with all the trees you lost earlier this year. But we're running short ourselves. The weather hasn't cooperated, and the summer drought really affected a percentage of our farm."

"I'm sorry to hear that," Granger said numbly, sensing

the bad news ahead. The farm in Virginia had all but promised to ship trees to Merry Mountain Farms. Talk about everyone disappointing him and letting him down.

"Sorry, buddy, but I can't make that shipment for you. I wish I could help."

"I understand," Granger said. After a few more polite exchanges, he disconnected the call but didn't move. Not until his girls dashed out the door with their book bags dangling off their shoulders. Then he smiled and kissed their foreheads. They'd gotten through a lot tougher times than this. They'd be okay, one way or another.

* * *

Joy's car had been humming around town all day as she completed errands that she hadn't gotten to do when it was in the shop. Now the back seat was full of art supplies, and she was finally on her way to Sugar Pines Community Center.

She pulled into the parking lot and climbed out. She unloaded her wheeled cart full of brushes and paints, paper, ribbon, Popsicle sticks—everything she could think of—and headed inside.

"Hey, Joy," the director, Donovan Tate, said as she entered the building. Joy wasn't exactly sure what he did. She guessed maybe he was akin to being the principal of a school. He walked around, joked, and looked stern when someone didn't clean up their messes. "Looks like you got your car back. The folks here are going to be so happy to have you coming in again." He gestured to the wall. "Look. I hung the group project you all completed in August."

Joy acknowledged the large abstract piece. It was now framed and centered on the wall to her right. "Looks great." About eleven senior citizens had participated on that one, each adding a little to it when she slid it in front of them. "I'm going to go ahead and set up, if that's okay."

Donovan nodded. "Your aunt Darby is already in there waiting for you. She caught a ride from my dad."

Darby rarely ever missed one of Joy's classes. She couldn't drive but she always found a way to get here. Joy usually picked her up herself but lately Darby was waving her off, preferring different company, she guessed. Darby herself was an artist and had been one of Joy's greatest inspirations growing up. She was also Joy's greatest supporter.

"Thanks." Joy pulled her cart of supplies and headed into the large, open room. The unmistakable sound of Darby's laughter filled the air, and Joy spotted Darby sitting in the back corner with Ray Tate, Donovan's father. Ray was old now but Joy remembered when he'd been middle-aged, flirting with every woman who'd looked in his direction.

Joy also remembered that he'd always flirted with Darby when her aunt had taken her out and about. Back then, Darby hadn't given Ray the time of day. Over the last year, however, Joy had seen Darby and Ray spending a lot of time together.

Joy cleared her throat, the sound echoing softly in the room. "Hi, Aunt Darby...Ray."

They both turned to look at her. Then Darby hurried over to give Joy a huge hug. "Joy! I've missed you so much. I've been so lonely without your visits." She pulled back and looked at Joy.

"I can see that," Joy said, side-eying Ray.

He smiled broadly. The smile was too perfect not to be caps. His hair and complexion were flawless too. She could see why her aunt was attracted to him. Joy just wanted Darby to be careful.

Darby looked at the rolling cart beside Joy. "Looks like we're being artists today." She turned back to Ray. "You promised, when Joy came back to teach, that you'd take a class with me."

He sighed and looked at Darby for a long moment. "You make me do things I'd never in a million years do on my own."

"I think that's called bringing out the best in you," Darby supplied with a giddy smile. Her cheeks darkened a shade as they exchanged a meaningful glance.

Joy blinked. *What is happening here?* If she didn't know better, her aunt was suddenly in a relationship with Ray. Joy's car had only been in the shop for a week and a half. But apparently, a lot could change in that amount of time.

* * *

An hour later, the community room at Sugar Pines was splattered with paint of all colors and torn strips of old newspaper. Nine people between the ages of fifty and one hundred had participated, which wasn't many but they'd all enjoyed themselves making a mixed-media masterpiece on small ten-by-ten canvases.

"I can hang this in my living room," Ray said. "It'll impress my family when they visit. Bet they never knew I was an artist." He looked over at Darby, who was sitting beside him.

Joy wasn't trying to eavesdrop but she couldn't help herself. She was fascinated by this new development. If she didn't know Ray's history, she might even be excited for Darby.

"Joy's the only family I have that cares enough to come

by," she told him. Then she looked at Joy, who pretended to be sorting the paint back into its carrier.

"Have you found a place to open your art gallery yet?" Darby asked.

Joy glanced in her direction. "Maybe. There's a FOR LEASE sign in the window of a place on Main Street. The old clockmaker's shop."

"Oh, that's a lovely location. I was thinking, when you get that store, you could sell our artwork for us. Not for much, of course. Maybe just for donations to the Sugar Pines Community Center," Darby suggested.

Joy grinned. "That is a wonderful idea."

Darby shifted in her seat and reached into her pocket, pulling out a crisp one-hundred-dollar bill. "Here. Put this toward your gallery."

Joy hesitated. "I can't take your money, Aunt Darby."

"You can, and you should. I wish I could give you more."

Joy didn't want a free ride though. She'd always earned her way on her own.

"It's an investment," Darby said. "This town needs more culture."

Joy took the bill and hugged her aunt. "Thank you."

"I wholeheartedly agree with Darby about needing more culture in Sweetwater Springs," Ray said.

Darby seemed to melt as she turned to him, her back and shoulders rounding softly. Then Ray tilted his head toward hers, resting his forehead briefly against her temple. Once again, Joy felt like she'd fallen into a time warp. A week and a half. That was the very definition of a whirlwind romance. And whirlwind romances didn't have a stable foundation. They fell apart. Joy knew this firsthand, and that's what concerned her.

She was still worried as she drove away from Sugar

Pines a little while later with a crisp one-hundred-dollar bill in her pocket to put toward leasing her gallery. Well, that was a start toward rebuilding her funds.

Joy's eye caught on two little girls walking on the sidewalk away from the local school. Sweetwater Elementary had gotten out forty-five minutes ago. Joy recognized the girls from behind. She slowed and pulled over to the roadside, rolling down her passenger window. "Hey, Abby. Hey, Willow. Are you walking home?" Surely they weren't. Their house had to be about three miles from here.

Abby pushed her glasses up on her nose as she scrutinized Joy. She was in mama hen mode, assessing the stranger-danger potential of this situation. Joy saw the girl seem to relax as she realized who Joy was.

Willow ran over to Joy's car. "Mrs. Townsend usually picks us up after school so we don't have to ride the bus two times in one day. She says that's one too many bumpy rides. She must have forgot about us today."

Joy's heart ached. Apparently, Willow didn't know that Mrs. Townsend had retired. Judging by the look on Abby's face, however, she did. "What about your dad? Why didn't he come get you?"

Willow shrugged. "He's working. So are Nana and Papa. Plus, they thought Mrs. Townsend was coming. Abby said if we went inside and told the principal we were forgot about, that he might call bad people who'll take us away." Willow's wide smile dropped. "I don't want to be taken away."

Joy's mouth fell open. Her gaze jumped to Abby, who looked down at her feet.

"I said that *might* happen, Willow," the older girl muttered just loud enough for Joy to overhear. "I mean, it *could*."

Joy's heart broke again, even as anger curled in her belly. Granger knew Mrs. Townsend wasn't picking the girls up. How could he leave them out here all alone to worry about things like social services and being taken into foster care? "Hop in, girls. I'll drive you home."

Willow jumped up and down and grabbed the car door handle but Abby hesitated. "What if Dad is just running late? And he shows up and we're not here? He'll be worried."

Joy offered a reassuring smile. "I'll call and let him know, okay?"

Abby nodded and then climbed into the back seat. Before taking off, Joy dialed Granger's number. No answer. She wasn't worried that he was going to show up. In fact, she was willing to bet that he'd forgotten all about his parental duties today.

"Buckle up," Joy said. "Let's get you girls home." And after that, she planned on having a chat with their father.

* * *

Granger headed away from the woods where he had gone for a walk to clear his head. Earlier today he'd called every tree farm he knew, and no one had trees to spare for Merry Mountain Farms.

What was he going to do? It was almost Christmas. Customers would be filing in and expecting their usual evergreens. And if he couldn't provide them, they'd have to go elsewhere.

Granger turned toward the sound of a vehicle coming up the driveway. He lifted his gaze and recognized Joy's car driving toward him. His heart gave a funny little jolt. He'd thought of her a couple of times since Halloween night.

Okay, he'd thought of her before that too. She'd caught his eye when he'd taken the girls for arts and crafts at the library. And when he'd seen her selling her art in various festivals in town.

Joy's car came to a stop, and Granger's mind was slow to process three doors swinging open. His daughters exited out of two of them.

"Daddy!" Willow said, hurrying toward him as if nothing were out of the ordinary.

Abby wore a thick frown, her pale brows furrowed as she latched onto the straps of her book bag, clinching them tightly to the middle of her chest.

Granger looked at Joy, who wore a thicker frown. His mind caught up, and his heart dropped. "Oh, I'm so sorry," he said, turning to Abby first.

"Not your fault, Daddy," Willow said. "Mrs. Townsend didn't remember to pick us up."

He swallowed past the familiar guilt. As a single father, he always felt guilty about something. There was always more that he could be doing or some ball in the air that he was letting drop.

Joy cleared her throat. "Girls, it's chilly out here. And Willow, you said you were hungry."

"I'll make her a snack," Abby said, not waiting around for any protests. Granger would gladly go make that snack for Willow but Joy wasn't heading back toward her vehicle so he suspected she wanted to talk to him.

"Thanks, Abs," Granger said. Tin left his side to go in with the girls, perhaps sensing that it would be a lot more fun in there than out here. Granger had a feeling Tin was right.

Joy waited to speak until the girls were out of earshot. Once the door was closed, she folded her arms across her chest and glared at him.

"I already feel awful, okay? I didn't mean to," he said immediately.

Her mouth dropped open. "Are you serious? They were walking home alone. Abby didn't want to tell the principal they didn't have a ride because she was worried about getting taken away by social services."

Granger shifted on his feet. "Principal Nelson knows me. He would've driven the girls here himself."

Joy shook her head. "It doesn't matter. Abby was scared, and she felt like she had to protect her younger sister. And you. You never should have put her in that position."

Granger held out his hands. "It's not like I did it on purpose. The day got away from me. And I'm used to having Mrs. Townsend get them. Otherwise, I would have gone and picked them up myself. Or asked my mom to help."

Joy looked away.

He knew she was judging him right now. And maybe he deserved it but he was doing his best. Even when his best wasn't nearly good enough.

"Anyway, thank you for helping the girls. I appreciate it." He turned to go inside, stopping short at the sound of Joy's huffing. Granger turned back to face her. "Is there something else?"

She narrowed her brown eyes, which seemed a shade darker than usual. "You haven't even told Willow about Mrs. Townsend."

"Not yet, but I'm doing that just as soon as I go inside. I was hoping to have a new plan to give her when I did, but..." He trailed off. There was no new plan. Abby would likely be taking care of her sister. And he and his mother would pitch in between trying to keep the farm afloat. "I'm going to call a few more contacts. I spoke to

Dawanda at the fudge shop earlier. She knows everyone in town so maybe she'll find a suitable person for the time being."

Joy shook her head. "I don't work in childcare anymore," she finally muttered.

"You made that clear the other night."

"I only take jobs involving art," she added.

Granger nodded and stepped closer. "Noted."

She stared at him for a long moment. Was he missing something? "So I'm only available if you want to hire me for art-related services."

Granger folded his arms over his chest, mirroring her now. "You're going to have to be clearer than that with me. What are you suggesting?"

Joy's expression softened. "Like I told you the other night, my parents were always working. I walked home alone more days than not. It's lonely, and I love your girls too much to watch them go through that."

"Forgetting them today was an honest mistake. I'm not going to let it happen again." He rubbed his forehead. "I'm doing my best."

Joy's expression softened a touch more. "I think that's true. And I don't mind coming over every day after school to nurture your girls' artistic skills."

"Art lessons?" Granger asked, thinking he was catching on.

"Exactly. And play is very creative. It feeds the imagination, which feeds the art. Snacks too. And artists need to keep their work space clean so chores are included."

Joy was being creative with her proposed job description but Granger wasn't going to argue with her. He was desperate, and he trusted Joy.

"Just until after the holidays," she added. "By then,

I'm hoping I'll have a place for my studio and gallery. I actually have my eye on a place on Main Street."

"Is that right?" Granger asked.

Joy nodded. "So I won't be able to keep coming after Christmas."

"I should be able to find a suitable nan— art teacher to replace you by then." Granger stuck out his hand.

Joy hesitated in reaching for it. When she slipped her palm against his, everything inside him came alive. And that sent off his internal warning bells. He needed her for his girls, not himself.

"Great. I'll start by picking the girls up from school tomorrow."

CHAPTER FOUR

Joy stepped into her town house later that night and shrieked as Chelsea launched a premeditated attack. Knowing her cat, Chelsea had likely been stalking the door for hours, waiting for Joy to arrive home.

Joy blew out a breath and laughed as she bent to pick up her lovable fur ball. "What kind of greeting is that?" she asked, flipping on the light switch and heading toward the kitchen. "How are you? Did you miss me?"

Chelsea purred loudly in her arms. Joy loved that sound. It was soothing, and it broke up the silence of living alone.

"I got a job today," she informed her cat, placing Chelsea back on the floor and flipping on the hot water kettle. She glanced over her shoulder and gave Chelsea a stern look. "It's an art-related job, just like the one at the library." She was trying to convince herself as much as her cat. The girls needed her, and Joy needed to replenish her funds so that she could lease that storefront on Main Street for her gallery.

She went through the routine of preparing a cup of tea and then sat down at the kitchen table to drink it with Chelsea vibrating on her lap. She pulled her laptop to her and decided to search for leasing details on Mountain Breeze Realty's site. Within a few clicks, she was staring at her would-be gallery on her screen. Her breath suspended in her chest as she scrolled through nearly twenty photographs. Not only was the location perfect but it looked amazing on the inside. Not too big, not too small. It was perfect for displaying her pieces on the walls and with easels as stands. And there was enough room in the back to hold small classes of six or seven.

Meow.

Joy ran her hand over Chelsea's fur, satisfying her pet. "I agree, Chels. It's the one." More likely, she was urging Joy to pay more attention to her instead of the computer screen. Joy couldn't tear her attention away from the old clockmaker's store though.

She scrolled farther down to see the price, and her heart deflated as if someone had taken a pin and popped it like a balloon. Fifteen hundred dollars a month was more than her town house's mortgage. Joy believed there was truth in that saying that you had to spend money to make money, and she was sure that she could bring in enough monthly profits to cover the expense eventually. It was just the start-up that would be hard. And she didn't have enough savings in her account to cover a few hard months.

Still...Joy could picture the gallery in her mind's eye. It was exactly what she needed to take her career to the next level.

Meow.

Joy nodded, running her hands through Chelsea's thick fur again. "You're right, Chels. It doesn't hurt to call and take a look." Before allowing herself time to second-guess, she picked up her cell phone and tapped in the number that she'd taken down earlier when she'd driven by—the same one that was on her computer screen right now.

"This is Janelle Cruz," a woman's voice answered a moment later.

Joy knew Janelle from the Ladies' Day Out group that she belonged to. The LDO, as it was affectionately called, was a group of women in town who got together for the sole purpose of having fun. It'd been a while since Joy had joined them in their outings but she had good intentions of doing so again soon. "Hi, Janelle. It's Joy Benson."

"Joy, it's so nice to hear from you. It's been a while."

"It has," Joy agreed. "I'm actually calling because of one of the properties you're representing on Main Street."

"Oh, you mean the old clockmaker's shop?" Janelle asked.

"That's the one." Joy nibbled on her bottom lip. It was a pricey property but it was perfect. "I was hoping that I could schedule a time with you to go look at it."

"Really? You're interested?" Janelle asked.

"I am. I've been looking for a place to open an art gallery all year."

"Oh, how exciting. An art gallery would be absolutely perfect there!" Janelle said, sounding over-the-top with excitement.

Joy was sure it was a Realtor's job to sound enthusiastic about all the ideas potential clients brought to her. Even so, Janelle was right—an art gallery would go perfectly in that location.

"I'd love to show the place to you. How would Friday be?"

Friday was a few days away. "I was hoping to see it

sooner than that," Joy confessed. Did that make her sound too eager?

"Let me see..." Janelle hesitated for a moment. Joy imagined her going through her booked calendar. She was apparently a busy woman. "Okay. I can meet with you tomorrow at one thirty if that would be better."

Joy exhaled a breath and smiled to herself. "Much better. Tomorrow would be perfect."

* * *

The next day, Joy glanced around the hospital cafeteria impatiently looking for "Dr. Mom," the nickname she only uttered for her mother in her mind. She was supposed to have met her here for lunch.

This was so like Dr. Mom. She was punctual for her patients but her daughter could wait.

Joy huffed. She knew she was being irrational. Her mom's patients needed her, and these days, Joy didn't.

Dr. Mom walked into the far side of the cafeteria, her gaze moving around the room until she located Joy. Joy lifted a hand and waved. She'd already gone through the line and had gotten their food. Her mom had requested a garden salad with grilled chicken—the healthiest option on the menu. Joy had gotten a hot dog with all the toppings and a bag of potato chips—not the healthiest choice, and she was certain Dr. Mom would make sure she knew it.

Her mom approached, looking pleased. "You're still here," she said, sitting across the table from Joy and reaching for her container of salad.

"Of course I am. We had a lunch date."

Dr. Mom nodded as she slipped the covering off her

plastic utensils. "I thought you might have something else to do other than wait me out."

She said it with a smile but Joy knew better. Her mom was subtly implying that Joy should be working. And by working, she meant a "real job." How many times had Joy listened to her stance on Joy's current occupation being a side job? A hobby? Not practical?

"Well, it would be rude to stand you up for a lunch date. I have better manners than that, Dr. Mom," Joy said. As soon as her mental nickname rolled off her lips, she felt her eyes widen. She gave a small, nervous laugh and shook her head. "I mean, um...Mom."

Her mom stiffened. Then they fell into silence as they began to eat.

"I do have plans this afternoon. I have an appointment at one thirty." No need to mention that it was with Janelle Cruz. Joy didn't want her mom's opinion on that front. "And I have a private class after that," Joy said, glancing at the time on her phone's screen. She had to be in the car pool line in front of Sweetwater Elementary two hours from now in order to pick up the students for their private class.

"Oh? Another class at the community center or at the library?" Her mom stabbed a piece of lettuce and looked at her with interest.

Joy shook her head. "Actually, I'm going to start giving art lessons to Granger Fields's daughters, Abigail and Willow."

Her mom continued to stare at her as she ate her salad. "How often will you be giving these lessons?"

"Every day," Joy supplied. "After school."

Her mom lifted an eyebrow. "So you're babysitting the girls?"

"No." Joy stiffened. "I'm giving art lessons."

"For how long?" her mom asked.

"What?"

"Every day after school for how long? I know that Mrs. Townsend recently retired. A colleague of mine told me. Has Granger hired you to be the children's new nanny?"

Joy felt all her defenses rise as she sat up straighter. "No, I'm not their nanny."

Her mom ignored her objections. "Well, I think that's good news. It's honest work, and you can still dabble in your hobbies while the girls are at school."

Joy felt like her head was going to explode. She felt like a teenager instead of a thirty-year-old woman. "Art isn't a hobby for me, Mom. It's a career. I'm not a nanny. I'm a full-time artist. And I'm about to lease a store for my gallery." So much for not telling Dr. Mom about her appointment with Janelle Cruz.

Her mom took a sip from her water bottle. "This is news to me. Where?"

"On Main Street."

Dr. Mom gave her an assessing look. "That's expensive real estate."

It was. But Joy had promised herself last night that she would do what it took to make it happen. A gallery was the next step in her career, and it was definitely time.

"I didn't realize your online store was doing that well," her mom said.

"I have more than an online store." But her mom already knew that. Joy also consigned her pieces at the Sweetwater Café that her mom frequented and in the hospital's own gift shop. "And yes, I'm doing very well." Joy was proud of her accomplishments. She just wished her parents could appreciate them too.

Dr. Mom's beeper went off. She looked down at it and frowned. "Oh, I'm sorry, dear. Duty calls. I guess I'll take the rest of my salad to go. My next patient is ready." She pushed back from the table and collected her things. "Thanks for meeting me. We'll have to do this again. Maybe for Thanksgiving in a couple weeks?"

Joy knew from experience that her mom meant that exactly the way it sounded. Thanksgiving here in the hospital cafeteria. Joy had agreed to that invitation many times before. Sometimes her father joined them, and sometimes he didn't. "Maybe," Joy said noncommittally.

Or maybe she'd prefer to spend her holiday at Sugar Pines Community Center with Aunt Darby, where she didn't have to prove she was worthy of sitting down to a meal.

Joy finished off her hot dog while sitting alone and then returned to her car and drove downtown. Janelle's navy SUV was already in the lot. Joy parked, hurried to the front entrance, and tapped on the glass door.

Janelle whirled to face her, smiling and waving immediately. She walked to the door and opened it. "Hi, Joy. It's so good to see you."

"Have you been waiting long?"

"No." Janelle shook her head, her short, cropped silver hair unwavering with the motion. Janelle wore a steel-gray skirt today with black tights, high heels, and a flowing silk blouse. She looked like an out-of-place New Yorker here in Sweetwater Springs. Which wouldn't surprise anyone. Several Northerners had found their way to this small mountain valley over the last couple of years and had never left. "I just showed this place to another prospect, actually," Janelle said.

Joy stepped inside the store and snapped her gaze up

to meet Janelle's. "What?" She guessed she shouldn't be surprised. The downtown area would be prime real estate for a business owner. "Who?"

Janelle offered an apologetic smile. "I shouldn't say. But I will tell you that this person is looking at a few locations right now. Not just this one. And I think this spot would be perfect for what you want to do with it."

Joy relaxed a bit. "Do you mind if I take a look?" she asked, gesturing around the store.

"Of course not. That's why I'm here." Janelle took a few steps and leaned against the wall to allow Joy freedom to walk around without her as a shadow.

Joy walked past her and took a closer look at the interior. It had little details that made her love it even more than she'd suspected she would. The ceiling was bordered with crown molding, and the walls were textured, making Joy want to run her hands over the surface. She hesitated only momentarily, and then unable to help herself, she ran her hands over the walls, letting the subtle bumps rub against her fingertips.

Joy's gaze swept down to her feet where the beige tile with rose-colored highlights was simple and perfect. It wouldn't distract from the art that she'd display on the walls.

Joy quickly walked across the small store area. There was a bathroom and a storage area in the back. The rest of the store was open. She could see placing a table along the far wall to have some group classes. It'd be perfect!

Joy turned to capture the view from the inside looking out. There was a window display area to set easels with her work. Looking past that, she saw folks strolling along the sidewalk, bags dangling from their arms. This was prime shopping area for locals and tourists. She could imagine people leaving their favorite stores and glancing in her window, spotting a piece of her art or another local artist's work, and being unable to resist stepping inside.

"I love it," Joy found herself saying.

Janelle looked pleased as she left the wall and stepped toward Joy, her heels clicking loudly against the beige-and-rose-tile flooring. "Well, I have another prospect coming by on Friday to take a look. So if you love it, you might want to consider acting fast."

Sudden panic set in. "Another prospect in addition to the one you just showed this store to?" Joy asked.

"Don't worry yet. The other prospect hasn't even seen the property yet. But if you're serious about wanting to lease this storefront as your gallery, tell me sooner rather than later. I'm not the only Realtor showing this place, and I've already gotten several calls on it."

Joy nodded. "Noted. Thank you, Janelle."

"Anytime." Janelle handed her a business card. "Call me when you're ready to make your move." She winked. "Realtor humor. That line works better for people buying houses, I guess."

Joy gave an obligatory laugh. Then she glanced at the time on her phone. "I will. I have to go pick up Granger Fields's girls from school."

"Oh?"

"I'll be giving them art lessons for a while."

Janelle nodded. "Interesting."

Joy knew her refusal to call herself a caretaker was silly. It was only temporary and Joy was willing to do any and all the odd jobs that came around if it meant opening her art gallery here at this location. "Thank you for meeting me today, Janelle. I'll be in touch."

* * *

Granger's patience was being tested right now, and he was getting a C at best.

"What about the Lewis Farms?" his father asked.

Granger shook his head. "I called them all. The only thing I can think is that we'll have a limited supply so we'll need to double our prices this year to make up for that."

"Double our prices?" His father looked appalled by the idea. Of course he was. "We haven't raised our prices in ten years. I'd like to keep it that way."

"Dad..." Granger sighed. He was distracted by the sound of giggling across the house. There was a lot more noise and laughter going on with Joy watching Abby and Willow instead of Mrs. Townsend. "If we don't raise the cost, maybe we could reconsider reopening the lighted hayride. We have the path and all the supplies. They're in storage in Grandpa's old woodworking cabin. It'll be amazing. We can call the newspaper and get them to run a story on it for publicity and—"

"No." His father shook his head, his jawline going stiff.

Granger wasn't finished arguing just yet. "I could run Grandpa's old tractor and pull the trailer of customers. You wouldn't have to lift a finger. I'd do everything. Then the community would gather not only to buy our trees but also to experience the hayrides they used to love. Those rides used to be a staple of Sweetwater Springs Christmas festivities." They used to have a slogan on their sign that read A LITTLE PIECE OF CHRISTMAS ON EARTH. His dad had painted over that a long time ago though. Now it just read MERRY MOUNTAIN FARMS, ESTABLISHED 1971.

His father frowned. "You want to start that up after that child got hurt on our property? We'd be crazy to subject ourselves to that kind of risk again. The Weizer family could have sued us for all we had. We could have lost the farm, you know?"

"We could still lose the farm, Dad," Granger said pointedly.

"No." His father shook his head. "We have savings. The farm can lose a little profit this year and still be fine."

What about the year after that too? It took a lot longer than a year for a tree to grow to full size. "If we don't do something, we risk losing our customers," Granger pointed out. "If they go somewhere else for their tree this year, they might not come back to us next time."

His father's steel-blue eyes narrowed on Granger. "You think our customers would trade decades of loyalty because we missed one year of providing them with a tree?"

Granger lowered his face to his palm. This was no use.

The girls' laughter carried into the room again. This was about more than Granger and his dad. More than one year or two. This was also about his girls. Merry Mountain Farms was the family's legacy. He wanted them to have the option of running it one day if they wanted to. He wanted them to look back at the memories here and consider it a little piece of Christmas on Earth no matter where life carried them.

Granger lifted his face and looked at his dad again. "Last year, you told me you were going to start handing over more of the farm's responsibilities to me. If you want me to be a partner in running this farm, then you should treat me like a partner. You need to at least listen to me."

"I listened," his father argued. "But the farm doesn't need your suggestions unless they're about how we can get more trees. Check with the farms to the west of us. In Georgia and Tennessee."

Granger stood. "I'll do that tomorrow."

"Where are you going?" his father asked.

Granger didn't face him. "Someplace where people actually listen to me." He headed into the kitchen where his mom was preparing the girls' lunch boxes for tomorrow. "You don't have to do that."

She glanced over her shoulder at him. "I know but it'll save you time. I have dinner baking in your oven too. Your father's dinner is in the oven at our place so I can't help you serve it. I told Joy to check on the wings in about thirty minutes."

Granger felt a little kick in his chest at the mention of his new nanny... art teacher.

"I made enough for her too," his mom said, not bothering to look over at him this time. "I already invited her to stay. I hope that's okay."

Granger sometimes wondered if he should move away from Sweetwater Springs. He was a grown man but his father wouldn't listen to him and his mom still pushed her agendas, which lately seemed to be nudging him back into the dating arena. "I guess it is."

"The girls seem to be really enjoying her company today. And Joy is so talented. You should see what they've created this afternoon."

Granger glanced toward the living room. "I'll check in on them in just a minute."

His mom zipped up the last lunch box and turned to look at him. She held out her hand and counted off her good deeds on her fingers. "Chicken wings in the oven. The rice is on the stove. There's also a pot of beans warming. And I made a pitcher of sweet tea. It's in the fridge."

"What would I do without you?" Granger asked, giving her a hug.

"I don't know. You'd probably start dating again."

Granger pulled back and gave his mom an exasperated look. "That's old-fashioned, Mom. I don't need a wife to cook and clean for me. I can do that myself or hire someone."

"You can't hire someone to love you though. To listen to you or keep you warm at night, hmm?" She lifted a brow.

Granger didn't really want to get into how lonesome he was when he went to bed. He reached for Tin who was only a couple of feet away and ran his fingers through the dog's thick fur. "Tin loves me, don't you, girl?"

His mom tsked. "A dog's love is wonderful, yes, but it's not the same as a woman's. Okay, I'm going home. Call me if you need me."

"Take Dad with you," Granger muttered.

His father stepped into the room, overhearing him. "I'm going, I'm going. And I'll think about what you said."

Granger straightened. "Yeah?"

"The part about raising the costs, not the other," he said.

Granger's mom put her hands on her hips. "Raising the costs?" she asked in mock horror. "We don't overcharge our customers. Our customers are our family."

"It's called supply and demand. It's business," Granger said.

"Family business," his father amended. "Family is the most important thing. Money, work, and profit—they all come and go. Family sticks together. And our customers are family."

Granger held his tongue. He'd argued with his dad enough for one afternoon. Instead, he kissed his mom's cheek and watched them leave out the back door. Then he turned toward the sound of Joy's and the girls' laughter, following it this time. He stopped to stand in the entryway of the living room, where the floor was covered in old newspapers. His girls were dressed in painted paper bags that had been cut to become vests and hats.

"Where are my girls and what have you done with them?" Granger asked Joy.

Willow whirled. "We're right here, Daddy," she said on a giggle.

Abby smiled. At nine, she was maybe too old for paper costumes but Granger suspected she was doing it for her sister's sake. And because she looked up to Joy. Abby had always loved to create art. "We did our homework first," Abby clarified.

Joy beamed. She was also wearing a paper hat. She lifted one up to him. "No need to be jealous. We made you one too. We're having a dinner party, and it is required tonight," she said.

"All right." Granger's fingers brushed against Joy's as he took his hat.

He was tired of arguing. He was also tired of pretending he wasn't wildly attracted to Joy. But he'd have to try. She was his only saving grace this holiday, and he wasn't going to risk losing her too.

* * *

Joy couldn't remember the last time she'd sat around a dinner table. And she wasn't sure she ever had wearing a brown paper bag hat. "Does your mom cook dinner for you guys every night?"

Granger looked up and laughed. "I wish. She cooks a lot better than me."

"You're not that bad, Daddy," Abby said.

His gaze slid over. "Not that bad, huh?" He looked back

at Joy, a teasing look in his eyes. "Not sure if that's a compliment or not."

"Sometimes your food is good," Willow added. "You make good peanut butter and jelly sandwiches."

Granger shook his head, a self-deprecating smile curling on his mouth. "You two are going to make Joy think that I'm an awful father."

"I don't think that," Joy said, sliding her fork through a mound of beans on her plate. "You must be pretty great because these two girls are always talking about you."

"And tomorrow, we're making a special project just for you," Willow declared. "It's a secret."

Granger looked at Joy. "A secret?"

"More of a surprise. Don't worry. It's perfectly harmless. The girls tell me that your birthday was a couple weeks ago, and they weren't able to get you anything."

Granger looked between Abby and Willow. "You made cards. That was perfect."

"But Joy is going to help us make you a present tomorrow."

"It might take a couple nights," Joy said. "But it'll be worth it. Homemade presents are the best. That's what my aunt Darby always says."

"You have an Aunt Darby?" Abby asked. "Where is she?"

Joy slid some rice into her mouth. She chewed and swallowed before answering. "She lives here in town. I go see her a lot, and we make art together too."

"Can I come one day?" Abby asked.

"Me too, me too!" Willow chimed in.

"I'm sure my aunt Darby would love that." Joy laughed softly. Darby had always been fond of kids. "She comes to my art class at the community center a lot. Maybe you could be my assistants for the class I teach there. If your dad agrees."

"Pleeeease, Daddy," Abby begged.

"Maybe so." Granger popped a piece of chicken into his mouth.

"Mrs. Townsend could come too," Willow said. "We can't leave her behind. She'd be sad if we left her out. Wouldn't she, Abby?"

The noise and motion at the dinner table came to an immediate halt.

Joy looked up at Granger. He couldn't keep putting his daughter off forever. She understood why he wouldn't want to disappoint Willow but she'd recover. Kids were resilient. A lot more so than adults sometimes.

"We'll see," Granger said. "Mrs. Townsend is older. She might just want to hang back while you girls help Joy that day."

Joy's mouth fell open. Why was he hesitating? Bad news was like a Band-Aid that needed to be ripped off. "And sometimes, when you get older, you retire from working altogether," she said pointedly.

Granger met Joy's eyes, his smile replaced by a grim line now. They stared at one another across the dinner table, warring silently.

"Daddy, is Mrs. Townsend going to retire?" Willow asked. The skin between her blue eyes pinched with concern.

Granger broke eye contact with Joy and turned to his daughter.

Joy swallowed, willing him to tell her the truth, even if it was hard. Willow deserved to know that Mrs. Townsend wasn't coming back as her nanny. The longer he waited to tell her, the harder it would be.

"Well, you see..." He moved his food around on his plate. "Mrs. Townsend is..."

"Mrs. Townsend already retired, Willow," Abby blurted, looking up and beating him to the punch. "That's why Joy is here."

Willow didn't say anything for a long moment. Her face was a blank canvas. Then she looked at her father. "Is that true?"

Granger cleared his throat, his gaze sweeping to Joy. And Joy got the distinct impression that he wasn't thrilled with her right now. "I'm afraid so, honey. But we should be happy for Mrs. Townsend. Now she gets to do whatever she wants, anytime she wants."

A hiccup escaped from Willow's mouth. "I thought she wanted to play with us. I thought she loved us. Why would she want to leave?" Tears began rolling down her flushed cheeks. "Why did she leave us?" Then she burst into gut-wrenching sobs that had Tin running toward the table to nudge her wet nose into Willow's thigh.

Joy felt gutted as she watched. This was why Granger hadn't wanted to tell Willow the truth. Joy had assumed that Willow could handle it but evidently, she couldn't.

Any woman who stepped into the girls' lives needed to be someone with staying power. At least when Joy was no longer caring for them after the holidays, she'd still be around to give them art classes. She'd also make a point to stop in for friendly visits. She hadn't realized what a big deal it was for Granger to trust her with his girls—and here she was tonight, already letting him down.

CHAPTER FIVE

*W*illow? I'm sorry, honey. I know you loved Mrs. Townsend." Granger knelt by her side.

Willow had her knees curled up to her stomach and her face hidden behind a shield of bent elbows as she sat on her bed. She hadn't looked up at Granger since she'd darted from the table and run in here.

"Will you say something? Please talk to me."

She sniffled quietly.

Granger reached out and touched her softly. "Willow?"

After several more moments, he stood up. "All right. I'll be in the kitchen when you're ready to come out and talk. Want me to send Abby in here?"

Willow peeked up from her arms. "She knew and didn't tell me. Just like you."

Granger swallowed. "She overheard me talking to Nana the other day."

"Nana knew too?" Willow cried. "You all treat me like I'm a baby. It's not fair. Just go away!"

Granger didn't move for a moment. "I'm sorry, sweetheart. I was just...I was just trying to protect you." Which was all he'd ever done. On a weary sigh, he headed back down the hall and entered the dining room where Joy and Abby were cleaning off the table.

"Is she okay?" Joy asked.

"Not really, thanks to you." His words came out harsh but what right did Joy have to push this issue? Yes, Abby was the one who'd actually told Willow but only because Joy had raised the subject. And Abby was a kid. All of this shouldn't lie on her shoulders.

"It's my fault," Abby said. "Want me to go talk to her?"

Granger shook his head. "Maybe we should just give her some time."

"I can talk to her," Joy offered. "Let me try. I'm not family, and sometimes that makes it easier. Please. I want a chance to fix this."

Granger stared at her. Against his better judgment, he nodded. "Fine."

"Thank you." Joy turned and headed down the hall to Willow's bedroom.

"Dad, I'm sorry," Abby said in a small voice. She sounded on the verge of tears now too. "It was just building up inside me, and it was like I couldn't keep it a secret anymore. It just exploded out of me. I'm really sorry. Are you mad?" she asked.

Granger walked over to his oldest daughter and wrapped an arm around her shoulders. "Not one bit. Willow needed to know, so you kind of did me a favor."

Abby furrowed her brow. "Then why were you looking at Joy that way?"

"What way?"

"Like you were mad at her."

Granger exhaled softly. "I'm not mad at her. Just upset with myself, I guess."

"You should make sure that Joy knows that too. So she'll keep coming back." Abby looked at her father earnestly.

"You like her, huh?" Granger asked.

Abby nodded. "She's a lot more fun than Mrs. Townsend was. And she likes art."

Granger already knew that Mrs. Townsend had frowned on making crafts because that required cleanup. "I'll be sure I talk to Joy tonight before she leaves," he promised. He didn't say what he'd be talking to Joy about, however. He and Joy hadn't really laid ground rules about this arrangement of theirs. His girls had been through a lot, and she needed to understand that. He also needed to make sure that Joy wouldn't be jumping ship anytime soon.

A few minutes later, Joy entered the room again, smiling this time. Willow was beside her, holding her hand.

"Hey," Granger said hesitantly. "Looks like you two had a nice talk. Everything . . . okay?"

"Better than okay," Joy said, looking from him and down to Willow. "Right?"

Willow's head bobbed on the air, a smile creeping up on her mouth. "It was a great talk. Joy said Mrs. Townsend is going to play with her friends now, just like I like to play with Chloe and Vala. And she's going to eat as much ice cream and candy as she wants now that she doesn't have to eat fruits and vegetables with us. Because we're growing up and we need fruits and veggies. Right, Joy?"

Joy's cheeks darkened a touch as she nodded and glanced up at Granger. "So you see, we should be happy for Mrs. Townsend. We'll miss her but we can still draw her pretty pictures and write cards and send them to her."

"I can't wait to draw her a picture with Joy," Willow said.

Kids were so resilient. Granger hoped the same was true for Abby.

"Sounds perfect," Granger said.

"And Joy said that we can probably eat some of that ice cream in the freezer. To celebrate with Mrs. Townsend from a distance."

Joy grimaced, and Granger had to laugh.

"I guess we can do that," he said.

"But not me," Joy said. "I'm afraid I need to head home. I need to prepare for our big surprise project tomorrow, remember?"

Granger noticed the way that Abby perked up. Whatever beefs he had with Joy, he was pleased with how well she interacted with Abby and Willow. "Can I, uh, talk to you outside for a moment, Joy?"

Her mouth formed a little O. What happened at dinner wasn't ideal but she'd made up for it by comforting Willow with her unconventional wisdom.

"I'll get the ice cream for Willow and me," Abby told Granger.

He nodded and followed Joy outside.

Joy turned to face him and started the conversation. "I am so sorry. I didn't realize Willow would be so upset. I wasn't thinking."

Granger shoved his hands in the pockets of his jeans and nodded. He headed down the steps, distancing himself from the house in case little ears were listening. "If you're going to work with the girls, we should talk." He glanced over at Joy, who matched him step for step. "For the past year, Willow has been asking questions about her mom. I guess I knew she would one day. She was just a baby when my ex left. Once she started getting older, she saw her friends with their moms and the questions began."

"How much does she know about why her mom left?" Joy asked.

Granger chuckled dryly. "I'm guessing not as much as you." He'd never told Joy his story but the same was true for most people in the town. And yet, everyone seemed to know. Or think they did. "Erin got really depressed after she had Willow. No matter what we did, she spiraled lower and lower." He stopped to stand by Joy's car. "Then one day, she just packed her bags and left." Granger looked down at his feet. No matter how hard he tried not to blame himself, he always did. Still. "I thought she'd come back but she didn't. Instead, she sent me divorce papers a year later, and that was it."

"I'm so sorry," Joy said quietly.

Granger met her gaze. "Me too... Sorry for my girls mostly. They need their mother but Erin doesn't see it that way. She was a great mom. No one ever would've thought she'd be capable of turning her back on us. I never would have thought that." He looked back at the house to make sure the girls were still inside. Then he turned to Joy. "So you see, they've lost enough. Especially now that Mrs. Townsend has retired without any notice. I know this arrangement of ours is temporary..."

"Just through Christmas," Joy said.

Granger nodded. "And we'll be up front with them about that fact the whole time. We'll make sure they know that when you're done here, you're not abandoning them."

"And I'll still teach arts and crafts at the library after the holidays. They can come to my studio and gallery for classes once I have it up and running."

Granger felt his body relax. "So we understand each other."

"Perfectly." Joy's gaze connected with his. "I'm not going anywhere, Granger. Trust me."

Trust was a tall request but Granger was going to do his best.

* * *

On Friday night, Joy and the girls were just finishing up their belated birthday surprises for Granger. Joy hadn't planned for the art pieces to be so intricate but Abby and Willow had really gotten into making and decorating their crafts.

"Daddy is going to love mine," Willow said, beaming at the tree she'd made out of an upside-down wire vegetable cage. The conical cage was used for growing tomato plants. Joy and the girls had spray painted it purple per Willow's request, tying large purple and gold ribbons to the wires that encircled it horizontally, and then she'd adorned it with plastic jewels, beads, and homemade ornaments.

"It really is beautiful," Joy said, not stretching the truth at all.

Abby's tree was made of a wire cage as well. Instead of ribbon, she'd decorated it with various items she'd found around the house. "Mine is kind of abstract," Abby said.

"I love abstract." Joy nodded at the creation. "It shows a lot of creativity."

"I've heard of a Christmas tree but never a birthday tree," Abby said.

Joy sat on the floor with the girls, admiring the finished art pieces. "When I was your age, my aunt Darby and I set up a tree for every occasion. Even Halloween," she said, looking at Willow. "And we made them out of whatever we could find. I made a tree out of a plastic soda bottle once."

"Whoa!" Abby said, obviously impressed.

"It was a lot of fun. Anyway, your dad is a tree farmer. He'll love the fact that you girls made your own special trees just for him."

From the kitchen, Joy heard the back door open and close.

"He's home!" Willow jumped up. "Can we give him our surprises now?"

Joy laughed and stood as well. "I guess so. We've been hiding these from him all week. I'm sure he's just as eager to see them as you are to show him."

Willow took off running toward the kitchen, her pale-blond hair blowing off her shoulders as she raced.

Abby stayed put. "This is the prettiest tree ever," she said quietly. "Thank you for helping us with these."

Joy smiled. "Of course, sweetheart."

Granger's heavy footsteps traveled through the kitchen until he was standing in the entryway of the living room with his eyes closed.

Joy's heart gave a soft kick. It'd been doing that every time she saw him this week. It had always done that when he'd brought the girls to the library. She was just seeing him more regularly now, and the feeling was becoming harder to ignore.

"Can I look yet?" he asked.

"Not yet." Willow turned to look at Abby. "Are we ready?"

Abby nodded excitedly.

"Okay! Yet!" Willow said, tugging on Granger's arm.

He opened his eyes, meeting Joy's gaze first. Her heart stalled. It was just a crush. One that she didn't need to nurture because he was a ready-made family waiting to happen. She'd been in a serious relationship last year, and she wasn't ready to jump into another anytime soon. In fact, she'd promised herself she wouldn't. This year was about furthering her art career.

"Well, what do you think?" Joy finally said, when Granger didn't pull his gaze from hers immediately.

He looked at the wire sculptures now, his expression shifting. His eyebrows lifted as he stepped closer.

"Wow," he said. "You guys did this?"

Willow bounced on her heels, clapping her hands at her chest. "Yes! All week! We worked so hard, Daddy."

"They did," Joy agreed on a laugh.

Abby sat proudly beside her tree. "These are your birthday trees. You're supposed to put them up for your birthday so people can put their presents under them but we're a little late."

"And the trees are your presents," Willow clarified. "But Joy said you can keep them out through Christmas."

Granger nodded and stepped closer. "These are incredible."

Joy felt a surge of pride for the girls. "I guess your dad likes his presents."

"I love them, actually," he agreed, looking at Abby and Willow. "They're so special. I can't believe you made these."

"And you can keep them forever," Abby said, her eyes bright behind her glasses.

"I definitely will." Granger looked at the trees again. "I think we should celebrate with some hot chocolate. Abby, can you and Willow make it?"

Abby jumped up, and Willow followed.

"Don't forget the marshmallows," Willow called as they darted toward the kitchen.

"I can't believe you did this with the girls," Granger said to Joy when they were gone. "You made these or they did?"

Joy wondered if he was upset with her. Last time he'd

gotten her alone it was after she'd pushed the issue about Mrs. Townsend. Did Granger not want his girls working with potentially dangerous materials? "It was completely safe. I handled the hot glue gun for Willow. And I helped her hold the spray paint can when we sprayed her tree. She even wore a mask and goggles."

Granger bent to admire Abby's tree, the motion bringing him closer to Joy. He smelled like evergreens, and without thinking, she inhaled deeply. "And it took you three days?"

"We started working on it Wednesday. We could've finished faster but the girls had homework and chores. This didn't keep them from any of their responsibilities," Joy added, in case that's what Granger was worried about. There was definitely something on his mind.

"These are special."

"You seem surprised. I am a real artist, you know," Joy said, her tone becoming just a tad defensive. She couldn't help it.

Granger looked at her and straightened. "You could teach others to make these?"

Joy nodded. "Of course. They're not that hard to make. They're kind of fun too. What are you thinking?"

Granger shrugged. Then the girls walked in.

"Your cocoa is ready at the kitchen table," Abby said.

"With lots of marshmallows," Willow added.

Granger redirected his attention to the girls and followed their lead, leaving Joy standing there momentarily. He'd been thinking something but she didn't think he was upset with her this time. She headed toward the kitchen as well.

"Well, I will see you two on Monday afternoon," she told the girls on her way out.

"Don't you want to stay?" Granger asked.

Joy turned back.

"There's a cup of hot cocoa with your name on it."
He gestured at the spot beside him. She suspected that the
right thing to do was make an excuse and leave. This was
his family time. The girls needed him—not more of her.

Despite her inner objections, however, Joy walked to
the table, pulled out the chair, and sat. "I can't resist a cup
of hot chocolate." And she was having a harder and harder
time resisting her attraction to Granger as well.

* * *

The house was dark except for the twinkle of the lights that
the girls had strung on Granger's new birthday trees after
dinner. He sat in his favorite chair and stared at them, ideas
bouncing around in his head. Crazy, insane ideas.

He hadn't brought the ideas up with Joy yet, and it would
all hinge on her willingness to help. She was already saving
him for the next two months by watching the girls.

Granger admired the trees. They weren't evergreens but
they were colorful works of art. They were festive, and they
would draw in a crowd to Merry Mountain Farms. People
would pay to come and create their own unique Christmas
tree with Joy as their instructor. Like the lighted hayrides
he wanted to bring back, these crafted trees were another
way to attract people to Merry Mountain Farms.

Excitement flickered in his chest. People would start
coming to buy their trees any day now. They had enough
trees to get through the first few weeks of the season maybe
but then the big rush would come and they'd sell out fast.
What would keep customers coming to the farm through
the holidays?

Perhaps if Joy were having classes and teaching the

crowds to make their very own trees this year, then they'd want to do that. Some, at least. In addition to a live tree farm, they could have a Christmas tree workshop here at Merry Mountain Farms this year.

"Daddy?"

Granger peered into the darkness at his oldest daughter. "What are you still doing up?"

"Can't sleep," she said quietly.

"Something on your mind?" Granger asked.

Abby walked over to him and climbed into his lap. He could feel the heaviness of her thoughts, which made his own breaths grow shallow. "Is Mama ever coming home?"

Granger knew that Willow was thinking about her mom lately but he'd thought that Abby had stopped hoping and wondering. Like him. Erin had made her choice. She'd cut them off, and he'd moved on. But maybe a daughter never did. "Why are you asking that tonight?"

Abby shrugged. "Joy just makes things a lot of fun. She talks to us like maybe a mom would." Abby swiped at the hair in her face, batting it away. "I know you said she's not staying so I was wondering if my mom would ever come back."

Granger wasn't sure how to answer that. He thought the answer was no but he couldn't rob Abby of any hope she might have. He also didn't want to get her hopes up just to be dashed. "No matter if she does or doesn't, you'll always have me."

Abby blinked at him. Maybe *he* wasn't enough. Then she kissed his cheek and stood up. She looked over at the trees that she, Willow, and Joy had made together. "They're really pretty, huh?"

Granger nodded. "They really are."

"I can't wait to see Joy again on Monday afternoon. I love her art lessons. My mom probably doesn't even like art, so..."

Granger reached for Abby's hand and squeezed it. "Your mom loved you, okay?"

Abby hesitated. "Maybe she doesn't know we want her to come back. Maybe she thinks we don't want her anymore."

Granger had made it clear to Erin that the opposite was true. But how could he tell Abby that? "Maybe so," he said instead. It probably wasn't the right thing to say but telling Abby that her mom knew they wanted her in their lives and still chose to stay away was far worse.

Abby nodded thoughtfully. Her eyes looked a little brighter so maybe he hadn't said the wrong thing after all. "Good night, Daddy."

"Night."

Tin got up and looked at Granger as if to say good night as well. Then, faithful dog that she was, she followed Abby to her room. Granger got up and retreated to his room as well. Sometimes it was better to keep hope alive. To believe in Santa and flying reindeer. And in moms who came home.

CHAPTER SIX

$\mathcal{G}$ranger had been watching the driveway from the living room window for the past half hour, waiting for Joy's car to pull up with the girls. Yeah, he was excited to see Abby and Willow. Of course he was. But he also couldn't wait to discuss his idea for the farm with Joy.

He'd considered talking to his dad first but he didn't want to give anyone a chance to shoot this idea down. It hinged on Joy. If she said yes, Granger would do whatever it took to convince his father. There was a large wooden shelter on the east side of the farm, where they used to have family barbecues and cookouts. It'd be the perfect place for classes. Granger could get some outdoor heaters to keep the crafters warm.

It was low cost and had the potential to make the farm money. And it would be good for Joy too.

Joy's car turned into the long driveway, and Granger's heart leaped into his throat. Yeah, some part of him wanted to lay eyes on Joy too. He stepped out of the house as the car came to a stop. The driver's side door opened and Joy stepped out. Then Abby and Willow pushed their way out of the car and ran up to give Granger a hug.

He chatted with them for just a moment and then distracted them with the promise of cookies inside.

Joy was about to follow, when he held up a finger.

"Just a second," he said. "They'll be fine for a bit."

Joy nodded. "Okay." She turned to face him, shoving her fingers in the front pockets of her jeans. "It seems like you're always trying to get me alone."

Granger felt his mouth drop open. "Uh..."

"Usually it's because I've messed up somehow."

"I seem to recall you pulling me aside when I messed up after not picking up the girls."

Joy grinned. "True. I guess we're even. Or we were until now. What's up?"

Granger sucked in a breath. He was really excited about this idea, and he wanted Joy to agree. "Those trees you and the girls made for my birthday..."

"You like them." A large smile spread through her cheeks.

"Love them," he said. "Can you do that again?"

Joy's brows furrowed. "What? With the girls?"

"With people. Merry Mountain Farms lost half our trees in a fire earlier this year."

Joy nodded. "I remember."

"We don't have enough stock, and I can't get any shipped in for the holidays. People will come here expecting trees, and we'll run out quickly." He'd been thinking about this all weekend. Now it was Monday, and the ideas were pouring out of him.

"I'm not following. Do you think I can help somehow?"

"I hope so. I'm trying to convince Dad to bring the lighted hayrides back to the farm."

"Oh, wow. I remember going on those as a little girl. My aunt Darby would take me, and I'd snuggle into the crook of her arm, and we'd just soak it all in. It was always my favorite part of the holidays. A little piece of Christmas on Earth."

"That's what the sign read," Granger said, surprised that she remembered.

"I know. And it was true…It still is. It's just"—she shrugged—"it's not quite the same. Sorry."

Granger nodded. "No, I agree with you. But my dad doesn't see it that way. A kid got hurt on the ride a few years back, and he's kept the ride shut down. But without trees, what will keep our customers returning to the farm?"

Joy shook her head. "I don't know."

"Well, the hayride, for one." Granger gestured at Joy. "And you."

"Me?" She drew back.

"You could help us provide more trees to the community by having a Christmas tree workshop. You could teach others to make their own unique trees, just like you did with the girls."

Joy's lips parted. "What?"

"You only want to be paid as a working artist, right? Well, this would meet that description. And you'd be saving Merry Mountain Farms in the process. I'd owe you. If people go somewhere else to find a tree this year, they may never come back. But if they come here and make a Christmas memory that they can cherish forever, they'll always return. I know it sounds like a lot but I need the help and you want to lease that store, right?"

"Yes," Joy agreed.

"Well, this is another way to make income. Not a lot, but you could also sell your artwork to our customers. With a holiday frame of mind, they'll be looking for presents. It'd be a win-win."

Joy's eyes were wide as she looked at him. "Are you serious?"

"Yeah. I mean, I've been thinking about this all weekend. It's all I could do not to go to your place and see what you thought."

"I'm flattered. But what about your mom and dad? Do they like this idea?"

Granger's excitement took a nosedive. "Well, I haven't run it by Dad yet. I wanted to talk to you first. To see if you were remotely interested in helping us."

Joy hesitated. "I'm interested. So I would be teaching people to make trees? And caring for the girls after school? Who would watch them while I teach the classes?"

"I'm thinking it'd just be one or two classes a week. Maybe just on the weekends."

Joy seemed to consider this. "The girls could be my assistants during the classes. They'd love it."

And Granger loved that she considered them first and brought them into the equation. That's why she was the perfect one to be caring for them this holiday season.

She nodded. "I'll stay with them on the weekdays and teach the Christmas tree workshops during the weekend."

"And you'll still have time for your library and community center classes while the girls are at school," Granger added.

"It'll be a busy season but it'll give me enough income to put a deposit on my store." Her eyes lit up. "Okay. I'll do it."

Granger wanted to wrap his arms around her and hug her. Because she'd just agreed to help him make Merry Mountain Farms a little piece of Christmas on Earth again.

And because some part of him was looking for any excuse to touch her. Instead, he shoved his hands in his pockets and smiled back at her. "Great."

* * *

"I don't want to do art today," Willow said, her bottom lip turning down a half hour later. "I want to play."

Joy had planned on making beaded items. "You know what? I don't want to do art this afternoon either."

Both Abby and Willow gasped.

"What?" Joy looked between them. "I like more than just art."

"Like what?" Abby asked.

Joy shrugged. "I like exercise. We could take a walk on the farm. You could show me around."

"We're not supposed to do that without an adult," Willow said. "But I guess you count as one."

Joy laughed. She would hope a thirty-year-old woman counted. But to a child, maybe the criteria for being an adult was different. Maybe you needed to be married with kids of your own. Or have a real job. That was certainly Joy's parents' perception.

"Put on your shoes and jackets," Joy said. "We'll head out. We all need some fresh air." She hadn't been able to think of anything else other than Granger's newest proposal anyway. It was an exciting proposition. And maybe it would be just the ticket to earn her enough money to lease her store.

The air was chilly as they left the house and circled the farm. Abby was a natural tour guide, pointing out the orchards, strawberry patches, and what was left of the family's tree farm.

"Daddy planted more trees this summer," she explained.

"But it takes two years for one to grow," Willow added. "That's what he told us. Sometimes even longer than that."

Joy found this interesting. "Wow. That's a very long time." That meant not only would the farm be struggling this holiday but it would be at a deficit for trees next Christmas as well.

"The fire was my fault," Willow said, looking down at her feet as she walked.

"Oh, honey. I'm sure that's not true." Joy glanced at Abby, who didn't disagree. How could one seven-year-old little girl burn down half a tree farm though?

"It was my mommy's birthday. I saw it on Nana's calendar. So I made her a mud pie because Mrs. Townsend said I couldn't use the oven to bake her a cake."

Joy's steps slowed as they walked. Tin ran up ahead, circling back every few minutes and wagging her tail excitedly. One time she darted off into the woods, staying gone for several long minutes. Abby said that Tin did that a lot but always came back so they continued forward on their path.

"I'm the reason our farm is struggling this year," Willow said. "I borrowed Daddy's matches and found a candle in one of the kitchen drawers so that I could put it on my mud pie. I didn't mean to catch a tree on fire. It just happened really fast," Willow explained. "And then another tree and another until there were so many flames."

Joy gasped, her imagination filling in the details. It must have been a horrifying experience for such a young child. And for Granger.

"Mrs. Townsend wasn't here that day," Abby said. "I told Daddy that I could watch Willow for an hour. He was only in the backyard. So the fire was kind of my fault too."

Joy's heart broke for Abby and Willow. They'd both been through so much in their short lives. Joy wrapped one arm around each girl. "Sometimes bad things just happen, and it's no one's fault."

Abby looked up at Joy. "If Mom had been here, then we would've had a real cake for her birthday. And she would've made sure that Willow didn't play with Dad's matches. She should have been here with us. We need her."

Joy didn't think Abby was blaming her mom at all; instead, she seemed to be missing her. "Well, my mom raised me, so I can't really say that I know exactly how you feel. But even though I had her in my life, she wasn't really there for me when I was growing up." Or now, for that matter.

Willow looked up at Joy. "Where was she?"

"At the hospital."

"Is she sick?" Willow asked.

Joy smiled. "No, she's a doctor. So is my dad," Joy said, watching Tin dart out of the woods at full speed. She had a lot of energy to burn off this afternoon. "They had busy schedules, and they didn't have time for silly things like playing dolls or creating artistic masterpieces."

"That's sad," Abby said.

"A little. But I had my aunt Darby. She always had time for me," Joy told them.

"We don't have an aunt," Willow said.

Joy looked at her. "Well, you do have a nana and papa close by. And you have me too."

"You're temporary," Abby pointed out. "Dad keeps making sure we know that."

Joy feigned insult. "You had me before I started caring for you two after school. You've been coming to the library for my classes for the last year. And after Christmas, you'll still have me. Sweetwater Springs is my home, so I'm definitely not just temporary."

Abby smiled at this, showing off a missing bottom tooth.

They walked past the last of the Christmas trees now and came up on Granger's parents' house.

"Let's go inside and see Nana," Willow said.

"Oh, I don't know. She might be busy," Joy hedged, but Willow tugged her forward. "She's never too busy for us. Come on. She has homemade apple cider. You're going to love it."

Joy started to knock on the back door but Abby turned the knob and walked right in with Willow and Tin following behind her.

Joy took a hesitant step inside as well, glancing around for any sign of the older couple. The kitchen was empty.

"I'll make us some cider," Willow said, opening the fridge.

"I'll get the cups," Abby added.

Tin trotted over to a dog bed in the far corner of the room and plopped down, making herself right at home as well. Evidently, the family dog had worn herself out in the woods.

As the girls prepared cider, Joy's attention diverted to male voices in another room. They were raised and sounded like they were arguing over something. Her breath stalled. Maybe they shouldn't be here. It sounded like Granger. He was probably talking to his dad, who Joy had met a handful of times. He was a nice man. Granger favored him, at least in the looks department.

"Uh-oh. Dad and Papa are fighting again," Abby said, her eyes wide.

"Again? They fight a lot?" Joy asked.

"All the time," Willow said.

Joy reached for the glass of cider that Abby slid in front of her and took a sip, adding a dash under her mental pros-and-cons list on Granger.

Pro: He's handsome.
Pro: He makes my heart skip around in my chest.
Con: He has a full plate, a lot of baggage with an ex-wife, and he argues with his father.

And since the last thing Joy needed was a complicated, drama-filled romance, that was reason enough to keep her eyes and heart to herself. Last Christmas had nearly broken her. Any forthcoming romance would be as temporary as Joy's job here at Merry Mountain Farms.

Granger appeared in the kitchen entryway, his face flushed and his jawline hard. He looked surprised that they were sitting at the kitchen island. "What are you guys doing here?"

"Drinking cider," Willow said. "And listening to you and Papa argue again. If Abby and I aren't allowed to argue, why are you and Papa allowed to?"

Granger frowned and looked at Joy, his expression softening. "Sorry."

"No, I'm the one who should apologize. The girls gave me a tour of the farm and then thought it'd be okay to come inside for something to drink. We didn't mean to intrude. I can take them home."

Granger exhaled a breath and walked to the fridge. "No, it's okay. I'll join you." He poured himself a glass of cider and took the only remaining stool at the island, which happened to be next to Joy.

Her heart skipped, and her body warmed. She reminded

herself of the con side of her list but those cons dimmed when he was sitting so close, his elbow bumping against hers as he lifted his glass of juice. "You're left-handed?" she asked, noticing that he held his glass closest to her right side. His left.

He faced her. "Yep."

"Picasso was a lefty."

Granger chuckled. "Believe me, I'm no Picasso."

"We'll see. Maybe you'll be my first student at the Christmas tree workshop," she said, hearing her tone of voice drop to something that sounded unintentionally flirty. She couldn't seem to help herself around this man.

Granger looked suddenly apologetic again. "About that…"

* * *

Granger was furious when he'd been talking to his father earlier. He'd kept his calm as his dad had shaken his head, refusing to even consider the idea of a Christmas tree workshop. His dad was the one to raise his voice, growing defensive as Granger pressed. His argument was futile though. His dad wouldn't even hear him out.

Now Granger felt guilty as he looked at Joy. He never should have brought the idea to her before discussing it with his dad first. Now her hopes were up, and he was going to have to be the bad guy who sent them spiraling back to Earth.

Her smile faltered. "That's what you and your dad were arguing about, isn't it? He doesn't like the idea?"

Granger inhaled deeply and then exhaled. "No. He doesn't like anything that isn't cutting down trees and loading them onto our customers' vehicles. I really thought the

Christmas tree workshop was close enough to that concept that he'd go for it."

"I see." She looked at her glass of cider, her shoulders rounding.

Granger had just brought the idea to her an hour earlier but she was obviously disappointed. "I'm sorry," he said quietly.

"No, it's okay. Not your fault," she said quickly. She wouldn't look at him anymore though.

Then Willow hijacked the conversation and started telling him about her day at school.

Granger nodded and listened, very aware of Joy's silence beside him. Finally, he looked at her. "I'm done with my work for today if you want to head home."

"Okay. Chelsea will be expecting me," Joy said, putting on a smile. Granger knew it was just for the girls' sake. "I can find my way back to my car." She stood and looked at Abby and Willow. "And I'll see you two lovelies tomorrow after school."

"Can we do something with art tomorrow?" Abby asked.

"You didn't have an art class today?" Granger asked.

Joy shrugged. "We decided to take a little break. Sometimes artists need fresh air and exercise to feed their creativity."

"I see. I'm...uh..." He had no idea what to say to make this better.

Joy held up a hand. "No need," she said, shaking her head and warding off any words of apology. "I've got to head home. I'll see you tomorrow." She waved at the girls, slid a look at Granger, and left.

"What did you do?" Abby frowned up at him.

"What do you mean?"

"Joy looks upset. Did you scare her off?"

Willow's expression twisted. "What? Joy isn't coming back?" His youngest daughter suddenly appeared on the verge of tears.

Granger shook his head. "Of course she's coming back. I didn't do anything." Except offer her a job and then snatch it away. The job wouldn't have brought in a ton of income but she was working hard to start up her art gallery. Every dollar counted, he guessed.

"You're sure she's coming back?" Abby asked, her expression wary.

Granger nodded. "Absolutely." Although the uncertain looks on his daughters' faces cast a shadow of doubt. Maybe he'd irreparably broken Joy's trust. And now she'd break her promise.

CHAPTER SEVEN

Joy changed into a tank top and pajama pants as soon as she got home. She wasn't leaving her townhome anymore today so why not? Then she checked Chelsea's food and water, poured herself a bowl of Lucky Charms cereal, and sat down on her couch to eat.

She lived alone. She could do things like eat cereal for dinner while seated in front of the TV. Only, the TV wasn't on. Instead, she was sulking for a reason she didn't understand. She didn't even feel like painting tonight, which was her usual nighttime activity.

There wasn't even a ton of money to be made running Granger's Christmas tree workshop. So why was she so upset?

Because the idea had excited her. It'd felt magical and like something she and Aunt Darby would've done once upon a time. And because Joy loved to teach art. She loved helping others find that satisfied whimsy that she herself found when she created.

Joy shoveled a spoonful of cereal into her mouth and stared at the wall ahead as she crunched loudly. And yeah, some part of her had been excited about having one more reason to see Granger during the week. What was wrong with her?

Her cell phone vibrated on the couch beside her. She glanced over and actually started laughing until milk dribbled off her chin. The caller ID said it was her mom. Of course it was, because Joy wasn't down in the dumps enough.

"I'm not answering, Mom," she told the phone as it continued to ring and vibrate. "You couldn't pay me to answer right now."

Then Chelsea leaped onto the couch and swiped her paw across the phone's screen perfectly.

Joy shot up, spilling milk down the front of her top.

"Joy?" her mom's voice called from the speaker. "Joy, are you there?"

Joy eyed Chelsea and set her bowl of cereal down. That's what Joy got for downloading the cat app on her iPad the other day. Now Chelsea was able to chase virtual fish on the screen. Evidently, she'd also mastered a good swipe and could now answer Joy's cell phone.

Joy reluctantly brought the phone to her ear. "Hi, Mom."

"Did I catch you at a bad time?"

Yes. "No, just eating dinner," Joy said.

"Oh, that's nice. What's for dinner?"

Joy didn't really want to answer that question so she ignored it and changed the subject. "What are you calling about, Mom?"

"Well, I'm on my way home from the hospital and wanted to touch base with you. There's a receptionist job opening at the hospital lobby area. It doesn't pay a lot but it offers benefits and it's steady. I told the chief of staff to hold off on advertising the position until I spoke to you first. He owes me a favor."

"Hiring me would be a favor?" Joy asked dryly.

"Joy, I've been worried. Your car has broken down, and several of my patients have mentioned seeing you walking around town. You can't even afford to drive now?"

"No need to be concerned. I have my car back," Joy told her.

"But what happens next time? Living paycheck to paycheck is all well and good until you have another emergency. It only takes one to put someone on the streets, you know. Not that your father and I would ever let that happen but we do worry about you."

"Unnecessarily," Joy said, forcing herself to take a breath. This conversation was already making her chest feel tight. "And as I told you before, I'm hoping to lease a place for my art gallery soon. I can't run my own business and be a hospital receptionist."

"How will you afford to lease a store on the money you draw in?"

Joy got up from the couch and grabbed a towel to dry herself off. "I'll afford it the same way I afforded to go to art school," Joy said, resentment rising. She knew her parents had only refused to pay for her college because they'd wanted her to choose a safer degree. One that would guarantee financial stability. That didn't ease the sting of feeling that they didn't support her though. Especially when her mom was arguing for her to take a job at the hospital.

The doorbell rang, and Joy whirled, looking at the opportunity as an escape. "Someone's at the door, Mom. I have to go."

"Just think about the position," her mom said before Joy said goodbye and disconnected the call.

Joy wasn't thinking about anything. Least of all who might be on the other side of her door as she opened it.

Granger stood on her porch, his hands tucked into his jeans pockets. He smiled, his gaze lowering. Joy looked down at her attire as well. She was wearing flannel pants with hearts and half a bowl of milk down the front of her tank top.

"What are you doing here?" she asked.

Granger looked taken aback. "I was hoping to talk to you. Can I come in?"

"Sure." She gestured him inside and then closed the front door behind her. "I'd offer you a seat on my couch," she said, "but I just spilled my cereal milk."

He gave her an amused look.

"Chelsea, my cat, spilled the milk, actually. She's very mischievous, especially when she's mad that I've been gone all afternoon."

Granger shook his head. "I don't need to sit down. I just came by to make sure I didn't totally mess up what we have going. If you don't come back to watch the girls tomorrow, they'll be devastated."

Joy furrowed her brow. "Why wouldn't I come back?"

"Because I offered you a job that you were excited about, and then I took it away."

Joy folded her arms in front of her. "So you think I would just not return to my commitment because you disappointed me?"

Granger looked vulnerable somehow as he watched her.

"That *is* what you think. Granger, I promised you that I'd stay through the holidays. I'm not backing out. Not even for a hospital receptionist position."

His brows scrunched.

Joy waved a dismissive hand. "I was just on the phone with my mother, and she was trying to convince me to apply.

The hospital's chief of staff apparently owes her a favor, and I get first dibs on a 'real job.' Lucky me." Joy rolled her eyes. "I'm coming back to Merry Mountain tomorrow and taking care of Abby and Willow. Don't worry."

Granger seemed to exhale a breath that he had been holding.

Joy wasn't sure why but she reached for his hand. "I made you a promise. I'm not going to break it, okay? No matter how many times you put your foot in your mouth or disappoint me."

He met her gaze. "Thank you. It's just, if I screw up, those girls will be lying on some couch talking to a counselor one day about all my inadequacies."

Joy laughed. "My parents have a lot of faults, and I've never done that. I just create abstract art that secretly relays how messed up I am because of them." She winked.

The magnetic pull of Granger's gaze seemed to intensify. She had a sudden urge to kiss him. A strong urge. When was the last time she had been alone in her living room with an attractive man at night? It was too far back to remember.

But she wasn't going to kiss him. Things were too complicated between them already. She let go of his hand.

"Thank you for helping with the girls. And for understanding. I'm not sure what I'd do without you right now."

"You'd be fine, I'm sure."

Chelsea strutted into the room to glare at Granger, her tail twitching.

Granger glanced down at Joy's cat. "I'm not a cat person. What does it mean when she's looking at me like that?"

Joy laughed. "Chelsea is very jealous. I'm hers, and you are encroaching on her territory."

Granger looked from Chelsea back to Joy, his eyes suddenly dark. "I wonder what she'd do if I came closer."

Joy held her breath as Granger stepped toward her, her heart beating erratically.

Granger's eyes slid to look at Chelsea, who continued to twitch her tail, her green eyes round. Then he looked at Joy again. "Should I be worried?" he asked in a low voice.

Joy swallowed. Her mouth was suddenly dry. Without thinking, she ran a tongue over her lips. "Sadly, Chelsea was already declawed when I rescued her from the shelter. But she still has teeth."

Granger grinned, his gaze still dark. There was an unmistakable heat there. "I'm taking my chances standing this close."

"You are," Joy agreed. Then Granger leaned toward her, drawing closer until he was one breath away from making contact with her lips. Every thought left her mind as she closed her eyes, let out a sigh, and melted into his kiss.

* * *

Granger had been wanting to kiss Joy since the moment they met but he'd been resisting for good reason. But all reason had escaped him now as he gently tugged her closer. She tasted sweet, and her body was warm. The temptation was too great, and after the day he'd had, he just needed to feel her in his arms.

Joy sighed against his lips. Then her body shifted beneath his hands, inviting them to explore. Slowly, one of his hands traveled up her side, taking the curves like that sports car he'd had when he was twenty years old.

Then in one quick second, Joy's cat launched herself at his lower leg. He drew back from the kiss as Chelsea landed at his feet, her wide green eyes locked on his in warning.

"Chelsea!" Joy bent and collected the large ball of fur into her arms. "That is not nice."

Granger looked at Joy and realized what he'd done. He'd kissed the one person in the whole world that he probably shouldn't have. Coming here, he'd worried that Joy wouldn't come back to Abby and Willow because of his stupidity. Now he'd done another stupid thing. "I'm so sorry. I didn't mean to..."

Joy's smile faded. "You didn't mean to kiss me?"

He shook his head. "No, I definitely didn't mean to do that. That was a mistake." And his mistakes kept coming, it seemed, because now Joy was frowning. "I mean, it was nice," he said. "But we shouldn't have."

"Nice," she repeated. "No, you're right, we shouldn't have done that. And now you should probably go...before you make another big mistake."

Granger swallowed.

"And before you ask," Joy said, "yes, I'm picking the girls up tomorrow afternoon and going back to the farm. Nothing has changed. Nothing at all."

* * *

Granger was in the middle of a great dream when he was startled awake the next morning by Willow bouncing onto the mattress beside him. He cracked an eye open and noted that she was already dressed and her hair was pulled back in a neat ponytail.

"Daddy, Abby says we're going to miss the bus if you don't wake up now."

Granger shot upright and turned to his nightstand clock. "What? Why didn't you wake me sooner?"

"Abby said you must not have slept good."

And Abby would be right about that. Granger stood and started grabbing clothes from his dresser. "I'll be ready in a minute. Did you brush your teeth?"

Willow nodded.

"Eat breakfast?"

She nodded again. "PB and J. And I took my vitamins too. Hurry up, Daddy. Let's go."

Granger disappeared into the bathroom and got ready in record speed. "I'm sorry," he told Abby as he darted into the kitchen. "You ready?"

She stood. "We tried to let you sleep as long as we could. You must have needed it."

So wise.

Granger grabbed his keys and headed to the door. Tin trotted over. "I'll get you a treat when I get back, girl," he promised his dog. Then he looked at his girls. They'd gotten ready all by themselves. He gestured them outside and pointed to the truck. "We'll drive to the bus stop today." There was no time for the five-minute walk.

The girls climbed in, buckled up, and Granger pressed the gas up the dirt path that led from his house to the road, reaching the end just in time to see the bus pull away.

Granger groaned and continued driving toward the school. He dropped the girls off and then headed back to Merry Mountain Farms, all the while trying not to think about that kiss with Joy last night. It'd been amazing and inappropriate. And then he'd made things worse by saying something that had obviously insulted her. Now he owed her yet another apology.

He drove past his house toward his parents' cabin farther down the dirt path. He also owed his dad an apology. They'd argued about Granger's idea for the Christmas tree workshop. Granger was still disappointed that his father wouldn't even hear him out but he never wanted to be at odds with his dad. His parents had gone above and beyond after Erin left. Merry Mountain Farms was a family business but his dad was ultimately the one in charge. If he didn't think the farm needed new income sources to survive, then Granger would respect that.

He parked and got out of his truck, heading toward the front door, stopping short when he heard his dad's voice calling out from the old abandoned cabin behind the house. It was where all the lighted hayride props were kept. What was his father doing there?

"Granger?" his dad called again. Something about the tone in his dad's voice had Granger picking up speed and running in that direction.

"Granger!"

Granger found his father sitting on a chair in the barn, his hand covering the left side of his chest. His dad's face was twisted in a deep grimace, and his eyes were slits of pain. "What's wrong?"

"Chest pain...Ow!"

Without hesitation, Granger pulled out his cell phone and dialed 911.

* * *

Joy wasn't sure why she felt guilty about last night's call with her mom. Her mom was the one who was out of line. Even so, Joy had texted her this morning to see if her mother was available for lunch at the hospital today.

The invitation was a peace offering of sorts. Joy was actually surprised her mom accepted the invitation, but she was pretty sure that their visit would become an opportunity for her mom to hound her about taking the receptionist position in the hospital lobby.

Joy slowed as she drove down Main Street, offering a longing look at the storefront for lease. It had only been a week since she'd viewed it but her excitement had continued to mount. This was the perfect location, and she could practically see herself on the other side of the windowpanes, staring out at the streets of Sweetwater Springs.

Movement caught Joy's eye, and she tapped the brakes. *Is that Janelle?* Was she showing the store again?

Joy's heart sank a notch. She didn't see anyone else in the store though. Maybe Janelle was just handling some upkeep for the owner. Joy hoped that was the case.

She wanted to stop but she couldn't keep her mom waiting. Instead, she continued driving, turning off Main and onto Red Oak, which led to a part of town with Sweetwater Springs' most popular pizza parlor and the hospital. If Joy worked at the same place as her parents, they'd be under each other's feet all day—another reason not to apply.

Joy pulled into the parking lot and got out. Her stomach growled as she headed inside, past the current receptionist who was apparently leaving the job to be a stay-at-home mom. That was the exact opposite choice her own mother had made. Joy's mom had taken being a mother as a reason to work longer hours.

Joy rounded the corner and took the familiar route to the cafeteria, where she headed toward the line to get her usual. She was already prepared to wait for her typically late mother. That was fine because Joy could use her cell phone to scroll through her Pinterest app and pin new art and craft ideas to do at the library, community center, and with Abby and Willow.

"Joy?"

Joy froze at the sound of her name behind her. She knew that deep voice and wondered if she was imagining it. She'd thought a lot about that magic kiss that she had shared with Granger last night. The one that had traveled from her lips down to her toes, melting her heart into one big puddle. Then Granger had gone and ruined it by calling it a mistake.

"Joy?" Granger said again behind her.

The voice was definitely real.

She turned, and her heart did a belly flop when she came face-to-face with him. "Granger. What are you doing here? Are the girls okay?"

He held up a hand. "Yeah. They're at school. I'm here for my dad."

Joy stiffened. "Is he okay? What happened?"

Granger shrugged. "I called an ambulance this morning. He was having chest pain after I got home from dropping the girls off at school."

"I thought they took the bus," Joy said.

Granger sighed. "This day just started off all wrong and hasn't gotten much better from there."

Joy narrowed her eyes. "What did the doctor say about your dad?"

Granger's eyes looked worried. "She's still running tests...It's Dr. Benson—your mom."

"My mom is treating your dad?" Joy's mouth dropped along with her stomach. She used to hate it when her mom treated her friends' family when she was growing up. Her mom was the best person for the job in most cases though. She was skilled, and any patient was lucky to have her.

"What a coincidence, huh?" Granger said.

"Yeah." Joy stepped up in line and ordered a salad and tray of fruit. She listened as Granger ordered behind her. Then they paid and headed toward the tables. "So I guess my mom isn't meeting me for lunch today after all."

Granger grimaced, his eyes apologetic. "She looked pretty busy on the cardiac unit when I was up there."

"That sounds about right." Joy picked a table against the wall and sat down.

Granger followed her to the table, but continued to stand.

She looked up at him and furrowed her brow. "Would sitting with me be a big mistake too?" she asked, referring to last night's kiss.

He cleared his throat, looking around the cafeteria momentarily. "I just wasn't sure where we stood...after last night."

Joy held up a hand. "Let's just forget about last night, okay? We're still friends—just friends. How's that sound?"

"I like the sound of that." Granger pulled out the chair next to hers and sat down. "I think that's better than before. I'm not sure I was even in your friend category until now. After my stupidity last night, I was worried that I had gone straight to your list of enemies."

Joy opened her fruit tray and unwrapped her plastic spork. "It's very difficult to get on my enemies list. You have to really tick me off."

Granger peeled the wrapper off his hot dog. "Who's on that list?"

Joy used her spork to stab a slice of strawberry. "There's only one. An ex."

"Yeah?" Granger's brows lifted.

Joy and Granger had been acquaintances through the years but she doubted he knew her dating history. "He's a doctor here, actually. My mom would've loved for us to have stayed together."

"What happened?"

Joy stabbed a cube of melon next. "While I was working

late painting pieces to place on commission in the hospital gift shop, he was staying late with one of the nurses here."

Granger stopped chewing. He held his hot dog in mid-air and seemed to be squeezing the dog out of its bun with his tightening grip. He lowered it back to the paper plate. "You're kidding."

"Nope. That was last Christmas. Mom begged me to give Dan another chance. Can you imagine? He cheated on me, and she made me the bad guy for respecting myself too much to take him back."

"So this guy wanted you to take him back?" Granger asked.

Joy narrowed her eyes. "You're really kind of good at unintentionally insulting me."

Granger pulled back as his eyes widened. "No, I didn't mean that he shouldn't want you back. A guy would have to be nuts to give you reason to leave in the first place. I just assumed a guy who was that crazy wouldn't realize a good thing when he lost her."

Joy swallowed, feeling her heart flutter around inside her chest. She looked down at her fruit. "You recovered that well."

"It was sincere."

Joy took a bite of salad and chewed. "Anyway, Chelsea is so much happier now that she has me to herself at night anyway."

"That is one jealous feline." Granger laughed. "I've never kissed a woman and gotten attacked by her cat before."

The tension between them was palpable. They were supposed to be forgetting about that kiss. Admittedly, that wasn't easy to do.

"So has this former relationship tainted your ability to trust all the guys that came after?" Granger asked.

Joy stabbed a leaf of iceberg lettuce now. "What guys?" she asked, looking up at him.

Surprise registered on Granger's face. "You haven't dated anyone since?"

"It hasn't even been a year." Joy was attacking her lettuce now. "Some artists feed off heartache but I have a hard time being creative after my heart has been ripped out. I'd prefer not to put myself through that pain again just yet."

Granger dabbed a fry in the little container of ketchup in front of him. "I get it. I haven't dated since Erin left us."

Joy stopped stabbing her salad. "That's a lot longer than one year."

"Well, I'm busy with the girls and the farm."

"So that kiss..." Joy trailed off. They couldn't seem to stop talking about it.

"You mean the one we agreed we'd pretend never happened?" A wide grin stretched through his dimpled cheeks.

She put her plasticware down as she mentally ran the math. "That was your first kiss in seven years?"

He winced softly. "It's embarrassing when you put it that way."

Joy didn't think it was anything to be ashamed of though. It said a lot about his marriage to his ex. His heart must have really been broken for him to stop dating for so long. "Will you ever date again?"

Granger met her gaze. She wanted to look away but she couldn't even blink. "Yeah. I've been thinking that it's time but things keep getting in the way. First the fire at the farm. Then Mrs. Townsend retired unexpectedly. Now Dad." He gestured upstairs.

"After what you've been through, a lot of guys might

not want to bother with another relationship," Joy said quietly.

Granger bit into a fry, nodding as he chewed and swallowed. "I see my parents together, and I want that kind of relationship with someone. They make each other happy. I want to have that."

Those flutters in Joy's chest intensified. She still couldn't tear her gaze from his.

Then Granger's cell phone buzzed to life on the table beside his food. He glanced down. "Oh. That's my mom. I guess I need to head back up to talk to Dad's doctor."

"My mom," Joy said, relieved that their lunch was being cut short. She liked spending time with Granger but it also made her uncomfortable. Her heart was racing, and her palms were sweating.

"Sorry to bail on you," he said as he pushed back from the table.

"No, it's fine. At least I didn't have to eat my entire lunch alone while I waited for her."

Granger collected his half-eaten food and stood. "I'll see you back home tonight?"

"I'll be there...Tell your dad I'm thinking of him," Joy said. "The girls and I can make some get-well cards for him as one of our art lessons."

"That'd be nice." Granger offered her a warm smile and then waved as he headed out.

Joy watched him go, her gaze dipping where it shouldn't. She pulled it back and focused on her lunch. She'd enjoyed Granger's company a lot more than her mom's anyway. Or anyone else's, for that matter. In fact, she'd enjoyed it far more than a woman with no desire to jump back into the dating game should.

CHAPTER EIGHT

Granger knocked lightly on his father's hospital room door and then stepped inside. Dr. Benson was still chatting with him. She looked back, and Granger saw a small resemblance to Joy. They had the same hair color and brown eyes, and a similar facial structure.

But her mom appeared to be all business as she rattled off a list of to-dos for his dad, where Joy had a relaxed way about her that enhanced her beauty.

"Today was a warning, Gene," she told Granger's father. "Your heart is sending you a message that you need to heed."

His father sat inclined in the hospital bed. "My old man died of a heart attack. I know better than to play around with my ticker."

"Good." Dr. Benson smiled but hers wasn't as warm as Joy's. Then she looked at Granger and his mom. "Will you make sure he remembers to slow down, get rest, and take care of himself?"

Granger's mom laughed as she sat in the bedside chair. "I'll try but Gene doesn't do anything that isn't his own idea. He's stubborn that way."

Granger had to agree with his mom. She was right. It was hard to be a partner in the family business when you didn't have any input.

"I'll be back to check on you later." Dr. Benson looked at her watch. "Right now, I have a lunch date with my daughter."

Granger considered telling her that Joy was probably gone by now but he supposed she'd find that out soon enough.

"Thanks, Doc," Granger's father called before she closed the door behind her, leaving them alone.

"I'm so relieved it wasn't anything more serious," Granger's mom said, exhaling softly.

"Me too." Granger took the chair on the other side of his dad's bed. "And I can handle Merry Mountain for the rest of the week while you get some rest. No need for you to jump right back into business."

His father turned his head and looked at him. "The rest of the week? I don't think so."

"Dad, you just promised Dr. Benson you'd take care of yourself," Granger reminded him. "Your health isn't anything to play around with."

"I know that. That's why I need more than a week."

Granger straightened. That was not at all what he thought he'd hear his father say. "How long do you need?"

"I was thinking I should hand the reins over to you for the rest of the season."

"Dad, the season just got started." And it was already looking bleak from where he sat. Shouldering that alone might put Granger in the cardiac unit himself.

His father reached for his hand. "I'm being serious. I want you to run the farm the way you see fit this Christmas. Put all those ideas of yours to work. I won't stop you."

"You're serious?" Granger asked.

"Dead," his father said, making Granger's mom swat his other arm.

"That's not funny. No death jokes in here…But I think this is a great idea, Gene." She looked up at Granger and gave him a wink.

"So do I. I was already going to give you the green light on the hayride. That's why I was in the barn in the first place. It's time. I was just being stubborn."

"Imagine that," Granger's mom muttered in a teasing tone.

"Go on and get started, son," his father said, pulling his hand back. "You have a lot of work ahead of you. Better get busy."

Granger wasn't sure he could do this alone. But his father's health, like Mrs. Townsend's, came first. He'd figure it out. Joy suddenly came to mind. Maybe he didn't have to do it alone—if she was willing to give him a second chance.

* * *

On Friday evening, Joy sat at Granger's kitchen island while the girls played a board game in the living room. Joy could hear them laughing together. She smiled to herself as she searched an online real estate listing for the shop on Main Street, just to make sure it was still available. Not that she had enough funds to lease it just yet. But hopefully, it would stay that way until she could scrape together enough money to get it.

A knock on the back door had Joy looking up. She went to answer and grinned at Granger. "This is your house. Why are you knocking?"

"I didn't want to barge in on anything private." He stepped inside and closed the door behind him.

"Don't worry—we're not making any special presents for you tonight."

"No, but I've been busy making something for you." Granger glanced into the living room where the girls were and then returned his gaze to Joy's.

"Something for me?" she asked. "What?"

"A surprise. Think you can step away from the girls for a minute?"

"Well, they're playing nicely. I'm sure Abby can watch Willow for a moment. Where are we going?" she asked.

"Not far. But you'll need your jacket. It's cold outside."

He didn't have to tell her that. She could feel the chill coming through the walls.

"I'll talk to Abby," he said. "Be back in just a minute."

Joy nodded. "I'll grab my coat and gloves."

Granger was back and standing in front of her by the time she'd pulled on her knit hat as well. "Ready?"

"I'm not sure. Surprises make me nervous."

Granger offered a boyish grin. "This is a good one. At least I hope so. Trust me," he said, offering her his hand.

She stared at it for a moment. It was just a friendly gesture, and it'd be innocent if it were anyone but him.

"It rained earlier, and with the cold front that's moved through this week, there's likely ice out there. I just want to make sure you don't break anything on the way to my surprise."

"Of course." Joy put her hand in his, the glove keeping them from skin-on-skin contact. She could feel his warmth, though, and the strength of his grip. He was worried about her slipping and breaking a bone but she was worried about a much riskier fall and breaking her heart.

They stepped out quietly into the night. There were a million stars overhead as they walked.

"Beautiful night, huh?" Granger glanced over.

"Uh-huh." She stepped on a patch of ice and skidded forward.

"Whoa!" Granger turned quickly, bracing her with his hands and putting them face-to-face, at a perfect distance for another kiss.

The night with its twinkling stars and full moon was made for romance.

"I'm okay," she said, her breath coming out in white puffs. Her chest was rising and falling quickly, and she was having a hard time looking away. Another second and they'd end up in the same predicament as the other night.

She pulled her gaze away and looked in the direction where Granger was leading her. "What is that?" she asked, noticing yellow fairy lights ahead. They were strung all over a large sheltered area with at least a dozen picnic tables underneath.

"That's your surprise," Granger said, leading her again.

"I don't understand."

"I'll make a sign that says 'Christmas Tree Workshop.' Or you can make the sign since you're the artist," Granger said. "We'll put some outdoor heaters at all four corners to keep your students warm."

"My students?" Joy looked over at Granger. "What are you talking about?"

"Dad put Merry Mountain Farms in my hands this Christmas. He gave me the go-ahead to do whatever I think is necessary to keep the business in the green this year."

"And that includes me?" Joy asked.

"I hope so."

Joy couldn't help but smile, even though she was hesitant after the rug had been pulled out from under her a few days ago. "It's really happening this time?"

"Yep. I've got some other ideas for the farm too. And there's not a whole lot of time. I need you, Joy. What do you say? Give me another shot?"

Joy looked out on the area he'd set up. "It's perfect. And it's beautiful. We could play some holiday music for the students while they work."

"And serve some hot cocoa and apple cider from the cider house."

Joy nodded. "It's going to be amazing."

Granger squeezed her hand that he was still holding. "So…is that a yes?"

She looked at him, so happy that she could throw herself into his arms and kiss him again. "It's definitely a yes."

Granger grinned. "Great."

"On one condition," Joy added. She pulled her hand from his. "We need each other too much to get messy like we did on Monday night. If we're going to do this, we have to be professional."

She meant every word but some part of her wanted Granger to argue.

He didn't. "You're right. And I can agree to that."

"Me too." She nodded, her excitement only slightly dulled by her own condition. But it was for the best. She looked at the twinkling lights again. "I'm so excited about this. It's going to be incredible."

"Yeah. The best Christmas ever…I just wish it weren't because my dad had a health scare today." He turned back toward the house, and they walked together again. When he reached for her hand, she didn't hesitate this time. It was icy outside, after all, and spraining or breaking anything would put a huge damper on this new project she was embarking on.

"How is your dad doing?" she asked.

"He's going back to see your mom on Monday morning." He smiled over. "I'm grateful that Dad has such a great doctor on his side."

Joy nodded. "My mom might not win any parenting awards but she's been the doctor of the year three years in a row. Your dad couldn't be in better hands."

They reached the house again, and Granger turned to her. "I've got it from here if you want to go home to Chelsea."

"She's probably stalking the door right about now," Joy agreed. "So when do we get started on our Christmas tree workshop?"

Granger gestured toward the farm. "I've already started. I don't know how your schedule looks but you're welcome to go back there and do whatever you want. The tree season is open now but really gets busy after Thanksgiving. I figure we can have our first workshop the Friday after."

Joy brought up a mental calendar. "That's two weeks from today."

"We don't have much time to waste. I'm starting the lighted hayride back up too."

"Wow. Merry Mountain Farms is having a complete makeover this season... I'll need supplies."

"Just make a list."

"I will. Tonight." She felt the tension dialing up between them again as they locked eyes. Would it be like this for the next couple of months? If so, how would she be able to resist him? "Well, good night." She stuck out her hand for him to shake, since they were being professional now.

His hand locked onto hers, warm and inviting. "Good night, Joy."

Time to go home to her cat.

* * *

The next day, Granger drove the farm's tractor down the old path they'd used so long ago, clearing it of limbs and debris and marking the locations where he intended to put out the lighted props.

The ride would start by going past a winter wonderland with lighted snowmen and snowflakes. Next, it would pass through a clearing of lighted candy canes. Granger planned to make a 'Peppermint Path' sign for that one. It would tour through Santa's workshop with lighted presents and elves and then past a large Christmas tree, lighted from top to bottom. He had lighted carolers and planned to stream Christmas songs through some speakers on the wagon as they rode. The very last stop on the hayride would be a visit to see Santa himself.

If Granger could find someone willing to play jolly Saint Nick. Granger would be driving the tractor so he couldn't wear the suit. He didn't want to ask his dad but maybe his buddy Jack Hershey would take the job. Jack was a local park ranger and definitely jolly since he'd gotten together with his first love, Emma St. James.

Granger exited the trail and headed toward his house around lunchtime. His mom was watching the girls today since it was Saturday. He parked and got off to go check in on them.

Granger walked into his house. "Mom? Abby? Willow?"

The house was oddly quiet, which was a rarity for his place. "Anyone home?"

When no one responded, Granger walked over to the counter and found a note in his mom's handwriting.

*We went to do a little grocery shopping for your bare
cupboards. Be back later!*

Granger had planned to do some shopping later but
this would save him time. He opened the fridge, poured a
glass of sweet tea, and leaned against the counter to take a
breather before going back outside to work. When he was
halfway through his tea, someone knocked on his back
door. He knew better than to think it was his mom. She'd
walk right on in. And if the girls were with her, they'd
barge in. His dad was supposed to be resting.

Granger walked over and opened the door, only slightly
surprised to find Joy standing there.

"I made a list," she said brightly.

He had to chuckle. "That was fast."

"Well, you said we have no time to waste, so..." She
held out a piece of paper.

He took it and scanned over the items.

"I was on Pinterest half the night looking at various
Christmas trees you can make. There are so many different types. I think offering a simple selection for people
to choose from will be best. Wire is very easy but if
people want to create a tree out of something different,
we can do that too." Joy stepped inside the kitchen and
walked over to the island where she plopped down on
a stool.

Granger guessed they were going to have an impromptu
meeting. "Would you like some sweet tea?"

"I'd love some." She hopped up and went to get her
own glass. Then she opened the fridge and pulled out the
pitcher. He guessed she knew how to make herself feel at
home at this point. "I'm thinking I'll need to premake a
few models for people to get ideas from. Then folks can

decide on what they want and use the materials available—wire, lights, rope, garland—and make it their own."

Granger nodded.

"Or folks can bring their own materials if they want. We might even offer one or two classes for ornaments to hang on the trees. That's something that adults and kids can do together."

"I like that idea. You might find yourself pretty busy over the holidays. Will your parents be okay with that?"

Joy huffed. "They've always been busy over the holidays. If you're not busy, something is wrong with you. Or me, in their minds. They'll be over the moon that I'm working, even if it is on art stuff."

Granger turned his attention back to the list. "I'll get this stuff tonight. It'll be here waiting for you on Monday. But you'll be watching the kids so I'm not sure when you'll get started."

"Actually, when you get the wire tomato cages, can you drop them by my town house? I'll work on a few model trees at night. It's just me and Chelsea. I'll have to find a way to keep her off them."

Granger nodded. "Sure. I can drop them by this evening. Mom will have the girls."

"Great."

Granger wasn't sure if being alone with Joy again was a good idea, considering what had happened last time. Then again, he was alone with her right now, and they were keeping their hands and lips to themselves. Just thinking about it made his gaze drop to her mouth.

"You're thinking about it again," she said softly.

"About what?"

She narrowed her eyes as one corner of her mouth kicked up. "The kiss."

The kiss. It was just one but it was enough to cause an avalanche of tension.

"I'm trying not to—believe me."

Her chest rose as she took a sharp intake of breath. "I am too. But when you're looking at me that way, it's impossible to forget about it."

"So maybe we don't have to fight it so hard. It happened, and that's okay. We're two single, lonely people."

"I never said I was lonely," Joy said.

Granger nodded. "Sorry. I guess that's just me."

Joy looked surprised. "How can you be lonely with those two girls around and parents who live on the same property?"

"You'd be surprised. A person can be lonely in a room with a hundred other people." He swallowed as his heart suddenly ached. He didn't think he needed Dr. Benson though. It was another Benson woman playing with his heart. "Or not lonely in a room with just one."

He hadn't meant that the way it'd sounded. Or he had but he shouldn't have been so honest. There was too much on the line right now.

He pulled his gaze away and cleared his throat. "So your place tonight? I'll deliver some materials, and you can get started." He stepped back and headed toward the door. "I promise not to give your cat any reason to attack me tonight."

"Right." Joy walked past him. "Thank you in advance for getting the items on my list."

"I'll make sure I check it twice."

Joy turned and smiled. "Sounds like you're vying for the role of Santa this Christmas."

"I don't think so." The only roles he was vying for were the ones he already had. Dad. Son. Tree farmer. And definitely not the role of a guy falling for the one woman he shouldn't.

CHAPTER NINE

*J*oy didn't like the feeling of waiting by the phone or the door. But that's what she was doing, expecting a delivery of supplies from Granger tonight. He hadn't given her a time, which meant she'd been expecting him at any moment for hours.

She glanced out the window once more and then returned to the kitchen where she was actually cooking tonight rather than having a dinner of cereal and milk.

Meow!

Joy's gaze fell to Chelsea, who pawed at her shin. "Is your bowl empty?" One glance in that direction told Joy it was. "I'm sorry. I've been MIA. And I really have no business letting myself get distracted by him, do I?"

Chelsea's eyes grew big as Joy spoke to her. Joy stirred the stew on the stove before heading over to refill Chelsea's food and water bowls.

"I mean, he's handsome, yes. And funny. And adorable with his girls." Joy smiled to herself. She'd always found a man who was good with kids attractive. "But he's a dad, and he has responsibilities. And I am really going to make my art gallery happen this year," Joy told her cat. "And when I do, you'll get to come with me to work every day." She bent and poured the kibble into the bowl as Chelsea purred loudly.

The doorbell rang, and Joy nearly dumped the entire bag of food. She caught it in the nick of time and stood to go answer, doing a quick inhale and exhale to calm her nerves. Then she opened the door and smiled back at Granger.

"Special delivery. Sorry it took so long. Willow was being dramatic this afternoon." He was wearing his signature jeans and long-sleeved T-shirt with the Merry Mountain Farms logo on the left side of his chest. Sometimes he accompanied the look with an unbuttoned flannel shirt that he seemed to have in almost every color. He also wore a ball cap with the Merry Mountain logo.

"That doesn't sound good. What was Willow upset about?"

Granger lifted a large box of wire vegetable cages from where he'd set it at his feet and stepped over the threshold. "Her Christmas list," he said, his voice strained under the weight of what he was carrying. "Where do you want me to set this down?" He glanced over his shoulder at Joy.

She pointed, and he headed in that direction. "Did Willow ask for too much?"

Granger set the box down in the corner of the room as she'd directed him and turned back. "It's not about the expense. That was fine. But she asked Santa to deliver her mother this year." He removed his ball cap and ran a hand through his hair. "I couldn't just ignore that and let her think that Santa was going to deliver. So I had to sit her down and explain that Santa can't do things like that."

Joy's heart broke for her little friend. "Poor thing. I'm guessing she took it badly?"

Granger choked out a humorless laugh. "That's an understatement. Finally, my mom came over and worked her magic. There's something about a woman's touch, I guess." His gaze held onto Joy's, making her breath hitch. He was obviously thinking about the other night when she'd calmed Willow down after learning that Mrs. Townsend had retired. "Then I went to the home improvement store to get your list. Mom said she'll stay until I get home and the girls fall asleep."

"These supplies could've waited until tomorrow." Joy followed Granger back outside to his truck where more supplies were waiting.

"We're on a tight timeline. I want to keep my end of the deal."

They both grabbed another box of supplies and headed inside.

"You can take the rest of the wire vegetable cages to your place. I just needed these basics to get started on a couple demos."

"You're going to make one tonight?" Granger asked.

"Yep. Right after I eat a bowl of vegetable beef stew."

Granger glanced toward the kitchen. "Oh, is that what I'm smelling? I bet it's going to be delicious."

Joy hesitated. It'd be rude not to offer him a bowl when she had such a big pot. "Would you like some? I made more than enough. It's my aunt Darby's recipe. She used to make it for me when I was a kid, along with a special PB and J sandwich."

Granger laughed. "Stew and a sandwich?"

"You'd be surprised at how well they complement each other. I know you probably need to head home and have dinner with the girls but you're certainly welcome to stay."

"Actually, they already ate without me. After the drama with the Christmas list, I needed to go ahead and get to the home improvement store. Mom fed them. Now they're likely on the couch watching TV or playing a board game."

Joy nodded. "Then it's my duty to feed you, I guess. You missed your family dinner because of me."

"Do I get a special PB and J too?" Granger asked.

Joy walked into the kitchen and stepped up to the stove to stir the pot, casting him a glance over her shoulder. "If you're lucky."

She reached into the cabinet and pulled out two bowls while Granger took a seat at her small kitchen table.

What was she doing inviting him for dinner? He could've grabbed fast food on the way home or had leftovers of whatever his mom had cooked the girls.

Her thoughts warred as she grabbed a loaf of bread and a mixing bowl for her aunt Darby's special peanut butter and jelly mix. It'd been a favorite of hers as a kid. She spooned a large dollop of extra-creamy peanut butter into the mixing bowl and then an even bigger dollop of grape jelly before stirring it all together. That was the secret to the perfect PB&J. It took a little extra time, and Joy's own mom would never make it that way. Only Darby would, and only for Joy.

A couple of minutes later, Joy slid a bowl of vegetable beef stew in front of Granger and one in the spot where she'd be sitting. "Here you are." She returned to the counter and grabbed the sandwiches on their paper plates. Lastly, she placed two glasses of fruit-infused water on the table and sat down.

"Where's your cat?" Granger asked, looking around. If she wasn't mistaken, he looked a little nervous.

She giggled. "She was at her bowl when you arrived. She's probably hiding somewhere, planning her next attack."

Granger's eyes grew a little wider as he looked at her. "Being attacked while eating hot stew could be dangerous."

"You're risking your well-being by having dinner with me tonight for sure," Joy teased. She picked up her spoon, dipped it in the stew, and blew on the steaming broth. She was aware that Granger was watching her now, and suddenly the act of eating stew felt sensual.

Granger mirrored her actions, dipping his spoon and blowing on his stew as well. Then he tasted it. "Mmm. That's . . . wow. That's really good."

Joy placed her spoon back in the bowl. "You sound surprised. You didn't think I had domestic skills?"

Granger shook his head. "It's not that. You're a talented artist, and you're great with kids. You can't be wonderful at everything."

She felt her cheeks growing warm, mostly because of the steam floating up from the stew but also because Granger had just given her a double compliment. She looked down into her bowl. "Well, I'm only good at a few dishes. I can't cook a full Thanksgiving dinner or anything."

Granger reached for his glass of water. "Will your mom cook for that?"

Joy laughed as she looked back up at him. "Oh, no. She has no domestic skills. She and my father will likely be working at the hospital that day. I usually stop in at Sugar Pines Community Center because that's where my aunt Darby is, and I volunteer at the early lunch there. The food isn't the best but the company couldn't be finer."

Granger nodded as he sipped.

"And what about you?" she asked.

"My mom runs the show on Thanksgiving. The girls and I contribute by making macaroni and cheese from scratch. We usually make a couple pies too. We have a midafternoon lunch so we're all starving by the time the food is put on the table. We tend to overstuff ourselves and lie around in food comas afterward."

Joy laughed. "Sounds fantastic."

"It is." Granger picked up his sandwich and took a bite, chewing and then swallowing. "Wow. I've never had a peanut butter and jelly sandwich like this."

"It's amazing how just mixing the PB and J changes the taste and texture, isn't it?" Joy reached for hers as well.

"Have you done this for the girls yet?" Granger asked. "Because if you have, it's no wonder they love you so much."

Joy nodded as she chewed and swallowed. "They went nuts over it too. Especially Willow. She begged for me to share the secret with you."

"I'm sure she did."

"And now I have. Your sandwiches will never be the same." Joy grew quiet as she ate her stew. Then, as if her mouth were possessed tonight, she said, "Since your mom is watching the girls, why don't you stay and help me make the first Christmas tree for Merry Mountain Farms?"

It was the polite thing to do. Just like inviting Granger to stay for dinner. It was perfectly all right because she fully expected him to say no.

"I'm not that artsy," he said with a little hesitation. "But okay."

* * *

"This tree is pretty convincing so far," Granger said, half an hour later. Under Joy's instruction, he'd placed an upside-down wire tomato cage inside of a large plastic planter full of dry soil. They'd wrapped garland from the wide base up the conical structure, securing it with a zip tie at the top.

"So this is what our customers are going to do," Joy told him. "It's really easy."

"And pretty fun." Granger nodded. "If a guy like me, with absolutely no artistic talent, can do this, then anyone can. I can see a lot of our customers really enjoying this. So what happens next?"

Joy bent and lifted some ribbon out of a box and handed it to him. "Next you make a bow for the top."

He chuckled. "You make it sound so easy."

"It is." She grabbed his hand and laid it on the ribbon and then reached for his other hand as she stood in front of him. "You just fold it and mold it."

The feel of her skin over his was hypnotic. His blood rushed, and his breaths slowed as he allowed her to move his clumsy hands. They weren't clumsy when it came to an ax and a tree. Or braiding his daughters' hair, which he'd gotten quite good at over the years. But when it came to art or Joy, his hands felt unsure of where they belonged. He knew where he wanted to put them.

"There," she said. "See? That wasn't hard at all." Her hands were still covering his, which in turn kept her body close. He could feel her warmth and smell the sweet aroma of her hair or lotion, he wasn't sure. "I don't know if I can do that on my own." He lifted his gaze, and their eyes locked, making another kiss seem like the next obvious step.

Joy removed her hands and stepped away. "Have a try."

Granger reached for a wire ribbon and bent it several times just like she had. Then he fanned it out to make it fuller. He had to admit it was a lot more fun when her hands were on his, guiding him.

"Just like that. You're a natural."

"I had a great teacher."

She grinned and grabbed a string of lights and handed them over. "I'm sure you know how to do this part already."

"As a Christmas tree farmer, I've done it a few times." He winked.

After the lights, they added ornaments, working quickly and quietly, bumping each other's elbows occasionally since he was a lefty and she was right-handed.

"Feels like we're working on a real tree," Granger said.

She placed the final ornament toward the top of the tree. "It does. I've always thought decorating a tree was romantic."

"Me too."

Joy side-eyed him. "Really? I'm surprised."

"Why? You don't think I can be romantic?"

She shrugged as she laughed. "You grew up on a Christmas tree farm. I would've thought all the magic and romance was drained out of decorating a tree for you."

"Never." He gestured at the tree. "It appears you and I make a great team."

She stood beside him. "It's beautiful. I just love it." She turned to him. "Do you think everyone else will love it and want to make one too?"

"Oh yeah. I really do." At least he was hoping so. This year he was betting everything on the success of the Christmas tree workshop and the lighted hayride.

"I'm excited about this. I just hope it works, and people come out."

Granger wasn't worried about that as much as hoping

that, after people came, Joy would stay. She'd given him no reason to think she'd leave but neither had his ex.

* * *

Granger unlocked the back door of his home quietly, just in case everyone inside was sleeping.

"You were out late," his mom's voice said from the kitchen table as he stepped inside.

Granger shut the door and faced her. "You said you'd watch the girls until they went to bed...Are they asleep?"

She nodded. "Oh yes. Their eyes closed while we were watching a movie. I just came in here to rustle around for a snack." She smiled up at him. "Did you have a good time at Joy's place?"

Granger had told her he was going over there to deliver her supplies. "What makes you think that's where I've been?" He could've gone out with his buddies to the Tipsy Tavern. He was overdue for that.

She gave him a knowing look. "Isn't it?"

Granger turned his back to her and headed to go make himself a hot tea. He flipped the kettle on and grabbed a mug from the cabinet. Then he turned to face his mom again from the counter. "I had to deliver the supplies, and she offered to let me stay for dinner since you guys ate without me."

"Wasn't that nice of her?" his mom commented. "Is she a good cook?"

Granger saw right through that comment. She was scoping Joy out to see if she was marriage material. "Yes. She made stew and peanut butter and jelly sandwiches." That should tell his mom everything she needed to know.

"Oh, that sounds interesting," his mom said.

"It was good. Best PB and J I've ever had. No offense to you."

"None taken."

He turned back to his tea, finished prepping it, and then walked over to the table to join his mom. "She has a few secret recipes of her aunt's."

His mom nodded. "Darby. I went to school with her, you know?"

Granger sipped his tea. "With Joy's aunt?"

"Joy reminds me so much of her. They're a lot alike. We weren't close but Darby was such a nice person. She never married or had kids, which I always thought was such a shame. I hope Joy follows a different path and meets a nice fellow."

Granger pointed a finger at her. "Now that I'm handling the farm this holiday, I don't have time for dating. At least not until the New Year."

She narrowed her eyes. "You don't need time. She's going to be here through Christmas, working right alongside you."

Granger took another sip of his tea. "I need her, and she needs me because she's low on work and income. It's a working relationship but nothing more."

His mom was giving him that look again. "So you had dinner with Joy and there were no..." She fluttered her hands around. "No sparks?"

Granger avoided looking at her. He was mulling over his answer but he guessed he took too long.

"So there were sparks," she said gleefully.

"Sparks that I plan to ignore. Half this farm went up in smoke this year because of a simple little spark. We could've lost everything."

His mom was frowning now. "Since Erin left, you've

given everything of yourself for your family. You've worked so hard and sacrificed so much. And I'm so proud of you, son." She laid a hand over his. "But, in the same way you want to see Abby and Willow happy, I want to see you happy. I'm your mother."

"I am happy."

She had that knowing look again.

Maybe he wasn't over-the-moon happy but relationships made people just as unhappy as they did happy. At least in his experience.

"You need to take time for yourself. Go out and have some fun. Date."

"I will. In the New Year."

* * *

The following Friday, Joy stood in front of her easel. She had two hours before she needed to pick up Abby and Willow from school. With nowhere to go and nothing to do, she decided to work on a new piece of art. Sometimes when her emotions were raw, painting helped. Hopefully that would be true today.

Before she dipped her brush into her linseed oil, her cell phone buzzed from the coffee table. The caller ID read Sweetwater Elementary—the girls' school. Granger had mentioned that he'd put her on the school's list as a contact, since she would be picking them up. If something changed in the school's schedule, they might need to call her and let her know.

"Hello?"

"Miss Benson?" a woman's voice asked.

"That's me," she said.

"Hi, this is the assistant principal at Sweetwater

Elementary. We have an issue here at the school. Abby is in a little bit of trouble, and someone needs to come get her."

"Abby? Is she okay?"

"Oh yes. She's fine."

Joy let out the breath she'd been holding. "Did you call her father?"

"We did but he's not answering his phone. No one on his list of contacts answered except you. Can you please come in?"

Joy put her paintbrush down. "Absolutely. I'll be right there."

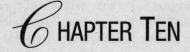

Chapter Ten

Granger had spent the last eight-plus hours deep in the woods behind Merry Mountain Farms. Now he came out hot, sweaty, and even more excited about his plans. The path was smooth, and all the lighted exhibits were put out. He'd changed more than two dozen bulbs and had completed a light check. It was ready.

He parked his tractor and got off, heading across the farm's property to his home. He needed a shower but he couldn't wait to tell Abby and Willow all about the displays. They'd been so small the last time the ride had been open. Willow had only been a toddler. Abby had some memory of the paths being lit up since she was older. When it got dark tonight, he'd take them for a ride. Joy too. He wanted to see the look of amazement on their faces as they bumped along what he had dubbed Peppermint Path.

He stepped inside the back door of his house and listened for voices. Tin got up and trotted over to him. That was Granger's first clue that no one else was home. Tin was always where the action was. "Hey, girl." He patted her head. "Where'd everyone go?"

Tin looked up and seemed to smile back at him behind her long, furry bangs. Then she barked as if to answer.

Granger turned back to the wall and glanced out the window. Joy's car wasn't here yet. Then he pulled out his cell phone and saw a slew of calls that he'd missed from Sweetwater Elementary School. Panic flared in his chest. The school didn't call often. Not unless there was an emergency.

He tapped the callback number and got a busy signal. Then he tapped on one of the voice messages.

Mr. Fields, this is Assistant Principal Melinda Pierce. There's been an issue at the school, and I've called your emergency contact Joy Benson to come get Abigail. I have a principal's meeting later this afternoon but I'm sending a letter home detailing today's incident. You can call or schedule an appointment to come talk to me if you want to discuss the situation.

Granger let his arm dangle down by his side. An issue with Abigail? She wasn't the type of child to cause trouble. Maybe another kid had caused trouble for her. He could find out the answer to that if he knew where she was. If Joy had picked Abby up, why weren't they here?

He pulled up Joy's contact and dialed. It went straight to voicemail.

Tin nudged her nose into Granger's palm, as if sensing that he was suddenly fearing the worst. That was his MO as a father. He paced the kitchen, trying to figure out his next move, when the back door opened. He spun, hoping it was Joy and the girls. Instead, he faced his mom.

"You look horrible," she said. "Is everything okay?"

And now his mom was fearing the worst.

Granger held out his arms. "Joy isn't back with the girls yet."

His mom's expression softened. "That's what I was coming to talk to you about. The school called earlier, and I couldn't get to the phone. Your dad and I were outside working on those signs you wanted us to paint, and the reception is spotty out there."

"It's not great in the woods either," Granger told her.

"I guess Joy got them?"

Granger shrugged. "A good guess is all we've got because she's not answering and she's not here."

His mom frowned back at him. "Well, if you trust her enough to put her on the emergency contact list to pick up your girls, you have to trust her enough to know that, wherever they are, it's okay."

Granger took a deep breath. His mom was right. He knew that but it didn't stop him from worrying. He grabbed his keys off the counter and headed out the back door.

"Where are you going?" his mom called, poking her head outside.

"To find my family and bring them home." Granger climbed into his truck, slammed the door, and cranked the engine. He could feel in his bones that he was overreacting but he couldn't seem to help it. After Erin had left, he'd promised himself he'd always be there for Abby and Willow. And he'd been MIA this afternoon when Abby had needed him. Irrational or not, he was kicking himself right now.

* * *

"Why did you bring us here? I thought Abby was in trouble." Willow looked over at Joy as she sat next to her at a table in Dawanda's Fudge Shop.

Joy had picked Abby up an hour earlier. They'd gone to the library because Joy had a meeting with Lacy Shaw to discuss upcoming events. Then Joy and Abby had gotten back into the car pool line to get Willow when the school day was over. Instead of going directly home as they normally would have, Joy had made a detour.

"She's not in trouble," Joy said, looking at Abby, who sat sullen faced across from her.

"But the assistant principal called you. That means she's in trouble," Willow argued. "Only the bad kids get called into the principal's office."

Abby looked down at the fudge square on her plate. She'd barely nibbled on it.

"That's not true. Sometimes you can get called into the principal's office for good stuff."

"I'm in big trouble, okay? Christmas is probably canceled for me," Abby muttered.

Joy still wasn't sure what exactly had happened. Abby wasn't the type of student who stirred up trouble. But apparently, she'd talked back to her teacher today. It wasn't like her at all.

"So we get fudge if we do something bad?" Willow popped the last bite of fudge into her mouth.

"No." Joy shook her head as she snapped her attention back to Willow. The last thing she needed was for Willow to start acting up because she thought it led to an afternoon treat. "But when I had a really bad day growing up, sometimes my aunt Darby would take me here. In my experience, chocolate makes the bad things seem not so awful." Joy offered a smile. Everything she knew about caring for a child came from how Aunt Darby had treated her. "Do you like the fudge?"

Abby gave a subtle nod. Her head was tipped down, making

her dark-blond hair pool around her face. "Yes. I'm just worried about Dad. He's going to be so disappointed in me."

"I doubt that," Joy said gently. "But it'll help if you tell him everything. He needs to know what you said to your teacher and why."

Abby looked up. "I told my teacher she wasn't my mom and I didn't have to listen to her."

Joy drew back. "Abby, why would you say that?"

"Because it's true." Abby looked down again. "And the girls at school are always doing things with their moms. They talk about how much fun they have together." She shrugged. "I want my mom back."

Joy wasn't understanding the reasoning here. "So you talked back to your teacher because you want your mom?"

"No." Abby looked at her like she had five heads. "I talked back to my teacher because I don't like how she treats some of the kids in the class. She talks down to them but no one ever talks back to her."

"So you did?" Joy asked, thinking she understood a little better now. Abby had her mom on her brain, and that's just what came out in her small explosion. "You were defending your classmates. Because you take care of everyone."

Abby dropped her gaze back to the fudge on her plate. "Then I told my teacher she was a bully, and she needed to talk nicer to us."

"I see." Joy couldn't fault Abby for that, although she suspected Abby should've handled her concerns differently. "Did you tell the assistant principal what happened?"

Abby nodded. "She said she'll talk to our teacher, and that we should never feel bullied at our school. She said I have to come talk to her next time instead of yelling at an adult."

"I think that's probably a good suggestion."

Joy met Abby's gaze. There was a lot more going on in Abby's head than protecting her classmates. She missed her mom, and she bore a lot of responsibility for Willow. Joy wished she could make the pain go away but she couldn't.

"Are you girls having a good afternoon?" Dawanda asked, walking to the end of their table. She smiled brightly, just as cheerful as she'd been when Joy had come here as a child.

"Well, it didn't start out that way," Joy said, "but it's looking up. Fudge makes things better. Don't you think, Abby?"

Abby took another bite of her fudge and nodded. "Thanks to you," she told Joy.

Joy felt a gooey warmness spread through her. She'd always enjoyed caring for children, and she'd missed this part of it. But this was the year she was supposed to focus solely on art.

Joy reached for another piece of fudge—because it made everything momentarily better.

A bell jingled on the door behind her, and Abby jolted upright. Joy sat up straighter too because she knew before even turning around who was standing behind her.

"What do you guys think you're doing?" Granger asked.

Joy turned to face him. "Eating fudge. What's wrong?"

His jaw dropped open as if that were an absurd question. "You're supposed to bring the girls home after school. Not take them out for fudge without my permission."

Now Joy's mouth was hanging open. "I didn't realize I needed your permission. And I called to let you know but your voicemail was full." Her tone sharpened as she continued to talk. "That's probably why the assistant principal had to call me. Good thing I was available, isn't it?" Joy stood now, talking to Granger face-to-face. She folded her arms over her chest.

Granger's expression softened a bit. "I...Yes, it's a good thing. Thank you."

Joy took a breath. "You're welcome. Please tell me you didn't really search all over town."

Granger shook his head, his gaze moving past her to the girls, who were still seated at the table watching them with wide eyes. Then he looked at her again. "I called all over town. Dawanda told me you were here."

"I was going to mention that to you," Dawanda said. "I had a customer, and then it slipped my mind. Granger is looking for you." Dawanda smiled innocently. "Granger, would you like some fudge?"

He shook his head. "No, thank you."

"How about a cappuccino?" she asked.

Granger held up his hands as if she were threatening him now. "Not today."

Joy laughed. She'd had one of Dawanda's famous cappuccino readings before, where Dawanda claimed to be able to read your fortune in the frothy foam. Joy's reading said she'd embark on a new endeavor and find success. Or something like that. That was eighteen months ago, and Joy had taken that to mean her art gallery, which hadn't come to fruition yet.

Dawanda pointed a finger at Granger. "One of these days."

"But not this one. Today, I think the girls and I are heading home," he said.

Joy looked at him, narrowing her eyes just slightly. Maybe she'd read this interaction wrong. Was she in trouble with him? "You're taking the girls? Not me?"

There were still hours left until dark, and it was her job to keep the girls until dinner.

He hesitated. "I wasn't sure if you needed a break. You picked them up earlier than usual because I didn't answer the call. I was thinking you might want to end your day earlier too..." He trailed off.

"You can't get rid of me that easily, Granger. I'm not going anywhere," she said. Then she turned back to Abby and Willow. "We haven't even had our art session yet. Today, I'm teaching you how to make origami."

Abby's eyes lit up, and it was almost as if the event at school had never happened. In Joy's experience, fudge and art made everything better. Well, almost everything. It hadn't worked as well for Joy last Christmas but this holiday was already looking brighter.

* * *

Granger turned to the sound of footsteps on the ground behind him. He'd been sitting on his tailgate under the star-studded sky for the last twenty minutes. He'd spoken to Abby about her behavior today. It was unacceptable and unlike her. She'd simply nodded as he talked. She didn't justify her actions, which would have made things better.

Instead, Granger was left wondering if he was somehow at fault. Maybe he wasn't giving her enough attention at home. Maybe she needed more from him.

"Are you wanting to be alone?" Joy asked. "Or do you need company?"

He thought about his answer. "Both and neither."

"You're not a contradiction at all, are you?" She continued walking toward him. "You can tell me to leave at any time. Otherwise, I'm going to join you. You should never tailgate alone," she said, feigning a serious expression.

"I think you mean drink alone."

She climbed up and sat beside him, her legs swinging gently off the edge. "Abby's at that age where she's going to push her boundaries and see what she can get away with. I'm speaking from experience. I was once a nine-year-old girl."

Granger was all too aware of how close his face was to Joy's right now. And of how her features seemed to glow under the moonlight. "I'm sorry about this afternoon." He searched for the right words to justify his actions, but just like Abby, he couldn't. There was no excuse. "I stormed into Dawanda's ready to blame you for doing exactly what I'd hired you to do—care for my girls."

"You were just protecting your family," Joy said. "I get it."

Granger laughed humorlessly. "Protecting them from you?" He shook his head. "No, you're letting me off too easy. You didn't deserve that. You've been..." He looked over, and his gaze stuck on hers. "You've been wonderful, Joy. I owe you a thank-you as well. And I won't question you again. I promise."

She narrowed her eyes. "Don't make promises you can't keep, Mr. Fields."

There was a hint of flirtation in her tone that didn't go unnoticed. "Mr. Fields is my dad. And you're probably right about not being able to keep that promise. But I promise I'll try."

"I'll keep you to that." She stared at him a moment. Then she tipped her face toward the sky, a sigh tumbling off her lips. "I love the stars. Every time I see a sky like this, it makes me want to grab my easel and paintbrushes and try to capture it. But it's impossible to ever do the night sky justice."

Granger looked up as well. "I don't look up as much as I should. It really is beautiful up there."

Joy nudged him with her elbow. "According to your mom, you don't do a lot of things as much as you should."

Granger pulled his gaze from the sky back to her, her eyes twinkling lovelier than the stars. "Oh no. Has she been talking to you about my dating life?"

Joy giggled softly. "Not just that. She says you work too hard to care for your family, and you need more fun in your life." A strand of her dark hair blew in the wind and clung to her cheek.

Granger's hand ached to reach up and swipe it away. To feel her skin against his again. Instead he shook his head. "I've told Mom to stop with that. With the holidays upon us, it's just not a good time for that kind of stuff right now." He said it casually but he also meant it for Joy. Just so there was no mistaking where he stood. The kiss they'd shared was in the past and wouldn't be happening again. Even if that's all he could think about doing in this moment.

"Well, a lot of women in town will be disappointed to hear that."

"And what about you? Your singleness has got to be breaking the hearts of men all over town."

"Better I break theirs than they break mine."

She said a lot in that statement. And he suddenly understood her a little better. He didn't have to worry about her pursuing a romance with him. And that relieved him as much as it disappointed him. Which made no good sense at all.

"I wanted to take the girls on the first lighted hayride

tonight but the timing seemed off. Abby is upset, and Willow is on a sugar high."

Joy grinned. "Sorry, not sorry about that last one."

Granger swallowed. They'd drawn the line in the sand and didn't have any reason to be worried about spending time alone together. "What do you say?"

Her brow dipped. "About what?"

"Want to be my first customer? The lights I've set up give those stars overhead a run for their money." And so did her eyes.

She smiled softly as her hair lifted in the slight breeze. "Well, that sounds like an offer I can't refuse. I would love a ride."

"Great. Come on." He hopped down and offered Joy his hand. There was that touch he'd been longing for. It was over as quickly as it'd started, and he wished he could continue holding her hand in his as they walked to the tractor. Joy started to climb on the trailer that was attached for pulling customers. "There's a seat up front beside me." Granger climbed back on the tractor and gestured to the open spot next to him.

"Okay." She headed toward the front. "Are you going to let me drive?" A wide grin spread across her face. "You said you trust me, right?" She was teasing him, and he knew it.

He gestured at the driver's seat. "Yeah, I do. I trust you a thousand percent."

Joy's teasing grin fell away. "Oh, no...I wasn't, um...I was just joking."

"Climb up. I'll teach you." Granger was teasing her right back now. "You trust *me*, right?"

CHAPTER ELEVEN

his is kind of fun," Joy said, white-knuckling the steering wheel. "It's going a lot faster than I would have expected."

Granger chuckled beside her. It was nice to hear him relaxed and having fun. The Granger she'd known so far was always working and worrying about his family. He deserved to let go and let someone else take the figurative wheel.

"So this is what I'll be doing all season. Easy job, huh?" he asked.

Joy looked over.

"Eyes on the road, miss," he teased.

She whipped her face forward. "Right. Sorry."

"Okay, turn here." He pointed. "This is Peppermint Path."

She turned the tractor and was met with a long path of giant peppermint sticks that towered at least six feet tall, lit up and shining bright. "It's so beautiful. Granger, this is amazing." She glanced over. "Sorry. Eyes ahead. And honestly, I can't take my eyes off this. It's a piece of art, Granger."

"I told you I'm not artsy."

"Well, you just proved that wrong." Joy steered the tractor down the lighted path, coming up on a scene of a snowman and snowwoman. And a snowbaby. There were lighted snow people throwing snowballs. And magical scenes of Santa and his elves. They rode for at least another ten minutes until they came to a clearing.

"We'll stop the hayride here and let the kids get off to talk to Santa."

"And who is your Santa?" Joy asked, pressing the brakes and bringing the tractor to a stop.

"Anyone but me. I'm just the driver," he said.

Joy clucked her tongue before her mouth spread into a wide grin. "Well, I can drive now. You can feel free to put on the red suit." She turned to look at him.

"No, you'll be teaching the Christmas tree workshop."

"Now that I have come to a complete stop, I can safely look at you," she said on a laugh. "And assure you that this is amazing. It's even better than I remember it. The people of Sweetwater Springs will love this."

"You really think so?" Granger asked.

The lights from the path reflected in his eyes, and staring into them was just as magical as staring at what he'd created on this path.

* * *

Granger leaned in closer to Joy. "So you think people will pay to come here?"

"Mm-hmm. Whatever you're charging, this ride is worth every penny."

"Except you didn't pay," Granger said, unable to take his eyes off her.

She giggled softly. Her laughter was the sexiest thing he'd ever heard. She was the sexiest thing he'd ever seen. She was vibrant and full of life.

"Well, you didn't pay to make the first tree sculpture the other night either," she countered.

He leaned some more. "I guess we can call it even, then."

"Seems we're always doing that."

This was one of those moments where the next right thing to do was to try to kiss the girl. There was eye contact, laughing, smiling. There was an undeniable sexual chemistry between them, even though he was doing his best to deny it. There was also a bone-deep desire to feel her mouth against his again. To hold her.

"So if I were playing Santa this year," he said, "what would you ask for?"

Joy's eyes turned dreamy. "That's easy. I'd ask for my dream store for my gallery." She sighed and looked away, breaking the moment if he wanted to kiss her. He wasn't going to anyway. At least that's the story he was telling himself. "But I don't need Santa for that. I'm going to make it happen all on my own. If no one else beats me to the punch."

"There are other stores," Granger said.

"Not like this one. The location is good. It's just small enough for myself and my art. I can't have a store that's too big. And I'd rather not get a place too far from downtown. I need to pull in the people strolling down the sidewalk. I want to get those impulse buyers."

Granger reached for her hand. Joy glanced down at his hand resting over hers. The gesture was one of support but now the tension was back, coiling and tightening between them. "I think your art is good enough that people would travel anywhere you opened your gallery to get it."

Joy's eyes grew glassy. He'd hit a nerve but he wasn't sure which one.

"Did I say something?" he asked.

"No . . . I mean, yes, but it's not bad. My parents wouldn't travel anywhere to look at it. They're too busy, and they don't seem as proud of me as even you. They're medical people, and the idea of their daughter wasting her life on art is just a thorn in their side. I am the opposite of a success to them. I'm a disgrace."

Granger's fingers wrapped around hers, squeezing tightly. "I doubt that. Speaking as a parent, you're always proud of your kids no matter how big or small their accomplishments."

Joy shook her head, finding that statement amusing, apparently. "I'm not being overly dramatic. My mom actually told me I was a disgrace when I dropped out of a nursing program."

"You're a nursing dropout?" he asked, pulling back just a touch to get a better look at her.

"And proud of it, thank you very much."

Something told him that wasn't true though. Not 100 percent. Her view of herself was clouded by what her parents thought. "I'm pretty impressed by you, if that counts for anything."

She raised a brow. "One minute you think I'm irresponsible and untrustworthy," Joy said quietly, "and now you're pretty impressed by me. Make up your mind."

Granger drew in a breath. "I think it's more that I don't trust myself. What if I hire the wrong person? What if I get it wrong?"

"Why do you question yourself so much?"

Granger took another breath. And another. He'd briefly gone to therapy after Erin left but had stopped after a few sessions. There was no time for counseling when he had two little girls to raise on his own. This felt good though—to share the heavy burden of his thoughts and fears.

"My ex had postpartum depression after Willow was born. I tried to help her but I was also working really hard. I had another mouth to feed, and I guess I thought she'd just get over it. She was seeing a counselor and her doctor, and I thought that was good enough. Everyone told me that mothers experience this after birth all the time."

Granger looked up at the stars now. "But maybe I failed her. Maybe it's my fault that she left and the girls don't have their mother. Should I have been there for Erin more? Or gone to one of those appointments with her? I guess I just don't trust myself to know what's best anymore."

Now Joy squeezed his hand. "That's a lot of burden for one person to carry."

He looked at her again.

"And from where I'm sitting, you've done a great job picking up the pieces. I'm pretty impressed with you as well."

He found it hard to breathe for a moment. Yeah, his mom told him all the time that he was doing a good job but it didn't carry as much weight coming from her. But from an outsider looking in, from Joy, it meant a lot.

"Every choice isn't going to make or break your family. In fact, I think you've proven that you guys are pretty solid. If you can get through what you already have, you can handle anything that comes your way."

"Thank you," he said. "I needed that."

"I'm not sure who helped who," Joy added. "I guess, once again, we'll call it even."

Granger's mouth was suddenly dry, and his heartbeat threatened to bowl him over. He wanted to kiss her again. Every choice wasn't a make-or-break, life-or-death move. One kiss wasn't going to bring his world down in pieces around him.

"Are you about to kiss me?" Joy asked.

"I'm thinking about it."

"That's one of your problems, Granger Fields. You think too much." Then Joy leaned in and pressed her lips to his, and suddenly he wasn't thinking at all.

* * *

Joy never wanted this kiss to end. Her body felt like a glass of bubbly champagne. Every nerve ending was sparkling, creating a satisfying buzz that ran from her lips to her toes. Granger's mouth was warm over hers, a welcome contrast to the biting cold around them.

His hand wrapped around her back while she reached one of her hands to explore his chest. It was firm beneath her touch. She'd noticed how broad and muscled it was but now she was free to touch him.

They both pulled back at the same time, coming up for air.

"Don't tell me that was a mistake this time," she said softly. "We both wanted that kiss."

"It wasn't a mistake." Granger looked at her. The brown of his eyes seemed darker suddenly. He was looking at her differently too. That had started before the kiss though, as the tension between them had started to mount.

"So what do we do now?" Because she wanted to keep kissing him. She didn't want to keep caging up this desire. But she didn't want to mess up the arrangement they had going either.

"I have no idea." He reached out and touched her arm. At least he wasn't pulling away this time. But maybe she should be. "We can't bring the girls into . . . whatever this is. I don't want them getting confused or getting their hopes up about us."

Joy swallowed. She didn't need to get her hopes up either. Just like their business arrangement, anything romantic between them would be temporary. A few kisses here and there. But why resist it? It felt good, and she needed to feel good right now. "While we're making this arrangement, let's make another promise."

Granger narrowed his eyes. "Okay?"

"When our chemistry fizzles out, we'll still be friends. No dramatics. I don't want things to be awkward between us, and I definitely don't want you to stop bringing the girls around if things get messy. I was theirs before I was yours."

"Mine," Granger repeated.

Joy cocked her head, her hair brushing against her cheek. "Figure of speech."

He nodded. "And I totally agree. Anything between us shouldn't affect Abby or Willow."

"Not that we're dating," Joy pointed out. "We just kissed. Two times." She looked at him, feeling hot and bothered and completely out of sorts.

"Let's make that three," Granger said, leaning in.

Yep, the desire was out of its cage now, and from this point on, it was going to be hard to keep their hands off each other.

* * *

The next morning, Joy awoke with a dreamy sigh. It was officially the weekend, which always brought a deeper level of relaxation. But this morning felt extra good because she'd made out with Granger for at least an hour under the stars last night.

That was real, right? Not a dream?

She slid her arm down by her side and pinched herself just to make sure. "Ouch," she said before breaking into a yawn. Then Chelsea leaped onto the bed and launched herself on Joy's midsection.

Meow!

Chelsea pawed her cheek gently. Joy smiled even wider. She'd forgotten how great the morning after a great kissing session was.

Chelsea walked up Joy's chest and looked her in the eye, purring loudly. Her body sounded like a small motor.

"If I were a cat, I'd be purring louder right now," Joy said, scooting Chelsea off her chest and sitting up. Even though it was the weekend, she still had work to do. Thanksgiving was this coming Thursday and the Christmas tree workshop got started the next day.

Joy had invited the Ladies' Day Out group to be her first customers, and most of them had seemed genuinely excited. If they enjoyed themselves, then they'd make sure that everyone in town followed suit between now and Christmas.

Joy scooted down the hall toward the coffee machine. There was a bounce in her step, and Granger had put it there. She was tempted to feel bad about their make-out session, but why? He was single, and so was she. They were both mature adults—mature, lonely adults who had needs. If it didn't get in the way of his family or their little working arrangement, what was the harm?

She watched the dark coffee pour into her cup. The potential harm lay with her heart. Just like Erin had done a number on Granger, Joy's ex had done a number on her too. There were still invisible scars on her heart from where he'd torn it to pieces last Christmas.

She just wouldn't let her emotions get involved this time. Kissing was just kissing, and she wouldn't let it go beyond that, she promised herself as she picked up her cup and brought it to the table.

After leisurely drinking her coffee, she dressed and got into her car. First stop was Sugar Pines Community Center. Joy's mind kept returning to Granger like a pesky moth to a flame as she made the short drive. Then she got out and headed inside.

Donovan met her at the door of the community center. "Good morning, Joy."

"Good morning to you. How are things over here?"

"Couldn't be better. We're having the monthly senior citizen breakfast this morning. Wanna join us?"

Joy mocked insult. "I still get carded when I go to the Tipsy Tavern, I'll have you know."

He chuckled. "Not saying you look a day past your twenties. Just willing to make an exception for you because we like having you here."

"Aw," Joy said. "Thank you."

"Will you be back for another art class soon?" Donovan asked.

Joy checked her mental calendar. "Well, this week is Thanksgiving. I'll be here to help with the lunch on Thursday as usual. And then Friday I'm starting a new venture just for the holidays." She quickly told him about the Christmas tree workshop.

"That sounds amazing. Maybe I can gather up a group from here to go on a field trip one Saturday or Sunday afternoon." He shrugged. "Or in the middle of the week if you're offering them then. What do you think?"

Joy hadn't even considered that. "Wow. That would be awesome. If you came in the afternoon, we'd finish up by dark, and everyone could go on a hayride through Granger's lighted path. Peppermint Path is very impressive." Last night with Granger was once again front and center. Peppermint Path was also romantic in her view, and it stirred up all the butterflies in her stomach.

"Being out after dark gets a little riskier for our senior citizen folks. There's a higher risk of falling for those who don't see well."

Joy nodded. "Right. Well, I'll talk to Granger. The ride won't be as beautiful in the daytime but I still think everyone would enjoy it."

"Just tell me when we can come, and I'll make the arrangements," Donovan said.

Joy grinned as she headed toward the large community room. Her mind exploded with ideas for a Christmas tree workshop for the people here. Perhaps wire cages weren't the best medium because of arthritic hands and decreased strength and coordination. They could do foam cones and spray paint them green. Or even red. Or papier-mâché trees. Then the folks could make little ornaments and attach them.

Aunt Darby looked up from her meal as Joy stepped into the room. "Joy! I didn't know you were coming today."

Joy slid into a bench in front of her. "I was just passing through and thought I'd come say hello."

"You've been so busy lately."

"Well, you've been busy yourself with a certain older gentleman." Joy watched her aunt's expression. "You really like him, huh?"

Darby blushed against her wrinkled skin. "I have a secret for you." She leaned in over her tray.

Joy leaned in as well. "I love a good secret. And I'm great at keeping them."

Darby giggled softly. "I've always had a little crush on Ray."

Joy pulled back. "What? Why have you waited so long, then?"

Darby shrugged and picked up her spoon, dipping it in her applesauce. "I never thought I wanted to be bogged down in the tangles of love."

Love?

Darby lifted her spoon to her lips. "But Ray makes me feel like I'm flying. I've been missing out." She slid the applesauce into her mouth now. "In fact, my artwork has even changed. And it's selling better than ever."

Even though Darby was getting older, she still created paintings and sculptures that she put up for commission in the same locations that Joy did.

"Yeah? That's great, Aunt Darby."

"It is." Darby gave her a serious look. "Love was the missing ingredient. It hasn't drained my creativity; it's increased it a thousandfold."

There was that *love* word again. Joy hadn't realized things were so serious between Darby and Ray.

"You should try it," Darby said.

Joy pulled back. She shook her head, speechless for a moment. "I have, Aunt Darby. Remember? Dan cheated on me with a nurse."

Joy swallowed back the bitter pain. Having her boyfriend go behind her back was one thing. Going behind her back when she was pregnant, another. Casual dating was one thing but she wasn't looking for love again anytime soon.

CHAPTER TWELVE

Granger knocked lightly on the front door of his parents' house on Tuesday afternoon. When they didn't immediately answer, he knocked again and then opened the door.

"Hello?" He continued walking through the front foyer until he reached the living room where his dad was snoring in his recliner.

Granger walked through the house some more, finding his mom napping as well. That was unusual for them but he knew his mom worked hard for Merry Mountain Farms. And his father was under doctor's orders to rest.

Granger started to walk back out the way he'd come.

"Granger? Where do you think you're going?" his dad asked gruffly.

Granger spun to face him. "To let you and Mom continue with your overdue afternoon nap."

His dad chuckled. "Overdue by a couple decades, I'd say." He sat up as the back of the recliner followed him.

"I came to update you on the farm," Granger said.

His father gestured to the couch. "By all means. Let's hear it."

Granger sat down and recapped. "Peppermint Path is done and ready to get started on Friday night. We'll have our first Christmas tree workshop that evening as well. Joy's gotten the Ladies' Day Out group signed up to be our first customers."

Granger's mom walked into the room as he spoke. "Oh, that's so nice. I used to go out with them all the time. Do you think I can join them and experience the workshop and the path myself?"

Granger looked up. "Sure."

"I mean, for the rest of the holidays, I was thinking of pulling out my old apple cider stand so we'd be more convenient to the folks taking the classes. Me and the girls would sell cider and hot chocolate. We can give the stand a fresh coat of paint tomorrow."

"That's an awesome idea." Granger looked at his father, who was frowning.

"You've done all this on your own?" his father asked skeptically.

"Joy's doing the Christmas tree workshop. It was just a matter of buying materials and making a sign for her. And we already had most of the materials for the lighted hayride. The tractor is shined and polished. The path is clear. I replaced a lot of bulbs. I just need a Santa." He looked at his dad hopefully.

His dad took a moment to respond. "You want *me* to play an overweight old man with a jolly laugh?"

Granger couldn't help but laugh. Half out of humor and half out of nerves. He wasn't sure his dad was joking.

"I love the trees," his dad said. "The real trees. The high-light of my year is watching families come out and pick the perfect one. That's what I'll be doing again this year. I'm resting like the doctor said but that doesn't mean I can't man the register, talk to our customers, and ring them up. Looks like you'll have to find another Santa Claus for this project of yours."

Granger nodded. "Fair enough. I've touched base with the guys from the Sweetwater Springs fire and police stations as usual. There were a few single guys from each who agreed to help load and deliver for us." Employees from both had been earning extra money helping Merry Mountain Farms for years.

"Sounds like we're all set for Friday afternoon, then," his dad said.

"Except for a Santa," Granger confirmed. The end of Peppermint Path was an elaborate place for his Santa to sit and talk to the kids. Now all he had to do was go down his list of friends who owed him a favor.

"Christmas is coming, yes," his mom said, interrupting his thoughts. "But first comes Thanksgiving. Granger, I was hoping you'd invite Joy to eat with us. The girls love her so much, and I'm not sure she has anywhere to go."

"She's going to see her aunt at the community center for lunch," he argued.

"Yes, but after that she can come here. Make sure you ask her." She gave him a stern look. "And before you jump to conclusions, I am not matchmaking. Thanksgiving is for friends and family, and Joy should be included this year."

"Sure, I'll ask her." In fact, he'd already considered asking but he'd worried that it was crossing some unspoken line. She wasn't looking for a relationship, and hanging out with his entire family wasn't exactly casual. But with the invitation coming from his mom, that made it less complicated.

"Oh, good. I hope she can join us. The girls think so much of her. I do too."

Granger looked at his father. "Her mom is quite the doctor too. I owe her a lot this season."

"Oh, maybe we should invite Joy's parents as well," Granger's mom said excitedly. "It's the more the merrier. And her aunt Darby. Ask Joy, won't you?"

Granger hedged. Asking Joy was one thing. Asking her whole family took it to a new level. Even if he did ask, he doubted they'd all come. According to Joy, her parents lived at the hospital. "I'll ask," he finally agreed.

As he headed outside, he saw Joy and the girls preparing cans of paint. He assumed they were getting ready to paint the beverage stand that his mom had mentioned.

Joy looked up from what she was doing and beamed at him. "Hi."

"Hi."

There was a charge in the air between them.

"Daddy!" Willow came barreling toward him. He braced himself for her bear hug. Abby took her time and gave him a quieter hug.

"Did you guys have a good day?" he asked.

They both nodded. It was the last day before their fall break. Tomorrow, they'd be home all day preparing for Thanksgiving on Thursday.

Granger looked up to see the mail carrier slowing down at his mailbox up the road. "There's the mail," he said.

Abby livened up and turned quickly to look. "I'll get it," she said eagerly. Her voice came out louder, which he found curious.

"Me too, me too!" Willow said.

Abby looked down at her younger sister. "Do you have to go everywhere with me? Stay here with Dad and Joy."

"But I want to go with you." Willow looked genuinely dejected.

And Granger was a bit surprised by Abby pushing her away. Abby was always a mother hen to Willow.

"You can stay with me, Willow," Joy said. "I might need your help while Abby is checking the mail."

Granger felt his heart squeeze. Seeing the way Joy interacted with his children made her attractive in an entirely different way. Combined with his overwhelming physical attraction to her, it was all he could do not to tug her toward him right now and kiss her silly.

* * *

Joy knew when someone was keeping something from her. Well, at least when a kid was. Men were another story. And Abby was definitely hiding something. Joy could see it in the way her gaze darted around. And the way she'd seemed completely deflated since she'd come back from the mailbox. What was going on?

"So we have to stay out here every night and sell drinks?" Abby asked, her mood sullen suddenly.

"Or you can help me with the Christmas tree workshop," Joy said. "I'll need an assistant. Willow can help your nana."

Abby seemed to cheer up a little at the idea. She glanced back toward the house where Granger and Willow had gone to get a glass of water. "Willow will probably pout about me not being with her," Abby muttered.

Joy put her hand on Abby's shoulder. "What's going on with you and Willow lately? Did something happen?"

Abby shrugged. "She just acts like I'm her mom. I'm not."

There was a tremor in Abby's voice, telling Joy that she was on the edge of her emotions. She'd told Joy that she was missing her mom lately. Maybe that was all it was. A girl her age needed a mother figure, and Abby only had her grandmother. Maybe Abby resented having to be that figure for Willow. It wasn't fair.

Granger and Willow came walking back outside where Joy and Abby were working.

Joy looked up at him. "You clean up nicely."

He looked down at himself for a moment. "I'm on my way to meet Jack and Luke at the Tipsy Tavern. It's overdue, and I need to collect on a favor from one of them."

Joy laughed. "Uh-oh. I have a feeling I know what that favor is."

"And you're probably right." He gestured back to his house. "My mom is inside. She's ready to take the girls off your hands anytime. They're out of school tomorrow, and my mom wants to spend some time with them. Then Thursday is a holiday."

Joy nodded. "Yes, it is."

"My mom was wondering if you could join us," he told her.

"Your mom?" Joy repeated.

Granger tilted his head from side to side. "And me."

"And me too," Abby agreed, suddenly looking a lot more cheerful.

"Yes, yes, yes! Pleaaaase," Willow said, grabbing Joy's hand. "I want you to come too."

Abby shook her head, her expression twisting. "You're copying me again, Willow!"

"Am not!"

"Are too!"

Joy held up a hand. "Well, it's hard to refuse such an enthusiastic invitation."

Her gaze fluttered up to meet Granger's. It was growing harder and harder to refuse him as well, which was part of the problem. "What can I bring?"

"Just yourself. Mom also told me to tell you to invite your parents and your aunt too."

Joy hedged. "I doubt my parents will make it. They're always so busy but thank her for thinking of them."

"Mom's a saint."

"She is," Joy agreed. "I'll ask Aunt Darby. She might prefer to spend the occasion with her new boyfriend though."

Granger shoved his hands in his jeans pockets. "My mom makes more than enough for an entire army if Darby wants to bring Ray."

Joy nodded. "You're sure you don't need me to bring anything on Thursday?"

"Positive."

Joy started backing up, feeling the need to distance herself. Not that distance eased the ache in her chest. It was just supposed to have been a few innocent kisses but she knew better. She had already started to develop feelings for Granger. What was she going to do about that? "Then I'll see you Thursday after I leave the community center."

"Yay!" Abby said. "Thanksgiving is usually kind of boring. But it'll be fun with you here."

"Thanks a lot, kid." Granger poked Abby's shoulder.

"No offense, Dad, but you usually pass out on the couch after eating two platefuls. I doubt Joy will do that."

"It's called the turkey coma. And everyone does that after stuffing themselves," Granger said. "Even Joy."

Joy raised a hand. "Guilty. Turkey gets me every time, I'm afraid."

"Well, you can stay and nap here with us," Willow offered. "You can even sleep over if you want," she said, bopping on the balls of her feet in the way that she did when she was bursting with excitement.

Joy didn't dare look up at Granger after that comment. A sleepover at Granger's place definitely wouldn't be happening this week. Or any week.

* * *

Joy left home bright and early on Thanksgiving morning. She planned to serve at the Sugar Pines Community Center at lunch but she wanted to stop by and see her parents at the hospital first. This was a day to spend with family after all.

She parked and headed inside, waving at the receptionist as she passed by. That job was still vacant as far as she knew. But she wouldn't be filling it. Not anytime soon at least. She stepped onto the elevator and pressed the button for the second floor. The door closed behind her and began to move. Yeah, she could've just taken the stairs and probably should have to make up for all the delicious food she was going to eat later. But just anticipating a battle of wills with her mom was exhausting.

Her mom would remind her about the open position here. She'd also likely insinuate that Joy needed a stable job. Or she'd imply that Joy needed a stable relationship. Someone like Joy's ex, Dan.

The elevator opened and...*Speak of the devil*.

"Hey, Joy," Dan said. He was in his white doctor's coat, and for a moment, her heart skipped a beat. She'd loved him once after all. Then her brain caught up, and she walked past him. "Joy?"

Ugh. Her conscience wouldn't let her continue walking.

She stopped and turned but didn't return his smile. Instead, she offered her best glare. "Yes?"

He stepped closer. She caught the whiff of his familiar cologne, much too strong to be appropriate at the hospital. It competed with the antiseptic smell on the floor but he had to impress the nurses, right? "Happy Thanksgiving."

"You too," she said curtly. "Have you seen my parents?"

He seemed to search his brain. "I'm pretty sure they both got called downstairs to the ER for an emergency consult."

Joy felt her good mood deflate another notch. An emergency consult for both an orthopedic and cardiac surgeon meant that someone was in pretty bad shape. It also meant she probably wouldn't get to see them today unless she stopped by later. That might give her an excuse to run away from Granger's house. She wanted to run from Granger for an entirely different reason than the one she had for eying the exits with Dan.

"I bought the piece of art that was hanging on consignment in the gift shop," Dan said suddenly.

Joy's gaze cut to his. "You were the one who purchased it? Why would you do that?"

"It was good. Really good." He shrugged a shoulder, something vulnerable flashing in his eyes. "And I wanted to support your art. I know every sale helps."

Joy felt her insides coil. She considered her art an extension of herself, and she did not want any piece of her on display at Dan's house. What could she do though? She couldn't put a restriction on who bought her pieces. "So it was a pity purchase?"

Dan looked taken aback. "Not at all. I've always loved your art. I consider myself lucky to get a piece at such a steal of a price. It won't always be so reasonable."

He was being nice for some reason that she didn't have the energy to investigate. "Well, if my parents aren't here, then I guess I'll leave."

She started to walk past him back toward the elevator but he grabbed her arm gently.

Joy yanked it away and glared up at him. "What do you want?"

"I don't know. I just ... I wish we could still be friends— that's all."

Was she supposed to feel bad for him? Maybe her mom did when he talked like this but Joy didn't. "After you cheated on me with that nurse behind my back? No, we can't."

"That's not fair," Dan said.

"Unfair is leaving me to grieve our—" Joy cut herself off. She wasn't doing this here with him. That was a year ago. She should be over this by now. "Bring my artwork back to the gift shop. I'll tell Shirley to refund you in full." Even though Joy could use that money to help put a deposit on her store.

She turned and started walking away again. Dan didn't stop her this time.

Joy was shaking as she stepped inside the elevator and silently begged the doors to close behind her. Once they did, she exhaled, and the tears rushed toward her eyes. *Get it together, Joy.* Today was a day to count her blessings, and one was the fact that Dan had shown her his true colors before their relationship had gone any further.

She couldn't bring herself to think that losing their baby had worked out for the best though. Yes, sharing custody of a child with that jerk would have been uncomfortable but she'd carried a child inside her. She'd felt an indescribable love for the life that she'd harbored. And then she'd lost it to some medical fluke she barely understood.

Joy stepped off the elevator and once again tried to conjure up a level of gratitude worthy of Thanksgiving morning. She had her parents. Her aunt. Her cat. And her passion for art. And that was enough.

She left the building and headed through the parking lot. After unlocking her car, she plopped down into her driver's seat, jabbed the key into the ignition, and turned it. The engine grumbled and refused. She turned the key again. The engine made another grumbling sound that flattened out along with the last of Joy's positive outlook.

Chelsea, Aunt Darby, her parents, and her passion for art couldn't jump her car for her. And no way was she going back inside and asking Dan for help.

Next on Joy's list of options was Granger. She really didn't want to call him and ask for help right now. But she knew he'd drop everything and come to her rescue. He was that type of guy. Then again, she'd thought the same about Dan.

* * *

Granger popped his truck's hood and stepped over to Joy's car.

"I'm so sorry. I hope I didn't pull you away from anything important," she said as she leaned against her car.

"You didn't. The girls are helping Mom in the kitchen, and Dad's watching TV. You didn't take me away from anything, and it'd be okay if you did. I need to get your car working so you can join us this afternoon, right?"

He reached into her driver's area and popped her hood as well. Then he connected a pair of jumper cables from his engine to hers. After that, he started his truck's engine and walked back over to her. "I'm guessing you came here to see your parents?" He looked over and studied her features. She seemed distressed, and he was willing to bet it was about more than just being delayed by a dead car battery.

She nodded. "But they're working in the ER right now. My parents, the superheroes."

"Your mom is definitely one to my dad. He's going to be able to celebrate with us today because of her."

Joy's lips fell into a subtle frown. "I'm proud of the good work she does. I just wish...I wish I knew her a little better. I wish she knew me."

"Is that why you look so gloomy today?" he asked.

"One of many reasons, none of which I want to talk about." She smiled now but he wasn't buying it. "I'm just thankful that you came to my rescue. Otherwise, I might be walking to Sugar Pines Community Center."

"You volunteer at the community center every Thanksgiving?" he asked. There was nothing to do except make small talk while her car charged but he also wanted to know more about Joy.

"Aunt Darby and I used to volunteer together when I was growing up. She taught me that when you feel helpless, the best thing to do is to help someone else. I stopped for a couple years as an adult. It's good advice though, and now I'm back to doing it."

Granger found this curious. "Who made you feel helpless?"

Her gaze flicked toward his. She'd told him about her ex that worked here at the hospital. Granger was an acquaintance with Dan but that was all. Dan came out to Merry Mountain Farms every year for a tree like most folks. He seemed nice enough.

Joy heaved a sigh as she looked out on the sparsely filled parking lot. "Today's focus should be on the good stuff. That's what Thanksgiving's about, right?"

"Yeah," he agreed. "And I like your aunt's advice about helping someone else. I'm feeling a little helpless these days too, especially when it comes to my oldest daughter who has had a mood transplant in the last week."

Joy laughed, the sound igniting all kinds of feelings inside him. "That's just the beginning. Wait until she's in the teen years."

Granger massaged a hand over his face. "I don't even want to think about it. I always thought she'd be exempt from any of the stages other people talk about. She's my little angel."

"And she's also a girl," Joy pointed out.

"Great. I feel even more helpless now." Granger grinned. "Maybe I can come to the Sugar Pines Community Center and volunteer with you this afternoon."

Joy's expression dropped. "You want to serve food with me?"

He shrugged a shoulder. He was feeling helpless when it came to her these days too. There was a pull between them, strong and unrelenting. Falling for someone who wasn't interested in a real relationship right now wasn't a good idea. He had a family to think about. And yet his heart was leading him right up to the edge of this invisible cliff.

The only hope he had to hang onto was that there wouldn't be enough time to fall in love with her. After Christmas, Joy wouldn't be coming around Merry Mountain Farms anymore. So it was safe to enjoy spending time together in the moment. That's what he was telling himself at least.

"What do you think? Let me tag along with you?" He stepped closer until he was standing right in front of her. So close he could smell the flowery scent of her hair. Close enough to see his own reflection in her eyes.

They were keeping their kisses private, which this parking lot was not. But there weren't a lot of people walking about on this chilly Thanksgiving morning either.

"If you work at Sugar Pines with me, you'll have to wear an apron," she teased. "And gloves."

"Done."

She grinned as she held his gaze, and then she lowered her eyes to his lips. He did the same. Standing this close, it was impossible not to feel the pull to kiss her. She nibbled on her lower lip.

Without even giving himself permission, he felt his body lean forward. Joy met him halfway, and then they were kissing. This kiss was different than the slow-building, shy kisses they'd shared before. This kiss was fast and needy. Granger needed to get his fill of her before she disappeared. And she seemed to need something from him this morning too.

Joy leaned back against the side of her car as he gently pressed against her, the kiss continuing as the car charged. Granger felt his own body charge from his connection with her. When they pulled away, they were both breathless. If this weren't a public space, that kiss might've gone further. And that might have been past the point of no return for him.

Someone cleared their throat from behind him.

"Joy? Granger?"

Granger turned toward several women, all part of the

Ladies' Day Out group here in Sweetwater Springs. "Alma. Janice...Good morning, Greta and Alice."

The women all stared at him and Joy.

"Well, this is something to give thanks for. It's about time that both of you find a little love in your life," Alma said. "After your wife took off, Granger, I worried myself sick about you."

Granger looked down at his feet. Alma meant well but sometimes people didn't understand that he didn't want to be pitied or reminded of the most painful event in his life every time he saw them.

"And Joy, Dan is my nephew but I'm still siding with you on what happened. He's too old for a spanking but he deserved one after he treated you so poorly."

Granger looked over at Joy.

She seemed surprised by the mention of her ex. "You know about what happened?"

"Of course I do. I'm his aunt. And to do that to you while you were pregnant no less."

All the color seemed to have drained from Joy's face now, leaving her pale.

"Pregnant?" one of the women whispered loudly to Alma. "I don't remember Joy ever being pregnant."

Alma's brows dipped, making deep lines on her forehead. "Oh no. Did I say something I shouldn't have? I thought people knew about that. Maybe I was supposed to keep that in the family. Oh, me and my big mouth. I'm so sorry." She covered her mouth with a shaky hand.

"Just stop talking." Greta swiped at Alma with her cane. "That's the past, and Joy is with Granger now."

"We're not..." Joy looked at Granger, her eyes pleading for help.

"We're not together," he told the group. "That was

just..." Now he looked at Joy for a little assistance. "That kiss was just..."

"A Thanksgiving kiss," Joy supplied. "I'm thankful that he's helping me with my car because it won't start."

The women stared at the two of them.

"That's the worst lie I've ever heard," Janice said. "A kiss is a kiss is a kiss. And you two were just caught kissing."

Granger didn't know how to respond so he ignored her and moved the conversation forward. "What are you four doing here on Thanksgiving?"

"Oh, we're visiting Linda May. She's an old friend of ours. She's got some stomach troubles, and the doctors are taking good care of her in there. We passed your father, by the way," Alma told Joy. "Don't tell me you're all alone on Thanksgiving."

Joy shook her head. Granger thought she still looked flustered from the kiss and the comment about her pregnancy. He hadn't known about that. She didn't have any kids underfoot so he wondered what had happened. He could tell by her expression that the situation had ended badly. "No, I'm, um, not alone for Thanksgiving," she said.

The ladies looked between Joy and Granger, their imaginations no doubt going wild.

"Well," Alice Hampton said, "we all are looking forward to your Christmas tree workshop tomorrow afternoon. My hands are old so you might need to help me out a little bit."

Granger saw Joy nod from the corner of his eye.

"I...yes, of course. I'll have Granger's daughter Abby assisting me as well. It'll be fun." Her words seemed to roll over each other. It was obvious to Granger that she was upset.

"And we're looking forward to your lighted path too, Granger," Greta added. "I'm so happy that you started that tradition back up."

"Me too. Have a wonderful Thanksgiving, ladies," he said. He turned to Joy as they started to walk away. "You know news of our parking lot kiss is going to spread to every person those four come in contact with today."

Joy offered a weak smile, her gaze unsure as she looked at him. He wanted to ask the questions that were racing through his mind but he felt the wall that Joy had put up. The women had uncovered a gaping wound, and Joy suddenly looked vulnerable.

"There's nothing we can do about any rumors that might get started. But when you feel helpless, help someone else, right?" he said softly.

Joy nodded. "Right."

"So we'll go to Sugar Pines and serve food together. Then we'll overindulge ourselves with my family." Granger reached for her hand and gave it a reassuring squeeze. "We can worry about everything else tomorrow."

CHAPTER THIRTEEN

Joy topped off a few glasses of tea and then placed the pitcher on the rolling cart at her side. The meal had already been served, and most of the diners were on their last bites.

Her gaze moved to Aunt Darby, who was giggling with Ray beside her. Joy had already spoken to them several times. They made a good match. Ray brought out a new side of Darby that Joy appreciated. All these years, Darby had been so independent, and she'd seemed sincerely happy. But seeing her laugh uncontrollably with Ray and allow him to help her, whether she needed it or not, was a nice change.

"Joy." Donovan stepped up to Joy and put his arm around her shoulders. "I don't know what we'd do without you always helping us out. You lift everyone's spirits around here."

She looked at him and smiled. Donovan had asked her out a couple of times, and she'd turned him down politely.

She was glad it'd never been awkward between them. Donovan wasn't the type of guy to get weird with rejection. In fact, Joy suspected that he'd ask her out again one day. Maybe if things were different, she'd have told him yes. He seemed like the kind of guy who married and had a big family. And this past year, that was the very last type of guy she'd been looking for. "Well, the people here lift my spirits as well," Joy said. "It's selfish on my part."

He chuckled. "I completely understand that. It's not a job if you love it."

Joy gave him a curious look. "That's what Aunt Darby always tells me."

"She tells me the same thing," Donovan confessed, making Joy smile. Her aunt Darby was such an inspiration to so many. Not just Joy.

Granger walked up, his brows gathering at the sight of Donovan with his arm draped over Joy's shoulders. Was he jealous?

Donovan removed his arm and held his hand out for Granger to shake. "And thank you, Granger. It was such a nice surprise having you help today. You've charmed all the ladies here, that's for sure."

Joy included. She would be trying to push him into the broom closet if not for Alma's slip of the tongue. Granger had several opportunities to ask about the pregnancy comment but he hadn't yet. Maybe he wouldn't, and Joy wouldn't have to recap the very worst moments of her life. Granger was just a guy she kissed after all, not one she told her life story to. "Well, we have to head to our next stop," Joy told Donovan.

The *we* got Donovan's attention, and just like the women from the LDO, he looked between Joy and Granger as if processing their togetherness. "I see. Well, don't worry about your aunt Darby. She and my dad will keep each other company."

"Oh, I know. They're inseparable these days." Joy was thankful for that; her aunt deserved love, happiness, and every good thing that came her way.

Joy and Granger said their goodbyes and headed back out into the parking lot.

"What was that about?" Granger asked.

Joy glanced over. "What?"

Granger held out his open palms. "He had his arm around you. I'd say Donovan Tate has a crush on you."

Joy laughed, which felt good on her raw emotions. "I suspect he does but the feeling isn't mutual."

Granger seemed to soften a bit. "Why not? He seems like a great guy. Friendly, and he has a stable job."

Joy narrowed her eyes. "I've never been one to fall into the mindset that a stable job equals a good person. He's just not my type."

Granger stopped walking as they reached her car, and he turned toward her. "Okay, what is your type?"

She met his dark gaze and had to remind herself to breathe. "The type that makes my heart skip a beat. Who makes me laugh. Who makes me want to be a better person." Her type was also the type that wouldn't expect commitment at the end of the day. She didn't want to go down that path again for a long time. The pain from her last serious relationship was still raw, splintering inside her heart every time she thought about it.

Granger continued to watch her.

Her heart skipped foolishly. He'd already made her laugh a half dozen times today. And watching him interact with his children and the people inside the community building definitely inspired her.

"You're one of the best people I know," he said quietly. "I don't think you can get any better."

Joy swallowed. A better person would have responded differently with Dan this morning at the hospital. It wasn't an apology but he'd tried to make amends. He'd said he wanted to be friends but she had walked away. Forgiving was easier said than done.

"I'll meet you at the house?" Granger asked.

She thought about shaking her head and telling him no. She was exhausted. It was more from emotional weariness than from the last two hours of serving food. Alma had opened an emotional wound earlier that she hadn't had time to deal with. It had festered over the last two hours while she'd ignored it, smiling politely and serving lunch at the community center. She couldn't ignore it any longer though. Joy didn't care that she'd lost Dan. But she did care about their baby.

Joy looked down at her feet, taking a moment to collect her emotions. She had to remind herself to breathe, in and out. In and out. Instead of growing calmer, her body began to shake. *Get it together. I'm not alone. Don't lose your cool yet.*

If she backed out of dinner at the Fieldses' house, Granger would ask questions, and some of those might be the very ones she didn't want to talk about. "Yes. I'll see you over there."

"You're in for a treat. Mom's turkey is the best I've tasted." His tone of voice made Joy know he couldn't see by looking at her how distressed she felt inside. She was good at hiding her emotions, painting over them with a smile and nod.

"I'm looking forward to it." She gave him a brief glance and then hurried to the driver's side of her car and got in, taking a few deep breaths.

Then, bursting from the inside out, she broke into tears.

* * *

Granger sat in his truck for a moment, unable to ignore the fact that he could see Joy crying in his rearview mirror.

Go to her or give her space?

He was pretty sure it was about what had been said in the hospital parking lot hours earlier. She'd kept it together but he'd been able to see the shift in her demeanor. She was tougher than she let on—he'd give her that.

His gaze flicked to the rearview again. Then, unable to help himself, he pushed open his truck door and got out, walking toward her. He opened her passenger side door and dipped into the seat beside her.

She looked at him, sniffling and swiping at her eyes. There was no hiding the fact that she'd just been crying though. "What are you doing?"

"I saw you crying and couldn't just drive away."

She reached for a tissue in the middle console and dabbed at her face. "It's n-nothing."

Granger reached for her hand. "Anything that makes you cry like that is something. Sometimes talking about things helps."

More tears rolled down her cheeks.

Granger grabbed a tissue and reached across the center console, his gaze lifting to hers as he dabbed her tears away.

She seemed startled by the gesture but didn't move to stop him. He wiped away one, then another, moving around her cheeks as his eyes stayed fixed on hers.

"It's just…a hard day, I guess. I'm supposed to be thankful, and I am. But sometimes I also feel so…empty." She seemed to hesitate about saying more.

"You were pregnant?" he asked, putting his arm back down to his side.

Joy looked away, turning her gaze to look out on the parking lot. "For a hot second." She took a breath and blew it out. "I was engaged and carrying a baby, and everything in my life seemed perfect for one moment in time. I didn't even know I wanted those things in my life...Then I found out Dan was also seeing a nurse." Joy hiccupped softly. "Nurse Nancy."

Granger treaded softly with his next question. He'd never been that close to Joy in the past. He hadn't even known she was engaged before. "And the baby?"

Joy's eyes welled. She pulled another tissue from the box and dabbed underneath her lashes. "It was what's called an ectopic pregnancy."

Granger shook his head. He'd never heard that term before. "What is that?"

"It means I was carrying the egg outside my uterus. The baby never had a chance of coming into this world." She snatched more tissues.

Granger reached for her arm again. "I'm so sorry, Joy."

Joy sniffled some more. "Anyway, that's my big, dark secret. It's not really much of a secret if the other women in town know." Her chin trembled as she tried to hold her emotions together. "I feel silly for sitting here and crying about it. It's been a year, and I don't even think about it as much as I used to. Really...I'm sorry. I'm keeping you from going to your family's Thanksgiving meal. You should go. Don't worry about me."

"You say that as if you're not coming too," Granger said.

"I'm afraid I'd be a drag this afternoon. I mean, look at me."

"I am looking at you." And he couldn't find any fault with anything he saw. Joy was the most beautiful woman inside and out that he'd ever known.

Joy shook her head. "I shouldn't."

He got that she didn't want to put a damper on his family holiday but she could only make it better, regardless of her mood. "You should," Granger insisted. "No one should be alone on Thanksgiving."

"I have my cat," Joy protested.

Granger chuckled softly. "You can return home to Chelsea right after you eat the biggest, most delicious meal you've ever experienced. Say yes, Joy." Suddenly he couldn't think of anything he wanted more in this moment. His Thanksgiving would be so much better with her by his side this afternoon.

She hesitated and then nodded slowly. "Okay. I'll go."

* * *

Granger saw the look that his mom kept giving him across the dinner table. Joy was seated next to him. Abby was on his other side with Willow to her right. They looked like one big, happy family.

But they weren't. He and Joy were friends, and he'd invited her to a family holiday dinner because she'd needed someone. The thought of her locking herself away in her house today and crying was unconscionable.

"I'm so glad you could come, Joy," his mom said. "Aren't you, Granger?"

"I am!" Willow answered instead.

"Thank you." Joy looked over at Granger. She seemed to be in better spirits now.

"It's such a shame that your parents couldn't take the day off," his mom continued.

"No, it's not," his dad defended. "If they took days off, I might not be here today. We need good doctors like them manning the ER."

Granger didn't really think his father had been at death's door a few weeks ago but he had been sick.

"What they do is very honorable," Joy agreed.

"No less honorable than what you do," Granger argued, looking over at her.

Joy met his gaze, her brows subtly lifting. "I make art." She said it as if that was the argument against her.

"And your art makes people happy. Happiness is just as important as being healthy."

"I don't know about that. There are plenty of grumpy but healthy people out there. We met a few this morning." Joy smiled.

Granger could feel everyone's eyes on them but he didn't care. He wasn't going to let Joy think that what she did wasn't just as important as anyone else's jobs. Joy mattered to him and his family. She was saving his Christmas this year. "What you do matters. Don't ever think it doesn't."

Joy looked at him for a moment, and his family at the table seemed to fade into the background. He'd been one of those people to think art didn't matter before her. It was just a glorified hobby that some made a living off of and some barely survived with before finally getting a "real" job.

He didn't feel that way after seeing Joy work with his girls and other kids at the Sweetwater library. Or after hearing the people at Sugar Pines go on and on about how much they enjoyed Joy's lessons. She added fun to their lives. She added fun to his too.

"Thank you," she said almost shyly.

"If Abby grows up to become an artist like she wants, I'll be proud," Granger added.

Joy looked down at her plate now.

Maybe he took his defense of her a little too far. What had gotten into him? "And if Willow decides she really does want to teach dogs to talk one day, I'll support that too," he joked, attempting to lighten the mood that had suddenly fallen over the table.

"Yay!" Willow cheered. "You hear that, Tin?"

Tinsel barked from the other room. Tin had been sluggish lately and wasn't following the girls around everywhere they went. Granger wasn't sure what was going on with her, but if it kept up, he might call the town's new veterinarian, Dr. Lewis, next week just to schedule her for a checkup.

"Can Tin sit at the dinner table if she learns to talk?" Willow asked.

"No," Granger's mom answered. "Dogs don't get to come to the table. That's a house rule. Even talking ones."

Everyone laughed, including Joy. Then the conversation slipped into talk of Christmas, which was a big deal in the Fields household.

"We always put a real tree up," Granger's mom said, "but I'm making one with you and the LDO this year instead," she told Joy excitedly.

"We put up a real tree," his dad argued. "Always. Real trees are our business."

She frowned at him. "Usually, yes. But things are changing this year. Our business is real trees as well as the kind you make with your hands and your heart." She winked at Joy.

Granger looked over just in time to see Joy smile. His heart kicked against his ribs so forcefully that he looked down at his plate for a moment, collecting his breath as he listened to the ongoing conversation.

"I'll put up two trees, then," his mom said. "A real one and the one I make at the Christmas tree workshop. How's that?"

Granger's dad nodded. "I guess I can't argue with more trees."

"And you've never been able to win an argument with me anyway," his mom added, winking at both Granger and Joy this time.

* * *

"You didn't have to help with the dishes," Granger's mom said, as Joy walked into the kitchen with her arms full of dirty plates.

"It's the least I could do. The food was amazing. Thank you so much for having me over, Mrs. Fields."

"I've already told you, call me Debbie."

"Debbie," Joy repeated. She guessed, after spending a family holiday together, they should definitely be on a first-name basis.

Granger's mom turned from the sink and leaned against the counter. "It's so good to see Granger finally moving on after all this time."

Joy felt her jaw drop. "What?"

"Oh, it's no secret, dear. We've noticed the way you two have been looking at one another. And Abby spotted you two kissing."

Joy's full stomach flip-flopped in her belly now. "She did? When?"

His mom nodded, her eyes warm. "I guess that means there's been more than one kiss," she said on a pleased smile. "Don't worry. Abby only told me, not Willow. It wouldn't be good for Willow to get her hopes up, of course...But to be honest, mine are soaring. You two make a wonderful match." Debbie stepped toward Joy and reached for both of her hands.

Joy shook her head. How did she explain kissing Granger when they weren't even together? "We're not...what Abby saw was a misunderstanding. Granger and I aren't..."

Debbie's wide smile wilted slightly. "But the way he defended you over dinner. A man doesn't rush to a woman's defense so fiercely unless he cares about her."

"I'm sure he does care about me but we're just friends." Friends who kiss sometimes. Friends who probably shouldn't kiss anymore. Joy had come to realize that Abby was just as fragile as Willow. Maybe even more so.

"Just friends?" Debbie let go of Joy's hands and walked over to the kitchen island to sit down on one of the stools. She waited until Joy did the same. "When Erin left, Granger made his life about keeping the rest of the family going at all costs. The girls mean everything to him, and he's not one to bring someone into their lives without losing several nights' sleep over the possible complications. And yet, you sat right beside him at our Thanksgiving meal today."

His mom shook her head. "No, I'm not buying that you're just friends." She held up a finger. "Don't get me wrong. I'm not saying you aren't being honest either. I just think you're selling yourself a story that's far from complete."

Joy wasn't sure what to say. She didn't want to lie to Debbie but the truth was complicated. "Granger has two little girls. He needs someone more—"

"Save your breath. I'm Granger's mother, so I know what he needs. It's my maternal instinct to know."

Joy didn't know much about maternal instinct. Her mom couldn't be bothered to even call her on Thanksgiving. And her one experience with being a mother was short-lived.

"What Granger needs is someone who makes him smile and laugh, and think about himself for a change. And that's what I saw him do today. With you."

CHAPTER FOURTEEN

*J*oy felt Granger following behind her, trying to keep up as she walked to her car.

"Hey. I feel like I'm chasing you," he said on a laugh.

She stopped walking when she reached her car and turned to face him. "Sorry."

He reached out for her but she moved so that his arm fell back down by his side. "You okay?" he asked, his expression pinching. "Did I do something wrong?"

"No." She shook her head. He'd done everything right today. In the hospital parking lot, he'd been there for her after she'd run into her jerky ex. Then when Alma had innocently mentioned her failed pregnancy, he'd been there. He was the reason she hadn't spent her holiday alone painting dark pieces of art. He'd been nothing short of amazing. "Granger, Abby saw us kissing."

Granger drew back, his eyes subtly widening. "What?"

"I think that's why she's been acting out. It's so unlike

her, and it came out of nowhere. Do you think she's upset because she saw us kiss?"

Granger shook his head. "She started acting out before that." He narrowed his eyes as if just realizing what she'd asked. "When did she see us kiss?"

Joy shrugged. "After we took the lighted hayride together. That's the only time she could have seen us. Your mom told me."

"My mom." Granger lifted a hand to his forehead now. "Oh, wow. This is not good."

"Willow doesn't know though. Not yet. I just think…" Joy's heart was racing. She didn't want to suggest what she was about to but she didn't feel like there was any other choice. "Maybe it's time to back away. We kissed and got each other out of our systems."

Except she hadn't. Kissing Granger only made her body ache for his touch even more. She loved the feel of his arms embracing her, holding her. It was something she hadn't even realized she'd missed. "Tomorrow starts the Christmas tree workshop and the lighted hayride so I think we should just focus on that. And your girls too, of course," she added, remembering what Debbie had said about how dedicated Granger was to his family. He would never do anything to risk their well-being. And being involved with Joy was a risk.

Granger hesitated before finally taking a small step back and increasing the distance between them.

Part of Joy had hoped he'd argue with her. She'd heard Debbie when she'd claimed that he had feelings for Joy. And part of her had believed it. A tiny sliver of her had wanted that to be true. But here he was backing away with just the slightest push.

It was the right thing to do, of course. He had no choice, and neither did she.

She stuck out her hand to shake. "So friends, then? Just friends. For real this time."

Granger looked at her hand and then slipped his palm against hers. *Big mistake.* Warm tingles ran from her hand up her arm and straight to her heart, making it kick against the current. Did he feel it too? Was it just her?

"Friends," he agreed, still holding her hand. "I guess I'll talk to Abby and make sure she understands what she saw."

How could a little girl understand though, if even Joy at thirty years old couldn't? "That's a good idea. Maybe you should talk to your mom too. I think she's rooting for us. We're apparently not that good at sneaking around."

Granger's gaze hung on hers. The night was cold, and she just wanted to step into him one more time. It couldn't have lasted anyway. They were from two different worlds. He was a family guy, and she was focused on opening her art gallery.

"You're still holding my hand," she said.

"Honestly, I'm having a hard time letting go."

Joy's breath hitched. "You saying that probably shouldn't make me feel wonderful," she confessed, breathless. "But it does."

"What if we didn't care so much about what we were supposed to do and feel? What if we just did what we knew we shouldn't for a while?" he asked.

Joy swallowed. Her mouth was suddenly dry. "What are you suggesting?"

"Dating you. Out in the open. Why not?"

"Well, because I'm not looking for anything serious. And you have a family to think of," she pointed out.

"People apparently want to see us both moving on with our lives. Why not now?"

"A pretend relationship for the benefit of the town?" Joy asked.

"Who's pretending?" Granger tugged on her hand, pulling her toward him and pressing his mouth to hers.

She closed her eyes and melted into the embrace, her heart hammering as it pressed against his chest. This probably wasn't the best idea but she wanted what he was offering her. She was just so tired of being alone.

He nipped at her lower lip as the kiss came to an end. Then her eyes fluttered open, and she looked at him. "I still don't want anything serious. I can't right now."

Granger glanced up at the sky for a moment, seemingly looking for answers in the clouds. Then he pulled his gaze back to her. "All I know is it feels good being with you. Better than good. It feels amazing."

Joy wound her fingers through his. "I agree."

"We'll take this at your speed."

"But your girls. I thought you were worried about who you brought into their lives. They've already lost so much."

Granger nodded. "That's true. But you're already in our lives. And they're going to see me dip my toes in the dating pool sooner or later."

"Might as well be me, right?" Joy asked.

"I can't think of a better person than you."

She swallowed. "Okay," she whispered, her breath making white puffs that faded into the night. "So what next? We go from stolen kisses to what, exactly?"

"How about we start with a date? Saturday is the Lights on Silver Lake event."

Lights on Silver Lake kicked off the Christmas season every year in Sweetwater Springs. It was a night when stores on Main Street stayed open later, showing off their

Christmas décor and offering sales to the night's shoppers. Then, after a group of carolers serenaded everyone with holiday tunes, the tree in the town square was lit, brighter than any star in the valley sky.

Joy had felt the weight of the upcoming holiday and had already decided not to go to the Lights on Silver Lake event for the first time in over a decade. But the thought of going with Granger on a date sounded like fun. "What about the girls?"

"My parents can take them," Granger said. "We shut the farm down that night anyway. We don't like to compete with something so important. My mom and dad can take Abby and Willow, and I can take you. What do you say?"

Joy thought about it for a moment. "If the girls want to go with you, promise me you'll cancel our date. I know what it's like to feel like your mom or dad has more important things to do than spend time with you."

Granger grinned.

"And that shouldn't make you happy. Why are you smiling at me like that?"

"The fact that you said that is one reason I'm not terrified to go on a date with you."

"Why?" she asked.

"Because you get what they've been through. It's not the same as with your childhood but you get it. And you're willing to put Abby and Willow first."

"I care about them. You have two of the sweetest kids."

Granger nodded. "No thanks to me."

Joy punched his arm softly. "All because of you."

Granger shook his head. "But I won't promise to cancel if they'd rather go with me."

"Grang—"

He held up a hand. "If that's the case, I'm guessing it's

okay if they just tag along with us. Not much of a date if a guy brings his kids, but…"

"It would be perfect. No kissing in front of them though," Joy said, putting up a finger.

"Only when they're not looking," Granger amended. "Or when we're standing under the mistletoe."

* * *

By the time Granger stepped inside, it was too late to talk to Abby. He knew he needed to. Maybe Joy was right. Maybe seeing him and Joy getting closer was why Abby was acting so differently lately, getting in trouble at school and snapping at Willow.

Tomorrow would be a busy day, being the first of the Christmas tree season, but Granger would make time to talk to Abby first thing in the morning. He didn't want to be alone forever; one day he'd have to move past his broken marriage. He'd thought the timing was all wrong right now but Joy made it all right.

"The girls are already tucked into bed. They brushed their teeth and said their prayers," his mom said. She'd walked them over here after dinner at her house. "Thanksgiving is a lot of work. But worth it," she added, patting his arm.

"Thank you for today, Mom. Everything was wonderful."

"Especially the fact that you invited a guest this year. I liked that part best."

Granger ran a hand over the top of his head and laughed. "She told me that you two talked earlier in the kitchen."

"And she explained to me that there is nothing going on and all the fireworks I'm seeing between you two is just a figment of my imagination." She narrowed her eyes at him.

"That was true. Partly. But Joy and I just changed our minds on what we are."

"Oh?"

He scratched the side of his chin where stubble was growing. "I asked her to be my date to the Lights on Silver Lake event Saturday. And surprisingly, she said yes." He couldn't control the smile that swept over his face. He was going on a date with a woman who made him feel more alive than he had in years.

"Not a surprise to me at all. Oh, Granger, this is wonderful. I have so much to be thankful for in this moment; I couldn't be happier." She wrapped her arms tightly around him, squeezing until it hurt.

A shuffle against the wall made her pull back, and they both turned toward Abby, who was watching from the dimly lit hallway. Watching and listening, which she had a habit of doing these days.

Granger guessed he'd be having that talk with his oldest daughter tonight after all.

His mom cleared her throat and collected a sweater she'd tossed across the back of his recliner. "I'll leave you two to talk. I need to get home to your dad anyway. Good night, Abby," she said.

"Night, Nana," Abby answered softly.

"Night, Mom." Granger walked his mom to the door and gave her another hug. "See you tomorrow."

"It's a big day. Your day," she said proudly. "You're changing the way Merry Mountain Farms does business, and I couldn't be prouder of you."

"Thanks." Granger closed the door behind her and turned to face Abby. "Wanna join me at the table?" he asked. "I can grab us some cider."

Without answering, Abby stepped toward the table, pulled out a chair, and sat down.

Granger took that as a yes and grabbed two glasses from the cabinet. He filled them halfway with some cider and sat beside Abby. "Here you go." He slid her glass in front of her. "Tell me what's on your mind."

He braced himself.

"You're dating Joy," she said.

Granger lifted his glass to his mouth and took a sip, readying his answer. "Is that okay?"

"No." She took a sip of her drink as well.

"No? Just no? Can I ask why? I thought you liked Joy."

"I do. But I like her for me and Willow. She's a lot more fun than Mrs. Townsend, and she does arts and crafts with us. I don't like her for you."

Granger nodded. "Well, I happen to think she's a lot of fun too. Isn't it okay for your dad to be happy too?"

Abby blinked as she stared at him stone-faced. "You have me and Willow to make you happy."

He felt like he was in a debate right now, and he really wanted to win. If he couldn't get Abby to accept his new relationship with Joy, could he even go through with his date planned for Saturday night? "It's not your job to make me happy, you know? Or to do the right thing or take care of your younger sister all the time. It's your job to be a kid, to learn and play and make mistakes."

Abby looked down at her hands. "What about Mom? What if she comes home and you're dating someone else?"

Granger sucked in all the air around him. "Your mom and I aren't getting back together, Abby. If she comes home, and I hope she does one day, it'll be for you and Willow. Not for me." And if Erin ever came back, she better be ready to prove herself before he let her have any kind of relationship with his girls.

"But what if Mom returns and she wants to live with

us again? Couldn't you give her another chance? You just said that mistakes are okay for me. What about her?"

Granger wasn't sure what to say. Where was this coming from lately? Abby had never opened this discussion before. "If your mom comes back, we'll talk about this at that time. But right now, she isn't here. We're here, and we've got to do the best that we can. It's Thanksgiving, which is a reminder to be thankful about what we've got. And we have a lot."

Abby's gaze flicked up to meet his. Granger could see the shine of unshed tears. She was working hard to hold them at bay.

"We've got each other," he said. "And now we have Joy in our lives too, and I'd like her to stay a little longer. What about you?"

Abby blinked, and one of her tears slipped down her cheek. She nodded quietly.

Granger reached for her hand. He'd met with a therapist in town once about how to deal with the girls' emotions about their mother. "It's okay to miss your mom. It's okay to be sad that she's not here. And anytime you ever want to talk about her or about how you're feeling, I'm here. Just say the word. I'll always be here to listen, okay?"

Abby sniffled, and another tear escaped. "'Kay."

"So I'm taking Joy to the Lights on Silver Lake on Saturday night. You can go with Nana and Papa or you can go with us if you want. It's up to you."

"I'll go with Nana and Papa," Abby said after a long moment.

Granger frowned. Maybe she wasn't going to accept him dating again.

"You and Joy should be alone on your first date. So you don't have to hide when you kiss her." She offered him the first smile of this conversation.

Granger reached over and ruffled her hair. "You have a big day ahead. You're Joy's assistant at the Christmas tree workshop tomorrow. Let's get you to bed."

She slid back from the table and stood. "You don't have to tuck me in. I'm a little big for that."

Granger stood as well and followed her down the hall. "You're never too big for that."

* * *

Granger always felt light on his feet on the day after Thanksgiving. Since as far back as he could remember, this was an exciting day—the first of the Christmas tree season. This was when the crowd started to trickle in, looking for their perfect tree.

Merry Mountain Farms had less to offer this year but it was still enough to fill the air with the scent of evergreen.

He took a deep breath as he headed outside, taking in the quiet excitement churning in his chest. Adding fuel to that excitement was the anticipation of seeing Joy and going on their first date tomorrow. It'd been a long time since he'd felt anything for a woman. And he felt more than just a little spark with Joy. The more time he spent with her, the more amazing he realized she was.

"Hey." He turned to see Joy walking up to him now from the large sheltered area where she'd be giving her first workshop in a few hours.

"Hey. I didn't think you'd be here so early."

"I wanted to make sure everything was all set for the Ladies' Day Out group when they came. I have a feeling some of the women are going to need a lot of extra attention."

Granger stepped closer to her. "You aren't second-guessing saying yes, are you?" He was talking about the Christmas tree workshop but he also wondered if she was having second thoughts about what she'd agreed to last night.

"Not one bit." Joy looked around and then stepped closer. "We don't have to hide anymore, remember?"

"You spoke to the girls last night?" she asked, pulling her hands to her midsection to fidget.

"Just Abby. Willow was already in bed."

"And?"

"And she wasn't thrilled about me dating but it has nothing to do with her love of you. That's intact. She's more worried about her mom coming home."

"Oh." Joy's mouth formed a little circle of surprise. "I didn't think that was really a possibility. I mean, she's been gone for a long time, right?"

Granger shrugged. "I guess it's a possibility, but the longer Erin stays away, the less likely she is to return. And she wouldn't be returning to me. I can't go through that again."

He shook his head as flashes of the past crossed his mind. He'd felt no control over the situation at all. For a long time, he hadn't even known where Erin had gone. She'd left him a letter that was both brief and incomplete. The waiting was the worst part. Every night he'd set her an extra place at the table. He'd kept the porch lights on in case she came in after dark.

Then the divorce papers had come. That was a clear message to him that he should stop waiting for her. He stopped setting her a spot at the table. He turned off the porch lights. And he did his best to let her go.

He didn't sign the papers when they first came though. Erin was on his insurance plan, and he had wanted to make sure she had access to the care she needed for her postpartum depression. Divorcing her would've meant cutting her off, and no matter how much she'd hurt him, she was still the girls' mother. Instead, he'd waited until he'd known for sure that she had gotten the help she needed.

"Abby will get used to the idea. She actually teased me a little about kissing you before she went to bed last night. I take that as progress."

Joy blushed slightly. Or maybe it was the cold nipping at her cheeks. "Well, I wanted to go grab a few more supplies at the store before the event. I'm going to head out." She looked around again, as if making sure that no one was nearby, and then she went on her tiptoes for what he knew she expected to be a brief kiss.

He held her to him though, deepening the kiss. Because if this was going to be his only close contact with her today, he wanted to make it count.

"What was that for?" she asked breathlessly once they pulled away.

"For good luck. It's an important day," he reminded her.

"Well, in that case…" She leaned forward and pressed her mouth to his again, not bothering to look around to make sure they were alone this time.

* * *

There were fourteen women from the LDO gathered for the Christmas tree workshop. She had more than enough supplies, and the ladies were being as creative as they were messy. It really wasn't a hard project in Joy's opinion. It didn't even take a lot of strength, which was good for this crowd.

"Oh, this is so much fun," Dawanda from the fudge shop

said with exaggerated hand movements, her smile stretching through her rosy cheeks as she wound the garland at the top of her tree. "I can't wait to string the lights and add the tinsel. This tree is going to be a great addition to my Christmas decorations."

"And it lasts a lot longer than a real tree," Joy pointed out.

"And you don't have to water it," Greta added, working at a snail's pace. Joy might have to step in and help her move things along if she didn't pick up speed.

"Well, I happen to love a real tree," Alice Hampton said as she worked on her own project. "This will be nice but I'm still getting a real spruce when I'm done."

Granger's mom nodded as she listened. She was making a tree today too. "That's good because we still have quite a lot of trees to sell. The fire might have taken some of our stock but those will grow back. And then we'll have real trees and art-sculptured trees."

"Oh?" A couple of the Ladies' Day Out group turned to look at Joy.

"I thought this was a one-time thing. Will you be coming back year after year?" Dawanda asked.

Joy shrugged. "Well, Granger and I haven't gotten that far in our planning yet." And Joy was hoping that next year, she'd have her own place on Main Street. She might have time to offer one or two classes here at the farm but probably not.

"Granger and I, huh?" one of the women asked. "Sounds like a Christmas romance to me."

Joy cleared her throat. She was tempted to deny that anything was going on with Granger. But they weren't hiding anymore. "We're actually going on a date tomorrow night."

The women made delighted sounds.

"To the Lights on Silver Lake event?" Alice asked.

Joy nodded as excitement swirled in her belly. "Yes."

"The Lights on Silver Lake event was where Ron and I had our first date," Alice said. She was a widow now. "It was the same night I fell in love with him, and I knew we'd spend the rest of our lives together."

Josie Locklear, who was sitting on her other side, put her hand on Alice's shoulder. "That's a nice memory."

"Yes, we had lots of nice memories." She looked at Joy. "They say it's good luck to have your first date at that event. I do believe Kaitlyn and Mitch had their first date there."

"Are you sure?" Greta asked.

Alice shrugged. "No, but I know several couples who did. If history is any indicator, it means you and Granger will have a long-lasting, love-filled relationship."

Now Joy was shaking her head. "I don't think...It's just a date." She laughed nervously, reaching for more wire ribbon. She wasn't even close to ready to think about anything long lasting.

Debbie gave her a pointed look. "Well, that's how every relationship begins. With a first date."

Joy fell speechless. Then she noticed Abby watching and listening to the conversation closely. She had a habit of doing that. "Abby, you're my assistant today. Would you mind helping Miss Greta with her bows?"

Abby stepped forward.

"Oh yes," Greta said. "I'll be here all afternoon if I don't get some assistance. And I don't want to miss the lighted hayride. It's going to be so pretty. I remember the hayrides. They used to be my favorite part of the season."

Abby picked up some ribbon and started making a bow, just like Joy had taught her to do last week.

"What do you think of your dad going out on a date?" one of the women asked.

Joy wanted to cover her face. Couldn't they talk about something other than her personal life?

"He's all grown up. He can do what he wants," Abby said, sounding like a little adult. "But my mom is coming back soon." She looked up at Joy, her expression apologetic. "I just don't want you to get hurt."

Joy was worried about the opposite though. She didn't want Abby to get any more hurt by wishing for something that wasn't very likely to happen. At least not according to Granger.

* * *

An hour later, there were just over a dozen wire-sculpture Christmas trees standing at four feet tall. They were all as unique as the women who had made them. The women had strung the lights and plugged them into the extension cords that roped around the shelter's perimeter.

"Okay," Joy said, standing in the center of the workshop with Abby by her side. "Are we ready to light your trees?"

"Sounds kinky!" Greta called out.

Joy's jaw dropped.

"Shh! There are little ears in here," Alice snapped at her older friend.

Joy glanced over at Abby and back to the women, deciding to ignore the comment and rephrase her question. "Who's ready for me to turn the lights on?"

"I bet Granger is," Greta called out, chuckling loudly.

Joy didn't even look at the older woman this time. Instead she gestured at Abby. "You can do the honors, sweetheart."

Abby reached for the On button on the main drop cord that all the others were plugged into and flipped it up, her expression brimming with excitement.

The women oohed and aahed as their trees twinkled.

"So pretty," one said.

"Beautiful," a man's voice said.

Joy turned to see Granger approaching the shelter. She smiled proudly. "Aren't they?"

He came to stand beside her, and his voice dropped to a whisper. "I was talking about you," he said for her ears only.

She warmed all over. She definitely needed to keep him around through the cold winter. "I'd say the first Christmas tree workshop was a success. These are amazing pieces."

"I'll load them in my truck and deliver them to you all tomorrow," Granger told the women.

"I want a real tree too," Greta said.

"Me too," another woman added.

He nodded. "You can pick one out on the lot and claim it. The guys will chop it down, string it up, and deliver it right to your door. But right now, I'm boarding the trailer for the first official lighted hayride of the season." Granger lowered his voice again, leaning near Joy's ear. "I saved you a seat next to me if you want to come along."

Thoughts of that night when they'd traveled the path alone came to mind. They'd kept each other warm with roaming hands and needy mouths.

It might be hard to keep her hands to herself with those memories at the forefront of her mind. She and Granger weren't hiding anymore but she'd never been a fan of PDA. She'd just have to keep her hands and lips to herself until later. Right now, it would be enough to occupy the seat next to him. "I'd love to."

From the corner of her eye, Joy saw Abby watching.

"Abby, would you like to sit up front with your dad?"

"Me too, me too," Willow said, running over. She'd been occupying the apple cider stand with her nana until now.

Granger frowned at Joy.

She leaned in this time. "You can give me a private ride later."

The brown of his irises darkened before he tore his gaze from hers to look at his daughters.

"Is Santa at the end of Peppermint Path?" Willow asked hopefully. "I have a list. I want to see him and make sure he knows exactly what I want this year. Last year, he got some of it wrong."

Joy cast a playful glance at Granger.

"Nobody's perfect." He shook his head. "Santa isn't here just yet but there's a mailbox where you can drop your list if you want."

Willow turned to her older sister. "Do you have a list, Abby?"

Abby glanced over at Joy, her expression once more apologetic. *What is that about?* "There's only one thing I want for Christmas this year."

And Joy got the distinct feeling that it wasn't for Joy to be sitting next to her father on this ride. No, Joy was fairly certain that Abby wanted her own mother to come home and occupy that space.

CHAPTER FIFTEEN

The moon was a sliver in the night sky with a chorus of stars around it. The LDO hadn't quite gotten this view when Granger had driven the path an hour earlier. The sun had just set, and it was dark enough to appreciate the lighted scenes but not black as it was now.

"I'd say today was a success." Granger looked over at Joy.

"Mm. I think so too." She met his gaze. "And it was a lot of fun. I've booked four classes for next week already."

Granger was only offering the hayrides on Friday, Saturday, and Sunday nights. The rest of the days, he'd be helping his dad to sell the live trees. "I'm already dreaming about new things for next Christmas, and it's only day one of the season. Assuming Dad lets me hold on to the reins after this year."

"Why wouldn't he?" Joy asked.

Granger shrugged, directing his gaze forward. "If I screw it all up, he might not trust me to run the show again."

"If today is any indication, you won't screw it up."

Granger reached for her hand. "Well, I have you around this year. I think that Christmas tree workshop is going to be a big hit. It could pull in people from surrounding towns too. We have something the other tree farms don't—you."

Joy laughed softly, the sound carrying in the breeze. "Well, next year I'll hopefully have my gallery open."

"Are you already starting to prepare me for the fact that you won't be coming back after December twenty-fifth?" He was teasing but a sudden ache resonated on the left side of his chest.

"Not exactly. I might be able to squeeze in some time for you next December."

"Good to hear."

"So, what are these new ideas you're thinking about for next year?" she asked.

Granger stopped the tractor and waved his hand in an arc in front of him. "Mistletoe Trail."

"I'm intrigued. What is that?"

Granger grinned. "A ride for lovers, with twigs of mistletoe dispersed along the way. There's lots of kissing involved."

Joy laughed harder this time. "I'm not so sure about that idea. Sounds like it could be problematic somehow."

Granger reached into his pocket and pulled out a sprig that he'd found on the trail earlier today. He'd been saving it for tonight with Joy. "Let's test it out." He held the sprig over both of their heads and looked at her.

Joy's gaze flicked to the mistletoe and back to him, a smile curling at the corners of her very kissable mouth.

Granger smiled too. "It's bad luck not to kiss someone if you're caught under the mistletoe."

"Bad luck? I've never heard that." She narrowed her eyes. "Is that true?"

"I don't know but I'd be one lucky guy if you did kiss me."

Joy leaned into him. "I was going to kiss you anyway, I'll have you know. You didn't need the mistletoe," she said, before pressing her mouth to his in a long, lingering kiss.

His hands ached to touch her but he kept them to himself. He and Joy were new, and he didn't want to get ahead of himself. It was as much because he wanted to be a gentleman as it was because he was wary of jumping into a relationship. She'd reminded him again and again that she wasn't looking for anything serious.

"I've been waiting for that all day," he said in a gruff voice once they'd pulled away.

"Me too," she sighed, kissing him again. And again. "Maybe we should slow things down. We haven't even had our first official date yet."

Granger leaned against the tractor's seat and wrapped his arm around her shoulders. "I'll just have to keep this sprig of mistletoe handy for tomorrow too."

"When does your new Santa start?" she asked after a quiet moment.

"Jack is starting next Friday night."

"Jack Hershey?"

Jack was one of Granger's best friends in town. "After the fire this past spring, he offered to do anything he could to help the farm out. I collected on that offer. He'll have to pad the suit, of course."

Joy grinned. "Will Emma be his Mrs. Claus?"

"I'm guessing she'll come down and dress the part with him if she's not running the Sweetwater Café that night."

"Mmm, hot chocolate from the Sweetwater Café would be amazing right now."

"The best in town, in my opinion," Granger agreed.

"And it's right down from my storefront."

"Your storefront, huh?" Granger reached for Joy's hand. "How's that going?"

"Well, I sold a few pieces tonight. And after a few more classes like we had tonight, I'll have a nice-size deposit to put down on the place. I'm really excited. I can see my artwork selling there and picture myself giving classes. I can even envision taking Chelsea to the store with me during the day."

"Chelsea, the attack cat?" Granger laughed. "You're not worried about her leaping at your customers?"

"She only leaps at the ones who threaten to steal my attention." There was a light in Joy's eyes as she looked at him with amusement.

"Well, when you get that gallery of yours, I'll be your first customer."

"Thanks." She pulled her gaze from his and looked around at the final destination on the lighted path.

"What do you think is on Abby's list?" Granger asked. "She was pretty secretive when she put her letter in that mailbox. She's been increasingly secretive these days," he added. "I guess that's part of her getting older."

Joy sighed softly. "Whatever is on her list, I'm guessing it's not more art lessons."

Granger knocked his arm against Joy's gently. "What makes you say that?"

"Just a feeling."

"Well, there's only one way to find out." Granger stood.

Joy reached for his arm. "Wait. What are you doing?"

"Getting her letter. In case you didn't know, I'm Santa Claus."

Joy grimaced. "Granger, you can't read her letter. That's private."

His brows dipped. "Yes, but she's my daughter. And how do you think I figure out what to get them every year?" Granger turned and looked at the mailbox again. "I've always read their letters to Santa."

Granger hopped off the tractor, jogged to the lighted mailbox, and opened the lid. Then he pulled out the letter from Abby and jogged back to the tractor where Joy was waiting. He sat back down beside her and passed her the envelope. "Here you go."

Her lips parted. "You want me to open it?"

"I'm making you my accomplice." He winked.

Joy hedged for a moment. Then she ripped open the top and pulled out the flimsy piece of paper with Abby's neatly printed handwriting. She opened the flashlight app on her phone to cast light on the paper. "Dear Santa," she read out loud. "All I want for Christmas is for you to bring home my mom. Before it's too late for us to be a family again."

Granger's heart dropped into the pit of his stomach. He'd always done his best to deliver what was on his girls' Christmas lists but that order was tall and out of his hands.

Joy's breath came out in visible puffs as she continued reading. "I believe in you and know you can help me. But please act soon before my daddy finds someone else. Love, Abigail Fields."

"Wow." Granger sat dumbfounded for a moment. "I don't know what's gotten into her lately. Nothing has happened to make her want her mother back all of a sudden."

Joy glanced over. "Something kind of has happened. Us. She saw us getting closer and then she saw our kiss on the hayride that night. And now you and I are going on a date. That's a lot for a little girl to take in."

Granger thought about that theory before shaking his head. "I'm sorry."

"Why are you apologizing to me?"

"I don't know. Because we were having a romantic night, and now we're talking about my ex."

"Can't you try to get Erin to come home? I mean, I know you say you've tried before but can't you try again? For Abby and Willow's sake?"

Granger clenched his jaw. "I have tried."

"I know, but what if she wants to come home, and she's just hesitating for some reason?"

Granger shook his head. "It's the busiest season of the year, and I'm in charge this holiday. It's not the time to do a missing-person search and recovery." And it wasn't the time for him to be going on first dates and losing his heart to the woman who was saving his Christmas this year but here he was.

"You're probably right," Joy said. "Sorry I mentioned it."

He blew out a breath. "And I'm sorry I got defensive." He reached for the letter that Joy was holding. "It's just I don't know what to do with this. I can't give her what she wants for Christmas this year."

"She'll be okay. Girls are tough."

Granger looked at Joy, suspecting she was speaking from experience. He didn't know a lot about her, despite having lived in the same town forever. He wanted to know more though. He wanted to know everything she'd ever been through that had made her into this beautiful woman sitting beside him.

She shivered as the cold seemed to overwhelm her.

"I guess I better get you back home. I don't want to turn you into an icicle before I get a chance to date you," he teased.

"It feels like we've already been on several dates," Joy said.

"It really does. I feel like we've been seeing each other for months." He started the tractor back up and set it into motion. Even though he'd done his best to smooth the path, the tractor still bumped along the trail, its motor making an oddly musical grinding sound.

"Well, we have been seeing each other for months," Joy pointed out. "Maybe not romantically, but I've been teaching the girls art for the past year."

"Who knew that all I needed in my life was a little canvas and paint to brighten things up?"

Joy laughed. "You need to work on your cheesy lines before tomorrow night."

"Cheesy?" Granger grinned. "Yeah, I guess I am a little out of practice," he admitted. "I'll work on it."

* * *

Joy sucked in a deep breath as she looked in the mirror to make sure there was no chocolate smudged on her lip after downing a piece of Dawanda's fudge, kept in the freezer for emergencies.

And a first date counted as a chocolate emergency in her book.

But this was Granger. She'd spent so much time with him lately. She shouldn't feel nervous. They'd kissed, held hands, and stared into each other's eyes. They'd even shared painful pieces of their pasts. If there was some playbook to follow, they were technically on the third or fourth date by now.

Maybe that's why she was nervous. What if they did more than just kiss tonight? What if the expectations were different? What if Granger came back to her house after the event and wanted to come inside?

She took in another breath. Then the phone rang, giving her a welcome distraction.

Joy pulled out her cell phone and glanced at the caller ID before answering. "Mom. Hi." She was actually surprised that her mom would be calling her right now. "Everything okay?"

"Oh, fine. I just didn't get to talk to you on Thanksgiving so I thought I'd call you now. Are you busy?"

Joy decided now wasn't the time to offer up that she was preparing for a date with Granger. Her mom had opinions on everything, and she wasn't sure she wanted Dr. Mom's opinion on whether or not Joy should be dating Granger Fields. "No, I have a few minutes to talk. What's up?"

"Well, you haven't applied for the receptionist position at the hospital yet," her mom pointed out.

Joy walked over to the edge of her bed and plopped down. "I don't think I ever said I would."

"You said you'd think about it."

Hmm. If Joy had said that, she'd meant that she'd think about how bad of an idea it was. "I have a job, Mom. Multiple jobs, in fact."

"Some of which are seasonal work, Joy. There's one month until Christmas, and then what?"

This wasn't really a conversation Joy wanted to have right before a romantic date. "And then I lease my gallery and start drawing in customers with my art and a few classes."

"Oh, start-up businesses rarely succeed, Joy," her mother said.

"It wouldn't be a start-up business, Mom. I've been making a living as an artist for a long time now." Like a decade. "It's an extension of what I'm already doing with my Etsy store and all the work I'm consigning around town."

Her mom seemed to ignore her. "That receptionist job won't stay open long, and it won't come around again for a while, I suspect. It has benefits, and you can still do your art on the side."

Joy closed her eyes as her mother continued. At some point, she forgot to listen, and she just waited for her mother to stop talking. Then Joy realized that her mom was waiting for her to respond. "I'm sorry, what was the question?"

"How is Mr. Fields? He's my patient, you know."

"Right. He's fine. I saw him last night at the farm."

"I hear you've spent quite a bit of time over there lately," her mother said.

Joy shouldn't be surprised. Her mother would no doubt know about Joy's date with Granger tonight within twenty-four hours too. That would at least give her mom something else to complain about the next time they spoke. Surely she must be running out of flaws to discuss by now.

"I just want you to be happy," her mom said on the other end of the line.

Joy held the phone away from her ear and looked at it for a moment. In what reality would Joy working as a receptionist equal happiness? "Mom," Joy said, "I am happy." Relatively at least. "Are you?" Joy had learned that trick from a therapist she briefly saw after her failed pregnancy. Turning the question around and echoing it back was a technique her therapist used on her often. And it had worked. That was therapy though. When Joy did it, it was technically deflecting.

"What kind of question is that?" her mother asked.

"A yes-or-no question."

Her mom didn't immediately answer, which Joy found surprising. Having a fancy high-profile job as a distinguished doctor apparently didn't equal happiness either.

The doorbell rang. Granger's timing was perfect. "I've got to run, Mom. I'll talk to you later. I love you."

"I love you too," her mom said.

After a quick goodbye, Joy disconnected the call and shoved her cell phone into her bag, which she looped over her shoulder. Then she hurried to the door and answered.

Granger was standing on her stoop wearing dark jeans and a brown leather jacket over his cotton T-shirt. He looked sexy, and part of her wanted to pull him into her town house, close the door, and enjoy some alone time with him. Before she could give in to temptation, she stepped onto the porch and pulled the front door shut.

"In a hurry?" Granger asked.

"I just don't want Chelsea getting ideas of escaping."

"I see." He walked beside her to his truck. "Has Chelsea escaped before?"

"Oh yeah. But she hates the cold, so I doubt she'd go far."

Granger opened the passenger-side door for her. She got in and fidgeted nervously as he ran around to the driver's side and got in. Then he quietly cranked the engine and pulled onto the main road, heading toward downtown.

"It's amazing how the town seems to transform overnight for the holidays," she said quietly.

"It's the most magical time of year."

She'd always felt the same way. But after losing her baby, a dark cloud had hung over her last Christmas. She'd thought this holiday would be just as difficult, but time healed, and Granger was doing a good job of lifting her spirits.

They parked in the public parking area and walked among the crowd, dipping in and out of shops as they strolled. All the storefronts were decorated for the season with lights and wreaths. Some sported mannequins wearing ugly Christmas sweaters.

Joy paused when she got to the empty window of her store.

"This is it, huh?" Granger asked.

While everyone else was admiring the decorations farther down, they stared into the empty space, the only decoration of this place a FOR LEASE sign in the window.

"This is it," she said on a sigh.

From the corner of her eye, she saw Granger nod beside her. "I like it. Not too small, not too big."

"Big enough to hold classes," she pointed out.

"And it's the perfect location to attract impulse shoppers, like you said."

"Exactly. And next year, I could have a festive store window for the Lights on Silver Lake event. Wouldn't that be fun?"

"It would." Granger reached for her hand.

She turned toward him, her heart leaping the same way it did every time she allowed herself to get excited about the prospect of having her own art gallery.

"I hope you get everything you want for Christmas, Joy Benson."

Looking up into his eyes, she discovered she wanted something else. Something she hadn't planned on. She wanted to keep Granger.

But she wasn't ready for anything serious right now. Her heart seemed to have a short memory but her brain didn't. She was finally feeling like herself again after last Christmas. She couldn't—wouldn't—risk that.

Granger held her gaze as he reached into his coat pocket.

"I know what you're doing," she said.

A smile curved along his lips. "Sometimes a guy needs a little help." He pulled out the sprig of mistletoe from last night and held it over her head.

She laughed as her gaze flitted up to the sprig and back down to him. Sometimes a heart needed a little help, too, because hers wasn't listening to all the reasons her brain was giving for why she shouldn't fall for Granger Fields.

He dipped and pressed his mouth to hers, wrapping his arms around her and capturing the warmth between their bodies. She melted like a snowflake against him, wishing she could stay here for the rest of the night. A restless ache weaved through her body as their kiss seemed to last forever. They were far enough away from the crowd that there was no reason to pull away or worry that they were making a scene. There was only so much one could do out here in the public eye anyway. Once again, her thoughts jumped ahead to what they might do when they were truly alone later.

"Hot chocolate?" Granger asked, pulling back from the kiss.

It took a moment for Joy to even process the question because she was floating in a dreamlike state, basking in the endorphins that were so much better than what chocolate could give her. "Hmm?"

"Would you like to go get some hot chocolate?" he asked again, a knowing look in his gaze. "Dawanda's giving out complimentary cups at the fudge shop tonight."

"The good news is that there'll be no time for her to force cappuccino readings on anyone," Joy said.

"That's true." The festive music grew louder along with the excited chatter of the crowd as they started walking in that direction.

"I owe Dawanda to let her give me another reading though." Joy wrapped her arms tightly around herself. Now that she was removed from Granger's arms, the cold felt even sharper. "She offered to put a sign-up sheet for the

Christmas tree workshop in her store for me. I gave her the days that we'll be offering it until Christmas, and she said she'd pass the word."

"That's nice of her," Granger said.

"It is. I don't think my art classes will make up for the loss of sales from the fire, but hopefully they'll help."

"Even with the hayrides, we might not cover the losses," Granger said. "But we're drawing in a bigger crowd already and creating a buzz. The local news is supposed to come do a story on our new events this coming week."

"That's great."

"I agree. I just hope it's enough to make my dad happy he put me in charge."

"I'm sure he doesn't expect you to pull in the same kind of profits as you would have if the farm had a full lot."

"If I don't, it'll give him justification to cancel the hayride again and get rid of any other attractions outside of just selling live trees. I don't want to leave any room for argument."

They reached Dawanda's storefront, which was lit up with multicolored twinkling lights. Granger opened the door and allowed Joy to step through first. With the offer of complimentary hot chocolate to tonight's patrons, Dawanda's shop was bustling, but not so much that she couldn't acknowledge them as they walked in.

She pointed to a table set up in the corner and winked at Joy.

Joy and Granger stepped over to the table. Next to it stood the wire-sculpture tree that Dawanda had made during the LDO's visit to the Christmas tree workshop. Joy looked at the clipboard and list lying on the table. It was a sign-up for Joy's class with twelve spaces for every night that Joy had told Dawanda she would be giving it until Christmas.

"Oh my goodness. I can't believe this." Joy looked up at Granger. "Nearly every space is full. And there's a check-box for if they want to stay for a hayride." Joy looked at the paper again, scanning over the list. "And they all do."

* * *

This night was more magical than any Lights on Silver Lake night that Granger had ever attended. Between kissing Joy and going into Dawanda's shop to find that both of their events were nearly booked, he couldn't imagine how it could get any better.

Or he could.

Granger walked Joy to her front door, the debate of whether he was going inside at the forefront of his mind. She might not even invite him in, but if she did, should he go? He wasn't a love-'em-and-leave-'em type of guy. In fact, he'd only slept with one woman in his entire life—the mother of his children. He'd thought he'd spend forever with Erin but that hadn't worked out. And he couldn't very well stay celibate forever. But he also wasn't willing to go to bed with Joy if this was still just a casual thing for her. Making love to a woman wasn't casual in his book. It meant something.

"Tonight was fun," he said as she turned to face him.

"Yeah, it was..." She pulled her keys out of her bag and gave him a hesitant look. "Do you, um, want something to drink?"

There was his ticket into her home. A ticket to more than just her living room, he suspected. Desire gathered inside him, quickening his heart. "Joy, I, uh...Things are going to get busy from this point on."

"Oh." Disappointment flashed in her honey-colored eyes.

He wanted to go inside more than anything. But he liked Joy. Sleeping with her would be a lot more than a casual fling for him. "I don't even know when we'll have a chance for another date," he added.

"I see. I mean, I was just offering you a drink," she said quickly, pulling her gaze away from him. "Nothing more than that."

He straightened. "Oh?" Had he read her signs wrong? Was she offended?

"I'm really tired anyway," she added, breaking into a yawn. "And you should probably get back home to the girls. To make sure they're okay." Joy wouldn't meet his eyes anymore. Yeah, he'd messed this night up.

"Right." He watched as she put her keys in her lock, her hand noticeably shaking. He reached for her. "I told you I was out of practice, and I think this is an example of that."

She looked at him, her lips parted just slightly.

"I had a great time tonight, Joy. The best time I can remember. And I'd like to see you again. I don't know when or how because the next month is busy. But I know our arrangement is only temporary, so if this is the only time I have with you, I don't want to waste a minute."

Joy hesitated. Then she took her hand off the key that was still in her lock and turned to face him. She reached into his coat pocket and pulled out the sprig of mistletoe, eying it in her palm before going up on her toes and suspending it over his head. "Sometimes a guy needs a little help," she whispered, repeating his words from earlier.

"Especially this guy," he said. Then he kissed her, savoring the private moment.

"Sometimes a girl needs a little help too," she whispered against his mouth, kissing him another time.

She didn't invite him inside again. Instead, they kissed at the door, ignoring the winter cold. Granger wasn't sure how long they stood there, holding and touching, kissing and whispering. All he knew was he never wanted to stop.

CHAPTER SIXTEEN

The next three weeks were a blur of activity. Everyone was rushing to the lot to get their live trees, fueled by the knowledge that there was a short supply this year. It'd been so chaotic that Granger hadn't gotten a chance for another real date with Joy. But she'd started staying for dinner after her art afternoons with the girls. And she and Granger had lingered at her car before she drove away at night. They'd also enjoyed a couple of more private hayrides, just the two of them snuggled together under the stars.

Granger planned to have another private ride with Joy tonight, after the crowd had gone home and the girls were fast asleep.

But first, he needed to update his father on progress and profits. He headed into his parents' living room and plopped down on the couch in front of his dad's recliner. "The good news is that we're ahead of schedule with profits for the season."

His dad's mouth stretched into a grim line. "What's the bad news?"

Typical that his father couldn't just take a moment to celebrate. "The bad news is we're running out of trees quicker than we expected we would."

His dad frowned. "Next year, we'll make sure to secure trees from other farms so we have enough."

Granger nodded. "And we'll continue to gain profits from the lighted hayride."

His father held up a finger. "I'm not sure about that. I only agreed to it this year because we were desperate. I want a plan B and C and even a D for getting live trees next Christmas."

Granger looked down at his boots, taking a moment to breathe past what felt like a punch to his gut. Then he looked up. "We're booked solid for the weekend. For the rest of the month. I might even have to add a couple Thursdays or keep the events open later to fill the demand."

"A greater demand means there's a greater risk for injury."

"One kid got injured, and his arm healed, Dad. I even gave him a hayride last week. He's not traumatized by what happened so why are you?"

His dad frowned. "Because we could've lost it all. This is your legacy. I'm leaving it all to you one day. Just like my dad left it to me."

"Your legacy is more than a farm, Dad. And Merry Mountain Farms has always been more than a farm. This place brings people together. It's the very essence of Christmas. People have missed the hayrides. They're part of what we do. And yeah, maybe there's a little bit of a risk but sometimes the benefit outweighs the potential costs."

Granger himself wasn't one to take risks, especially ones that affected his family. But the additions to the farm were exciting, and he wanted his girls to see how magical this place had once been. The way it was again this year.

Dating Joy was a risk too. She could leave and break all their hearts, not just his. But what if she didn't?

His dad looked at him long and hard. "This is why I'm letting you take over the farm this year. And next year too. You have the farm's best interests at heart."

"Next year too?" Granger asked.

"Well, I'll help, of course. A little cardiac scare won't keep me down. Truth is, that boy falling off the ride hurt my heart a whole lot more than the heart attack. I'm putting you in the lead, not just this year but from now on. It's time."

"Wow. I wasn't expecting this." Granger had been expecting to go head-to-head with his dad about continuing the hayride next year. And possibly the Christmas tree workshop. "Thank you."

"I should be thanking you," his dad said. "What you've done for Merry Mountain Farms this season is nothing short of amazing. It's made me remember the way it was when you were a kid. Bright and festive. A little piece of Christmas on Earth."

Granger smiled. "That's Mom's line."

His father chuckled. "I understand what she meant. That's what it is again and what it should be from now on."

Granger swallowed past the lump in his throat. He'd just been hoping to satisfy his dad with how well he ran the farm this Christmas. But this was a high compliment coming from his father, and it meant a lot. He cleared his throat, hoping his mounting emotions weren't obvious. "I've got to head out and prepare for tonight."

"Not before giving me a hug." His father stood and held open his arms.

Granger swallowed past another lump and stood. He stepped over to give him a hug. After pulling away, they shook hands and Granger headed toward the back door. He passed his mother on the way.

"Joy and the girls just got home. They're helping me sell cider tonight," she told him.

Granger nodded. "Thank you for taking care of them."

"Oh, they're helping me. Merry Mountain is much busier than normal this year. We never sell this much cider," she said.

"We'll have to continue selling at the stand again next year," Granger told her. And he didn't have to run that idea by his father to get permission. It would be up to him now.

His mom smiled. "Yes, we will," she agreed.

When Granger was outside, he sucked in a breath, pulling the oxygen deep into his lungs as he walked.

"That bad, huh?" Joy asked, crossing the lawn from his place to her vehicle. She was going to get something out of the trunk of her car.

"The opposite actually. It's that good." He looked around. "Are the girls inside?"

"Abby is helping Willow with homework. There's only one more week of school before the break but her teacher is not letting up on sending work home." Joy stepped toward him, her forehead wrinkling softly with concern. "What's going on?"

"My dad just handed over the reins to the farm. Permanently." Granger removed his ball cap and ran a hand through his hair.

Joy touched his arm. "Granger, that's amazing! Wow. Congratulations on your big promotion." She went up on her tiptoes and gave him a celebratory kiss.

Granger wrapped his arms around her, holding her captive. "And you're the first person I wanted to share the news with." She was the first person he thought of when he opened his eyes in the mornings these days, and the last person he thought of when he went to bed.

"I'm honored," she said, tilting her head to the side. "And I know what you mean."

"Yeah?"

She nodded as he released his hold on her. "I sold a piece of artwork today, and I have more than what I need to put the deposit on the store on Main Street. I left a voicemail for Janelle Cruz to call me as soon as she can."

Granger was even happier for Joy than he was for himself. "Joy, that's terrific."

She beamed. "And you were the first person that I wanted to share my news with."

"Sounds serious," he said, treading lightly. She'd made it clear that she wasn't looking for serious. Looking or not, he was pretty sure they'd found it.

She lifted one shoulder slightly. "It feels serious."

Granger's heart knocked around in his chest. Sometimes taking risks led to great things. "Maybe that means you'll let me hang around a little longer in your life?"

Her eyes widened just a touch. "Only if you let me hang around in your life a little longer," Joy finally said, the corners of her mouth lifting softly.

"The girls would insist on that...I would too." Granger reached for her hand, needing to touch her. "I want to make sure I'm not misunderstanding. We're talking about staying together past the holidays, right?"

Joy nodded. "Yeah. Those kisses of yours are addictive. I'm not sure I could stop you at this point."

Granger took that as a hint to pull her in for another

kiss. A little longer could mean until January. Or next Christmas. Or forever. All he knew was that it didn't have to end anytime soon. And that was enough—for now.

They pulled away at the sound of a car's tires rolling over the dirt path. Granger didn't recognize the burgundy midsize SUV, and it was the wrong entrance for Christmas tree customers.

Joy stepped even farther away, heading back to the car. She removed Abby's book bag and shut the trunk.

Granger headed in the direction of his guest, his steps slowing as he got a better glimpse of the woman sitting behind the steering wheel. He thought his eyes were playing tricks on him at first. But as the driver cut the engine, opened her car door, and stepped out, his thoughts were confirmed.

"Mom!" Abby cried, bursting out the back door and down the porch steps toward her mom.

Willow followed behind her, but paused once she reached the ground.

"Mom! I knew you would come," Abby said. She threw her arms around Erin as she started sobbing.

Granger held his breath, waiting to see what Erin would do, relieved and also furious when she wrapped her arms around their daughter and hugged her back. What was she thinking coming back here without contacting him first? Without giving him a chance to prepare the girls for her visit? To prepare himself.

* * *

Joy felt out of place in this sudden family reunion.

Willow stood on the sidelines as well, looking as if she felt the same way. She had likely seen pictures, but she didn't know this person any more than Joy did.

Joy's gaze flitted to Granger's. His expression was stoic, and his eyes a little sad.

"Hi, Erin," he finally said.

The woman looked up.

Joy was surprised at how beautiful Granger's ex-wife was. In her mind's eye, Joy had painted the woman who left her little girls when they needed her most as something ugly—a monster. But Erin was far from unattractive. She had light-brown hair and the lightest brown eyes that Joy had ever seen.

"Granger," Erin said shyly, looking down for a moment and then looking over at Willow. Her gaze was hesitant, and Joy wanted to feel sorry for her. Then she reminded herself that Granger and the girls were the victims here. They'd been abandoned by this woman. Erin had left her children when Joy would have done anything to hold her own. Erin didn't deserve sympathy. She deserved someone to tell her to get back into her car and return to wherever she'd been hiding all these years.

"You got my letter, and you came," Abby said, looking up with a large smile.

"What letter?" Granger asked.

Abby looked proud of herself as she turned to look at him. "I found Mom's address in your private drawer. I know I'm not supposed to go in there but I just knew that if I wrote to her and told her how much we needed her, she'd come. I knew it," Abby repeated, looking back up at her mom. Joy wasn't sure she'd ever seen Abby so happy.

Joy looked at Granger again. She wasn't sure if she'd ever seen him so...upset. She couldn't blame him. The girls would be devastated if their mom came back for a visit only to disappear from their lives once more. He had to be terrified right now. And angry at Erin for not talking to him first.

Erin looked at Willow. "Hi, sweetheart."

"Hi." Willow's voice came out small.

"Willow, give Mom a hug. She came back to us," Abby said.

Willow took a half step forward. Then her mother broke away from Abby and kneeled in front of her.

"Hi." Erin held open her arms. "You've gotten so big. I can't believe it."

That's what happened when you left a newborn. They got bigger every day until they were no longer recognizable to a person who should've been there all along.

Joy bit her lower lip. Who was she to judge? She wasn't a mother. She'd never gotten a chance to hold her own baby in her arms.

Willow took another step and then she fell into Erin's arms.

Emotion clogged Joy's throat, making it hard to take in a full breath. She turned to Granger. "I should probably...should probably go inside so you all can be alone."

Erin looked up and met Joy's gaze. "Who are you?"

"I'm, um, I'm..." For a moment, Joy couldn't even remember her own name. The girls' mom had come home. Was she here to stay? To stay at the same house? Did she want to reunite with Granger too? The thought made Joy's chest feel like it was caving under the emotion. She hadn't wanted anything permanent with Granger. Or she hadn't thought she did.

"She's our babysitter," Abby supplied with a bright smile.

Joy shook her head, wanting to say no. No, she was not the babysitter. That was never the deal. She was the art teacher. And she had become more than that. To all of them. Hadn't she?

"This is Joy Benson," Granger told Erin. "She's been giving the girls art lessons. She's also teaching a Christmas tree workshop here at Merry Mountain this year."

Erin nodded slowly, looking between him and Joy as if filling in the blanks.

"I see. Nice to meet you, Joy." Erin said it in a friendly tone, even if Joy didn't get warm fuzzies from her. "That sounds wonderful. Art, huh?" She turned back to Abby, who nodded proudly.

"I love art," Abby said, the desperation to please her mother evident in her small voice.

Joy gave Granger another look. "I'll be inside to watch the girls when they're ready," she told him.

"No, that's okay," Abby said, overhearing. "Mom can watch us. Can't you, Mom?" Abby turned back to her mother with a hopeful look that it would be impossible to say no to.

Erin looked at Granger. "I'm sorry to intrude. I know I should have called."

"Yeah, you should have," he bit out coldly. "You can't just show up whenever you want. We have plans. I have to work tonight."

"But Mom doesn't. She can watch us," Abby said, overcompensating for Granger's demeanor by putting on an even bigger smile.

Granger shook his head. "Stay out of this, Abby."

Erin's mouth popped open at the rise in his tone. Joy wanted to run to his defense but that wasn't her place. She had no idea what was right or wrong in this moment but she didn't blame Granger for how he felt. "I need to get ready for the crowd tonight," he finally said. "If I had known you were coming, I might have suggested a different time," he said, not bothering to hide his resentment. "I can call Mom to come supervise a visit," he said. "She's running the cider stand with the girls tonight but there are a few hours before that time."

Erin wrung her hands in front of her. "Supervise. Right," she said quietly. "Yes, that would be wonderful. Thank you, Granger."

Granger looked at Joy, something apologetic passing across his gaze. Was he sorry because he was cutting her work with the girls short today? Or for some other reason? "Joy, it looks like you're free until it's time for your workshop."

Joy breathed past the hurt suddenly spreading through her chest. She wasn't sure what she had wanted him to say. They certainly couldn't discuss how this would affect their relationship right now in front of Erin and the kids. She handed him Abby's book bag that she'd retrieved from her car a few minutes ago. "I can go home and grab a bite to eat."

Granger took the bag. "Sounds good." He gave her a fleeting glance. It felt like he looked through her instead of at her this time, which left her feeling cold inside.

Joy pulled her keys out of her pocket. "Bye, girls. I'll see you later."

Abby didn't even look at her. Willow did though. She still looked wide-eyed and pale. Joy wanted to go over and reassure the little girl that everything would be okay. But she wasn't sure that was true. Joy wasn't sure of anything right now.

She got into her car and pulled out of the driveway. She'd been so busy lately that she hadn't had time to go grocery shopping. So instead of going home for the next hour, she decided to drive down Main to grab a bite. An added bonus was that she could drive by her store. Janelle Cruz still hadn't returned her call. If she didn't hear from her in the next hour, she'd try again.

Joy slowed her car as she passed the old clockmaker's shop a few minutes later. It looked different somehow. It took a moment for her to realize what was missing. The FOR LEASE sign that had been in the window was now gone.

"No." Joy pulled over and reached for her cell phone in the passenger seat. She pulled up Janelle Cruz's number and pressed Dial.

"Janelle Cruz," the real estate agent said in the receiver a moment later.

"Janelle, this is Joy Benson." Joy's heartbeat felt erratic. Panic was overtaking her like quicksand pulling her under. "I'm on Main Street."

"Right. I've been meaning to return your call. The place you've had your eye on went under contract yesterday morning. I'm very sorry, Joy."

* * *

Granger had spent the last couple of hours zombie-driving down Peppermint Path and Santa Street. His thoughts had been somewhere else the entire time, and he wasn't even sure how he'd managed to give the ride. Now he sat parked at the end of the final ride as Santa came walking toward him.

"You okay?" Jack asked, pulling on his fake white beard.

Granger blinked him into focus. "No."

"You wanna sit on my lap and tell me what you want for Christmas?" his friend teased.

This made Granger smile despite himself. "Not so much, buddy."

Jack climbed into the tractor seat beside Granger where Joy had sat so many times in the last couple of weeks. The crowd had gotten off at their exit and headed to their cars. Now Granger was expected to go back to his house where Erin was likely still sitting with the girls. His mom had called in a friend to help with the cider stand tonight and had stayed at the house to keep a close eye on them.

Granger didn't think Erin would hurt the girls. Or take them. Or anything like that. But he also wasn't comfortable leaving them alone with her. It was the emotional repercussions he was concerned with.

"Erin's back," Granger told Jack, looking over in time to see Jack's smile fall.

"Since when?"

"Since this afternoon." Granger sighed. "She showed up after the girls got out of school. She's with them right now."

"Wow. And you didn't know she was coming home?" Jack asked.

"She's not coming home. She can't stay at the house," Granger said, even though he understood that Jack hadn't meant it that way exactly. But that's the very thought that had been bumping around in Granger's mind along with the tractor and trailer down the lighted path. "I've always told her that she can return when she's ready. But there's a way to do it and a way not to. I needed to talk to the girls first. I needed to talk to Erin and make sure she was in a good emotional place to spend time with the girls. She can't just waltz back into our lives like nothing happened."

"Is that what she's trying to do?" Jack asked.

Granger shook his head. He wasn't sure. He hadn't had time to sit down and have a discussion with Erin yet. He'd needed to prepare for tonight, and it was obvious there was no way Abby was going to let her mom out of her sight immediately. "Abby said something about writing Erin a letter. She got the address from my private drawer."

Jack clasped his hands in front of him. "So she appealed to Erin to come home, and it worked. Makes you wonder what Abby said or what made this time different."

Yeah, that was another thought that had been rattling around in Granger's brain for the last couple of hours. He had no idea but the look he'd seen Erin giving Joy made him suspect Abby had taken action because of his new romantic relationship.

He blew out a breath and ran a hand through his hair, tugging softly on the roots.

"What does Joy think?" Jack asked.

Granger shook his head. "I haven't had a chance to talk to her either. Abby called her a babysitter and told her she could leave. Joy came back for the Christmas tree workshop but we only had time to wave at each other before the crowds arrived."

"You two are an item now, right? I heard it through the grapevine so it must be true," Jack said sarcastically.

Granger swallowed. He and Joy had discussed continuing to see each other past the holidays. But that was before Erin had shown up. This new change of events complicated things. He thought the girls would be okay with him dating again, but now that their mother was back in the picture, they might have a harder time understanding.

"Well, buddy, you're not going to know anything until you go inside and talk to Erin," Jack finally said. "And Joy too."

"I didn't know Santa was in the business of doling out advice."

Jack chuckled and stood. "This Santa is heading home to his other half." He was talking about Emma. He and Em had started dating this past summer, and Granger was glad to see his friend happy.

"Thanks for playing Santa, bud."

"I'd say anytime but that would be insincere." Jack let out another dry chuckle. "I have heard so many toy and video game requests tonight that my head is spinning. I'll probably dream of the stuff... Good luck, buddy. We need to meet up at the tavern again sometime soon."

"We will."

After Jack had descended the tractor steps and disappeared toward the parking lot, Granger drove the tractor to its barn, parked, and got off. He scanned his gaze over the parking lot looking for Joy's car as he walked toward his back door. She was already gone. He needed to talk to her but first he needed to talk to Erin.

He stood outside his home, staring in for a long moment. His family was inside. He wanted to do right by them, but for the life of him, he wasn't sure what that was. Was it sending Erin out of here? Or welcoming her to stay?

CHAPTER SEVENTEEN

Joy awoke the next morning with a sense of loss bearing down on her so heavy that it was hard to breathe. And for a moment, she couldn't remember why she felt so awful.

Then it hit her like two large blocks of ice over her head.

Granger's ex had returned yesterday. And Joy's dream store had gotten leased. All in a day's time.

Joy rolled into her pillow and buried her face. She had a long to-do list today that didn't give her the luxury of sulking. This day couldn't possibly get any worse than yesterday so she might as well rise, shine, and smell the coffee.

She shuffled down the hall to her coffee brewer and opened the container of grind. Empty. Joy frowned. "Bah humbug," she muttered as Chelsea came meowing into the kitchen. Chelsea's meow seemed to reflect the same sentiment. At least she had her catnip. Joy's catnip—coffee—wasn't immediately available. And there was no way Joy was braving the world without her morning caffeine so the only thing to do was get ready and head down to Sweet-water Café. Emma's coffee had a way of transforming Joy's mood anyway. Hopefully that would be true today.

A half hour later, Joy was headed toward the front counter at the local café.

"Hey, stranger," Emma said, perky as always. Even perkier these days, thanks to Merry Mountain Farms' new Santa.

"Starving artists can't afford to buy fancy coffee every day," Joy said.

Emma shook her head. "You're hardly a starving artist. From what I hear, your work is selling all over town, and your Etsy store is taking off." She waved a hand. "Today's coffee is my treat. But only if you agree to sit down with me. I'm taking a break, and one should never drink alone." Emma turned to her employee Dina. "Can you cover the counter?"

Dina nodded. "Of course. Go chitchat."

"Thanks." Emma made two cups of coffee and gestured toward an empty table.

Joy wasn't exactly close to Emma. They'd both grown up here and crossed each other's paths regularly. But they didn't usually sit down together. Some part of Joy just wanted to be alone after yesterday but another part needed the distraction of another person to take her mind off herself.

"So how've you been?" Emma asked. "I've seen you and Granger getting cozy over the last couple of weeks. And I've heard the talk around town."

Joy sighed. She couldn't get away from her problems even for a moment. "I'm helping Merry Mountain Farms this year because of the fire. We came up with the Christmas tree workshop as another way to bring in customers."

"That helps you too," Emma pointed out.

Joy sipped from her beverage. "That was the plan. I had my eye on the vacant store down the street. I wanted to open my own gallery."

"The one that just leased?" Emma asked, her skin pinching just above her eyes.

"Yep. Do you know who leased it?" Not that Joy needed to know. Knowing might make her feel worse.

Emma nodded. "Hearsay is that it's a vineyard owner from the West Coast. I think they're setting up a wine shop maybe?"

Joy raised a brow. Her art gallery was going to be a wine shop? And not even local wine?

"At least that's what I've heard. You can't sneeze around here without everyone hollering, 'Bless you.'"

Joy laughed.

"So you and Granger aren't a couple?" Emma asked.

Joy tilted her head. "Am I talking to you or the town?"

Emma drew back. "Come on, Joy. You know me better than that. I hear everything but I never repeat it. My lips are sealed." She fastened an invisible zipper across her lips.

Joy's shoulders rounded forward. "Sorry. Yes, I know I can trust you...Granger and I were teetering on the line between friends and more, but then...his ex returned to town yesterday afternoon." Fresh pain poured over Joy. It wasn't like with Dan, who'd cheated on Joy behind her back. Granger hadn't done anything wrong. But Joy still felt cheated.

"Erin has returned?" Emma's back went rod straight. "Wow, I never thought I'd see the day."

"I didn't either," Joy said. "The girls are thrilled."

"I imagine." Emma reached for Joy's hand. "You don't have to worry about Granger. He let Erin go a long time ago.

I remember when he'd come in here and order coffee and hot chocolate for the girls. For a while, he was broken. Then he gradually came back to life." Emma shrugged. "I see that stuff standing on the other side of the counter. And then he started seeing you, and he's a new man. I've seen that too."

This made Joy smile. She felt like a new woman these days too.

"You really like him, huh?"

Joy nodded. "More than I wanted to let myself."

"That's how it happens." Emma let go of Joy's hand. She giggled and sipped her coffee. "I'm really happy for you. Maybe we can go out on a double date or something in the New Year. Me and Jack and you and Granger."

"That sounds fun," Joy said with a smile. The thought of Erin was still bothering her but Emma had eased her mind a bit. Just because Erin was back didn't mean that she was losing Granger. She'd just found him. She wasn't ready to let him go, which both surprised and terrified her.

"Well, I better get back to the counter. Coffee breaks around here are short and sweet. But come back again next week, and let's do this again."

"I'd love that," Joy said. She watched Emma return to the counter for a moment. Then she collected her coffee and bag and headed down Main Street for a little window-shopping. She wasn't one to give store-bought gifts to others. Homemade was best. But she didn't mind buying a little something for herself. Maybe something new to wear when she went out with Granger on their next date.

The old, fearful Joy would be canceling that date now that Erin was back in town, thinking that she couldn't trust Granger or her heart if someone else was in the picture. Joy definitely felt like a new woman these days. The doubts might come but she was doing her best to push them away.

She had feelings for Granger, and she wasn't going to let a little fear of heartbreak and rejection lead her astray.

* * *

Granger sat in the stiff vinyl booth of a diner just outside of Sweetwater Springs. He was anxious and hungry. Last night when he'd gone inside the house after the hayride, Erin had already left. She'd left a number where she could be reached and a note asking him to meet her for breakfast. He'd texted her when he'd found it this morning to make arrangements, and they'd chosen a place far enough removed from the valley where they were unlikely to run into anyone they knew.

"Can I get you something to eat?" a waitress asked.

Granger looked up at the older woman. She'd already asked him once, and he'd told her he was waiting for someone. That someone wasn't here yet though. And maybe Erin wasn't coming after all.

Granger blew out a breath. Maybe last night had been a fluke, and Erin had run away again. Maybe she had no intention of returning to the farm and teaching Abby how to knit like Abby had gone on and on about before bed last night.

"Would you like a plate of biscuits while you wait?" the waitress suggested.

"I, uh…"

A bell rang on the entry door to the diner, and Erin stepped inside. She looked around for a moment before spotting him. There was a note of hesitation in her eyes as she headed in his direction, dressed in a heavy wool coat with a brightly colored scarf around her neck.

"Looks like your date arrived," the waitress said with a

smile. "I'll leave the menus here and be back to take your order in just a minute."

Granger wanted to tell her this wasn't a date. If he didn't, he'd feel a little disloyal to Joy. But the waitress had already stepped away, leaving him and Erin alone.

Erin slid into the booth across from him. "Sorry I'm late," she said. "I guess I forgot how to get here."

Seven years would do that to a person.

This was the spot where he and Erin used to come when they'd first started dating. They hadn't wanted anyone to intrude on their new romance. They'd wanted to keep it to themselves as much as possible. What had Granger been thinking when he'd chosen this place? He didn't want any romantic ties to Erin. He just wanted to be removed from the public eye.

"You're not that late," he said, studying her face. He hadn't gotten a good chance yesterday afternoon. He'd been too taken aback that she was actually standing in front of him. But now, he looked at her more closely. It had been a long time since he'd laid eyes on her. She looked healthy. And just as attractive as ever, but he didn't think of her that way anymore.

"It's not okay," he finally said. "Coming back without discussing it with me first isn't okay, Erin."

Her lips parted just slightly. "You told me that I was welcome back when I was ready."

"Yes, but there's a right way and a wrong way. We have to think about the girls. They come first. Yes, they need to see you but don't you think it would've been good for me to prepare them before you breeze back into their lives? To prepare myself?"

"I...I..." She looked pale and frightened suddenly.

Guilt slammed into him for making her look that way. He lowered his voice. "I'm sorry."

She held up a hand. "Don't be. I deserve it," she said quietly. "I'm lucky you're even allowing me to see the girls."

The waitress reappeared at their table. "Can I get something for you two?"

Granger looked up. Judging by the woman's pinched expression, she'd heard him raise his voice. She didn't know the dynamic here, and she wouldn't understand even if he tried to explain it. "Eggs and bacon for me, please."

"I'll have the same." Erin kept her gaze on her folded hands. "And a coffee."

"Coming right up." The waitress walked away.

There was a moment of silence between them before Erin lifted her gaze and spoke. "I should've called you before I came. I don't know what I was thinking." She shook her head. "I've just been trying to get up my nerve to come visit for a while now. I've gotten in the car so many times, driven down your road, and almost turned in. I was just trying to get there before I could talk myself out of it."

"Willow has been asking questions about you lately. And Abby has been missing you too. I could hardly get her to go to sleep last night, she was so excited," Granger said.

Erin's lips turned up at the corners. "She's gotten so big. I can't believe it. I can't believe how much I've missed."

Granger had sent Erin a lot of pictures over the years. Anytime the kids had a formal portrait taken, he'd put one in the mail to Erin. He didn't have to but some part of him felt like he owed Erin. She was the reason his girls were in this world. Whatever Erin did or didn't do, he would always be in debt to her.

And he'd read up on postpartum depression a million times. He'd even gone to a counselor after Erin had left the family. He understood that depression could last a long time, even years. He also knew that Erin had been through a lot growing up. Her own mother had left her, and when they had gotten married, Erin swore she'd be the best mom in the world. She'd set the bar high, and he had no doubt that when her depression kicked in, she'd blamed herself.

Granger looked down at his hands, which he noticed were shaking. "So what made you finally decide to come back?" He lifted his gaze back to Erin.

The waitress slid a cup of coffee in front of Erin. Once the waitress had walked away, Erin reached for it and took a sip. "Abby's letter brought me here."

Granger had heard Abby say something about that last night. "What did she say?"

"She said she loved me and missed me. And that she wanted me to come home for Christmas."

Granger nodded. "All the things you'd expect."

Erin nibbled her lower lip. "Except I didn't expect her to say that. When I opened the letter, I expected her to tell me that she hated me. And how awful a mother I was for leaving her and Willow. I expected her to tell me that I'd ruined her life and that she never wanted to see me again."

Erin looked away for a moment. "I guess that was what I thought I deserved from her. That's how I felt after my mom left me. But I really have been working on myself and my thoughts. So I read her letter again and again. Until I believed it."

"She didn't tell me she was writing you."

"She probably knew you wouldn't have let her," Erin said.

Granger clenched his jaw, holding back his first response. He wasn't the one who had kept Erin and the children apart all these years. "Look, I'm happy that you're doing better these days—I really am. But my responsibility and loyalty go to the girls first. I just want to know what your plans are. You're here but for how long?"

The waitress returned and slid their plates in front of them. "Anything else?"

Granger shook his head. "Not for me."

"No, thanks," Erin added.

"All right. Just holler if you do need something." The waitress looked between them, and Granger knew she was trying to decide what they were to each other. A couple? Business partners?

He waited to speak again until he and Erin were alone. "I want you to be a part of Abby and Willow's lives but you can't walk in and out. If you're walking back out, it's best that you're not in at all. For their sakes."

Except even as he said it, he knew it was already too late. Erin had visited with the girls, and if she disappeared again, Abby and Willow would feel abandoned and rejected. In that case, Granger would likely have to put them in counseling.

Erin used her fork to move her food around on the plate but she didn't take a bite. Granger hadn't touched his breakfast yet either. "I'm moving back."

"Moving back?" he echoed.

Erin swiped a lock of hair behind her ear. Once upon a time, he'd loved that gesture of hers. He'd loved the way she'd looked away shyly even when there was no reason to be shy around him. "I work from home so it doesn't matter where I live. And I've already made an appointment with a therapist here just to keep myself moving in the right direction. For the girls and myself."

She swiped her hair out of her face again, looking vulnerable. "My last therapist told me that I will always regret leaving. But I don't have to also regret never coming back." Her voice choked with emotion. She moved her food around on her plate some more. "Anyway, I'll be at the new inn on Mistletoe Lane while I look for somewhere more permanent."

Granger nodded. "The Sweetwater Bed and Breakfast. It opened about two years ago."

"That's the one. It's cozy. The owner, Kaitlyn, is really nice too."

"She married Mitch Hargrove," Granger told her, making small talk and moving the conversation around the way Erin was moving the food on her plate.

"I saw Mitch. He looks great," Erin said. Granger and Erin had both gone to school with Mitch, Jack, and the current mayor of Sweetwater Springs, Brian Everson. Erin was as much a part of this town as Granger was, and he had no right to tell her not to return. Even if that's exactly what he wanted to beg of her right now.

"I can't stay at the inn forever. It's reasonable but I'm ready to get settled here."

Granger had so many mixed emotions about that. Things were good at home. This would disrupt the balance, but if there was a chance for Abby and Willow to have both parents, it was worth the risk, right?

"Janelle Cruz can help you," he finally said. Janelle was great at helping people find the perfect home. That wouldn't be easy in this situation though. The perfect home should be where your family was but that wasn't going to happen in this case.

"So you're okay with this?" Erin asked. "With me coming back?"

"It's going to take some time for me to let my guard down," Granger said. "It's not because I'm trying to hurt you. I'm just trying to protect the girls."

Erin nodded. "I knew coming back that it would be a long row to hoe. I'm stronger than I used to be, and I'm going to prove myself to you. And your mom and dad. Everyone who has Abby and Willow's best interests at heart."

Granger scooped some grits onto his spoon and nodded. "I'll be honest. I'm wary, Erin...But I'm also rooting for you."

*   *   *

What is Dan doing here?

This was Joy's Christmas tree workshop, and he had no right to be here. Except, apparently, he did. Tonight, she was giving a workshop to the men's group at a local church, and Dan was a new member. The group was making trees for the children's home an hour away.

Ignoring Dan, Joy walked over to Pastor Phillips and put on a smile. "Wow, these trees look amazing. The kids are going to love having their very own tree in their rooms."

Pastor Phillips stopped what he was doing and faced her. "They'll need these trees to put their gifts under. The Hope for the Holidays auction chose the children's home as their recipient this Christmas. And the Ladies' Day Out group has generously offered to go shopping for the kids with the money earned. Our men's group is tasked with delivery."

Joy had already heard that the children's home was this year's Hope for the Holidays recipient. Usually the town chose a person in need but this year it had chosen the orphanage. It was a bigger job but it would benefit the kids so much.

"What are you donating to the Hope for the Holidays auction this year?" Pastor Phillips asked.

Joy shrugged. "I don't have much to offer. I guess just a private art class."

"You have more to offer than you think," the pastor said, returning to his work.

Joy had only meant financially. But his words hit her with a soft punch. Until lately, she wasn't sure she had what it took to invest in another relationship. But Granger had made her think otherwise. Maybe it wasn't too soon to consider something serious again. Maybe she could fall in love and have it actually work out this time.

At least, that's what she was thinking before Erin came back. Now her thoughts were a jumbled mess.

Joy continued walking around to look at the trees, chatting with various guys in the group, continuing to avoid Dan. Not going over to speak to him, however, would imply that she cared about him. And she didn't. With an inward groan, she headed over. "Looks good," she told him with all the insincerity she could muster.

Dan held a can of bright-pink spray paint in his hand. She'd put out a rainbow of colors for her students to paint the trees tonight, thinking that the young recipients would love that. "Thanks."

"Since when are you in a men's group?" she asked.

Dan gave a humorless laugh. "Since about three weeks ago. I'm trying to make some positive changes in my life."

Joy's mind couldn't help but come up with a list of changes she wanted to suggest for him. She truly believed that people could change, but somehow, she thought he was the exception. He'd betrayed her, broken her for a while, and in her mind, he was beyond saving.

As if reading her thoughts, Dan nodded. "At least, I'm going to try. I have good motivation to want to help the children's home. And to want to be a better man."

"Oh?" Joy folded her arms over her chest, barring the cold and guarding herself from this man who'd hurt her heart so much.

His expression looked apologetic, and something told Joy she didn't want to hear what he was about to say. "Nancy is...well, she's pregnant."

Pain poured over Joy, stealing her breath and threatening to buckle her knees. Not because she still loved Dan. No, she didn't. But he was getting his second chance at love and a family, and he was changing for Nancy the way he hadn't found Joy worthy of changing for.

"Are you okay?" Dan asked.

"I'm fine." Joy held up a hand. "Congratulations on the baby. That's wonderful news. I'm happy for you two."

Dan nodded and looked down at the can of spray paint in his hands. "For what it's worth, I am sorry about what happened between us."

"Which part?" Joy asked, knowing that she should be a bigger person. He was apologizing. She should accept it graciously and move on. "The part about lying to me and telling me you loved me? Or the part where you cheated on me with one of your nurses? Or maybe the part where we..." She trailed off.

He was a doctor, and he hadn't held the baby inside him. He hadn't had time to even get attached to the idea like she had. Then when she'd found out it was an ectopic pregnancy, he'd talked about it as a medical event. Like having a gallstone. Inconvenient and unimportant. But it'd been more than that to her.

"All of it." Dan frowned and nodded as if he expected her anger. "This pregnancy is why I've wanted to make amends with you lately. When you're faced with something like parenthood, it makes you look at your life. I want to be my kid's hero, and a hero takes responsibility for his actions. I was a jerk—I admit it. I treated you badly, and I'll always regret that... I'm sorry, Joy."

Joy wasn't sure what to say. She couldn't very well hate him now. "I, um... thank you. And congratulations." She sucked in a breath, realizing now that it was unusually quiet. She knew without turning around that people were watching and listening to their conversation. *Crap.* She didn't like airing her dirty laundry even if Dan had just made a noble attempt to clean it.

She put on a smile and turned to the group.

"Hi, Joy." Local newscaster Serena Gibbs and her cameraman stood a couple of feet away. "I heard this is one of the most talked about places to be this Christmas, so I wanted to make sure I got a good story." Her gaze jumped from Joy to Dan, who was standing behind her now.

Oh no. That was old news. It was in the past, where Joy would leave it and her resentment for Dan from now on. He was moving forward, and she wanted to do the same. That was the only way she and Granger had a chance. A second chance at love for both of them.

Joy put on a bright smile to match the newscaster's as the camera pointed at her. "Welcome to the Christmas tree workshop."

CHAPTER EIGHTEEN

Joy slipped off to her car as soon as the workshop was over. She'd seen Granger chatting with several customers and hadn't wanted to bother him. Plus, she'd known that Willow was inside biting at the bit to talk to him about something that had excited her. Erin was in there as well.

Joy took a deep breath, trying not to feel jealous. Because that would be immature and silly. Granger had told Joy he wasn't interested in reconnecting romantically with his ex, and Joy didn't need to worry.

Instead, she drove home and carried the small tree she'd purchased for herself into her little townhome. She planned on decorating it while she binged on Hallmark Channel holiday movies. If she couldn't have real romance tonight, she'd live vicariously through the characters on her TV.

First things first though—she poured herself a deep glass of wine from a local vineyard in the valley—not some far-off place in California—and took a healthy gulp. "Ah, that's good."

Chelsea poked her head out from under the couch. *Meow.*

"Don't worry. The coast is clear. There are no children or men in tow," Joy told her cat. "Just you, me, Hallmark, and wine."

The doorbell rang.

"And an unexpected visitor." Joy headed to the door, wondering who was on her porch. It could be her mom—who she wasn't in the mood to see right now. Or her elderly neighbor, who regularly knocked to ask for milk, eggs, or even toilet paper.

Or it could be Granger. But he was likely with his family by now. And she knew how important family time was to him. There was no way it was him, even if that's the only person she wanted to see tonight.

She opened the door, and her heart did a free fall into her belly.

"Hi," Granger said, standing on her porch. He was dressed in jeans, a T-shirt, and a long-sleeved flannel shirt per usual, and he was the sexiest man alive in her opinion.

"What are you doing here?"

"You left tonight before I could talk to you."

Joy gestured him inside. "Come on in. It's cold out there." She closed the door behind him, and immediately, Granger's arms wrapped around her.

"And it's warm in here," he said. "I came all this way just to kiss you good night."

Joy's breath caught as she looked up at him. "Really?"

"You sound surprised. Nothing's changed from yesterday when I told you I wanted to keep this thing between us going," he said, voice lowering.

Except a lot had changed. Erin had returned, and his family needed him more than ever.

Seeming to read her thoughts, Granger sighed and

kissed her forehead. "Okay, it's a little more complicated than it was but I've never been one to back away from a challenge."

Joy grinned. "Are you calling me a challenge, Mr. Fields?"

Granger's arms wrapped more tightly, squeezing her softly in a hug. "The challenge is keeping my hands off you every time you're near." Granger looked around. "Am I going to be attacked by a cat if I kiss you right now?"

"There's a good chance," Joy said with a tiny laugh. "But Chelsea comes with the territory. If you want to be with me, you're stuck with random cat attacks."

Granger nodded. "And my family comes with my territory."

Joy already knew and accepted that about him. But she wasn't sure if his family now included Erin. She was the girls' mom after all. Instead of kissing him, Joy wiggled free from his arms. She fidgeted momentarily and then gestured at her kitchen. "Would you like some peppermint tea?" she asked, needing to be busy. She didn't wait for him to respond. Instead, she turned and headed to the small open kitchen of her townhome.

Granger sat on a stool at her kitchen island and watched her work. She prepared and carried the mugs of tea to the island and took the stool opposite him.

"I guess we need to talk before kissing, huh?" Granger finally said.

Joy curled her fingers around her mug, soaking in the warmth and letting it soothe her frayed emotions. "Is Erin...back?"

Granger reached for his tea. "Yeah. Looks like it. She's actually moving back for good, so she says."

Joy stiffened. This should be good news, and she felt a

wave of guilt for being disappointed by it. "Wow. That's a big turnaround."

"And unexpected. I just wish she had told me she was coming so I could have prepared the girls. But it's a good thing for them. At least if she stays."

Joy couldn't help being hurt somehow. "So you're just letting her back in that easy?"

Granger lifted a brow. "It's not easy for me to let Erin back in. It's hard. But what kind of father would I be if I denied my children the chance to have their mother in their lives?"

"You're a wonderful father," Joy said quietly. And it was her own jealousy talking right now. "What about you?" she couldn't help asking. "I'm sure Erin is hoping to return to more than just the girls."

"No." He shook his head. "I told her over breakfast that we were over. She accepted that."

"Over breakfast?" Joy asked.

Granger narrowed his eyes. In the dim lighting of the kitchen, she saw flecks of amber swirling with the honey brown. "We needed to talk privately. I made sure she knew it was over between us, and she agreed. She's only interested in reconnecting with Abby and Willow."

Joy wanted to believe him but she also wanted to be smart. She'd been dumb when it came to love once before. "So where is Erin staying, if she's moving back?"

Granger lifted his mug and took a sip. "Last night she stayed at the Sweetwater Bed and Breakfast."

Joy got the feeling he was holding something back. "And tonight?"

He sighed and placed his tea back on her counter. "Tonight, she's staying at Merry Mountain Farms."

Joy stood and started walking toward the front door, leaving Granger at her island.

"What? Wait a minute."

"I think you should leave," Joy said, suddenly short of breath.

Granger followed behind her. "What would you have me do? Erin hasn't found a permanent place to live yet, and if she spends all of her available funds on temporary dwellings, how does that help her or my kids?"

Joy could see his point but she didn't like the idea of Granger and his ex staying under one roof together. She'd been down a similar road last Christmas, and she didn't want to travel it again.

"Joy?"

She turned to face him and blew out a breath. "This was supposed to be casual and fun. Easy." Her eyes started burning. "There weren't supposed to be tears and heartbreak or any of the awful stuff that relationships have."

Granger looked at her. "Comes with the territory when feelings get involved." He reached up and swiped his finger across her cheek now. She hadn't even realized there was a tear there. "You didn't let me explain. Erin is staying in my parents' guest room. Across the lawn in a completely different house. And only until she can find a place of her own to stay, which will hopefully be sooner rather than later."

Joy folded her arms at her chest, applying pressure to her aching heart. She didn't know whether to toss Granger out in the cold or kiss him.

Kissing him sounded like a lot more fun.

As if reading her thoughts, Chelsea flew out from under the couch and attacked Granger's leg.

He stumbled a little, doing his best not to step on her paw. Then she darted off, no doubt to plan her next attack. "I think your cat is starting to warm up to me. She didn't hiss this time."

Joy laughed. Chelsea hadn't hissed last time either. "She's a good judge of character."

"Joy, I want to be completely transparent with you. I'm not going to break your heart. Not if I can help it."

She nodded. "So I'm overreacting?"

"Not at all. My ex is back, and that's a big deal. But I like you. I didn't expect to fall as hard as I have. I can't seem to help it though. It's been a really long time since I've felt anything for a woman. And I feel a whole lot of things for you."

Chelsea flew out from under a chair and attacked his leg again.

This time he didn't look away. His gaze held steady on Joy's.

Her heart throbbed in her chest. She felt a whole lot of things for him too, and that's what scared her. "Okay," she finally said, at a loss for anything more.

"Okay what?" he asked.

"Okay, you can kiss me now," she whispered, stepping toward him. Then she cupped her hands over his cheeks and pressed her mouth to his.

* * *

Granger held on to Joy, loving the feel of her in his arms. Loving the sweet taste of her lips, like wine and Christmas. This woman was all he wanted this holiday season, and now that he was holding her in his arms, he never wanted to let her go. This was anything but casual for him. It was complicated and messy—getting messier by the moment. And falling for someone was risky to his little family who needed security and stability. It was his job to give them that.

His body silenced his mind with all its worries and fears, giving his hands permission to run over Joy's back, feeling her curves beneath his touch. She seemed to come alive beneath his fingers, her mouth increasingly needy as they kissed.

Movement stirred under their feet, and Granger was sure that Chelsea had made another attack. But all he cared about was Joy. Little moans left her as they kissed, adding fuel to his overloaded senses. The taste, the sounds, the feel of her.

He lifted his head and opened his eyes, breaking away from the kiss. His breathing was heavy, as if he'd just jogged across the parking lot. "I want you," he whispered. If his mind were in control, he definitely wouldn't be saying that.

"I want you too." She looked up at him with dreamy, half-closed eyes. Her lips were swollen, a deep rose color from their kiss. He just wanted to dip his mouth to hers again and kiss all night. That would lead to more than kissing, though, and possibly to all the things he meant when he told her he wanted her.

"But we probably shouldn't," Granger said.

"Where are the girls?" Joy asked.

"With my parents." And Erin too, but he left that part out. It didn't feel right to even utter another woman's name at this moment.

Granger took a step back, distancing himself from Joy.

Her brow furrowed softly. "What's wrong?"

"I want to pull you in my arms and stay here all night. But…"

"You need to get back to your family." She stared at him for a moment and then nodded. "Okay. So then what should we do?"

Granger chuckled because he couldn't believe what he was about to say. "I should probably go home now. Staying would only test my willpower. Another ten minutes and we'd be kissing again." And kissing would lead to roaming hands and discarded clothing. He headed for the door. "Don't run off after your workshop tomorrow evening." He looked over his shoulder as he reached for the doorknob.

She tilted her head, a questioning look in her eyes. "Another hayride?"

Granger shrugged. "Are you getting tired of my moves already?"

She grinned. "I don't think I'll ever tire of sitting with you under the stars."

He was tempted to read a lot more into that than he thought she intended. That sounded an awful lot like forever to him. And he was pretty certain he would never tire of Joy either. "Good. I'll see you after closing." He turned around and then dipped to give her a soft kiss, pulling away before things got out of hand this time. "Good night, Joy."

"Night."

He opened the door and stepped outside. As he walked to his truck, he heard her front door close. He'd been a breath away from losing her tonight. And a breath away from making love to her.

And he was long past falling in love with Joy Benson.

He unlocked his truck and got in. Then he drove the short distance home and hurried through the biting cold into his house. His mom was sitting at the kitchen island with a book in front of her. She turned and gave him a visual assessment that ended with her smiling. Could she see Joy's fingerprints on him? Did his mouth reveal that he'd been kissing someone?

"Thanks for watching the girls," he said as he removed his coat.

She closed her book and stood.

"You don't have to thank me. You know that. And I didn't do much. Erin made popcorn, and they watched holiday movies all night."

"Is Erin over at your place already?" he asked.

His mom shook her head. "No. She fell asleep on the couch with the girls. I think it's best if we don't wake them, don't you?"

Granger looked past his mom toward his living room. He didn't see how Erin staying under his roof overnight was best for anyone. He also couldn't see waking her though. That would only stir the girls. He ran a hand through his hair and tugged.

His mom swatted him. "Stop that. You'll be bald if you keep pulling at your hair . . . Were you at Joy's tonight?"

"Yeah."

His mom nodded and smiled. "Good. Joy makes you happy, and that makes me happy. Everything else will fall into place just like it should."

His mom's perspective never ceased to amaze him. She could make a root canal sound like something positive. "You make it sound so simple."

"It should be simple. The heart knows that. It's the mind that gets in the way."

Granger chuckled. "The two are kind of inseparable, you know."

"Yes, but they're complete opposites. That's what makes them perfect for one another." She winked up at him.

Something told him she was referring to him and Joy more than the heart and the mind. "You're anything but subtle, Mom."

"Subtlety is for the young with time to spare for mis-understandings." She headed toward the back door. "I'll see you in the morning. I'll cook breakfast."

He knew she was also making sure that Granger didn't have to deal with Erin being under his roof alone. He was thankful for that. His mom had always understood him the way his father couldn't seem to.

"Will you try to drag Dad over here too?" Granger asked, stepping onto the porch behind her. The cold rushed around him, making his frozen breaths visible. "This year doesn't feel quite the same with him taking a back seat at the farm. I miss talking to him."

"I think he feels the same way. I'll drag him over. I'm sure he'd love to see Erin as well. We might not approve of her choices but we'll always love her. We'll always do our best to support you too." She nudged Granger softly.

"Just like you always have." Granger kissed her cheek. "Love you, Mom."

"I love you too, son. Good night." She started walking home. Granger watched her for a moment and then headed back inside. He stopped in the entryway of his living room, where Erin was sleeping. He'd told Joy that Erin was stay-ing at his parents' place tonight, and yet here she was in his living room. Should he text Joy and let her know? He hated keeping secrets.

He picked up his phone and brought up Joy's contact but hesitated. This was no big deal, really. And what Joy didn't know wouldn't keep her up tonight. She needed her sleep. For full transparency, he would just make sure he told her as soon as possible tomorrow.

* * *

Granger was up early the next morning, careful not to wake anyone as he tiptoed toward the kitchen. He needed that first cup of coffee before he could deal with any of what the morning would bring. Erin was still asleep in his living room with Abby and Willow curled against her. For a moment, Granger stopped to look at them. The girls looked so peaceful.

Granger turned the coffee brewer on and listened as it grumbled to life. Wow, he never realized how loud this thing was until he needed it to stay quiet. He tossed a glance over his shoulder, hoping not to wake Erin before his parents got here. He didn't want to be alone with her. Not because he was attracted to her. Just because, well, he didn't feel like he knew her anymore. She felt like a stranger in his house—one that he'd once known intimately.

He retrieved a mug from the cabinet and turned to bring it over to the pot.

"Can you make that two?" a woman's voice asked.

Caught.

He looked over and met Erin's watchful eyes. "Morning."

She looked away shyly, using one hand to tamp down her sleep-ruffled hair. "I guess I fell asleep here last night. Sorry."

"No need to apologize. It's fine," he said quietly, although now he didn't mind if he woke the girls up. Their chatter would ease the tension between Erin and him. "Mom will be over with Dad for breakfast in a bit."

Erin nodded and looked at the coffee again.

"I'll grab another mug," he said.

"Thank you." She looked down the hall and gestured. "I'll freshen up and be right back."

Granger nodded, realizing that they'd have to share a cup of coffee together when she returned. Just like the old days. A heavy sigh rattled through his chest. He suddenly felt exhausted, even though he'd had a full night's sleep. He poured two mugs and carried them back to the kitchen island. Then he adjusted the stools so that he and Erin wouldn't be sitting too closely.

When she returned, her hair was neatly brushed, and her skin was fresh. The only evidence that she'd just woken was the faint pillow crease running diagonally across her lower cheek. "Thank you." She sat on the other stool and pulled her mug to her mouth.

Granger did the same, and they sat quietly together for a long moment.

"So Abby tells me that you're dating their babysitter."

Granger choked on his sip of coffee. "What? No." He shook his head. "Joy isn't the babysitter. She's helping with the girls temporarily until I can find a new nanny to watch them after school. It's more of a favor on her part."

"But you are dating her?" Erin seemed to search his face.

He hesitated before nodding. "Yeah. It's new."

Erin looked down into her coffee. "So I guess that's where you were last night?"

He cleared his throat. "Yeah." Not that it was any of her business.

She looked up. "For what it's worth, I'm sorry, Granger. For everything."

"Me too," he said. "But I'm glad you came home. The girls need you in their lives."

"I need them too." Erin held his gaze for a long moment. Granger wondered if things would be different if he hadn't started seeing Joy right before Erin came back. Would he have tried to go down this road with her again? He didn't think he would.

"Do you have someone special in your life?" he asked.

"No." She gave her head a quick shake. "I've been working on myself in counseling. But I'm not ready to be with someone else. I'm not sure I'll ever be ready. But I am here for our kids. You don't need to find someone else to watch them anymore. I can handle their care after school, and I want to."

Granger took a sip of his coffee. He wanted to say yes but his girls came first. Their safety got priority over what they would want. "Let's see how the next couple weeks go first, okay? Then we'll talk."

Disappointment colored her expression. "I get it. I'll just have to show you that I'm ready. And I will."

* * *

Joy had finished her workshop thirty minutes ago but she couldn't find Granger anywhere. Her day had been unexpectedly busy, and she hadn't gotten a chance to see him all day. Instead she'd taught a class at the community center and the library and then had made a run to the art supply store for more materials to use at her Christmas tree workshop tonight.

Joy spun around, looking in all directions. Last night before he left, Granger had asked her to meet him tonight after the crowd had gone. He seemed to have disappeared with them though.

Joy knew the girls were inside with Erin. Maybe he'd gone to check on them. She headed in that direction. Joy didn't really want to talk to Erin but she had promised Granger that she wouldn't run off tonight like she'd done last night. As she drew closer to the house, she heard sniffles coming from the front porch. Joy bypassed the back door and headed in the direction of the sound, pausing for a moment when she saw Willow crying.

Willow was usually such a happy girl. It broke Joy's

heart to see her cry, her little body twitching softly as she tried to take in air.

"Willow? You okay?" Joy climbed the steps and headed toward the little girl.

Willow blinked up through her big tears, and despite her sadness, she smiled.

That turned Joy's heart to mush. This was the sweetest little girl in the whole wide world. Her and Abby both.

Joy sat on the swing next to Willow, her elbow bumping against Willow's shoulder. "Wanna talk about it?"

Willow lifted her forearm and used the sleeve of her shirt to wipe beneath her nose.

Joy laughed softly. No doubt that snot would be all over her own clothes when they hugged in a minute. Not that she minded.

"I asked Santa to bring me a new mom." She looked up wide-eyed at Joy. "And he got it all wrong."

Joy pulled back to look at her. "What? But your mom is here."

"I said I wanted a *new* one." Willow shook her head, her body trembling again. "Not the old one who doesn't even want me," she squeaked out.

Joy pulled her in close. "Oh, honey. What makes you think she doesn't want you?"

"Because that's what the kids in my class told me. Last year, when I asked the teacher why I was the only one without a mother for the Breakfast with Mom at school, my friends said it's because my mom didn't want me...So I don't want her either."

Some friends. "Is that why you asked for a new mom? Because of the kids at school?"

"And because my old mom is sick. At least that's what Daddy told me." Willow hesitated. "But she doesn't look sick to me. I even asked her if she felt okay, and she said yes."

Joy reached for Willow's hand and gave it a gentle squeeze. "Sometimes you can't really see when someone is sick. They don't get a fever or sneeze or anything like that. But your mom seems to be doing well now. I think the doctors have helped her feel better." At least Joy hoped so for this little girl's sake.

"I just... When I asked Santa for a mom, I meant new. Why couldn't he have picked you?" Willow asked with a sniffle.

Joy sucked in a sharp breath. "Me? I'm just the baby-sitter," she teased, regurgitating Abby's words from the other day. It was strange that Willow was the one pushing her mom away. Joy would've expected this from Abby, who had counseled her sister on stranger danger. Erin was their mom, but they didn't know her.

But on the contrary, Abby was doing everything she could to win her mom's attention.

"You would've been a good mom for us," Willow said, throwing her arms around Joy for a big hug. There went that snot all over Joy's clothes. "You are the best babysitter in the whole world. And the best art teacher. In my letter, I also told Santa that I wanted you to stay forever."

Granger must not have gotten ahold of that letter yet.

Joy hugged Willow back. "Santa can't bring everything, you know."

Willow pulled back and lifted a brow. "Yes, he can."

"Well, his sleigh is only so big, sweetheart."

"But it's a magic sleigh," Willow countered. "It can fit everything on everyone's list for the whole entire world."

Joy looked down into Willow's hopeful eyes. Willow was too young to see how illogical that was, and perhaps that was a good way to be. To believe in your dream instead of what you deemed to be reality. Joy's own dream was starting to crumble in the real world's hands. Her gallery on Main Street was leased, and another place might not become available until this time next year. "Maybe you're right."

"I am," Willow said. She pulled her arms back and looked down at her lap. "But Santa might be very disappointed in me this year. Maybe he won't bring me the rest of what I want for Christmas."

"Why is that, sweetheart?"

"Because I haven't treated my mom very nicely." Willow looked up. "I haven't been mean to her or anything."

"Of course not. You're not a mean girl."

"But I haven't given her lots of hugs and stuff like Abby has."

"That's okay," Joy said. "It might take a little time. She knows you're happy to see her."

"Because adults know everything?" Willow asked.

Joy laughed and wrapped her arm around Willow's shoulders and squeezed once more. This was one misconception that Joy could debunk. "Hardly. We know a lot but there's a lot that we don't know. But you have so many grown-ups in your life. You can always talk to one of us about anything on your mind, and we'll do our best to help you, okay?"

Willow nodded solemnly.

"Don't worry about Santa. You, of all kids, are on his good list. You want to go inside and have some hot cocoa?"

Willow hopped off the swing in response. Then she grabbed Joy's hand and started to pull her up. "With marshmallows?"

"Of course."

They headed through the front door instead of the back door for once, stepping directly into the living room. Willow ran off into another room as Joy closed the door behind her. Then Joy inspected the messy living room with blankets and clothing tossed about. As she looked closer, she noticed an adult woman's cardigan. A scarf. There were some earrings lying on the coffee table. These were Erin's things.

Abby came into the room. "Willow says we're going to make hot chocolate?"

Joy greeted the older girl with a wobbly smile, her mind still processing the items. "Yes, that's right. I have time before I go home. I'm supposed to meet your dad before I leave. Is he here yet?"

Abby shook her head. "My mom went to meet him too. He's probably with her."

"Your mom?" Joy repeated.

Abby nodded. "Those are her things on the floor. She slept over last night."

"Did she?" Joy asked, taking a closer look. The clothing was on the couch. Hopefully that's where Erin had stayed, far away from Granger. Joy was tempted to jump to conclusions, but she forced herself to give him the benefit of the doubt. Even if doubt was always her knee-jerk reaction. Granger was a good man. And he was hers, not Erin's.

CHAPTER NINETEEN

Granger walked fast, shining his cell phone's flashlight at the ground to make sure he didn't fall on his face in the dark. He was running late to meet Joy for their romantic hayride. He'd been looking forward to it all night. Hopefully, she hadn't given up on him and gone home already.

"Granger?"

He froze and looked around, seeing the shadow of a woman coming toward him. "Joy?"

"No...It's Erin," his ex said as she stepped into the beam of his flashlight.

He should've known it wasn't Joy. Their voices weren't similar but Joy made the most sense right now. "Erin, what are you doing out here? It's freezing, and you don't have a flashlight." Or a proper coat, for that matter.

She continued to walk in his direction, stopping when she was just a couple of feet away. "I came out here to find you."

"Is everything okay with the girls?" he asked, panic flaring.

"Yeah, they're fine. Your mom is with them right now."

"Of course she is. I don't know what I would've done all these years without her help." He didn't mean it as a guilt trip but he knew Erin took it personally as soon as the words came out. He wouldn't have needed his mom to help so much if she had been here.

"Well, I plan to help a lot more," she said. "She'll get a much-needed break."

Time would tell if that was true. "So then why did you want to come see me?"

Erin looked up at him. She stepped even closer, standing only a foot away now. "I've been thinking a lot since I've gotten back. I know I should have called you."

"You've already apologized for that."

She held up a hand. "Yes, but it's worth repeating. I came back because I realized that it's never too late to be the mom I wanted to be. I wanted to be the fun mom, the energetic and understanding and cool mom. I wanted to be the mom who taught my girls to be confident."

"There's still time," Granger said.

Erin nodded. "I know. Although, I think you've done an amazing job helping them grow."

Granger swallowed. "That means a lot to hear you say that."

Erin looked hesitant. "When you and I got married, I also had an idea of the kind of wife I wanted to be. I wanted to be the supportive wife. The kind of wife who made you want to come home at night."

Unlike her own mother, Granger knew. Erin's father hadn't wanted to go home, because her mother was verbally and emotionally abusive.

"I wanted to be a woman you felt lucky to have in your life."

"Erin…" Granger shook his head. "We don't really need to get into this."

"I just wonder…" She blew out a breath. "I've been wondering…"

Granger watched as she struggled to find the right words. Then she reached into her pocket and pulled out a sprig of mistletoe.

"I found this on the kitchen counter."

It was the sprig he'd been carrying around for Joy. It'd given him a little extra help in dating her, and he couldn't bring himself to discard it. He reached for it but Erin didn't let go. Instead, their hands came together, connected by the sprig.

He was about to ask what she was doing, but somewhere inside, he knew. His thoughts were struggling to keep up as she pulled the sprig from his grasp and lifted it above his head, went up on her toes, and pressed her lips to his. Her body pushed against him in the movement, and he had no choice but to brace his hands around her waist to keep her from knocking him over.

He stood frozen as she kissed him. Before he could even process or figure out the answer, Erin pulled away and returned to flat feet and pulled the sprig of mistletoe back down to her midsection.

"What was that?" he asked.

She shrugged and looked down at her hands shyly for a moment before returning to meet his gaze. "I guess I just wanted to make sure it was truly over between us. That there weren't any sparks left to fan. Or any reason to fight for what we had."

He remained silent.

"And there doesn't seem to be." Her smile fluttered on her mouth, like a butterfly trying to land but unable to find its footing. "You're in love with Joy now."

Granger didn't hesitate. The answer was immediate in his mind. Yes. He was so in love with Joy. She was the only one he ever wanted to kiss in the moonlight, under the stars, or under the mistletoe.

Erin nodded. "She's a lucky woman to have you. I hope she knows that." Erin's eyes turned glassy.

"It's going to be okay." Granger reached for her hand. "The girls want you here. And so do I. Maybe not romantically, but we can still be a good parenting team. We'll make this work, Erin. I'm not going to turn my back on you."

She sniffled quietly. "You've never turned your back on me. I'm a lucky woman to have you in that regard. And I know it." She handed the mistletoe back to him. "I won't try that again—I promise." She tilted her head and gave him a full smile now. "And just so you know, there were no sparks for me either."

He chuckled. It had been seven long years, and they'd both changed so much. She wasn't a stranger to him like he'd thought this morning. He remembered her, and she was still the woman he'd once fallen in love with— even if he wasn't in love with her anymore. "That's good to know."

"In fact, it was a lot like kissing a dead fish."

Now he gave a full belly laugh that rivaled the one Jack had been putting out in his role as Santa here on the trail. "Is that so?"

"It is," Erin said, teasing him and punching him softly in the stomach. Something loosened in his chest in that moment. Everything was going to be okay between them. Erin had her humor back, and she wasn't going to be rejected by him and run away. She was here to stay for the girls, not him. And he was free to follow his heart wherever that led. "Maybe we can just stick to hugging from now on," she said.

Granger nodded. Then he opened his arms and pulled
her in. It felt like a hello as much as a goodbye. It felt like
a new beginning for both of them.

* * *

Joy was having a hard time breathing as she stood frozen
in the woods, watching Granger with his arms around Erin.
A moment earlier, she'd seen them kiss. She'd seen it with
her own eyes. And while it hadn't looked like the most
romantic of kisses, their lips had touched, and now their
arms were encircling each other.

Joy wasn't about to walk in on this happy moment. If
she did, she might combust into tears. Or fits of anger.
She might find herself in the local jail for Christmas if she
came out of the shadows right now.

Instead she turned and hurried back along the path to
Granger's house. Her breaths were shallow as she walked.
She could feel the sobs collecting at the base of her throat.
And the feeling felt familiar. It was only last year when
she'd accidentally happened on Dan and Nurse Nancy
kissing in his office at the hospital. Joy had been having
cramps. Something hadn't been right. Worry had niggled
in her stomach along with a foreboding feeling that something bad was about to happen.

She wasn't even sure if she'd knocked before stepping
into his office. She'd needed to see him. He was a doctor.
He would know what to do. He could settle her mind and
reassure her that her pregnancy was normal. There was no
reason to be upset. But instead of finding comfort, Joy had
walked in on Dan and Nancy in a heated embrace.

Just like tonight with Granger and Erin.

Joy reached her car and unlocked it with a trembling

hand. The girls were already tucked into bed inside. Mrs. Fields was with them. All Joy needed to do was go home.

The kiss Joy had just witnessed between Granger and Erin wasn't exactly the same as the one she'd seen last year between Dan and Nancy. Tonight's hadn't looked as passionate. Maybe the kiss hadn't meant anything. Maybe Erin had kissed him. Joy wanted to trust that Granger would never cheat on her but that meant distrusting what she'd seen with her own eyes.

Tears dripped down Joy's cheeks. She needed to get out of here before someone knocked on her window and tried to talk to her. Before Granger came back. She got in her car and cranked the engine, not bothering to wait for it to warm. Then she drove home, careful of the icy roads due to the earlier rain shower. When she got home, she peeled off her clothes and traded them for some warm pajamas before climbing into bed.

Chelsea launched on her stomach and stared her squarely in the eyes. *Meow.*

"Granger would never hurt me," Joy told her cat, speaking to herself as well. She knew Granger, and he would never purposely do anything to make her feel the way she did right now. And yet, here she was, feeling like someone had socked her in the heart. Her brain was trying to be rational though, searching for ways where that kiss and hug made sense. No matter what possibilities she came up with, though, they all hurt. Everything hurt. Maybe she was coming down with the flu on top of a broken heart.

Her phone buzzed on her bedside table. She lifted it and read the text from Granger.

Where did you go? I thought we had plans to meet tonight.

She stared at her screen for a long moment as Chelsea swatted her paw at the words. Joy never should've introduced Chelsea to that cat app on her iPad. She didn't know how to respond to Granger's text. His tone was as if nothing had happened. Shouldn't he be leading with, I need to tell you something. Or Don't freak out.

I had a piece of mistletoe with your name on it in my pocket.

Bitter emotion rose in Joy's throat. Did he also have one with Erin's name? Instead of starting an argument, she replied, Sorry to leave so soon. I was tired.

She watched the dots on her screen begin to bounce as Granger texted back.

I can understand that. We can talk tomorrow.

Joy stared at the message. Maybe things would feel different in the morning but right now, since Erin was picking up the girls after school, Joy had no intention of seeing him tomorrow. Or the day after that. She also had no intention of playing the fool again this Christmas.

CHAPTER TWENTY

Granger woke with the sound of birds calling outside his window on the Monday before Christmas. The big day wasn't until Friday, so he still had time to finish shopping.

"Mom is watching us again today?" Abby asked, standing in the doorway.

Granger sat up in bed and looked at her. "Is that okay with you?" He frowned as he looked at his daughter. "I thought you'd be happy about your mom being around."

Abby stepped inside his room and plopped on the edge of the bed beside him. "I am."

"Well, you don't look happy."

She sighed and looked up as she lay back, her hair fanning out all around her. She still looked like a child but her deep sigh and eye roll gave away the fact that she was growing up. "I just thought that when she was here, you'd be here too. Like a real family. Except, whenever she's watching us, you're not here. You're off doing something else. With someone else."

Ah. Granger thought he understood now. "Come here." He tipped his chin up to gesture for Abby to sit back up. She did, and he wrapped his arm around her. "First off, we *are* a real family. We've always been a real family."

Abby frowned. "No. A real family has a mom and a dad. We've mostly just had you."

Granger sucked in a deep breath. He felt like he'd been having various versions of this conversation for years. But he'd have it as many times as his girls needed it. "A family is as big or small as the people you let in. It can be two people or a hundred. It's not about the size; it's about the love. It was you, me, and Willow. And Nana and Papa too. Now your mom is back. Maybe things aren't the way you thought they'd look but we're still a real family, and we all love you and Willow very much."

"What about Joy? Is she part of our family?"

Granger pulled in a breath. That was a tough question, and he didn't want to say or do anything to give Abby false hope one way or another. "Right now, she's a friend of the family. And a very good friend of mine."

"You said family was as big as the people you let in. Are you going to let her in?" Abby asked.

It sounded like a simple yes-or-no question, and maybe it was. He had deep feelings for Joy. He loved her...And love didn't come along every day. She already felt like family to him.

Granger blinked Abby into focus. "What if I did let Joy in? Would that be okay with you?"

Abby took a moment to think. "I really like Joy. And if you're not going to marry Mom again, I think it's good if you marry Joy."

Granger chuckled quietly. "Who said anything about marriage?"

"That's what people do, right? When they want someone else to join their family? Cami at school got a new
mom when her dad married his girlfriend."

Granger nodded. "Well, you already have a mom. So
even if I did...marry Joy, she wouldn't take your mom's
place. She'd be more of a..."

"Stepmom." Abby shrugged. "So I'd have two moms."

"But Joy and I aren't getting married," Granger clarified,
thinking the idea should sound crazy. Joy had only just
walked into his life. He'd been taking the girls to art and
fighting his attraction to her for a year but it wasn't until
last month that he'd invited her into his home. And his
family's Thanksgiving. And into his heart.

Granger swallowed. "You're a good kid, you know that?"

Abby grinned. "So I guess I made Santa's good list
this year?"

"I'm thinking so." Granger stood. "Your mom will be
here any minute, and then I'm heading out. You're okay?"

Abby fidgeted with her hands in front of her. "Yeah. It's
just a few days before Christmas, and my mom is home.
I'm better than okay."

Granger was too. He was heading up Merry Mountain
Farms, and things were in the green. His girls were happy
and healthy. He hadn't heard from Joy today but tonight,
they were going on a real date to the Hope for the Holidays
auction. He wanted to bid on a lot more than a few items
to support the orphanage though. He wanted to place a bid
on Joy's heart.

* * *

Joy glanced down at her phone as it pinged with another
incoming text from Granger. She'd have to respond to him

soon and either call off their date or keep it and confront him about what she'd seen last night. She wanted to give Granger the benefit of the doubt but it was difficult to explain away a kiss on the lips.

Without sending a reply text, Joy shoved her phone back inside her purse and carried her lunch tray to where her mother was sitting at one of the tables. "Hi, Mom."

"Joy!" Her mom looked happy to see her, which took Joy by surprise. "I've missed you."

"Well, you've been kind of busy lately," Joy pointed out.

"Yes, I have. I'm training a new physician right now though. Hopefully, she'll be able to cover some of these emergencies that I get called in for. That should free up a lot of my time."

"That would be nice."

Her mom smiled happily. "It would, wouldn't it? So fill me in on what I've missed in your life lately. I hear you're dating Granger Fields."

Joy took a sip of her soda. "We've been out a few times. That's different than dating exclusively." Maybe Joy should have given herself more time before jumping back into the dating pool. Relationships always ended badly, and her heart wasn't ready for another blow.

Joy's mom reached across the table. "I know Dan broke your heart last year. He's one guy though. Don't let your experience with him taint this new thing you have with Granger."

Joy's mouth dropped. "I thought you were on Dan's side when we broke up."

Her mom pulled her hand away and shook her head. "No, of course not. He's a colleague but you're my daughter. I'll always be on your side. I just want you to be happy."

Right now, there was a deep ache in Joy's chest making it really hard to feel happy. "I want the same for you too, Mom."

Joy met her mom's gaze, recognizing something sad there. If she didn't know better, she'd say her mom felt a deep ache in her own chest. "Mom? You okay?"

"Me? Oh yeah. Your father and I just feel like two ships passing in the night lately." Her mom looked down at her drink for a moment and then back up to Joy. "We just need to make more time for each other. And I guess I need to work on my own happiness."

Joy tilted her head. "You work too much already. And being happy isn't supposed to be work."

"Maybe your father and I should take up art."

Joy laughed. "You could join Aunt Darby and Ray at the community center and take a class with me."

Her mom nodded. "I think that sounds like a wonderful idea. Maybe I'll sign us up."

* * *

After working all day, Granger left his house early enough to make a trip to the Little Shop of Flowers on the way to pick up Joy for their evening out. For some reason, she hadn't responded to his texts today, which left him unnerved. Joy was reliable though. She would have canceled if she wasn't feeling well or if something was wrong. She'd probably just gotten caught up in painting one of her masterpieces.

Granger parked his truck and nearly sprinted into the flower shop, the scent overwhelming him as soon as he stepped inside. He breathed it in as he headed toward the counter.

The shop's owner, Halona Locklear, looked up and smiled brightly. It was good to see her so happy these days. She'd fallen in love with Alex Baker this time last year, and now they were planning a wedding. Maybe that would be Granger and Joy next year.

Slow down, cowboy.

"Hi, Granger. Fancy seeing you here," Halona said. "I'm guessing you want flowers for the lucky lady in your life."

"That I do."

Halona hesitated. "We're talking about Joy, right?"

The question took Granger by surprise. "Of course."

She shrugged, softening back into an easy smile. "I saw that Erin was back in town so I wasn't sure. I know I've heard rumors about you and Joy though. And I think that's great. Joy is so sweet. She comes in here all the time, you know?"

Granger shook his head. "No, I didn't know."

"She gets flowers for her aunt. Sometimes she gets a couple extra bouquets for the other women at Sugar Pines Community Center too. She's such a thoughtful person."

"I did know that part," Granger said. Joy was thoughtful and caring—just as beautiful on the inside as she was on the outside.

"What are these flowers supposed to say?" Halona asked, reaching for her florist shears. "Not that they talk, of course. But different flowers say different things. Yellow roses say you're good friends, and red roses say..." She trailed off.

Granger knew exactly what red roses said. "I'll take a dozen red," he said without hesitation.

Halona's lips formed a little circle. "Oh. Does she know?"

"Not yet. But I plan to tell her tonight."

"Oh my goodness. Well, this is wonderful news. And my lips are sealed. Florists' confidentiality."

"Is that a thing?" Granger leaned against the counter as they talked.

"Totally. You wouldn't believe some of the things I've heard standing behind this counter. None of them I repeat because they're shared in confidence." She lifted a brow. "But I'm hoping that Joy stops in next week to give me the second part to this story. I want to know how she reacts to her roses."

Granger hoped Joy would react by reciprocating how he felt. She'd been unusually quiet since last night though. He'd thought maybe she'd fallen asleep by the time he'd texted her. But she would've contacted him this morning to respond. Something about that wasn't sitting right.

"Give me ten minutes," Halona said, turning to her flower cooler. Granger watched as she set about making a beautiful bouquet. When she was done, he paid, and she wished him luck. He didn't really feel like he needed it. He was already the luckiest guy he knew. At least in Sweetwater Springs.

Half an hour later, he pulled into Joy's driveway. It was six p.m., and the auction would begin soon. He grabbed the bouquet of flowers from the passenger seat and sucked in a deep breath. Then he got out, climbed the steps, and rang the doorbell.

There was a flutter of noise inside before Joy opened the door and looked at him. His smile faltered slightly as he took in her sweatpants and oversize T-shirt. Her hair was a bit of a mess, and unless he was mistaken, she looked like she'd been crying.

Joy folded her arms over her chest, her eyes narrowing. She usually greeted him with a smile and lately a kiss. But not today. "Oh, I forgot to cancel our date," she said, her tone of voice just as chilly as her stance.

Granger cocked his head. "Is everything okay?" Maybe she was sick. Or she'd gotten into a fight with her mom. Was that why she hadn't replied to his texts all day?

"No." Joy's eyes suddenly glistened. "Nothing is okay right now."

"Maybe these will make things better." Granger held out the bouquet of roses but she stepped back. "Joy, you're worrying me." He set the bouquet on the ground beside him and reached for her. She took another step back, letting his arm fall back to his side. "What's wrong?"

Her chin trembled as she gritted her jaw. "Oh, you know, I caught the guy I like kissing his ex-wife."

Every muscle in Granger's body tensed. "What are you talking about?"

Joy narrowed her eyes. She looked as angry as she did sad. "Please don't lie to me, Granger. I deserve better than that."

"I haven't lied to you. Ever." A wave of panic crashed over him. He'd come over here with flowers, hoping to tell Joy how much she meant to him, and now, suddenly, they were at odds.

"Not telling me that you kissed Erin is basically lying. You just didn't think I'd find out. But I saw you and Erin kissing under the mistletoe last night, Granger. I saw you, so please don't deny it."

Granger held up his hands. "You have this all wrong. It wasn't the way you're thinking."

Joy put her hands on her hips, her chin lifting slightly. "I'm thinking she kissed you."

"Yeah. *She* kissed me." Granger was relieved that Joy understood that, but if she did, why did she still look so broken? "I didn't kiss her. I didn't even want her to kiss me."

"But you didn't push her away. I was watching. You didn't even look too unhappy about it from where I was standing."

Granger opened his mouth to speak but no words came out for a long time. He never wanted to be called a liar. He wanted to be completely honest. "For years, I spent every night wishing that Erin would come home. But she never did. She kissed me, and maybe I let her. Maybe I needed to see if there was anything there. There wasn't. For either of us. Nothing at all."

Tears brimmed in Joy's eyes as she looked at him.

"You're the one I want. The only one, Joy."

"You didn't even tell me that you kissed."

"I didn't have a chance. We haven't even spoken since last night."

Joy narrowed her eyes. Then her gaze dropped to the bouquet of roses in his hand. "So you were bringing me flowers and planning to tell me you kissed your ex last night."

Granger hesitated. No, he'd been planning to tell Joy he loved her tonight. But that didn't seem appropriate at the moment.

Joy shook her head. "You weren't going to tell me. How can I trust you after that, Granger? I'm not sure I can."

Granger felt like he was suddenly on trial—and he was. "I'm not sure if I was going to tell you. The kiss didn't mean anything. Nothing at all. And I would never want to willingly break your heart. That's the last thing I would ever want."

"And yet..." Joy's chin trembled again, and he knew she was trying not to cry.

"I have not broken your trust, Joy," he said gently. "If you can't trust me, it's because you've never trusted me. I think some part of you has been waiting for me to let you down."

Joy's lips parted. "You're going to turn this around on me?"

"No. But I'm not the guy you're making me out to be. I'm not the bad guy."

"Well, you're not the good guy right now either."

Granger felt his defenses rise. Here he was with flowers, wanting nothing more than to love Joy, and she was grouping him with all the other people in her life who'd hurt her. Well, he'd been hurt too. "I have spent the last few years wondering what I did to make Erin leave. What I didn't do to bring her back home. And what I've finally realized is that it wasn't me. It was never me, and I'm not going to play that blame game again."

He stepped toward Joy, noticing how her body stiffened. She didn't step back though. Not this time. "I didn't do anything wrong here. The only thing I have done is fall in love with you."

Joy gasped softly.

"I love you, Joy. And you know what? I think that's the real issue here. I think you're scared to trust your heart to someone again. I think you're waiting for the other shoe to drop, and you're ready to believe that's happening now to save yourself the future pain that might cause."

Joy stared at him, eyes misty. A tear rolled off her lashes, clinging to her cheek. He wanted to pull her in but he was pretty sure she wouldn't let him right now.

"Maybe that's true. But things were never going to last between us anyway."

"What are you talking about?" Granger asked. Anger

was rising inside of him, warring with the sudden ache in his heart.

"I just...I'm not ready for any of this. All I ever wanted was a casual relationship. I didn't want the heartbreak. I honestly can't take another Christmas like last year's."

"Nothing about what's going on between us is like what you experienced last year. I meant what I said. I've fallen in love with you. I want a relationship with you. There doesn't have to be any heartbreak this time."

Tears slipped down her cheeks as she listened. She hugged her arms around herself. He just wanted to pull her into his arms and hold her. "There already is, Granger. I cried myself to sleep last night because of you and Erin. My heart hurts so much right now I can hardly breathe." More tears slipped off her eyelashes, making a slow descent down her ruddy cheeks.

She seemed to shiver as she stood there, watching him. Then she shook her head and stepped back. "I can't do this. I just...can't. I need you to go."

CHAPTER TWENTY-ONE

Joy had woken feeling hungover this morning, even though she hadn't had anything more than apple juice before bed. She'd tossed and turned all night and had barely slept a solid hour. Whoever said breaking up was hard to do wasn't kidding. And she didn't plan to let herself go through it ever again.

She'd said that after Dan though. Apparently, her heart had a mind of its own and disregarded any common sense her mind offered up.

She steered her little car down the street and pulled into the public parking space near the Sweetwater Café. She grabbed her laptop because she was applying for the hospital receptionist job this morning. She'd promised herself that she'd open her art gallery this year, and she hadn't. Maybe it was time to get what her parents would call a "real job." It didn't mean she was giving up on her art.

Joy locked up her car and headed down the sidewalk. Maybe fancy coffee would make applying for the position go down better. Perhaps it would take away her heartache over breaking up with Granger too. Joy pushed through the front entrance, immediately accosted by the scent of gingerbread and coffee. She breathed it in as her stomach rumbled.

Emma looked up from the counter and smiled brightly. "A tall regular coffee with our seasonal peppermint creamer coming right up!"

"Sounds amazing. Can I add a blueberry muffin?"

"You got it!"

"Thanks." Joy paid at the counter and then looked for a seat while she waited for her food.

A moment later, Emma slid a cup of coffee and a muffin in front of Joy. "Is it okay if I join you for a moment?" she asked. "Dina offered to watch the counter for me."

Joy reached for her cup of coffee. "Of course it's okay," she said, even though she wasn't in the mood for socializing. She guessed that's what she got for coming to a public place.

"Are you done with your Christmas shopping?" Emma asked. She had her own cup of coffee in front of her and seemed oblivious to the fact that Joy had spent a sleepless night. Maybe Joy didn't look as bad as she felt.

"I make all my presents. I'm almost done." She just needed to finish a painting she'd started for Willow, but other than that, her Christmas list was complete. She might not even see the little girls before the holidays anyway.

"I love homemade presents," Emma said on a sigh. "They're the best. I tend to give café gift cards and specialty coffee grinds as gifts. But that won't work for Jack. I haven't figured out what to give him just yet."

Joy looked over her drink as she tipped it back for another sip. "Christmas is only three days away; you better figure it out soon."

"I know. He's a hard one to buy for though," Emma went on. "He's a man of nature. He likes things you can't buy in the store."

"Maybe wrap yourself up and give it to him," Joy said, only halfway teasing. She waggled her brows playfully, and Emma offered a mischievous grin.

"That's not a bad idea." Then her gaze dropped to Joy's laptop. "What are you working on this morning?"

Joy sighed. "I'm applying for a receptionist job at the hospital, actually."

Emma's brows scrunched. "Really? Just because the store you wanted was leased to someone else?"

"That's not the only reason but it didn't help matters. At the start of this year, I promised myself that I'd find a way to open my own art gallery. It felt like the next step in my career. But that hasn't happened and...I don't know. Maybe it's a sign that I need to do something safer. More practical. I can still sell my artwork on the side." Just like her mom had always told her she could.

Emma tsked. "This café wouldn't be Sweetwater's favorite if I'd allowed myself to be safe and practical. Instead, I'd be working as a store clerk or in a school somewhere. Not that there's anything wrong with that, if it's what I truly wanted to do. But my passion is coffee. I love serving others, and I love being my own boss. Starting up a café wasn't a safe decision but I'll never regret it."

Joy turned to watch the passersby outside for a moment, their arms full of shopping bags. "The difference is things fell into place when you decided to open your café. The opposite has happened for me. The stars aren't aligning perfectly. I just want life to be simpler." Joy blew out a breath. "For my career and my love life."

Emma laughed and reached for her drink. "Don't we all?"

Joy found this curious. "You and Jack aren't simple?"

Emma shrugged. "Not really. But he's worth any challenges that come along. So what's going on with you and Granger?"

Joy laughed but there wasn't any humor in it. "I guess you could say it's complicated. We broke up."

"What? No," Emma said with a growing frown. "And right before Christmas too. Are you all right?"

"Not really," Joy said honestly, surprising herself.

"Well, I know you have your parents but if you need a place to spend the holiday, you can come over to my dad and stepmom's place. Jack and I will be there. His mom and sister are coming too. It's the more the merrier at the St. James house."

Joy smiled, grateful for the invitation even if she didn't plan to take Emma up on it. "Thanks. I'll probably go visit my aunt Darby but I might stop by."

Darby was happy and in love these days though, which Joy was grateful for. She had a lot of things to be thankful for this season, and she was doing her best to convince herself that the application on her laptop screen was one of them.

"Well, I better get back to the counter with Dina. I just wanted to catch up." Emma scooted back from the table and grabbed her coffee. "I mean it. Come by my dad's place if you're free on Christmas. We'd love to have you."

Joy nodded. "Thanks."

Joy guessed Emma knew she wouldn't come because she added, "Or stop in next week, and we'll have coffee and chat again."

"I'd like that." Joy watched Emma wave and walk back behind the counter. She pulled her laptop close and started working on her application, her heart sinking with every word she typed. Was she really going to do this? Sitting behind a desk eight hours a day sounded like torture.

A bell dinged as the front door opened with incoming customers. Joy didn't look up until she heard the familiar voices calling her name.

"Joy!"

Abby and Willow skipped ahead to greet her with a hug.

Joy reflexively opened her arms, laughing as they rushed in. Then she looked up at Erin, who was also standing with them. Joy guessed that was better than having to run into Granger this morning, but not much.

"Hi," Erin said, almost shyly. "The girls wanted to come in for hot chocolates this morning, and I could use a coffee."

Joy released her tight hug on the girls. "It's good here."

"I remember," Erin said. "It had just opened when I..." She trailed off, her gaze moving to the girls. "Anyway, it's good to see you."

"Yeah," Joy lied. Maybe coming out to the coffee shop this morning wasn't such a great idea.

"Mommy." Willow tugged Erin's top. "Can we go ahead and see Miss Emma? She knows what we want. Can we go?"

Erin looked at Abby. "Do you mind taking her?"

Abby looked between Erin and Joy. "Sure," she finally said.

Joy waited for the girls to reach the counter before saying anything more. "Abby is so good about taking care of her younger sister."

Erin nodded and then gestured at the chair that Emma had just been sitting in. "Mind if I sit for a moment?"

"Not at all." Joy watched Erin take the seat.

"I wish I hadn't put Abby in that position all these years

but you're right. She takes great care of Willow. They're really good girls."

"They are," Joy agreed. "I'm sure they're glad to have you home."

Erin swept her hair out of her face, looking down for a moment. "I want to talk to you about that kiss between me and Granger."

Joy's heart stopped. "He told you that I knew?"

Erin looked up. "I'm part of his life again. Part of the girls' lives. I saw him upset, and he told me that you two had broken up."

"Well, when your boyfriend is caught kissing another woman, it's kind of a given that you're going to part ways," Joy said. Her words flew out before she could rein them back in.

"I kissed him," Erin said. "It wasn't the other way around. It was me."

"But he didn't tell me about the kiss either." Joy looked away, turning her gaze outside once more. "He probably wouldn't have had I not caught him... It doesn't matter. It's over between us."

Erin reached across the table, signaling Joy's attention. "I'm sorry I kissed him but I had to know if there was still a spark between us. Maybe that's what he needed too—why he didn't push me away." She nodded. "And now we both know. It really is over between us. I've accepted that. And he has too—a long time ago. I think that's why he didn't tell you about the kiss. It didn't matter to him. It didn't mean anything."

"Well, it meant something to me," Joy said.

Erin fidgeted with her hands on the table in front of her. "Granger is a dream guy. Any woman would be lucky to have him. And he's a good guy. He would never do anything to intentionally hurt you. I know that for a fact. After all I've put him through, he's never been anything less than a great guy to me."

Deep down, Joy knew Granger hadn't meant to hurt her. She also knew he was a good guy. Maybe that's one of the things that scared her. He was real. He wasn't going to let her down.

"I also know that any woman who'd walk away from him is a fool," Erin said.

Joy didn't want to feel sorry for the woman sitting in front of her but she did. "You weren't a fool. You were sick. Everyone knows that."

Erin smiled, this time with more confidence than she'd shown before. "I was talking about you."

* * *

It was two days before Christmas, and the snow was finally starting to blanket the ground. It would be a white Christmas this year. Granger had always found those magical when he was growing up. He used to run through the tree farm, leaving snowy footprints in his wake, making snowmen and snowwomen and knocking them down with his snowball fights.

Granger looked over at Abby and Willow now as they sat at the kitchen table with a couple of sketchbooks that Joy had given them. "Don't you want to go outside?"

"Not really," Abby said. "It's cold out there. And we're finishing up pictures for Joy."

"For her Christmas present," Willow said, looking up with a gap-toothed grin. "She says homemade presents are the best. They're the ones from the heart."

Granger felt a big kick in his own heart. "That's nice."

"When we're done, can we go over and give them to her?" Abby asked, looking up from her work. She lifted a finger to push her glasses up on her nose.

Granger shifted uncomfortably. He didn't want to break it to the girls that he and Joy had parted ways. "I'm not sure. The weather on the roads isn't great right now."

The town got snow every year, and local folks knew how to drive on the roads. He hadn't seen the salt trucks go out yet though, and he didn't want his girls out there if they didn't need to be.

"I'll take the gifts to Joy myself if you want. I'm going out to meet Jack once your mom gets here." Granger was supposed to meet Jack at the Tipsy Tavern, which had become a Christmas tradition for them. The snow had Erin running behind though, which meant he'd be running late as well.

Abby paused what she was doing. "We made gifts for Mom too. I hope she likes them."

"I'm sure she will," Granger said, stepping over and ruffling her hair.

She swatted at him but she giggled too. She was growing so fast. But maybe he had a little more time with her as his little girl. He could hope.

Erin knocked on the screen door.

"Come on in," Granger called.

She shook off her boots on the bottom step before stepping inside. "Hi." She looked at him and then the girls, stepping closer to admire what they had drawn. "Oh, you two are such artists!"

"Joy taught us," Willow said.

Granger searched Erin's face for any jealousy. She just smiled and nodded, continuing to look at the pictures.

"Done!" Abby said, putting her colored pencils down.

"Me too!" Willow added, doing the same.

Granger waited for Abby to growl in frustration at her little sister's constant shadow. She didn't this time. All the frustration she'd felt at the start of the month had dissipated, and for now, she seemed satisfied.

Abby looked up at him. "Now you can take these pictures to Joy."

Granger looked at his oldest daughter. "All right." He didn't plan on going inside Joy's town house though. She'd ended things with him. Unfairly, in his opinion. And one thing he'd learned from his relationship with Erin was that he never wanted to spend his life waiting in vain for someone to return. That took too much emotional energy.

Instead, he'd leave the presents from the girls at Joy's door and text her that they were there. Right after he met up with Jack for drinks.

"I need to head out." Granger kissed the girls' foreheads, collected their artwork, and headed out into the snow. There was just an inch on the ground but by tomorrow there'd be a half foot. He cranked his truck and traveled down the driveway, turning onto the road.

The Tipsy Tavern was only fifteen minutes away. Granger owed Jack a drink after playing Santa at the farm for the last few weeks. Jack didn't drink alcohol so he'd buy him a soda.

Jack was already nursing his first Dr Pepper when Granger took the seat across from him at the tavern table. "There you are," Jack said. "I thought maybe I was being stood up on our Christmas tradition of beer and Dr Pepper."

A waitress walked over and took Granger's order. Once she was gone, he looked at his friend.

"Not skipping our tradition, especially this time. I could use a couple drinks."

Jack pointed a finger. "Not too many. I'm cutting you off at two. When you have too many, you do stupid things."

Granger nodded. "Two is all I need."

Jack frowned. "So what's going on with you and Joy? If you're needing a drink, I'm guessing it's not good."

The waitress put Granger's beer in front of him. Perfect timing. He reached for it and took a sip. Then he recounted the story.

"So Erin kissed you under the mistletoe and Joy saw it?" Jack asked, crunching his ice now.

"That's right."

Jack blew out a breath. "That is bad timing. So she's ticked, and you're in the doghouse?"

Granger scrunched his brow. "For a reason that isn't my fault. Erin kissed me. I didn't do anything to deserve Joy's anger."

Jack chuckled. "Joy saw your lips locked, right?"

Granger nodded. "Yeah. Erin held up a piece of mistletoe and kissed me." To make his point, Granger reached in his pocket and pulled out the sprig he'd been carrying around for Joy's sake. "This stuff grows rampant on the tree farm. It's everywhere."

"But you aren't kissing everyone," Jack pointed out. "Just your ex."

Granger didn't like the way this conversation was going. He'd fully expected a little commiseration from his friend. "Whose side are you on anyway?"

"Yours. Always, buddy. I want you to be happy, and Joy seemed to be doing that for you."

Granger nodded. "But if she's willing to toss away everything over something so minor—"

"A kiss isn't minor," Jack interrupted.

"Are you listening, man? I didn't kiss Erin back. I don't want anything romantic with Erin. I want Joy."

Jack reached for the sprig of mistletoe that Granger was holding, rolling its stem between his fingers. Then he pushed away from the table and stood.

"What are you doing?" Granger set his drink down and watched his friend walk over.

In one quick motion, Jack dangled the mistletoe over Granger's head and bent in to kiss him on the cheek.

"Whoa!" Granger said, nearly falling out of his chair to get away. "What the hell are you doing?" he practically shouted, making a small scene in the bar.

Jack bent over with laughter. You'd think he was drinking more than soda but Granger knew him better than that. "I'm proving a point," he said when he could finally catch his breath. Then he slapped the sprig back on the table and sat back down in his chair, looking proud of himself. "That's how you react when you're kissed by someone and you don't want it to happen. You should've seen your face." Jack started howling with laughter again.

Granger blinked across the table at his friend. He wanted to laugh too but he didn't think this was funny.

"I took you by surprise, and you still had time to fall on your butt," Jack said.

"I didn't fall on my butt."

"Near about. And it would've served you right too."

"I thought you said you were on my side," Granger muttered, reaching for his beer again.

"I am. And sometimes being a good friend is showing you what an idiot you are. Joy has every right to be upset if she sees you kissing your ex. I would've told you to walk too if I were her. And I would only take you back if you came crawling in with an apology. A really big one."

Granger couldn't speak for a moment. He hadn't apologized. He hadn't even admitted that he'd done anything wrong, not even in his own mind. He'd felt justified and put out by Joy for no fault of his own. But now...now he just felt like a jerk. "You're right."

Jack cupped a hand to his ear. "Say that again."

Granger shook his head and stood. "Not happening."

"Wait, you're walking out on our Christmas tradition?" Jack asked, no longer laughing.

"We had our drinks. You had your fun." Granger pulled out his wallet and put down a twenty-dollar bill.

"It was pretty fun," Jack agreed. "Now I can go home to Emma." He stood as well and reached out a hand to shake Granger's hand. "While you go home to a cold, empty bed," he teased.

His friend wasn't going easy on him tonight, and Granger couldn't be more thankful.

Jack was right. He'd been such an idiot. He hadn't done everything he could to avoid the kiss. He'd let it happen. It was as much his fault as it was Erin's. "I'm not going home just yet."

"Going to find Joy?" Jack asked. "Just be prepared to beg, plead, and grovel."

Granger nodded. Now that he'd had some sense knocked into him, he was prepared to do whatever it took to win Joy back.

* * *

The Christmas party at Sugar Pines Community Center was maybe the liveliest in town. If the people of Sweetwater Springs only knew the festivities they were missing here, they'd be breaking down the doors.

But instead, it was just a small group of senior citizens and several women from the LDO and their husbands.

There was a huge live tree from Merry Mountain Farms in the corner of the community center's main room, decorated with lights, tinsel, and ornaments. Donovan Tate sat at the piano in the back, playing Christmas tunes while some of the folks sang along. Others ate the food from A Taste of Heaven catering, the scents wafting in the air and making Joy's stomach rumble.

Joy had busied herself with serving meals for the last hour. Now Darby caught Joy's eye and waved her over.

"Why are you avoiding us?" Darby wanted to know once Joy was standing beside her.

"I'm not. I just didn't want to be a third wheel."

"Nonsense." Darby gestured to Ray on the other side of her. "I see this big lug all the time but I don't see you nearly as much as I used to. I'm just not sure if that's a good thing or a bad one."

"It was busy this month with all the extra Christmas tree workshops," Joy told her aunt.

Darby nodded. "Yes, I know. Were they a success?"

Joy sat in the chair on the other side of Darby. Ray didn't seem to mind sharing his girlfriend's attention. In fact, he looked just as interested in the conversation as Darby was.

"From what I hear, the farm made its normal profits, plus a little extra. Between the live trees, the workshops, the hayrides, and the cider stand, Merry Mountain Farms was hopping this season."

"Oh, that's so nice to hear." Darby reached for her hand and gave it a squeeze. "Will you do that again next year?"

Joy hesitated. "I actually applied for the receptionist job at the hospital," she admitted.

"What?" Darby pulled away as if Joy had told her she was going to prison. "Why on earth would you do that?"

Joy shrugged a shoulder. "I don't know. I guess it feels like maybe it's time. And I can still do my art on the side."

"No, you can't. Art is life. The receptionist job will suck you dry, and there'll be nothing left. Believe me."

Joy offered a wobbly smile. "It'll be okay, Aunt Darby. My dream store on Main Street was just a dream. It's been leased now. It's time to face reality." And Joy was tired of having her heart broken.

"The reality is that you're a talented artist. More talented than I ever was. And you're a wonderful art teacher. You have so much to give, Joy. Don't convince yourself otherwise just to fit into a mold."

Joy met Darby's gaze. "I don't want to disappoint you. Especially on the eve of Christmas Eve."

"You could never disappoint me," Darby said automatically, her voice and posture softening. "You make me just as proud as if you were my very own daughter."

Joy wished her own parents would say how proud they were. But if she wanted to make them proud, she needed to take the receptionist job.

Ray was quiet as he sat and listened to their conversation. Then Darby looked back at him. "Should we tell her now?"

His mouth curved softly. "Good time as any, I guess."

Darby returned to looking at Joy. "We're moving in together," she practically squealed.

"What?" Joy looked between the new couple. "That's a big step," she said, disbelieving her ears.

"Life doesn't wait for those who second-guess. Life is now. I'd say that's especially true when you're my age." Darby looked at Ray. "Ray asked me to move in with him, and all I know is my heart was ready to paint the town red. So I said yes."

"Where will you live?"

"Ray's house is bigger," Darby said.

"Darby will have her own room, of course," Ray added.

Joy felt her brow pinch, and Darby laughed.

"That doesn't mean I have to use it all the time. But I'm used to my own space, and Ray doesn't mind."

Joy held up a hand. "I don't think I need all the details. All I need to know is that you're happy."

Darby leaned over and kissed Joy's cheek. "I'm happy." She looked into Joy's eyes, and Joy could immediately see that it was true.

"You can live with us," Ray offered out of nowhere. "If that would save on your expenses and allow you to lease a store for your gallery."

Both Joy and Darby looked at Ray.

"Aw, that's so sweet." Then Darby threw her arms around his neck and kissed his mouth. "I love you, you know that?"

A broad smile stretched across his lips. "I do know it. But you can remind me as much as you want for the rest of our lives."

Tears pressed behind Joy's eyes. This thing between her aunt and Ray was real. There wasn't any doubt in her mind. "Thank you, Ray. That's an amazing offer but you don't need a thirty-year-old woman moving in with you." They might have their own rooms but Joy suspected that they'd be making good use of every room. "I appreciate the gesture though," Joy said.

"Yes, Ray. You are the nicest man I've ever known," Darby told him.

Joy smiled as she watched, even as an ache moved over the left side of her chest. Despite her fears, she wanted that for herself. She wanted to follow her heart without second-guessing if it would lead to heartbreak. "I better go," Joy told the couple as she scooted back from the table. "I'm happy for you both."

"Thank you. Ray and I will be together on Christmas. Will you come over?" Darby asked. "Or are you spending it with your parents?"

Joy shook her head. "You know they don't really make plans. They're so busy."

"Too busy for their own daughter?" Ray asked.

Joy laughed. "It's hard to compete with saving lives." And she didn't blame them as much as she used to. They could be more loving and doting but they were who they were, and she had to respect that. "I will be going to see them at the hospital tomorrow. And I'll try to make it to your place for Christmas," she told Darby. "Or would that be Ray's place?" she asked.

"My house is our place now," Ray said.

"When we said we were moving in together, we meant effective immediately. We're not getting any younger." Darby winked.

Joy nodded. "Good night, Aunt Darby. Good night, Ray." She waved and then headed into the parking lot, now covered in a soft layer of newly fallen snow. Her boots sank to the earth with every step, her thoughts swirling around in her head and her emotions bubbling in her heart.

She got behind the steering wheel and cranked the car, turning the heat up high. The heater probably wouldn't kick in until she was almost home. She'd make some hot chocolate when she got there and snuggle under a fleece blanket. The thought sounded cozy. And lonely.

Joy pointed her car toward her town house and started driving, still thinking about Darby and Ray and her earlier conversation with Erin. There were so many jumbled thoughts in her head—nothing felt clear.

Then Joy's mind went blank as her car fishtailed and started spinning. She squeezed the steering wheel and tried to gain control of the vehicle. Had she hit ice? It felt like she was spinning forever, her life flashing before her eyes. Then her car jerked to a sudden stop.

Joy clutched the wheel, her breathing just as out of control as the car had been. Her gaze darted to the rearview mirror to make sure she wasn't about to be hit by a car. The road was empty though.

She patted her heart and forced slow, deep breaths as she pulled to the roadside and let her emotions go into their own sort of tailspin. Aunt Darby was right. Life was for now.

She was so tired of being disappointed. In her parents and Granger, but most of all in herself. The person she'd always been was someone who followed her heart no matter what. That's what had led her to quit nursing school and to work to put herself through art school. She fought for what she wanted and never threw in the proverbial towel. And she wasn't going to start now.

She didn't want to be a hospital receptionist. She didn't want to give up on her art gallery, even if her time frame for achieving that goal had expired. She'd put it on her list for next year and wouldn't give up until she succeeded.

And she didn't want to give up on Granger either. What they had was worth fighting for, even if there was a risk she might get hurt again.

* * *

Granger needed to talk to Joy tonight. It was time to grovel like he'd never done before. He missed Joy, loved her, and he didn't want to lose her over his own stupidity.

He pulled into the driveway in front of her town house, noticing the empty space where her car should be. She wasn't here.

He pulled out his phone and considered calling, but last time they'd spoken, it hadn't been pleasant. He should have fallen on his knees in that moment, but instead, his foolishness and pride had gotten in the way.

Granger groaned at the memory. He'd let his past affect his future. That's why this wasn't a conversation that could be had on the phone. It was too important, and he needed to look Joy in the eyes when he apologized. And when he told her he loved her.

His cell phone rang. For a moment, he hoped it was Joy. Then he saw Erin's name flash on-screen. "Hey," he said, answering immediately. "Everything okay?"

"No, I don't think so," Erin said, her voice a little shaky.

Granger's internal alarms started sounding. "Are the girls okay?"

"Yeah, we're just worried about Tinsel. She's not acting right. I think something is wrong with her."

"What do you mean?" Granger watched the rearview mirror, hoping to see Joy's lights pull in behind him.

"Tin is lying down, and she won't get up. And she's whining a lot. I think maybe she's in pain, and I don't know what to do, Granger," Erin said. "The girls are expecting me to fix this, and I can't. I don't want to ruin their Christmas."

Granger didn't want that either. "Just sit tight. I'll be right there," he promised, giving the rearview mirror one last glance before reversing out of the driveway and heading home.

CHAPTER TWENTY-TWO

Granger drove as fast as he could safely get away with, knowing that there was ice on the yet-to-be salted roads. When he got home, he rushed inside, his heart thrumming against his ribs.

"Daddy!" Willow cried, rushing into his arms. Her cheeks were wet. "Something is wrong with Tin! She won't get up or eat or play. If she dies, it will be the worst Christmas ever!" Willow wailed.

Granger gave her a quick squeeze and then peeled her off him so he could assess the situation himself. Hopefully it wasn't as dire as Erin and the girls feared. "I called Chase on the way here," Granger told Erin as he knelt at Tin's side. She was laid out on her dog pillow against the wall. Normally, she'd have met him at the door with her tail wagging.

"Chase Lewis?"

"He's a veterinarian here now," Granger told her, focusing on his dog. Tin definitely looked out of sorts tonight.

With the busy season, Granger hadn't given Tin a lot of attention. The girls had been responsible for looking after her, and from what Granger had seen, they'd done a good job. Tin's food and water bowls had stayed full, and he'd seen them walking her daily around the farm.

But Tin was not in good shape right now. Granger pressed his hand around his dog's belly, palpating it gently. It was round and firm—definitely not normal. Tin let out a soft whimper of pain under the touch, and Granger moved his hand to her head instead, massaging her gently behind the ears. "It's okay, girl," he said softly. "We've got help on the way."

Granger looked back at Erin, who had her arms wrapped around her girls now. It was as if she'd never left. But she had, and things were different between Granger and his ex. But fortunately, kids were resilient. They bounced back, forgave, and forgot.

Granger had forgiven too. He didn't even blame Erin anymore. But he hadn't forgotten the pain he'd felt after she'd left. He still vividly remembered the struggle and his feeling of total inadequacy in raising his small family alone. Love was hard—*so hard*. And yet, here he was plunging into its depths again. He hadn't signed up to fall in love with Joy but he had. And now here he was in pain again.

"Mind getting Tin some water?" Granger asked the girls.

"I'll get it," Abby said, quickly going to the sink.

"Thanks." Granger turned toward the knock on his back door.

"I'll get that," Erin said, moving to answer.

Granger watched over his shoulder as she opened the door to Dr. Chase Lewis. Chase was in his thirties. He'd been a year ahead of Granger in school but he'd always been nice to him. As a teenager, Chase had worked on the farm during the holidays, cutting trees and loading them into customers' vehicles. "Hey, Doc," Granger said, reaching out his hand to shake.

Chase took it but his gaze moved immediately to the patient. "What's wrong with Tinsel?"

"Not sure. She's just lying here. She won't get up to go outside or eat."

Chase knelt beside the dog as well. Granger usually took Tin to the veterinary clinic but it was closed due to the holiday.

Chase palpated Tin's belly for a moment, speaking softly to her as she panted. Usually Tin's tail would be wagging excitedly at the sight of her favorite veterinarian. Chase typically had dog treats in his pockets, and she knew she was only one "good girl" away from getting one.

Not today.

"What's wrong with her?" Granger finally asked, unable to wait patiently anymore. "Is it bad?"

Willow let out a little whimper now from behind them. Granger heard Erin's voice soothe her.

"Well"—Chase looked up, his gaze bouncing from Granger to Erin and the girls—"it looks like your family is getting a little bigger this Christmas."

"What do you mean?" Granger asked.

"Tinsel here is going to have Christmas puppies. Tonight." Chase grinned up at them.

Suddenly Abby and Willow were jumping up and down, cheering so loudly that Granger's parents could probably hear them from across the lawn.

"I want one!" Willow said.

"Me too! Me too!" Abby agreed.

Granger's shoulders rolled forward as he exhaled. Now

wasn't the time to tell the girls that they couldn't have three dogs, or keep however many Tin was going to have tonight.

"Me too," Erin added, her voice softer than the girls', but her face shone with just as much excitement.

Granger met her gaze. A puppy would keep Erin company in her new place. "I think that's a great idea. You'll give one of these pups a good home."

Granger looked from Erin to Chase, just in time to see the veterinarian's frown. Whatever Chase was thinking, he kept it to himself though. Other people's opinions were one of the hurdles that Erin would deal with if she was moving back to Sweetwater Springs. For a while, people would judge her for leaving her girls, for returning, and for everything in between. The folks in town were amazing people but it was human nature to make assumptions and to form opinions before you knew what was truly going on. It wouldn't be easy for Erin but Granger really hoped she'd endure it. And he wasn't going to let her go through this alone. He planned on being her friend through it all.

"How long until the puppies are born?" Abby asked, stepping near Chase.

"Not long. They'll be here before morning. All we can do for her now is make her comfortable and give her a little privacy."

"Of course." Granger got up and started gathering old blankets. They dimmed the lights in the kitchen, leaving just the soft glow of the lit Christmas trees to illuminate the living areas. Granger saw Chase to the door and thanked him again as he left. Then he turned back to Erin. "The snow is still coming down heavy, and it's dark," he told Erin. "You should stay the night. You can take the bedroom."

Her eyes widened. "Are you sure?"

Granger shoved his hands in his jeans pockets. "I'll change the sheets and sleep in the living room to be close to Tinsel."

"Can I sleep with you tonight, Mama?" Willow asked.

"And me too?" Abby added, sounding like a little girl again.

Erin laughed. "I guess that's okay." She looked at him, her eyes going soft. "Thank you, Granger."

"Of course." Then he went about preparing the sleeping areas for the night. He might not get much shut-eye but that wasn't all because of Tin and the forthcoming puppies. His thoughts were circling around Joy too, wondering when he'd see her again so he could apologize and hoping she'd hear him out. After all, Christmas was the season for hope, miracles, and second chances.

And for him, this Christmas, it was also his season of Joy.

* * *

Joy bundled up against the cold and headed out into the snowy Christmas Eve morning. She had a lot to do today. First on her list was meeting her parents at the hospital cafeteria. After that, she intended to find Granger so they could talk.

She got into her car and cranked the engine, letting it warm for several minutes. As she waited, she was very aware of her racing heartbeat.

Last night's fishtailing on the ice had cleared her thoughts on more than what she was doing with her career. It had also set her straight on what she wanted for her life. She'd gone online and had deleted her application at the hospital. Then she'd spent the rest of the night thinking about

Granger. She'd pushed him away because of the kiss—yes. But also because she was scared. Terrified, actually. She hadn't wanted to fall into that dark hole of heartbreak and loss ever again. But she was tough. She could get through anything, as long as she knew she'd given it her all.

She was a passionate woman. That's why she couldn't spend a portion of the day behind a desk. Why she created art. Why she taught others to do the same. And why she couldn't walk away from Granger just yet.

When the snow and ice on her car were melted enough, Joy pulled onto the road and drove to Sweetwater Springs Memorial Hospital. She parked in the parking lot and headed inside to meet both of her parents. Joy traveled down the well-lit corridors toward the big, open cafeteria. It was bustling today with noise and people, and there was the faint sound of Christmas music streaming in from the overhead speakers. Joy glanced around and saw her parents seated at a corner table.

She quickened her pace, heading over to them. "Hi, Mom. Dad."

Her dad stood first and gave her a big hug. He was a tall man, towering over six feet in height. And these days, he was balding—a sign of intelligence, he liked to joke. "You look beautiful," he said just like he did every time he saw her.

"Thank you." Joy looked down at her jeans and sweater and guessed at what her hair must look like after coming inside from the cold, windy weather. If he was saying she looked beautiful right now, then she lost faith in all the other times he'd ever said it.

Joy turned to her mom next. Her mom opened her arms and pulled Joy in as well. Reflexively, Joy inhaled her mother's scent. It wasn't floral or sweet like one might imagine a mother to smell like. Her mom smelled of anti-septic; it was the distinct smell of a hospital.

"Merry Christmas," her mother said. "I'm so glad we could get a chance to see you." She pulled back and gestured at the table. "We already got you a plate."

Joy glanced down at the three full-size meals. "Wow. So you guys have time for a real meal?"

Her father laughed and shared a look with her mom. "Well, it is Christmas Eve," he told Joy.

"I'm sorry I didn't cook it myself," her mother said. "One of these days, when I retire, I will cook the grandest Christmas Eve meal you've ever had."

Joy pulled out her chair and sat down as well. "Who are you kidding? You two love what you do. You'll never retire."

"If you love what you do, you'll never work a day in your life," Joy's mom said.

Joy glanced over with interest. "That's Aunt Darby's line."

Her mom nodded. "Yes, it is. I should have listened to her a long time ago. And I never should have pushed you to apply for that receptionist job here if you didn't want it."

Here we go.

Joy blew out a breath and reached for the tea they'd purchased for her. "So I guess you heard that I pulled my application from consideration." She waited for the *but* in her mom's conversation. Her mom never should have pushed her to apply *but* it's a good job. With benefits. It's practical. Responsible. It's time.

"Actually, I'm glad you pulled it," her mom said instead, surprising Joy. "Your father and I... well, we don't often act impulsively, but..." She looked over at Joy's father, sharing another look. Joy wasn't sure what was happening right now but there was something brewing in the Christmas Eve air.

"What's going on?" Joy asked, looking between them.

"Well, we went to look at some property yesterday," her father finally said.

Joy's mouth dropped. "You're moving?"

"Oh, no, no. We're not moving out of the house that you grew up in. I couldn't bear it. You're my bundle of Joy, no matter how big you get." Her mother beamed across the table at her. It was unusual to see her so happy, which only confirmed Joy's suspicions that something was off.

"Why did you look at property, then?" Joy asked.

"It's an investment property." Her father pushed his glasses up on his nose. "A store on Main Street. The old clockmaker's shop."

Chills rode up Joy's spine. "Oh?" That wasn't possible. That shop had been leased.

"We were thinking about opening an art gallery," her mom said excitedly.

Joy furrowed her brow. Was this a joke? "But you don't make art."

"No, but our very talented daughter does. And who knows? I might need a hobby in my retirement. Maybe I'll take up sculpting or painting."

Joy blinked, trying to process everything her mom was saying.

Then her mom reached for her hand. "I know it was never just a hobby for you. Your father and I both know it. And I know we're a little late but we want to support you."

Joy shook her head, momentarily at a loss for words. "I can't let you buy me an art gallery. I'm not a kid anymore. I'm an adult, and if I want this, it has to be something I do for myself." She looked between her parents, who stared back at her, their smiles subtly slipping off their previously excited expressions.

The disappointment was thick but not because they were trying to force her to do something she didn't want anymore. This time it was because they were trying to support her and she was refusing their help.

But there wasn't anything wrong with accepting help. It was about trust and faith, two things Joy needed to work on.

She took a breath and looked between her parents. "I'll lease the store from you at a fair price," Joy said finally. That's what she'd been planning all along anyway. "And I'll pay just like any other tenant would."

Her mother smiled, her gaze moving back to meet her husband's before returning to Joy. "Of course. And I'll pay for my art lessons just like any other student would."

Joy swallowed back her emotion. "Did I hear you right? Are you retiring, Mom?"

Her mother reached for Joy's father's hand now. "We both are in the New Year. Life needs to be lived, and we're still young enough to enjoy it."

"We've missed out on a lot of time with you over the last few years," her father added. "With our careers and promotions. We don't want to miss any more."

Joy felt her eyes sting with tears. "Well, this is definitely something to celebrate. And if you ask me, it's the best Christmas ever, even if we're having it in the hospital cafeteria." She giggled softly and reached for her plastic fork.

"Next year, it'll be in my kitchen," her mom promised. She wasn't even retired yet but she already looked a lot more relaxed. "And Darby and Ray can come. And you can bring Granger and his girls if you like."

Joy's excitement deflated slightly. She wasn't sure if Granger would still be in her life. Maybe her lack of trust and faith had pushed him away. "That would be wonderful," Joy said, keeping her smile pinned in place. This was her parents' moment, and she didn't want to ruin it by bringing up her problems. "I can't wait."

* * *

"Daddy, can we keep all the puppies?" Abigail asked, looking up at him.

He had just checked on the new fur family and was now sitting down for a minute with a much-needed midmorning coffee. "I think your mom wants to take one with her."

"With her? Where is she going?" Abigail's expression scrunched into one of worry. No doubt she was fearful that Erin would slip away to some far-off place again. Granger had similar fears, although he thought they were groundless. Everything Erin had shown him supported that she was doing well these days.

"Somewhere in Sweetwater Springs. I'm sure she won't be far, wherever she settles down," Granger assured her.

Abigail visibly relaxed. "And Willow and I will split our time between you and her?"

Granger reached for her and pulled her toward him, wrapping her in the crook of his arm like he used to do when she was so much smaller. When had she gotten so big? "You know your mom and I aren't going to be a couple again, right?"

"I know," she said in a small voice.

"But we're going to stay good friends. She is welcome over here anytime. You're never going to have to choose between us. I promise."

Abby hesitated as she seemed to think on this. Then she nodded and reached up to push her glasses higher on her nose. "Okay. But what about the puppies? They don't want to be separated either. They're a family too."

Granger didn't know how to respond to that one. He couldn't have six dogs. Could he? "They're small right now. They aren't going anywhere for a long time. And we'll talk about it later, okay?"

"Dr. Lewis told me that if we name them, it means we're keeping them," Abigail said.

Granger chuckled. He'd have to thank Chase for that little tidbit later. "Let me guess. You and Willow have been naming them already?"

Abby shook her head, a mischievous smile growing on her face. "Not yet. I told Willow we had to wait to see what you said. But I did name the littlest one Miracle. Because I think that's what they are. I also think Mom coming home for Christmas was a miracle. Don't you?"

Granger wrapped his arms around her tighter. He loved his little girls so much. "Yeah, I really do."

Abby narrowed her eyes as she watched him. "I'm not a baby anymore, you know. I know you and Joy are going to be a couple and probably get married one day."

"What?" Granger pulled back. "Where on earth did that come from?"

She shrugged a shoulder. "It's pretty obvious. But I looked under the tree, and I also know that you didn't get her a present. Dad, you have to get the woman you love a present."

Granger looked at his daughter for a long moment. She might still fit in the crook of his arm but she was right. She wasn't a baby anymore. "I do have feelings for Joy," he confessed. "And you're right. I didn't get her a present. It's Christmas Eve though. Not much I can do about that."

Abby thought for a moment. "You have to give her something. No matter what. You could make her a piece of art."

"I'll think about it," Granger said. They talked some more as he finished his coffee and then he checked on Tin and the nameless puppies once more. "You're doing a good job, Tin," he told his dog, rubbing behind her ears. If he wasn't mistaken, there was a look of pride in Tin's eyes. He suddenly couldn't imagine breaking this canine family up, and the farm was big. Big enough for six dogs.

He changed clothes and headed back through the house to get the girls. "Nana is coming over for a little bit. She's going to help you bake cookies for Santa."

"Yay!" Willow practically flew off the couch.

Granger looked at Abby. "I'll see you later, okay?"

"'Kay. But take your time. I can help Nana with Willow."

Granger swallowed back his pride. She and Willow had been through a lot but he had the sense that everything was going to be okay. He hoped the same was true for Joy and him.

* * *

Joy had rarely left Sweetwater Springs Memorial with a smile on her face like the one she wore now. She was so happy for her parents. They'd worked so hard, and they deserved to take time for themselves. And she was looking forward to seeing them more. She also couldn't believe that they'd bought a store on Main Street.

Not just any store. It was the place she had her heart set on. Apparently, the deal with the first potential leaser had fallen through. And when it did, the owner had decided to sell instead. Joy's parents had swept in and made an offer that same day. Her mom had listened when Joy had talked about her dream store. Her parents were finally being supportive in the way she needed, which felt like a tiny Christmas miracle in Joy's eyes.

There was only one other thing that could make this holiday complete. One person who could complete her.

She got in her car and cranked the engine, giving the motor time to warm against the bitter cold. Then she pointed her vehicle toward Merry Mountain Farms. She was going to find Granger, lay her heart on the line, and tell him exactly how she felt. Hopefully by the time she arrived, she'd have the words to articulate what that was. She felt alive when he was around. Invincible. Amazing. Loved.

She was also terrified. Anxious. And a million other things. She felt everything—the whole gamut. But the one emotion she knew for sure was love. She was *in love* with him, and that didn't happen every day. It was rare and special. And worth the risk.

Joy drove slowly, careful not to take another spin on the ice. When she finally pulled into Granger's driveway, his truck wasn't there. Erin's car was, however. And it was surrounded by a layer of thick, untouched snow. Too much to have just fallen this morning. The only explanation was that Erin had stayed the night.

Joy swallowed past her emotions. But she wouldn't let them lead her in this instance. Maybe there was a good explanation.

The door to the house opened, and Mrs. Fields stepped out. She looked over and seemed surprised to find Joy sitting in her car. No backing up and leaving without being noticed now.

"Joy! It's so good to see you!" Mrs. Fields said as Joy got out of the car and trudged through the snow in her direction. "Did Granger know you were coming? He might have forgotten."

"No. No, it was…a surprise." If he'd known, maybe he would've shooed Erin away. Or maybe not.

"Well, he's gone to get supplies for Christmas dinner tomorrow. Won't you come and eat with us? We loved having you at Thanksgiving."

Joy shook her head, even though she wanted to say yes. She couldn't say or do anything without talking to Granger first. She needed to know where they stood. "I really need to talk to Granger. Do you know where I can find him?"

Mrs. Fields's brow dipped. "Maybe the grocery store on Red Oak Street. Or he might be at the pet store getting supplies for our new puppies."

"Puppies?" Joy asked.

"Tin was pregnant, and we didn't even realize it. Isn't that wonderful? We have a house full of puppies."

Joy smiled. "Wow. I'm sure the girls are over the moon."

"Oh, indeed. Between having their mom and a litter of wiggly fur balls, they're just thrilled. They miss you though." Mrs. Fields nodded. "And Granger does too. He'll be back in a couple hours or so."

Joy needed to talk to him as soon as possible though. Preferably without Granger's mom, his girls, and his ex watching.

"You can call him and see where he is, I suppose," Mrs. Fields suggested.

"I'd rather talk to him face-to-face," Joy said.

Granger's mom gave her a knowing look. "Face-to-face is always best. You can wait for him inside if you want. I'm sure the girls would love to see you."

Joy shook her head. "I'll come visit them soon—I promise."

Mrs. Fields reached for Joy's hand. "Maybe tomorrow. I'll set you a spot at the table just in case. Your parents too," she offered.

Joy hugged the woman tightly. "Thank you. If you don't mind, I'm going to drive my car up to the Christmas tree workshop and gather up some of my supplies."

"Of course. And if you change your mind about coming inside, just head right in."

Joy thanked her and then turned. She glanced over at Erin's vehicle as she walked past. Joy wasn't going to jump to conclusions.

If Granger told Joy that Erin had stayed over but it was all innocent, Joy would believe him. She would trust him. A relationship couldn't stand without trust, and Joy wanted a relationship with Granger. She wanted him in her life more than she'd ever wanted anything on her Christmas list before.

She got inside her car and drove it to the Christmas tree workshop. Then she got out and stepped over to the pavement, shaking off her boots before turning on one of the space heaters that they'd set up for her classes.

Not ready to clean up just yet, Joy headed over to the supplies and pulled out a few. According to her aunt Darby when she was growing up, a tree was for all occasions. Birthdays, Christmas, even Halloween and Thanksgiving. Joy righted her wire cage in front of her, and she started working on another tree. Her aunt Darby had always taught her that handmade gifts were from the heart, and Joy intended to use all of hers to make this next one.

CHAPTER TWENTY-THREE

The sun was on the descent as Granger made his way home. He'd swung by Joy's house on the way to Dr. Lewis's veterinarian office but her car wasn't there so he'd stopped again on the way back. Once again, she'd been gone. He supposed she might be visiting family.

He pulled into his driveway at Merry Mountain Farms, noticing that Erin's car was no longer there. Granger got out and headed toward the back entrance, hearing Willow's and Abby's excited voices inside. His heart lifted a notch. No matter what was going on in his life, he was a lucky man. He had two beautiful little girls in his life and parents who supported him fully. There was a lot to be grateful for, even if he couldn't help wanting more. He wanted someone to spend his life with, to experience all the ups and downs with. He wanted Joy.

He stepped inside the house and breathed in the scent of home-cooked food. "Whatever it is, it smells delicious," he said in lieu of hello.

"Daddy!" Willow leaped off her stool and came barreling toward him like a mini hurricane.

He wrapped his arms around her and squeezed tightly. She smelled like sugar and Christmas spices, and he guessed she'd been helping prepare whatever had his stomach rumbling. Abby stepped toward them and joined in the hug, making his heart squeeze even harder.

"What's all this?" he asked on a small laugh. "Have I been gone that long?"

"Yes, and the girls missed you." His mom turned to watch them from the stove, a smile stamped across her face. Her cheeks were rosy from cooking, and her eyes were bright.

"We thought you'd never come back," Willow said. "Mommy has been gone all day too."

Fear gripped Granger's chest. He remembered that Erin's car wasn't in the driveway. Maybe that's why he was getting this exaggerated homecoming. Had the girls' mother already ditched town? "Where's Erin?"

"She left," Abby supplied.

Granger looked down at her. "What? When?"

Abby shrugged, seemingly unbothered. "A few hours ago."

"Is she coming back?" Granger asked, his breaths growing shallow. His gaze snapped to his mom. He didn't want to have to piece together the broken pieces of his girls' hearts this holiday.

"Relax." His mother stepped over. "She's not coming back tonight but she'll be back tomorrow."

It took a few seconds for him to process the new information. Then Granger felt the breath he was holding whoosh out of his mouth. "Tomorrow," he repeated as his shoulders relaxed.

His mom nodded. "Yes. Erin found a place to live. A nice little town house close to where Joy stays. She says it was already furnished and move-in ready. She's there tonight getting herself settled, and she'll be coming back early in the morning. To spend Christmas with us. I told her that was okay. I hope you agree." Her eyes looked suddenly worried.

"Of course." Granger took another breath, in and out. For a moment, he'd thought that Erin had really left. But she hadn't. She was here to stay.

"Did you talk to Joy?" his mom asked. "Will she be coming over tomorrow as well?"

Granger shook his head, releasing his hug on his girls. They stepped away and returned to decorating cookies at the table. "I stopped at her house a couple times but she wasn't there. I tried to call but I kept getting an out-of-service message." And he didn't really want to have this conversation on the phone. He wanted to look Joy in the eye and gauge how she felt. He wanted to be able to pull her into his arms and hold her when he told her he loved her.

"Well, cell phone reception isn't good out there at the Christmas tree workshop, you know. That's probably why."

Granger watched his mom turn back to the stove. She pulled the oven door open and looked at another batch of cookies. How many were they making? "What are you talking about?" Granger asked. "There aren't any classes going on tonight. It's Christmas Eve."

His mom glanced over her shoulder, straightening as she closed the oven's door again. "I think she's still out there. She was there half an hour ago when I brought her some hot cocoa and a couple of our cookies, fresh from the oven."

"Joy is here?" Granger straightened. "She's at the Christmas tree workshop?"

His mom nodded.

"But her car isn't here," Granger said.

"Oh, you probably just didn't see it. She pulled over to the shelter with her supplies. She's making trees out there."

Granger's heartbeat sped up. "Trees? What for?"

"Us, Daddy," Willow said. "She told Nana it was a surprise so we couldn't watch. She's making us our very own tree from her." Willow bopped up and down on her toes. "I can't wait to see what kind of tree she's making for me. I'm going to set it out so that Santa will know exactly where to place my gifts when he comes to our house tonight."

"She's making our gifts because the best gifts come from the heart," Abby added. "Did you get her a gift yet, Daddy?"

"No." There hadn't been time. This holiday season had been a roller-coaster ride. One of ups and downs, magic and wonder. And at this point, he wasn't sure Joy would even want a gift from him. Maybe she never wanted to see him again.

Abby held up a finger. "Wait. I have something you can give her." She turned and ran down the hall toward her bedroom. A moment later, she returned and held out her palm. "It's origami. Joy taught me how to do it during our art class."

Granger stared down at the origami flower made from delicate blue paper. "I can't take that."

"Yes, you can," Abby insisted, her lips curving into a wide smile. "I can make more. Joy taught me how to do it. And I don't want you to mess things up with Joy."

Granger lifted his brows. He didn't want to inform his daughter that he'd already done that in a big way.

"I want her to keep coming back," Abby continued. "We need Joy in our lives. All of us."

* * *

Time seemed to slip away when Joy was creating art. Even if it was something as simple as making these little Christmas trees. She wasn't creating cookie-cutter trees like the ones she'd taught at this workshop all season. She'd worked on making a half dozen trees this afternoon, each one as unique as the person she planned to give it to. Now the sun was dropping behind the mountainous skyline, and the lights that were strung around the covered area twinkled brightly in the growing darkness.

Joy stepped back to admire her work.

Instead of using tinsel and ribbon, the tree that Joy had made for Willow was decorated with artificial wildflowers. Abby's tree was decorated with paper hearts, cut from the pages of old books that Joy had gotten from the recycle bin of the library. Joy had loaded the box of books in her car earlier in the week, planning to incorporate them in some mixed-media artwork of hers. But this was perfect. Abby was going to be so thrilled with her gift.

The tree that Joy had made for Aunt Darby used vine that Joy had collected in the woods beyond the farm. She'd wrapped it tightly around the wire vegetable cage and had used it as a canvas, painting it a dark-blue color with bright-yellow dots to give the appearance of a starry night. The kind that might represent the very first Christmas.

Joy had made Erin a tree too. She doubted Erin had a tree this year. Joy doubted Erin would be receiving a lot of gifts either. And while Joy had cut ribbon and plied wire, she'd also worked through her emotions. Art had always been her form of therapy.

Erin was here to stay, and Joy was happy for her. There was no reason to be jealous because Granger and Erin had both told Joy they weren't interested in each other romantically. Otherwise, she'd make herself miserable.

Joy had needed Mrs. Fields's help to make Erin's tree. Joy looked at it now, her gaze running down the collection of photographs of Abby and Willow. She'd made copies of the originals and had used laminating paper to protect the images so Erin could enjoy the tree for years to come.

Joy looked from one tree branch to another, each reflecting the girls' beaming faces at various times in their lives. They were smiling, happy, beautiful girls. And Joy loved them. She loved their father too.

"Joy?"

Her emotions were already high, thinking about all these people who meant so much to her. Granger most of all. She turned to face him, steadying her breath and trying to keep her tears at bay. She had so many feelings bubbling out of her.

"I've been looking for you. I didn't know you were out here," he said, stepping closer.

"I've been here most of the day." She shrugged. "I came here looking for you earlier."

"And apparently never left." Granger took another step, his gaze fixed on her. "Aren't you freezing out here?"

She shook her head, even as a chill ran through her. "The space heaters are keeping me warm. And I've been working steadily out here. The view makes for good inspiration. I love a white Christmas."

"Me too."

They stood a couple of feet apart, looking at each other. Just a couple of days ago, they would have greeted each other with a kiss. They wouldn't have been able to pry their hands from one another. Now their hands were shoved in pockets or fidgeting in front of them.

There were so many things Joy wanted to say but she couldn't figure out where to start.

Granger blew out a white puff of air as he looked around. "What have you been working on out here?"

Joy looked around as well. "Trees."

Granger smiled back at her. "I thought I was the one in the Christmas tree business."

She cocked her head to one side. "I guess you and I have a few things in common."

"More than a few things, I'd say." He moved closer. She watched him take a breath as a cast of micro expressions rippled over his face. "I was a jerk."

Joy's lips parted. "No, you weren't."

He held up a hand. "I let one of the best things to happen to me in a long time walk away. And I regret it. That's why I've been looking for you all day. I want another chance."

"There's another thing we have in common. That's why I was looking for you too," Joy said. "I should have trusted you when you told me Erin kissed you. I should've trusted myself. I was just…" She shook her head, looking for the right words. It felt like Christmas depended on saying this right. It felt like the rest of her life would be determined by what happened in this moment. "You were right—I was looking for you to do something wrong. I was expecting it."

"Because you've been hurt in the past. It makes sense."

Joy swallowed. "Maybe, but that doesn't make it right.

If we're going to be together, we need to trust each other. I'm sorry, Granger."

He kept his gaze heavy on her. She wanted to look into these eyes for the rest of her life. Was that too much to ask?

"So," he said, "can we maybe start again?"

Joy hesitated and then shook her head. "That's not what I want."

Disappointment flashed across his unwavering gaze.

She reached for his hand. "Starting over would mean erasing this entire December, which has been the best month of my life. This is the month that I fell in love with you. I don't want to lose that for anything."

"Neither do I." Granger grabbed her other hand and squeezed them both. "I fell in love with you too, Joy. Deeper and harder than I ever expected. I've loved every second I've gotten to spend with you, and call me selfish, but I want more. I'm not sure if I'll ever get enough of you."

Joy smiled, feeling an overwhelming feeling of relief and excitement. She went up on her tiptoes to kiss him, stopping short of his lips. "Wait. Not yet."

Granger gave her a questioning look as she laughed, her breaths coming out in white puffs.

"I have a present for you." She gestured for him to follow her to one of the trees she'd worked on today. Like her aunt Darby's tree, this one was wrapped tightly with thick vines from the woods. She hadn't painted this one though. Instead, she'd taken every sprig of mistletoe she could find and had woven them into the folds of the conical structure. "I know you want a mistletoe path for lovers but I thought this year we could have a mistletoe tree. For us."

Granger's smile seemed to grow as he admired what she'd made for him. "A mistletoe tree?"

She nodded. "Do you like it?"

He turned to face her. "I love it. And I have a present for you too," he said, reaching into his coat pocket. He pulled out the origami rose that Joy had helped Abby make. "I know I didn't make this myself but it's still coming from my heart." He held it out to her. "Merry Christmas, Joy."

She took the paper flower, remembering how careful Abby had been in folding the paper. She'd worked with precision, and Joy had been so proud of her. She was such a sweet girl to give it to Granger as a present for Joy.

Emotion swelled at all the implications. Abby accepted her. Willow did too. And Granger wanted her. It was complicated and simple, all at once.

They both looked at the tree again. It twinkled brightly with the mini lights that Joy had strung around it.

"Does this mean I get to kiss you now?" Granger asked. "I mean, I have plenty of mistletoe to help a guy out."

Joy grinned. "The nice thing about being a couple is that we can kiss each other anytime we want. No mistletoe required."

Granger's eyes narrowed. "A couple, huh? That sounds serious."

"Definitely," she said.

The corners of Granger's lips curved. "That's good because you are all I wanted for Christmas this year."

Joy pulled in a breath. Her chest felt full with so many emotions—all wonderful. There was no fear. Not anymore. Just excitement, anticipation, and a whole lot of love. "You are all I didn't know I wanted. And more," she whispered.

Granger looped his arms around her waist as he stared into her eyes. Warmth gathered between them. She could stay here forever and not be cold, no matter how hard the snow came down. "I guess sometimes Santa gets it right."

And sometimes her heart did too. All the time, if she listened closely.

Pressing her body to his, Joy went up on her tiptoes once more, waiting for Granger to dip his lips to hers. Then they shared the first of many magical Christmas kisses to come.

$\mathcal{E}$ PILOGUE

$\mathcal{A}$ million tiny lights sparkled against the dark Christmas night. Joy shivered underneath the heavy burlap blanket that Granger had laid across their laps.

"One last time down Peppermint Path?" He looked over with a handsome smile. It warmed Joy from the inside out. It'd only been one year since she and Granger had started dating but it seemed like forever.

Granger reached for her hand and cranked the tractor's engine, its motor quietly grinding along with the faint sound of holiday music streaming in from the speakers attached to the back for any passengers on the trailer. There were no passengers tonight. It was just Granger and Joy.

They rode for a long time in silence, watching the lights. Tomorrow, Granger would take them down and put them in storage for next year. The big day had come and gone with all of its excitement and wrapping paper. There'd been carols and handcrafted gifts made from the heart. And lots of family and friends, reminiscing of past Christmases.

"This time last year, I was worried that you'd be leaving in the New Year." Granger glanced in Joy's direction. "You told me you were only staying through the holidays."

Joy shook her head. "That was before."

He lifted a brow, pretending not to know what she was talking about. "Before what?"

Joy knocked her body softly against him. "You know exactly what it was before. You're fishing, Granger Fields."

He grinned, carving out deep dimples in his cheeks. "Maybe. But sometimes a guy needs to have his ego stroked."

Joy giggled and tipped her head up to the sky. A million stars danced up there, all for them, it seemed. "That was before you stole my heart like a thief in the night."

Granger laughed lightly. "Oh, I don't remember it that way."

She looked at him again. "No? How do you remember it?"

Granger stopped the tractor, freeing up his hands to take hers. "The way I'll tell the story one day, many Christmases from now, is that *you* stole my heart."

Joy swallowed as chills rode up and down her spine. She loved the thought of being with Granger many Christmases from now.

"From the very first moment I brought the girls into the library for one of your art classes, my heart was yours."

Joy shook her head as a small laugh bubbled out of her. "That's not true."

Granger squeezed her hands. "It is. I knew as soon as I saw you. There was just something in the air between us. A spark. I knew if I spent any amount of time with you, I'd be a goner. I was scared of getting hurt again though. I was a broken man, and somehow you put me back together again."

Joy wasn't sure why she was suddenly crying but tears streamed down her cheeks. "Funny. I thought you put me back together again." She smiled as he leaned in and kissed her softly. His lips were warm and inviting.

"So there you have it—we can argue about what really happened every Christmas from now until we're one hundred. Do you think you can put up with me for that long?"

Joy thought he was joking at first but then she caught the look in his eyes. He was waiting for her to answer him. "You're being serious."

Granger's eyes narrowed. "Yeah. You stole my heart, and I don't want it back, Joy. I never want it back. All I want this year, every year, for Christmas and every other day for the rest of our lives is you."

More tears slipped down her cheeks. She didn't want to cry but she couldn't seem to help herself.

"Are you okay?" Granger asked, his eyes worried.

She squeezed his hands this time. "Better than okay," she finally said, sniffling. "You're all I want for Christmas, and forever too."

"Good." He grinned at her. "I lied."

Joy furrowed her brow. "What?"

"I actually do want one more thing," he said.

Joy started laughing, even as she continued to cry happy tears. "You need to get some new tricks. I know exactly what you have in that coat pocket." She reached in ahead of him, expecting to find a sprig of mistletoe. But this time, her fingertips hit a piece of smooth, cool metal. A gasp tumbled over her lips. "What is this?"

Granger shrugged, his gaze unwavering. "Pull it out and see."

Joy trembled as she brought the ring out of his pocket and looked at it in the starlight. "This isn't mistletoe."

"No. I'm aiming for much more than a kiss tonight."

Joy looked at him. "This is a ring."

Granger nodded. "And if it's too soon, you can tell me to wait. I just wanted to show you that I'm not going anywhere. I'm here to stay."

Joy shook her head. "It's not too soon. It's perfect, actually."

"Yeah?" Granger took the ring from her hand and held it to her finger. "Warning. I come with two little girls and six dogs."

"And I come with one jealous cat," Joy added on a laugh.

"Sounds like one big, happy family to me."

Joy nodded and looked down at the ring as Granger slid it on her left hand.

"It's not homemade but it does come from my heart. This was my grandmother's," he said.

"It's beautiful." Joy wiped away her tears. "I couldn't have drawn up a more perfect ring for myself."

"I'm glad you love it." Granger tipped his head back down to his coat. "Okay, now check the other pocket."

Joy narrowed her eyes. Then she reached into the other side of his coat, and her fingers hit a small sprig of mistletoe. She pulled it out and held it over his head, and then leaned in to press her lips to his. "This is the best Christmas ever," she said, echoing what Willow had shouted out in the living room this morning as she'd unwrapped her presents.

Granger brushed his lips over hers in tiny kisses as he spoke. "Until next year. What do you say? Same time, same place. We can get married right here under the stars on Peppermint Path."

Joy looked around, taking in the idea. "It is pretty magical out here."

"We can make it a small affair for family and friends. You in a white dress..."

She looked at him and smiled. "And you in a checked flannel shirt and jeans?" She couldn't imagine anything more perfect. "I say yes," she said. Then she snuggled in closer, tucking herself into the crook of his arm as they both looked out on the night, dreaming of Christmases past and Christmases to come, and every moment in between.

MERRY MOUNTAIN FARMS'
FAMOUS APPLE CIDER

There's nothing better than a cup of tasty goodness fresh from Merry Mountain's orchards to warm your heart during the holidays! It's the perfect beverage to have while trimming and decorating the tree (hopefully live from our tree farm).

Ingredients:

- 12 medium-size apples (Fuji apples are great for sweet cider. Granny Smith apples are a good choice for those who like their cider on the tart side.)
- 2 peeled oranges (sectioned)
- 2 teaspoons ground cinnamon
- 1 tablespoon ground cloves
- Optional: 1 tablespoon ground ginger and/or 1 tablespoon ground nutmeg
- 1 gallon filtered water
- Brown sugar to taste (the sweeter the better when the grandchildren come to visit!)

Instructions:

1. Wash, core, and slice the apples. Add the apple and orange wedges to a large slow cooker. Add the spices and pour water into the slow cooker until it completely covers the fruit by a good inch.
2. For the patient chef, cook on low heat for 7–8 hours. Added benefit: Your home will smell like Christmas! If you're in a hurry, cook on high heat for 3 hours.
3. After cooking, use a large wooden spoon to mash the softened fruit as much as possible—squeeze out every last

drop! Drain the liquid from the leftover pulp (but save the pulp for homemade applesauce).

4. Time for a taste test. Add more sugar for sweetness, if desired.

5. Serve your cider warm on a cold winter's day. Refrigerate the rest for up to a week. It tastes so good that you'll be lucky if it lasts a day. It certainly doesn't when friends and family come to visit.

> * Don't forget to add the secret ingredient before serving—lots of love! Shhh—don't tell.
> Happy holidays from Merry Mountain Farms!

About the Author

Annie Rains is a *USA Today* bestselling contemporary romance author who writes small-town love stories set in fictional places in her home state of North Carolina. When Annie isn't writing, she's living out her own happily ever after with her husband and three children.

Learn more at:
   www.AnnieRains.com/
   Twitter: @AnnieRainsBooks
   Facebook.com/AnnieRainsBooks
   Instagram: @AnnieRainsBooks

Rosalie Reyes has big plans to open her new pet shop during the Christmas parade. But it seems like Everett Bollinger, the new town manager, is determined to be a Scrooge and sabotage the parade—and her business too. With the help of the local matchmakers and a rambunctious Saint Bernard named Remy, Rosalie is about to unleash the town's holiday cheer and make it a paws-itively amazing Christmas for all.

Please turn the page to read the bonus story *The Christmas Wish* by Melinda Curtis.

FOREVER

To Remington, a loving Saint Bernard who thought your business was his business and made you believe the same.

$\mathcal{P}$ROLOGUE

$\mathcal{H}$ow did it get to be Christmas again so soon?" Bitsy Whitlock organized her cards while her friend's granddaughter serenaded the card players. Bitsy had a pair of threes, an ace of spades, plus a jack and eight of hearts. In other words, *nothing*.

"*Ho-ho-ho. Cherry nose.*"

"Time flies when you're a widowed grandma." Mims Turner set down her cards, casting a grin toward her granddaughter, otherwise known as their songstress—Vivvy, a blond cherub cuddling a plush Santa.

"*Ho-ho-ho,*" Vivvy crooned from her seat on Mims's hearth. "*Cherry nose.*"

Cute as Vivvy was, cute as Bitsy's own grandchildren were, cuteness didn't make up for the empty space in Bitsy's king-size bed. At the holidays, the loneliness of widowhood tended to creep up on her.

"Are we finishing the game now? Or taking a break?" The red-and-green tie-dyed shirt Clarice Rogers wore hung loose on her shoulders compared to the last holiday season. "I think the eggnog needs more nog."

"*Ho-ho-ho. Cherry nose.*" Four-year-old Vivvy sang louder. She'd inherited her loopy blond curls from Mims. "*Gammy, sing!*" As well as her grandmother's take-charge attitude.

"*Hat on head,*" Mims warbled dutifully, with head-shaking, gray-curl-quaking intensity.

"*Eyes so red!*" Clarice sang at the top of her seventy-something-year-old lungs.

"Those aren't the words," Bitsy murmured, staring at her cards.

"Go along with it," Mims urged before singing, "*Special night.*"

"*Beard bright white!*" Clarice may have gotten the Christmas carol wrong, but she got an A for enthusiasm, just like Vivvy.

Won over by cuteness, Bitsy hummed along.

It was Black Friday, and instead of shopping, the three grandmothers in Sunshine, Colorado, were playing poker. There was business to be taken care of in addition to holiday planning. Business that rode on the outcome of their poker game.

Matchmaking business.

Bitsy, Mims, and Clarice made up the board of the Sunshine Valley Widows Club, which was open to anyone who'd suffered the loss of a spouse or partner. But they were playing poker as the sole members of what they privately called the Sunshine Valley *Matchmakers* Club. The winner of the pot of pennies earned the right to decide who they were going to help find love this holiday season.

Bitsy had someone in mind—a young widow who probably laid a hand on an empty bed pillow every night like Bitsy did and wished...

"*Must be Santa.*" Little Vivvy rocked back and forth. "*Must be Santa.*" She got to her feet and danced with her plush Santa. "Gammy, sing again."

Mims obliged her granddaughter, embellishing the song with arm movements and googly eyes that made both Bitsy and Vivvy giggle.

"My eggnog needs more nog." Tossing her gray braids over her shoulders, Clarice hobbled to Mims's kitchen, where they'd left the bourbon.

At this rate, the trio of matchmakers would be passed out on the floor with Vivvy at naptime, game still unfinished. Bitsy was fond of Vivvy but the sweet girl stood in the way of serious matchmaking decisions. If only she could be distracted long enough for them to finish the poker game.

But how?

Bitsy rummaged around in the black leather bag at her feet. She may be thrice widowed, but she was always prepared—Band-Aids, hair spray, clear nail polish, antacids, and... "Vivvy, I have a candy cane in my purse. Would you like it?"

Vivvy gasped, dropped Santa, and ran across the wood floor, blond curls bobbing. She put her little hands on Bitsy's leg and bounced up and down, no longer interested in singing.

Clarice returned with a bottle of bourbon just as Bitsy unwrapped the cane and handed it to Vivvy.

The little angel took a lick and then spun away like a ballerina, chanting, "*I love Bitsy. I love Santa. I love Christmas.*" And then she was silent.

"Back to the game, ladies." Clarice topped off their eggnogs and settled into her chair. "Per the rules, once we start the game, we must finish the game." Clarice was their secretary and the keeper of club rules. She nodded toward little Vivvy. "Nice save, Bitsy."

Bitsy inclined her head. "I think we need to add an event to the Widows Club schedule. Our account balance is low." As treasurer, Bitsy managed club funds. She sipped her eggnog and glanced at the cards she'd been dealt. She had a feeling about that ace. She kept it and the pair of threes, weak though they might be.

"Let's postpone new events until next year." After reviewing her hand, Mims discarded two cards. Didn't mean the club president had three of a kind. She had a tendency to keep face cards, even if they didn't match or were different suits. "I'm warning you gals. I have a good hand and a person in mind who needs Cupid's help."

Cupid, aka the Matchmakers Club.

"You should get better at the bluff." Clarice ran her fingers down one of her long braids and then discarded one card. Just one! She had a competitive hand, all right. "Last game of the year and it's going to be mine."

It wasn't an idle threat. Bitsy's pair of threes were worth nothing. She wasn't going to beat Clarice without some bluffing.

Clarice dealt their replacement cards. Bitsy glanced at hers. *For the love of Mike.*

She'd received another three and a jack.

Why didn't I keep that handsome jack?

Bitsy bit her cheek to keep from frowning. No sense emboldening her opponents. "Are we doing a gift exchange this year?"

Mims rubbed the worry lines from her forehead. She had bubkes, for sure. "I liked what we did last year. Lunch at Los Consuelos."

"Boring." Clarice inserted her cards into her hand. She had something, all right. Either two pair or a full house. Nobody sorted a garbage hand.

Despite sagging spirits, Bitsy kept biting her cheek.

Clarice tapped her cards on the table. "Ladies, are you in or out?"

"I'm in." Bitsy went big, tossing in ten pennies, working the pretense of a good hand.

Mims folded.

Clarice slanted Bitsy a sideways glance. "You're looking to end the game on this hand."

"I've got some shopping to do." Another bluff. Bitsy had done all her shopping online this year.

Instead of folding, Clarice counted out ten pennies. "Let's see what you've got."

The moment of reckoning had come. There would be no more bluffing.

"Three of a kind." Shoulders drooping, Bitsy fanned her cards in front of her. "All threes. Pathetic, I know."

"My hand is more pathetic than yours." Clarice huffed and tossed her cards down. "Three of a kind. Mine are twos."

"I won?" Bitsy couldn't believe it. "With threes?"

"Merry Christmas," Mims mumbled. She'd been on a losing streak lately. In fact, Bitsy couldn't remember the last time the club president had won.

"I got sticky hands." Vivvy flexed her little fingers as she walked toward Mims, candy cane eaten.

With Mims about to go on grandma cleanup duty, Bitsy didn't waste time gloating. "I choose Rosalie Reyes." The widow who reminded Bitsy of herself.

"The gal with the dog?" Clarice sat back in her chair.

"I love puppies." Vivvy held her hands in front of Mims. "Sticky, Gammy."

"Rosalie is the *widow* with the dog," Bitsy confirmed. "She's only just come back to town. I was thinking Doc

Janney would be perfect for her." He was so patient and intuitive. He'd know when a memory of a lost love lingered, and he'd be big-hearted enough not to be jealous.

"It's flu season." Mims stood and gathered Vivvy into her arms, careful of her candy-cane-coated fingers. "Doc Janney is too busy for love this time of year. What about Noah Shaw? He's handsome and—"

"Not ready to settle down." Clarice scrunched her thin features. "What about that new man at town hall? What's his name?"

"Everett Bollinger?" Bitsy couldn't think of a reason why the man wouldn't work except "He seems like a bit of a stick in the mud."

"Scrooge-like," Mims agreed, clapping Vivvy's sticky hands together.

"Scrooge?" Clarice chuckled. "What better Christmas present for Ebenezer than the gift of love?"

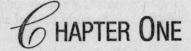

CHAPTER ONE

*E*veryone in town knew Rosalie Easley Reyes.

And today, two days after Thanksgiving, Rosalie was making sure everyone in town *saw* her.

It was snowing, but only just, as if the sky above Sunshine, Colorado, couldn't decide if it should or shouldn't.

Shouldn't, please.

Rosalie walked the length of the town square, trying not to shiver.

Pearl, the oldest waitress at the Saddle Horn diner, came out of the pharmacy bundled up for the cold. "Well now." She handed out one of her rare smiles. "Don't you two have the Christmas spirit?"

"Yep." Rosalie glanced down at Remington, her dog, and kept walking. And walking.

Past the bakery. By Los Consuelos. Down Sunny Avenue. Up Center Avenue and past the dilapidated, empty warehouse. Back to Main Street and around the town square.

She approached the town hall, where the Widows Club

board stood huddled as if planning their next event. They waved.

Shoppers got out of her way. Kids stared. The younger ones stopped playing in the snow in the town square and gawked.

"Are you Santa's helpers?" one of the kids asked, running over.

Two other boys joined the first, cheeks red from the cold.

"We are." Rosalie slowed, risking freezing. Her green flannel elf onesie wasn't as warm as Remington's thick fur coat. "This is Remy." She straightened the Saint Bernard's antlers and smoothed his plush sweater so the words *Merry Christmas from Sunshine Pets* were more easily visible.

"There's no reindeer named Remy," the young ringleader scoffed.

Before Rosalie could answer, Remy did. As dogs went, he was a talker, working his vocal cords up and down the spectrum like a baritone in the opera.

Ra-roo-roo-roo-arumph.

"Yes, Remy. I know." Rosalie leaned down as if imparting an important secret to the children. "Remy says he's no reindeer. He's Santa's dog, here to remind you not to forget your pets this Christmas. They need a gift under the tree too, which can be found right around the corner at Sunshine Pets."

"Subtle." The deep, familiar voice from behind Rosalie was loaded with sarcasm.

And just when she'd been about to hand out pet store flyers for the little tykes to give their parents.

Rosalie turned, bringing Remy around with her so she could face her nemesis—Everett Bollinger, the new town manager and all-around killjoy.

"Hey, kids," Everett said without taking his eyes off Rosalie, "there are free candy canes at the town hall."

The children scampered off.

"Free?" Rosalie gasped dramatically, which in the cold nearly gave her a shiver-spasm.

Everett had been hired to balance the town's budget. Nothing in Sunshine was free anymore.

"To promote the town hall toy drive." Everett was tall, broad-shouldered, and disapproving where he should have been tall, broad-shouldered, and kind. He had the appearance of a nice guy—balanced features, gray eyes behind wire-rim glasses, brown hair threaded with occasional strands of gray. It was just when he spoke that the façade of kindness cracked, and you knew ice flowed in his veins. People in town had taken to calling him Scrooge. "I admit, free candy canes were inspired by your Black Friday promotion."

"But you hated that idea." She'd given out a hundred candy canes on Friday, threading their red-and-white stems through white felt kitten faces. When he found one discarded kitten face in the snow, he'd claimed Rosalie was contributing to litter and had made her stop.

Since she'd opened her pet shop a few weeks ago, Everett had constantly trounced her efforts to market the business. The signs she put up on the way into town were against code. The sandwich board placards she placed on the corner of her street were trip hazards to shoppers. The flyers she'd left on car windshields were against the town nuisance ordinance.

Someone was a nuisance, all right.

Scrooge gave her a tight smile. "I made the candy cane idea fall within Sunshine's guidelines."

"Without branding," Rosalie pointed out, patting Remy's front flank, drawing him closer as the wind from Saddle Horn Mountain whipped though Main Street.

Remy stared up at Everett and spoke: *Aroo-arumph.*

Everett glanced from Remy to Rosalie.

Rosalie gave her adversary a half grin. "Remy says using my idea is stealing."

Everett's mouth formed a grim line.

Too late, Rosalie remembered Everett's history. "I'm sorry I...I shouldn't have said that."

It began to snow in earnest—slow, silent flakes that swirled around them as if trying to block out the kids playing in the snow, the shoppers hurrying from store to store, and the painful memories of the past.

"You should get inside," Everett said in a husky voice.

"Walking my dog isn't against any ordinance in Sunshine." She gripped Remy's leash in her red-mittened hands. "Why are you trying to sabotage my business?"

"Rosalie." Everett moved closer and gave Remy a pat on the head, being careful of his antlers. "You're out here without a jacket, and it's below freezing."

He hadn't answered her question.

"Santa's elves don't wear jackets." Despite her best efforts, Rosalie shivered.

Everett sighed. "Santa's elves have Christmas magic to keep them warm."

Her chest constricted.

He'd mentioned Christmas magic, a clue that there might be a heart buried beneath all that frozen tundra.

Impossible.

Rosalie lifted her chin. "If you want to see Christmas magic, you should come to Sunshine Pets."

He sighed again, but it wasn't an angry sigh. In fact, a smile seemed to be lingering at the corner of his mouth.

She waited for that smile, despite snow and wind and cold. She waited and wondered if his smile would have the same impact as his use of the words *Christmas magic*.

The smile didn't come. "Don't you ever give up, Rosalie?"

"Nope." Rosalie smiled brightly at her adversary because no one ever beat city hall by shouting. "I'm looking forward to our next Holiday Event Committee meeting." The group he'd formed to plan celebrations of holidays year-round. "What time is it again?"

"Monday after you close up shop for the day." Everett left her on the sidewalk and headed toward the bakery.

"See you around." Rosalie breathed easier now that his back was to her. "Come on, Remy. Let's spread more holiday cheer"—and awareness of her pet store—"before I lose feeling in my legs."

Besides, there was bound to be an ordinance against frozen business owners on the sidewalk.

She traipsed around the town square at a good clip.

"Merry Christmas." One of the Bodine twins emerged from the bakery in a T-shirt and brown apron. The Bodine twins were identical, and it was impossible to tell whether this one was Steve or Phil since they both worked at the bakery. "Mr. Bollinger said to give you this." The tall teen handed her a cup with a lid.

Rosalie stopped. "Mr. Bollinger?" *Scrooge?*

Everett was nowhere to be seen in the bakery but the Widows Club board sat at a table near the window and waved to her. A toddler with blond curls and a wide smile sat in Mims's lap, waving too. The group caught Remy's attention. He pressed his face against the glass and gave them a doggy grin.

Rosalie accepted the cup, cradling its warmth in both hands. "Is it coffee?" A latte would be heaven about now.

"Hot chocolate with extra whip." The teen grinned. "Mr. B. wanted you to have something hot and sweet."

"Probably because I'm out here burning off too many calories," she mumbled. "I need the sugar to avoid freezing." Everett seemed the practical sort.

"No, no. Mr. B. said you needed a drink to warm you up and that you deserved something as sweet as you were on the inside." The Bodine boy darted back in the bakery, stopping to talk to Bitsy before returning to his place behind the counter.

Rosalie met Remy's gaze.

Her dog shook his head, a loud flapping of ears that knocked his antlers askew.

The candy canes. The mention of Christmas magic. And now this gift.

Rosalie straightened her dog's antlers. "I think you're right, Remy. It's hard to believe, but I think Everett Bollinger has a heart after all."

"I've gone soft," Everett muttered as he entered the town hall.

He no longer tolerated rule benders and rule breakers. And Rosalie…She challenged him on every ordinance, every regulation.

Which was why it made no sense that he'd spoken to Rosalie about Christmas magic.

At least I had the presence of mind to refuse the Widows Club suggestion that I buy her a hot chocolate. Still…

"I've gone soft," he muttered again as he removed his coat. Soft wasn't in his plans.

"Ev, you are anything but soft." Yolanda, his assistant and the front desk clerk, was decorating a Christmas tree in the lobby. She brushed back her shoulder-length gray hair, revealing dangly Christmas tree earrings. "I have people tell me that every day. Scrooge is the nicest name they call you."

"I'm not taking that personally." Everett hung his coat on a hook by the door, reminded of Rosalie, coatless, with gloves so thin they were unraveling, walking around outside in green long johns and freezing her heinie off. "I was hired to be the bad cop to Kevin's good mayor."

He'd been contracted to increase Sunshine's coffers, something Mayor Kevin Hadley had struggled with because he was a nice guy.

I used to be like him.

But nice guys always finished last. Everett wasn't going to be anyone's nice guy again.

He paused, surveying Yolanda's work. Twinkling lights on twisted cords, shiny balls that had seen better days, small paper snowflakes. Up close, he was pleased with the cost-cutting décor. "Where did you get the tree?"

"Never fear, oh mighty Ebenezer." Yolanda delivered her words with humor, not sting. "It's fake and came out of storage. I didn't spend a penny of the town's money on it. You know, you're taking all the fun out of Christmas."

"I like to think I'm cutting the fat from the budget." And none too soon. But Everett wasn't a total wet blanket when it came to Christmas. He went into his office and returned with a plain brown cardboard box and a simple sign that read, TOY DRIVE.

Yolanda glanced up. "Oh. That's nice. And just when I was convinced that I didn't like you."

"Contrary to popular belief, I don't reject Christmas." Everett placed a tin on the counter with child-size candy canes he'd bought with his own money. "Remember, I signed off on the expenditures for tree decorating in the town square."

"Uh-huh." Yolanda smirked. "Only after the mayor requested it."

Before Everett could reply, a man in his early thirties came in the front door. Beaming, he greeted Yolanda and then introduced himself to Everett with a firm handshake. "I'm Haywood Lawson, local real estate agent. I hear you're the one to talk to about special events."

"This ought to be good," Yolanda muttered, sprinkling the tree with tinsel.

"You want to hold a special event?" Everett leaned on the counter, unable to resist guessing what that event might be—beer fest, outdoor concert, community yard sale? Haywood had a strong grip. Maybe he was the athletic type. "We're in the initial planning stages for a mudder," Everett said. The outdoor obstacle courses challenged competitors physically and emotionally.

"It's not that kind of event." Some of the shine came off Haywood's smile, but then he brought it right back to beam-strength. "I want to propose to my girlfriend in the town square after the tree-lighting ceremony on Friday. The choir is going to be there and has agreed to sing when she says yes."

"You don't need my permission for that." *Or a permit of any kind.* Everett straightened, preparing to retreat to his office and the stack of paperwork that awaited him.

"Whew." Haywood grinned. "I'd heard—"

Yolanda coughed.

"And...um..." Haywood seemed to think better of what he'd been about to say and grinned some more. "Back in the day, my dad proposed to my mom in the town square, and then the town bells rang." At Everett's blank look, Haywood added, "There are bells in the town hall's belfry. They haven't been rung in years."

Everett glanced at Yolanda. "And that would be because..."

"It's a long story," his assistant hedged.

"And yet I have time." Not really, but enough time to hear why the town bells weren't used.

Yolanda gave Haywood an apologetic glance. "The last time they were rung... Well, it was over a decade ago. There was this group of athletic boosters from the high school. They'd been celebrating Kevin's recruitment to play quarterback at Western Colorado University. But they jammed too many people in the belfry, and things got a little... *squishy*... for the occupants as the bell swung back and forth."

Everett sucked in air and held himself still, preparing to hear the worst.

"No one was killed," Haywood was quick to point out, allaying Everett's fears.

"Understandably, we stopped allowing citizens to ring the bell after that." Yolanda made a weak attempt at a smile. "But this is different. We can have someone on staff ring the bell when Haywood pops the question."

That would be very Kevin-like, soft on regulations and protocol.

Everett frowned, not like Kevin at all. "I'd have to calculate the cost."

The pair blinked at him.

"What cost?" Haywood was no longer smiling, not even a little bit.

Everett didn't care. He didn't feel a twinge of remorse for being fiscally responsible. "I imagine this would take a fifteen-minute commitment from a town employee, so an increment of their hourly rate."

"I'll volunteer my time to do the bell ringing." Yolanda gripped the tinsel as if it were Everett's neck. "After all, it's for love."

And what fools did for love…

"I can't authorize that, Yolanda." There was nothing soft inside Everett. Nothing at all. "If you aren't on the clock, if things get…*squishy*…the town of Sunshine will be liable for your injuries—or death, should it go that far."

"It won't go that far." Yolanda shook her tinsel. "It'll just be me and the bell, which will give me about two more feet of clearance in the belfry." ·

Kevin came downstairs from his office. "What's up?"

"We're discussing the fee for bell ringing," Yolanda said darkly. "Things in this town didn't used to be so complicated."

Everett leaned on the counter and brought the mayor up to speed. "There are two issues here: liability for *squishiness*"—he raised his eyebrows Yolanda's way—"and *precedent*. If we ring the bells for Haywood without charge, we have to ring them for every happy couple who walks through our door." *Our.* As if he were staying.

He wasn't.

"Precedent? You mean when our constituents enter expecting a small service for free?" Kevin smiled. He was a politician, and it was a good smile. But it was a smile that had nearly pushed the town into bankruptcy. "That's a good precedent to set."

"I'll pay," Haywood blurted, clearly uncomfortable. "Will fifty dollars do it?"

"I think that's fair." Everett took a candy cane from the tin and handed it to the would-be groom. "And now we know the going rate for bell ringing. Yolanda, can you take Haywood's money and write him a receipt?" He told her which fund to deposit it to. "Kevin, when you have a minute, I'd like a word."

The door opened again. A uniformed deliveryman entered

with a clipboard. "Is there an Everett Bollinger here? I've got a delivery in the truck."

"That's me." Everett reached for the clipboard, trying to remember what he might have ordered and drawing a blank.

"I can't tell you how happy I am to find you," the deliveryman said. Once in possession of his clipboard, he hurried back outside.

"We can talk in my office when you're ready." Kevin disappeared upstairs.

There was a commotion outside, like the sound of fingernails on chalkboard or . . .

It can't be.

Everett's view was obstructed by a tree. He rushed to open the door, facing his worst fear. "I can't accept that." He had to shout to be heard above the scruffy little dog inside a plastic crate, who was yapping her displeasure with hoarse vocal cords.

Tinkerbell hated her crate.

"Too late." The delivery guy thrust the small cage into Everett's arms. "I drove over a hundred miles with her. You signed. She's all yours." He practically ran out the door, calling, "Merry Christmas!"

Yolanda said something Everett couldn't hear over Tinkerbell's protest.

He turned, hoping to be able to read her lips.

"No dogs in the workplace," she shouted, grinning. "Even on Saturdays."

"She's not my dog." But Tinkerbell was his problem.

Everett hurried into his office and closed the door. "Tink, calm down." His ex-wife's dog pressed her button nose through the bars and sniffed. Her little tail wagged over the remains of what looked like a pink sweater. "Come on out." Everett set down the crate and opened the door.

The brown terrier mix leaped out and piddled in the corner.

"Tink," he scolded, grabbing wads of tissue and mopping up the puddle.

Tinkerbell raced around him, yapping. There was no telling how long she'd been in her carrier. A quick search of the crate revealed nothing—no water bowl, no leash, no food. Only the remains of that sweater.

Kevin opened Everett's office door. "Everything okay in here?"

Tink barked and panted and ran in circles around Kevin's feet until Everett snatched her up.

"It's my ex-wife's dog." Sitting on the edge of his desk, Everett poured water into his empty coffee mug and then gave her a drink. "Lydia's mother was supposed to keep Tink while she was...away." Something must have happened.

Tink stretched to lick Everett's chin as if to say, *It wasn't my fault.*

"I'm sure this is just temporary." Everett adjusted his glasses with his free hand.

"I don't know if it should be." Kevin stepped inside and closed the door. "This is just what you need."

Everett was quick to disagree. "Tink is..." High maintenance, like his ex-wife. "I work long hours. It's not fair for me to have a dog." Which was why his ex-mother-in-law had agreed to take Tinkerbell in the first place.

A few scratches behind the ears and Tink stopped giving doggy-shouts of displeasure.

Kevin settled down too, sitting in a chair on the visitor's side of Everett's desk. "Do you remember when we first met?"

"Yes." Everett fought a frown, confused by the change in subject. "At a conference in Denver."

His boss nodded. "You were speaking about the balance between fiscal responsibility *and* community building."

"Yes." That was back before Lydia had been arrested for embezzling from the city Everett had been managing. Before her conviction and the confiscation of 99 percent of their worldly possessions to repay what she'd stolen.

"Hiring you was a risk given what your wife..." Kevin trailed off. He'd been good about avoiding the topic, as had Everett. And then the mayor gave Everett his winning smile. "Hiring you has paid big dividends. You've done a great job finding places where money was leaking or where we can ask our businesses and constituents to pay for Sunshine's services. Your outreach for business development out by the highway has been stellar. For the first time in a long time, there's potential for growth in Sunshine's future."

Everett's chest swelled with pride. When he'd been hired, Sunshine was a town on the verge of bankruptcy. In nearly six months, he'd worked miracles. If he could unload one piece of property from the town books, there'd be a surplus in the budget and a shine to his tarnished reputation. And then he could make a move to bigger things and a bigger town.

"But, Everett, I didn't just hire you to adjust our financial course. What we're lacking here is the balance between the two—financial stability and community services." Kevin's smile sharpened to a point where Everett's pride was punctured. "I need community building, or come the next election cycle, I'm toast."

Everett would be long gone before the next election. "It hasn't all been about the finances. I started the Holiday Event Committee." The goal of which was to add events to Sunshine's municipal calendar that generated revenue year-round. But he'd also put events on the calendar that cost nothing, like Rosalie's upcoming evening dog walk through Christmas Tree Lane.

"You and I both know that's not enough." Kevin had a way of looking at Everett that cut through all the bull. "Yolanda needs to be empowered to grant small, personal requests like Haywood's."

"Like ringing the bells when someone proposes?" Soft. It was soft and lacked the structure to protect the town's economic interests.

Kevin nodded. "Or giving Yolanda more than one hour to decorate the office for Christmas. On a Saturday, no less."

"Strict performance guidelines means no one will shout about nepotism." The way they'd shouted at him after Lydia's crime had come to light.

"I'm willing to foot a few hours' bill to show some holiday cheer." Kevin's tone was cajoling. "The goodwill gained is worth it. Christmas spirit goes a long way around here."

Tinkerbell perked up her ears and tilted her head as if confused.

Everett could relate. "I don't follow."

Kevin stood. "Decorate your apartment's exterior for the season, for one. In a small town like Sunshine, people notice these things."

"But...I'm never there." Except to sleep.

"The bare minimum will do. Put a wreath on the door. Frame your window with holiday lights on a timer." Kevin patted Tinkerbell on her tiny head. "I'm not saying you have to get a tree. Unless of course you're planning to hold one of your committee meetings at your place."

"No." Everett's apartment was plain. Cast-off furniture

and bare walls. As part of the agreement to turn state's evidence against Lydia, he'd had to turn over all their possessions. He'd come here with only a used car he made payments on and a suitcase of clothes. "No meetings at my place."

Kevin stared at Everett's shirt and tie. "And maybe you should loosen up and wear a tacky holiday sweater. I know you have a sense of humor. You should show it."

Everett stroked his designer tie, resisting the urge to try to loosen it. He was holding on to the few things the government had let him keep, his squeaky-clean image not being one of them. "Next thing you know, you'll be telling me to date."

"Great idea. It would prove you have a heart." Kevin moved toward the door. "But Tinkerbell is evidence of that too. It's clear that dog loves you. Why don't you bring her to the office these next few weeks? Show this town what you're really made of."

What Everett was made of was slugs and snails and puppy-dog tails, as his grandmother used to say, reciting a child's poem when he misbehaved. "You don't really want me to bring Tink to work." The noise and prancing would be a distraction.

"I do. I can't enforce a tight budget without some semblance of compassion." Kevin's no-nonsense tone reinforced that the point was non-negotiable. His boss hesitated, hand on the doorknob. "What was it you wanted to talk to me about?"

"Nothing." There was no way Everett was going to broach the subject of end-of-the-year layoffs after receiving a lecture like that.

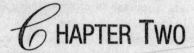

CHAPTER TWO

$\mathcal{T}$he bell over the front door to Sunshine Pets echoed through the store.

Remington turned his big, furry head to see who'd entered but remained seated next to Rosalie, who was lying on her side trying to connect the water supply to a pet fountain. He thumped his tail though, indicating he knew her visitor.

"Rosalie?" Her younger sister, Kimmy, came to lean over the counter.

Rosalie realized she'd been hoping it was Everett who'd entered the store. Sometimes it was the simplest of gestures that touched her. That cup of hot chocolate... Since she'd stopped walking Remy an hour ago, she hadn't been able to stop thinking about Everett. Had she misjudged him?

"This place looks the same as when I left." Kimmy had watched the store while Rosalie was out playing elf with Remy. She ran the deli and lunch counter at Emory's

Grocery store during the week and had been helping Rosalie on the weekends. Kimmy tugged off her green mittens and unwound her matching muffler. "Where is everyone?"

"Everyone as in customers?" Rosalie gave the pipe connector one last, good twist. After adding more ornaments to the store's Christmas tree, she'd tried filling the pet fountain, and water had gone everywhere. No way was she making that mistake again.

"Yes. The sidewalk over by the town square is busy with shoppers." Kimmy shrugged out of her jacket and laid it next to her scarf and mittens on the sales counter. "Stores on Center Street have good traffic. Is it too late to move your business onto Main Street? There's a space open by the thrift store."

It wasn't too late to move. It just wasn't an option. She was emotionally attached to this location. It was on this street that she'd decided she was going to marry Marty. Granted, they'd both been in high school at the time. And granted, she'd never imagined that years later she'd be widowed, her life forever changed by a bullet aimed at Marty and his badge.

"Earth to Rosalie." Kimmy rapped the counter with her knuckles, bringing Rosalie back to the present.

"I made a few sales." Most people seemed to be shopping for their two-legged family and friends instead. "And I've got a great idea to bring in more customers before the tree-lighting ceremony."

Rosalie turned on the spigot, her hand hovering over the handle. Thankfully, the pet fountain filled with a gentle gurgle of water this time, not a leak in sight.

With a soft grumble, Remy stood and lapped water spilling into the bowl.

"Do you know what's missing in this pet store?" Kimmy

glanced around with a twinkle in her eye, fiddling with her long brown hair.

"There's nothing missing." Rosalie caught sight of her reflection in the decorative mirror on a nearby wall. She and Kimmy used to stare in the bathroom mirror and marvel about how much they looked alike. They both had the same brown eyes, the same friendly smiles, and the same long brown hair. But since Marty's death, Rosalie's reflection had changed. Her eyes were flat, and she'd cut her hair. When she looked in the mirror—heck, when she looked out on life—there was something missing, inside and out. And she couldn't quite put her finger on what it was.

"Nothing is missing," Rosalie reiterated, glancing out to the historic fountain on a brick island in the middle of the road before stowing her husband's tools in his beat-up red metal toolbox. The store was perfect. It was something inside of her that was incomplete. "I've got a great variety of merchandise." Collars and leashes. Pet beds and pet food. Key chains, T-shirts, and sweatshirts for humans. Fuzzy pet sweaters and snow booties, like the ones Remy had worn on his walk.

"I agree. You've stocked everything here a pet owner would want." Kimmy straightened Remy's sweater. "Except pets. What about people who don't have a fur baby? Or want another one? Isn't that why you built those enclosures in the front windows?"

It was. But that was Rosalie's expansion plan. She wanted to establish the pet-supply business first. "I don't want to bring in puppies, kitties, or baby bunnies and not have customers here ready to take them home." Because if they didn't find homes by Christmas, Rosalie would adopt them all. Not wise when she, Remington, and Kimmy were sharing the small apartment above their parents' garage.

"I think you should help rescue animals find homes." Kimmy waved toward the door. "And look. It's Eileen Taylor." Kimmy glanced back at Rosalie. "And before you say anything, yes, I asked her to meet me here. She works at that animal rescue on the outskirts of town. You want a business with heart? You can form a partnership of some kind and bring in animals ready for adoption."

On cue, Eileen entered the store lugging two pet carriers. "Merry Christmas, Rosalie."

Arr-aroo. Remington trundled toward their latest visitors, his big, bushy tail wagging.

"Merry Christmas, Eileen." Rosalie grabbed Kimmy's arm and whispered, "I hope you have it in your heart to take on whatever she's bringing in here." In case they failed to find a home for them due to a lack of customers.

"Trust me." Kimmy pried herself free.

"I brought some sweethearts in the hopes you can find them forever homes." Quiet and unassuming, Eileen was a sweetheart herself. She was several years younger than Rosalie and had been rescuing animals since she was a kid. "A pair of lop-eared bunnies the color of cinnamon toast. And a trio of kittens, including a three-legged darling."

"Bunnies and kittens." Kimmy grinned at Rosalie. "No one can resist bunnies and kittens. Just wait until we post pictures on social media."

"Okay." Rosalie relented because the animals were adorable. "If you're willing to trust them to my care, Eileen, we can put them in the window boxes and see if we can't find them forever homes."

While Eileen and Kimmy prepped the window space under the watchful eyes of Remy, Rosalie unpacked her latest delivery—holiday pet sweaters.

The front door opened, and Everett walked in.

All three women stopped what they were doing to stare. He stared back, adjusting his glasses and studying them as if they were an exhibit in the zoo. Remington meandered up to greet him, sniffing the air like a bloodhound.

Rosalie found her voice. "Can I help you?" Because he hadn't come bearing a gift of hot chocolate.

"Yes." Everett didn't sound happy. He unzipped his thick red jacket, revealing a small Yorkie mix with a happy dog smile and long, thin hair. "I need to equip my dog."

"You have a dog?" Kimmy blurted, cradling the three-legged gray tabby to her chest.

Rosalie couldn't fault her sister's outburst. She hadn't taken Everett as an animal person at all. Up until this afternoon's hot chocolate treat, he'd been Scrooge.

"Clearly, I have a dog." Everett drew the little thing from inside his jacket and held it to his chest with one arm. "This is Tinkerbell."

The dog shivered against what was certainly the cold outer lining of Everett's jacket. Remy stretched and touched his nose to Tinkerbell's delicate toes.

"We'll start with sweaters." Rosalie fought to contain her excitement. She could sense the opportunity for a big sale because Tinkerbell had hair, not fur. She'd need a wardrobe to keep warm. Waving Kimmy and Eileen back to pet duty, Rosalie leaped into action. She held up a small red sweater with a Christmas tree knit on the back. "I just received some thick holiday pullovers. But I also have plain pink fleece."

Everett winced at the word *pink*. He joined Rosalie at the box of sweaters and touched the red one. "I'll take this and a black fleece, if you have it."

While Rosalie hurried to check her display for a fleece jacket in Tinkerbell's size, Everett moved to the rack of hanging leashes, followed by Remy.

Rosalie could contain her grin no longer. Sunshine was a small town, and Everett was a prominent figure who made the local rounds. If she outfitted Tinkerbell well, it'd be great promotion for the store.

"I don't have black fleece but I found a red one." Rosalie placed her find on the sales counter, sweeping Kimmy's jacket, scarf, and gloves underneath.

"That'll do." Leash in hand, Everett moved to the aisle with bowls. He selected a set of copper ones, which weren't cheap. This was going to be her best sales day yet.

"Dog food and pet beds are mostly on the back wall." Instead of joining him, Rosalie went to the display of leather-soled dog booties and selected a pair, adding it to the pile on the counter.

Facing the choices in bagged dog food, Everett set Tinkerbell down.

Yap-yap-yap.

Tinkerbell raced toward the pet fountain. She stood on her hind legs and stretched over the edge but she was too short for a drink because the water level was still low. Continuing to bark, she hopped in. She cringed and barked louder as the water splashed her.

Eileen rushed to the little dog's rescue. The last thing she needed was Everett annoyed because his dog was being made fun of.

Garumph-aroo. Remington moseyed over and put one foot in the water, as if in solidarity with Tinkerbell.

"Oh, no you don't." Rosalie grabbed the Saint Bernard's collar and urged him back while Tinkerbell continued to let them know she wasn't happy.

Yappy-yap-yap-yap.

"Tinkerbell," Everett chastised, carrying a bag of premium dog food toward the counter, "get out of there."

The small dog faced her master, yaps targeted at him.

"She's stubborn," Everett said loud enough to be heard over Tinkerbell's complaints. He paused at a display of pet beds.

"I think she's just anxious in a new place." If he wasn't going to make a big deal out of his wet dog, neither was Rosalie. She plucked a small towel with Christmas wreaths from a nearby rack and then picked up Tinkerbell and dried her off.

As soon as the dog was in Rosalie's arms, she quieted.

When Everett joined them at the register with the dog food and a fuzzy brown pet bed, Rosalie set Tinkerbell on the floor and then held up a bag of dog treats. "These too?"

Everett nodded. While he paid, Tinkerbell barked and pranced adoringly around his feet.

"Thank you for the hot chocolate earlier." Rosalie rang up his purchases. "That was very thoughtful."

Everett opened his mouth but hesitated a moment before answering. "You say that as if you didn't think I had it in me." He stared down at his canine chatterbox with a long-suffering sigh.

"I've always thought you had kind eyes." Rosalie wanted the words back as soon as she'd uttered them.

"Kind eyes? My self-image is shattered," Everett said. But there was a look in his eyes or perhaps the beginning of a smile on his face that belied that statement. He picked up his dog and scratched behind her brown, silky ears.

Over at the window, Kimmy and Eileen were grinning.

Remy sat near Everett, glancing from Tinkerbell to the man with an occasional contented rumble deep in his chest. It was an approving sound.

If Rosalie had been able to growl in her throat, she'd

have been doing it too. "You know, with a little work, Tinkerbell would get over some of her anxiety."

"Tink is untrainable." There was mutiny in Everett's tone, as if he was daring her to contradict him.

"No dog is untrainable... if their owners can be taught." *Right back at you, Scrooge.*

Kimmy made a strangled noise and tried to hide behind a kitten snuggle.

"Owner training?" Everett raised a brow. "Your dig is duly noted." He zipped Tinkerbell into his jacket as he headed for the door. "Can you deliver my stuff to my apartment after five thirty?"

"Yes." Everett didn't tell her his address, and she didn't ask. This was Sunshine. She knew where he lived. His apartment was in a small complex. His door visible from the street. But... he'd left all his purchases on the counter. "Don't you want to bundle Tinkerbell up and put on her leash?"

"You'd be surprised what I want," Everett grumbled as deeply as Remy but he stared at Rosalie when he said it, pausing with the door open.

A gust of wind rushed in.

But Rosalie's goose bumps had nothing to do with the cold.

"You need to grow up, Tink." Everett strung lights in his apartment window while Tinkerbell ripped apart the cardboard wrapper they'd come in. "You might get a day or two at the office but then it's home alone for you."

Tinkerbell tore a long cardboard strip free and then abandoned it to pounce on the empty light-timer box. Everett knew as soon as she lost interest in the cardboard, the barking would begin again.

The barking...

Tink had yapped up a storm the day Lydia had been arrested. The terrier had barked her upset at the world until her voice was a raspy squeak. And Everett had sat in a kitchen chair holding her as they'd led Lydia away, as the rug of his life had been yanked from beneath him.

"You can be on your own," Everett told Tink. He plugged the colorful Christmas lights into the timer. They came on, racing around his window frame like a video game in an arcade. "You can be quiet and a good dog." Just as Rosalie thought Tink could.

Rosalie. The petite beauty was a dreamer. She probably still believed in pots of gold at the ends of rainbows. He should have confessed that he hadn't been the one to buy her a hot chocolate. What had the Widows Club been thinking to treat her in his name? He'd heard rumors of their matchmaking but one look inside her store with its pampered-pooch merchandise and Everett knew he and Rosalie were like orange juice and toothpaste.

Tink stood, ears forward, cardboard dangling out of half her mouth.

Footsteps sounded on the stairs.

Yap-yap-yap!

Tinkerbell bounded toward the door, destroyed boxes forgotten on the carpet.

Yap-yap-yap!

The little dog stood on her hind legs and pressed her front paws on the door, only to drop back down to all fours, circle, and continue to bark.

The doorbell rang.

Everett scooped Tink into his arms. Immediately, the barking stopped. He opened the door.

"Nice wreath." Rosalie swung the bag of dog food

inside and followed it in, closing the door behind her and depositing a bag of goods next to it. "You left the price tag on it though." She glanced around, eyes widening.

The apartment was clean but dated—from the kitchen cabinetry and countertops to the used furniture he'd bought locally when he'd moved here.

"You were expecting a black leather sofa and glass coffee table?" He raised his brows in challenge.

"You aren't a stereotypical bachelor so why would I expect you to furnish your place like one?" She plucked Tinkerbell from his arms and knelt with her next to his dog supplies. "Honestly? I expected antiques covered in white sheets." She tugged the Christmas sweater over Tinkerbell's head.

"You expected Scrooge's mansion." Not a question. This Scrooge thing was going to haunt him until he left Sunshine.

Rosalie guiltily raised big brown eyes to his face.

"I know what people call me." He didn't much care what the populace of Sunshine thought of him. But Rosalie? For some reason, he cared about her opinion. "So you think of me as Scrooge too." Also not a question.

Rosalie tugged Tinkerbell's sweater into place and didn't answer.

He stared down at Rosalie's short, dark hair. It curled around her ears. And her long, dark lashes curled across her cheeks. And her optimistic determination tried to curl around his heart.

Don't go there. She thinks I'm Scrooge.

"I think my feelings are hurt." He hadn't meant to say that. He hadn't meant to say anything. He adjusted his glasses but he couldn't adjust his response toward her.

Rosalie stood, cradling a merry-looking Tink and flashing a half grin. "You have feelings?"

"If we're doing inventory of what I possess, you can start with a dog." Everett tried to smile, as if this was one big joke. But there'd been so little to smile about in the past eighteen months that he was sure his expression was on the fritz.

"A dog is a fine place to start after what happened to…" Her half grin flatlined. "Sorry. I didn't mean to bring up your past. I don't like it when people remind me of mine."

More than his smile was broken. There was his pride too. But the remnants of his pride also made him tell her, "You can say it." A part of him didn't want her to. A part of him wanted to believe that Rosalie hadn't searched out his history online. "I'm not running from what happened."

That wasn't exactly true. He wasn't running but he was regrouping.

And it was working. His shock over Lydia's crimes no longer haunted his dreams. He didn't wake up feeling hollow every morning. He had a reason to put one foot in front of the other.

Cuddling Tink close, Rosalie searched Everett's face as if looking for something she'd lost.

Being a man who'd lost everything, he knew her search would come up empty.

Sighing, she set Tinkerbell on the floor.

Tink began to bark, sounding like a broken record.

Almost without thinking, Everett bent to return her to his arms.

"You should really do something about that," Rosalie said unnecessarily.

"My ex-wife got Tink a month or so before she was caught." Everett stroked Tinkerbell's small head. "I think Lydia was worried things were about to go south. She had a doctor prescribe the need for a therapy dog." Which was literally a whole different animal than this one. "She carried Tink everywhere."

"And now you can't put her down." Rosalie nodded. "We can fix that."

We.

Everett stilled, aware of the warm woman who smelled of Christmas trees a few feet away, the small warm dog next to his chest, and the warmth blossoming where his heart used to be.

He should point out that there was no partnership between them, no *we*.

He should point out that he wasn't looking for anything long term, no *we*.

Instead, he said, "My wife's hobby was dressage."

"That's an expensive hobby." Rosalie opened the dog treats. She held a nugget in one hand where Tinkerbell could see it. With the other hand, she pointed her index and middle finger at her eyes. "*Watch.*" The word came out like a growl.

Tink's ears pitched toward Rosalie, and she stared at her with bird-dog-like intensity.

"Good girl." Rosalie gave Tink the snack and then brushed a hand over her head, touching Everett's arm in the process.

Her touch immobilized him. It made his heart race. It was irrational. Rosalie was a permanent resident of Sunshine, a business owner. She had roots, whereas he had no intention of staying.

"Dogs want to have a purpose." Rosalie dug out another treat and said in that same growly voice, "*Watch.*" Repeating the hand gesture toward her own eyes.

Again, Tink's attention focused on Rosalie. Again, she

received Rosalie's praise and the snack. Again, Rosalie's hand brushed over Everett's arm.

His lungs burned from a lack of air. He couldn't move, not even his eyes. He couldn't remove his gaze from the delicate lines of her face.

"We just need to give them a role in our lives—companion, protector." Rosalie took Tinkerbell from him and put her on the floor, where the dog immediately began to yap and romp at their feet. "*Watch*," Rosalie growled.

Tink stilled, staring up at Rosalie.

Everett stilled, staring down at Rosalie.

"Good girl." Rosalie knelt to give Tink a treat and praise.

All that affection…

It wrapped around Everett and made him long for a comfortable couch in front of a blazing fire with Rosalie by his side. He cleared his throat and straightened his glasses, trying to bring order to his wayward thoughts. *I'm too old for infatuations.*

Maybe Kevin was right. Maybe Everett should date. He could spare a night or two out, and there was probably a single woman in town his age who was looking for casual company.

As soon as Rosalie stood, Tink started barking again, albeit half-heartedly with one eye on her.

"You try, Everett," Rosalie said above Tink's complaints, pressing a small dog treat into Everett's palm. Her fingers were as soft and warm as the look she gave him. "Use a rumbly voice to tell Tink you're the top dog here and she needs to keep an eye on you instead of barking so much."

Everett didn't have much faith in the exercise, but he dutifully said, "Tink, *watch*."

The little stinker sat down and panted at him.

"Wow, look at that." Everett laughed.

When he didn't immediately give Tink the biscuit, she stood and barked at him. Once. Sharply.

Everett started to give her the reward but Rosalie stayed his arm.

"Tell her to do it again." Rosalie gave his biceps a squeeze, and even through his dress shirt he could feel the unexpected strength in those small fingers. "Repeat the command, and then be fair and feed her if she earns it."

Tinkerbell waited for Everett to speak, watching him the entire time. It hardly seemed fair, like she knew the drill. But since the dog was staring at him when he said, "Tink, *watch*," he gave her the treat.

"It's a miracle," he said. Now he could take Tink to work with fewer concerns that she'd disrupt the workplace and derail his carefully reconstructed image. "You're a lifesaver, Rosalie."

Before she could say any more, before he said something he'd regret to her, and before Tink could have another meltdown, he ushered Rosalie out the door.

And when she was gone, his apartment seemed as sterile and unaffected as before.

Except for the vaguest impression—like the scent of a Christmas tree—that warmth and happiness had been within reach.

"What took you so long?" Kimmy asked when Rosalie climbed into the passenger seat of her older-model car.

The gray, three-legged kitten was asleep in Kimmy's lap. Rosalie's sister had fallen for one of Eileen's furry orphans and was taking her home.

"I was about to text you to see if you needed rescuing." Kimmy smirked. "Or more time with that handsome man. Spill. Which was it?"

Remy's curiosity was in sync with her sister's. From the back seat, the dog nuzzled Rosalie's shoulder, emitting a grumble as soft as the snowflakes falling on the windshield.

"I gave Everett some dog-training tips, that's all." Rosalie wasn't going to admit he'd shared some insight into his past. If she told her sister that, Kimmy would get ideas about romance and second chances. Rosalie was at peace with widowhood, her plate full with the launch of Sunshine Pets.

Kimmy's gaze searched Rosalie's face, as if she already had romantic ideas and was looking for proof. "I'd hoped Scrooge was asking you out."

"Please. Let's not go there." Rosalie could admit to herself that she felt attracted to Everett but the last thing she wanted was for her sister to latch onto the idea. She'd never hear the end of it. "Does Everett look like the kind of guy who'd ask the delivery girl out?"

"No." Kimmy backed out of the parking space. "He looks like the kind of guy who'd overthink a first kiss." She pulled out of the parking lot and turned toward the south side of town and home. "He has that intense stare. I saw him stare at you back at the store. I can imagine how it'd be. Your gazes would linger while the wheels of his brain would turn."

Holy how-to-read-a-situation. There had been prolonged gazes.

But Kimmy wasn't finished. "And you'd be staring into his eyes waiting to see what would happen, because you're polite and a little clueless."

And because I'd be slow on the uptake, focused on the dog.

"And then Everett would swoop in for a kiss you'd have had no inkling was coming."

Rosalie resisted the impulse to touch her lips and give her sister's fantasy credence. Nevertheless, the notion of kissing Everett had been planted in Rosalie's mind.

The clouds above them parted. A star twinkled in the velvet sky. A single star as bright and shiny as Marty's love for her had been.

Her eyes burned with tears.

My future wasn't supposed to be like this. In my thirties. Alone. Starting over.

But it was. And even the memory of her dead husband's love couldn't wipe away the attraction she felt for a quiet man with a loud dog.

"Or I could be misreading the town Scrooge completely." Kimmy laughed, unaware of the tenor of Rosalie's thoughts. "After all, I'm the woman in the car who's never been married."

CHAPTER THREE

"It's my first meeting, so I brought fudge." Bitsy Whitlock set a plate of fudge in the middle of the town hall's conference room table and sat next to Rosalie.

Everett liked Bitsy. Fudge. No more needed to be said. He hadn't had dinner yet.

"And I brought dog treats." From her seat next to his, Rosalie passed a small plastic bag to Everett. Despite the upbeat impression made by her green Christmas sweater with Rudolph's blinking nose, Rosalie seemed tired. Her big brown eyes had circles under them that were nearly as dark as her short hair. She opened her mouth to say something and then paused and cocked her head. "What's that sound?"

Everyone on the Holiday Event Committee went silent. Muted yapping could be heard down the hall.

"It's...uhh..." Everett wondered how he could phrase the truth without looking like a jerk. "I put Tink in time-out in the bathroom with a dog chew." Because she panicked in her crate, and regardless of what Kevin said, Everett needed to project a businesslike impression with his committee. "The *watch* command you taught me only worked during the first hour this morning. And before you judge, she's only been in there about ten minutes." He'd waited until the last possible moment to put Tinkerbell away, hoping she'd take a nap.

"Oh, poor thing." Rosalie stood and swiped the treat bag. "Moving is super stressful for pets. I'll get her."

"Make sure you bring my guilt back with you too," Everett called after Rosalie, who quickly returned with Tink barking excitedly at her feet.

Everyone admired Tinkerbell and her holiday sweater, not seeming to mind her prancing about and yapping. Finally, Rosalie sat between Bitsy and Everett with Tink in her lap. The little dog wagged her tail and stared adoringly at Everett until he gave her a friendly pat, and then she was all about the dog treats Rosalie slipped her.

"We'll start with the events this month before moving on to events for the first half of next year," Everett said, dragging his attention back to his agenda. "This Friday is the tree-lighting ceremony and—"

"The Widows Club usually sells hot chocolate." Bitsy extended the full plate of fudge in front of Rosalie and toward Everett.

Finally.

Everett extended his hand. And then the meaning of Bitsy's words sank in, and he paused midreach. "Did your club pay the city for a permit?" He didn't recall one being issued.

"No." The warmth left Bitsy's tone. She withdrew the plate. "We donate all proceeds to charity."

"That doesn't mean you don't need a permit." Everett

spoke slowly and deliberately, the way he did when he suspected someone wouldn't be happy with his enforcement of a law.

Rosalie leaned toward Bitsy, slanting Everett an it's-coming-back-to-bite-you smirk. "Town hall has declared the tree-lighting ceremony a commerce-free event. Everett wouldn't let me hand out free dog biscuits that night or flyers about my organized dog walk through Christmas Tree Lane."

Tension balled in his chest. Rosalie was making him out to be a heartless ogre. "I explained—"

"Everett nixed me too." Paul Gregory nodded. He ran an extermination business in town. "I was going to pass out magnetic chip clips with my logo."

Everett had no problem explaining town ordinances to Paul but he wasn't going to be the one to tell the man that a cockroach logo on a chip clip was in poor taste.

"What the Widows Club does isn't commerce." Bitsy's smile stiffened, and she drew the fudge into the circle of her arms. "It's charity. I can't remember a year the Widows Club didn't sell hot chocolate at the tree-lighting ceremony. Permitless, I might add."

Everett glanced toward the mayor's wife, who was his boss's eyes and ears on the committee.

Barb raised her finely arched brows as if to say, *If you're picking an argument with the Widows Club, you're digging your own grave*.

If that wasn't an indication of the power and popularity of the Widows Club in Sunshine, Everett didn't know what was.

"Perhaps we can make an exception for charity," Everett allowed carefully, eyeing the fudge. "I'll have to check with the mayor."

Bitsy passed the treats away from Everett to Paul.

"Moving on. There will be a marriage proposal at the end of the tree-lighting ceremony," Everett continued, giving Tink more pats despite her sitting in Rosalie's lap. He was finding he couldn't resist the tiny dog's big, pleading eyes. "And the bells will ring when the proposal is accepted."

"How romantic," Bitsy said.

"Super sweet," Rosalie agreed.

"That seems to be the consensus." Stomach growling, Everett eyed the plate of fudge, which was being passed around the table and had only a few pieces left. "Moving on to the Christmas parade. Did we garner enough volunteers for the event, Paul?"

"Yes." Paul waved a sheet of paper. "Volunteers will be stationed at the high school, where the parade begins, and at the town square. The latter is the toughest job since volunteers have to make sure when the parade ends, everyone disperses quickly and efficiently. We don't want a backup like we had last year. It took over an hour to unclog the streets and sidewalks in the center of town."

"I have a suggestion." Rosalie raised her hand. "Why not have the parade wind around the town square and end on Sunny Avenue?" Where her shop was located. She smiled her unflappable smile, tired though it was. "It eliminates the logjam."

And showed favoritism to businesses on Sunny Avenue. Everett's spine stiffened.

"What a lovely idea." Bitsy patted Rosalie's arm. "Isn't that a lovely idea, Everett?"

Everyone was agreeing it was a lovely idea, just like everyone agreed ringing the town hall bells after a marriage proposal was romantic.

Everett fought back a frown. "I'll have to conduct

an analysis and run it by the mayor for final approval." Heaven forbid Everett found some cost associated with a new parade route.

"I'm sure everyone will appreciate the change." Barb was as open to pleasing constituents as her husband was. "It makes things easier on the *community*."

Everett didn't miss her hidden message or the gentle reminder that Kevin wanted to strengthen their community.

"Oh, and don't forget the Widows Club has a hot chocolate stand in the town square during the parade too." Bitsy's voice was as gentle as her smile. "Benefiting charity, of course. And speaking of which, we work a wrapping booth for charity at the local mall. Please don't tell me we need a permit for that."

The local mall being a three-story brick building on Main Street housing multiple small, independent retailers.

"No permit for that," Everett reassured her.

The fudge plate bypassed Everett and returned to Bitsy with one piece remaining. "We'd appreciate you volunteering for a wrapping shift, Everett."

How could he refuse? Unfortunately, it didn't earn him that last piece of fudge.

Next on the agenda was the committee's homework—compiling ideas for Valentine's Day. They did a good job creatively—from wine tasting in the local library to a Cupid-themed scavenger hunt with the town's businesses. The group was a bit deflated when Everett pointed out that none of their ideas required town hall's formal participation.

"Remember that we want events to build both a sense of community and Sunshine's coffers." Everett's comment was about as well received as Scrooge telling Bob Cratchit he could put only one lump of coal on the fire.

They finished the meeting by talking about Sunshine's Easter Egg Hunt. The committee felt it should continue to be free. Everett disagreed. Had none of them checked the price of eggs recently? Rather than argue, Everett tabled the decision pending financial review and made a mental note to seek sponsorships to offset the cost of eggs.

"Rosalie, can I have a word?" Everett asked after he adjourned the meeting. "About the parade..."

Perhaps having heard his words, Bitsy turned at the meeting room door and stared, holding the plate with that one last piece of fudge wrapped in cellophane.

"About the parade..." Everett lowered his voice and moved closer to Rosalie.

"You're going to veto my suggestion." Rosalie put Tinkerbell on the floor.

Yap-yap-yap.

Tink raced around the meeting room, from Bitsy to Everett to Rosalie and back again.

Yap-yap-yap.

Everett caught Tink as she circled his feet, bringing a welcome silence.

"You shouldn't pick her up." Rosalie crossed her arms over her chest. She plucked the small dog from his arms and set her down once more. "Let me tell you why ending the parade on Sunny Avenue is a win for you." She barely paused to take a breath before making her argument over the sound of Tinkerbell's barking. "There are charming and historic features on Sunny Avenue, places that are great for selfies and to start conversations. The lamppost clock, the barbershop pole—"

"The bench dedicated to the town's founding fathers," Bitsy cut in, also at a near shout.

Rosalie nodded. "The historic fountain in the middle of the street."

"And what should I tell other businesses on other streets?" His head began to pound from the shouting required to be heard. It had been an all-day occurrence, after all—people shouting over Tinkerbell's barks. "What should I tell the businesses that aren't going to have a parade finish nearby?"

Tink showed no sign of quieting, although neither did Rosalie.

"Tell them you'll end the parade elsewhere next year," she said.

"That's a brilliant idea." Bitsy moved to Rosalie's side.

"And fair." Rosalie nodded. "Plus the parade will look like a well-orchestrated event. This is a win for you and town hall."

The pressure to agree closed in on him. Simultaneously, the pressure to hold his ground kept his shoulders square.

Yap-yap-yap.

The soundtrack of his life lately. His temples pounded harder.

"I tell you what." Rosalie started to smile, as if preparing to sweeten the pot. "You're obviously too busy and stressed to make a decision now." She gestured toward Tink, who'd stopped running the racetrack and was prancing in front of Everett. "Let's take her for a walk to Sunny Avenue. You can see it through my eyes, and I'll give you some more training tips."

"Do not offer me free training," he said quickly. No way would he allow himself to be put in a situation where it might look like he was playing favorites. "I'm open to tips." From one business associate to another. Unable to stand her barking anymore, he picked Tink up. "I'll walk with you, Rosalie, because this dog needs an outlet. This has nothing to do with the parade or comped services."

"Of course not." Rosalie was quick to agree. "Why don't you suit up Tinkerbell in her booties? I'll go get Remington. He's still at the store."

Rosalie hurried out the door before Everett's stomach growled again.

"I'm so glad you two found common ground." Bitsy handed him the last piece of fudge and wished him a Merry Christmas.

CHAPTER FOUR

The temperature was falling. Rosalie's breath created visible clouds.

But the cold couldn't reach the warm feeling of excitement inside her. Everett was considering changing the parade route, which would help build store awareness and sales. That explained her eagerness, not the fact that she'd be walking with Everett.

She rounded the corner and saw him standing outside the town hall holding Tinkerbell.

Remington gave a soft grumble and picked up his pace.

"Put her down and let's walk," Rosalie instructed when she was a few feet away.

"Are you sure?" Everett glanced around. "I tried to walk her this morning, and she wouldn't stop barking."

There were several shoppers entering and exiting stores. They greeted Rosalie warmly, frowning at or ignoring Everett. He didn't seem to mind being snubbed but it bothered her.

"Put her down." Rosalie shoved thoughts of Everett aside, focusing on Tinkerbell. "Once we get in a rhythm, she'll quiet down."

Tinkerbell didn't prove Rosalie's theory. She yapped her way down the block next to Remington, who pitched his ears forward as if he was inwardly wincing. Likewise, Everett hunched his shoulders higher up toward his ears with each step.

"You know," Rosalie shouted above the barking as they neared a corner, "dogs can sense when your stress is off the charts."

Everett blew out a breath. "If that's true, old Remington should be woofing nonstop like Tink."

"What do you mean?" She patted Remy's shoulder, not breaking stride. "I'm perfectly fine."

"Liar. You look like you haven't had a good night's sleep in weeks." They turned down a street toward Sunny Avenue. Everett glanced at her. "I've always heard starting a business is stressful. Go on. Admit it. It's not like anyone can hear us above Tink."

Before she could deny she was stressed, Tinkerbell stopped barking.

"Do you hear that?" Rosalie asked, grinning.

"No," Everett grumped. And then he looked down. "Oh."

"That is the sound of a happy dog." One that didn't bark. "Maybe you're the one who needed a walk. Are you feeling less stressed?"

"That's a chicken-and-egg question." His lips rose in an almost smile. "Did our walk relieve my stress? Or am I more relaxed because of Tinkerbell's silence?" He stared at her the way Kimmy had described. Lingering. Thoughtful.

Is he thinking about kisses?

Rosalie had trouble breathing.

"And what about you?" he asked. "I've seen you walk all over town with your dog. Why?"

"Besides the fact that he needs exercise, I…" She shouldn't say anything. "I…" For sure, Everett didn't want to hear about her feelings. "I wake up angry," she said anyway.

Everett's eyebrows arched.

"I'm angry at the kid who shot my husband, although I ache at the thought of him spending his life in prison." Rosalie should stop there but she couldn't. The anger that interrupted her sleep had invaded her mouth. "I'm angry at my husband for letting his guard down while on patrol, although he died doing a job he believed in and that makes me proud. And—"

Aruff-aroo.

Remington didn't like it when she released all these messy emotions. He crossed into her path, slowing her down.

Rosalie guided him back to her side. "And I'm angry with myself for wanting Marty to pick up an extra shift." She patted Remington's shoulder again. "I wanted to buy a new dining room table. I shouldn't have cared what we ate on. I should have been patient or found something used online. I should have been happy with what I had, because now what I have is anger and regret in the middle of the night."

They approached the corner at Sunny Avenue. All the landmarks came into view—the clock, the barbershop pole, the wrought-iron bench and historic street fountain.

Everett's silence said more than words. She'd made him uncomfortable.

Rosalie slowed and measured out an impromptu sales

pitch. "This street is as wide as those around the town square, providing plenty of parking. And it's charming, don't you think?"

His gaze roamed the street. "I hear the fountain doesn't work."

Rosalie glanced up at Everett. "My husband hit the fountain years and years ago." The day she'd decided she was going to marry him.

Everett's eyebrows resumed the surprised position. "Joyriding?"

"He was learning how to drive, and I was walking our family dog."

"You stopped traffic." There was a teasing note in Everett's voice.

She elbowed him gently, as if they were longtime friends. "I had fewer miles on me then."

"You don't have many miles on you now."

Her cheeks heated. "But they're hard miles. I feel older than thirty-four."

Kimmy would be crowing at Rosalie fishing for Everett's age.

"Wife of a cop. Widowed." He shrugged. "Fair mileage."

He wasn't going to tell her how old he was? She tried to tell herself it didn't matter. She wanted him to change the parade route, not make a pass.

"Age is relative," Everett added slowly, coming to a stop in front of her store. "The day after Lydia was arrested, I could barely bring myself to get out of bed. Coming here...Let's just say I feel much younger now." He may have been looking at her shop but he didn't seem to see anything.

The chalkboard sign invited folks in. The bunnies and kittens were cuddling as they slept. The Christmas tree lights twinkled next to pet-themed ornaments. It was a beautiful façade.

She caught sight of his reflection in the window. He wasn't smiling.

His reflected gaze met hers. "I understand the anger. I understand sleepless nights and second-guessing. But what happened . . . You can't change that. You have to move forward with a more careful tread."

Watch your step.

The reason for all his rules became clear. She'd read about his past. His wife had been a city's longtime controller. He'd been hired to straighten the finances, same as in Sunshine. And according to the press releases, his wife hadn't stopped stealing after he'd come on board. She hadn't watched her step but Everett now made sure everyone around him watched theirs.

Tinkerbell barked impatiently, prancing. By unspoken agreement, they resumed their walk. They rounded another corner, heading back up Center Avenue toward the town square.

Everett slowed, staring across the street at the vacant warehouse.

"Does the city still own that warehouse?" At his nod, she said, "I've always thought it would be cool to turn that place into loft apartments with shops or restaurants below."

Before he could answer, a group of high school kids drove by in a car with the windows down, singing the *five golden rings* line at the top of their lungs. The rest of "The Twelve Days of Christmas" faded as they turned at the next intersection.

"Kids." Rosalie chuckled, although it sounded bittersweet.

"Lydia didn't want to have children," Everett admitted quietly, squelching Rosalie's desire to laugh. "Her horses were her babies. And then Tink, of course. Afterward, I was grateful we hadn't been parents. What do you tell a child about their mother when she goes to jail? What do you say when..."

"Their father is killed in the line of duty?" The words came out on a tight thread because Rosalie was angry about being childless too. "We always felt like we weren't at a place to afford children yet."

Aroo-ruff. Remington had something to say about that. Or perhaps he thought she'd said too much already.

They reached Main Street. The town square was dark. The trees wouldn't be lit until Friday. But the stores along the town square were open late, shop lights warming the sidewalk. Townspeople were bundled up and scurrying about with shopping bags. For them, it was just another normal holiday season.

But for Rosalie and Everett...

"There's something about you..." Rosalie couldn't look at him. "I tell you things I should keep to myself." Things she hadn't even told Kimmy.

"Who says I don't want to listen?" Everett took her hand, the one that didn't hold Remington's leash. He slid his thumb over the hole in her mitten, touching her skin with his bare hand because he didn't wear gloves. "Or that I didn't want to be heard?" He stared into her eyes. There was no Scrooge, no ice, no frozen tundra.

Rosalie held her breath. Was he thinking about kissing her?

Why was *she* thinking about kissing *him*?

Somewhere nearby, a child belted out an energetic rendition of "Must Be Santa."

Somewhere, deep in her chest, Rosalie's heart belted out a strong cadence of attraction—*him, him, him*.

It's okay to move on. Marty's voice, as if he were reading a line from the love letter she'd found after he died.

Rosalie sighed.

"I'll see you around." Everett released Rosalie and walked toward the town hall. "Here's hoping you don't wake up in the middle of the night angry."

Rosalie stood staring at his retreating back, unable to move.

What was happening here? This morning he'd been Scrooge, more concerned with pennies than people.

It didn't matter what she'd thought of him this morning. The attraction…It wouldn't go away. It validated her hunch that there was more to Everett Bollinger than what he showed others.

Snow began falling. Several inches were predicted to come down before morning, enough to cover their footprints in the sidewalk and conceal all evidence that indicated Everett Bollinger had a heart.

Yap-yap-yap.

No matter how much Everett walked Tink, she was still yappy every time he put her down when they were inside.

"*Watch.*" He gave her a treat and then walked out of his office to the printer to collect the pages of a proposal for the town council to sponsor a mudder. The costs associated with setup were minimal, while the entry fees would generate much-needed income. Building and housing values in Sunshine were stagnant and had been for years, which meant tax dollars didn't increase when the town hall's spending increased. And then there was the vacant warehouse.

When Kevin's father had been mayor, he'd purchased that warehouse from a friend and proposed developing it into a second mall. The rents were supposed to pay the mortgage, and then tenant sales were going to be taxed. He'd claimed it'd be legal double-dipping. But while they were remodeling the building, there'd been a fire and a worker had died. Several years and one lawsuit later, the abandoned warehouse was a rock around the town's neck.

Kevin couldn't find a company who'd be willing to invest in the building and Sunshine. Without a buyer, the path to a balanced budget was nearly impossible. And without a balanced budget, the town wouldn't qualify for federal funding, which they needed to provide residents with other services.

Yap-yap-yap.

Tink pranced around his feet in her holiday sweater. She followed Everett back to his desk, where he put her in her pet bed, currently residing on the corner of his desk.

Feeling masculine much, Bollinger?

He'd seen Rosalie every morning and every night as they walked their dogs. They'd call out hello and by mutual agreement head in opposite directions, as if they regretted the confidences they'd shared on their walk around the block.

I regret it.

And yet his thoughts drifted toward Rosalie when he clipped on Tink's leash. Would she be out walking? Was the hole in her mitten unraveling further?

Unproductive, these thoughts. Not to mention soft. He was the hatchet man, not the mayor.

"Of course we still have places in the parade," Yolanda was telling someone in the outer office.

Everett pressed his lips together. The deadline for

inclusion in the parade had been the Wednesday before Thanksgiving. Deadlines were rules and meant to be honored. He stood up and put Tink on the ground.

Yap-yap-yap.

"*Watch.*" Everett gave her a treat. Crunching the kibble, she followed him happily to the service counter. "Late entry?"

Twin teenage boys stood at the counter with paperwork and cash. They were the same boys who worked at the bakery after school.

Yap-yap-yap.

At Yolanda's frown, Everett scooped Tink into his arms.

"We forgot to turn in the paperwork." One teen tried to look contrite but he was doing a bad job of hiding a smile.

"It's for our FFA club at the high school," his twin said, doing a better job of looking meek and apologetic. He elbowed his brother.

"You're letting them in?" Everett fixed Yolanda with a stare. "Were you going to charge them a late fee?"

Yolanda had a hard stare of her own, one he'd been on the receiving end of from her all day. "You want to charge a late fee to students?" She crossed her arms over her chest and *tsk*ed. "During the holiday season?"

"We just want to make it right," said the first teen.

"Yeah," echoed his twin. "Just because we screwed up doesn't mean the rest of the kids should suffer."

Kevin would have given them an understanding grin and relented. Everett wanted to refuse them entry, teach them a lesson about responsibility, and send them on their way.

"We brought a toy." The first teen dug in his backpack and put a new Frisbee in the toy drive box.

It was the only thing in the toy drive box.

"You're gonna make them pay a late fee when they brought a toy?" Yolanda made another disapproving noise, strong enough to send her Christmas tree earrings swaying. "I need to consult with a higher power. And I don't mean God." She meant Kevin. She picked up the phone and punched in Kevin's extension.

"Hang on." Everett pushed down the phone button, blaming his sudden soft spot on Rosalie, who was kind to everyone. "I think there's a lesson to be learned here."

Yolanda's eyes narrowed.

"Boys." Everett fixed them with a no-nonsense smile. "We're trying to build a stronger sense of community in Sunshine. You missed the deadline to sign up for the parade, late or otherwise."

"Here we go," Yolanda muttered, picking up the phone once more.

"But..." Everett waggled a finger at Yolanda. "I'm willing to make an exception if you help us with the town hall toy drive." He rattled the near-empty box.

"You'll waive the parade fee completely?" Yolanda asked suspiciously.

"We'll take their fee, and if they fill this box with toys by the tree-lighting ceremony, we'll let them be in the parade."

"Toys in lieu of a late fee?" Yolanda still looked dubious.

"Exactly." Everett nodded. "No one gets special treatment around here."

Except maybe Tinkerbell.

CHAPTER FIVE

"You know, this is ridiculous." Rosalie stopped on the corner of Sunny and Center Avenues and called across the street to Everett. It was Thursday and the third night in a row she'd seen him walking Tinkerbell after she closed for the night. "We're the only ones out here walking dogs. We should walk together."

The sheriff's car drove slowly toward them. It had snowed earlier, and the roads and sidewalks were slick. Sheriff Drew Taylor waved to them both as he passed. He had one of his deputies in the passenger seat.

"I don't think walking together is a good idea," Everett said, but he crossed the street toward her anyway.

"Why? Because you haven't decided about the parade route? You know it's a good idea."

Oo-oo-aroo.

"And Remy agrees with me." Rosalie patted Remy's shoulder.

Everett stopped a few feet away, staring at her. "And

this is why I don't walk with you. I don't like to talk shop after hours."

"Please." Rosalie turned toward the south end of town and home. "You don't walk with me because you have your secrets, which you don't want to tell."

"And you have yours." He fell into step beside her. "Which you don't want to tell."

Rosalie could feel his gaze upon her face, as tangible as a caress. Her pulse quickened.

"The circles under your eyes are gone." Everett looked ahead. "You've been sleeping well."

She had been. Their conversation had loosened anger's hold on her dreams. "And you've been up to your old tricks in town."

He glanced at her. "Tricks?"

"Blackmailing kids into supporting the toy drive. Charging another couple to ring the bell after they become engaged in the town square." Rosalie whistled, long and low.

Both dogs perked up their ears.

"What is it with you and money?" Rosalie gently bumped Everett's arm with her elbow. "If I didn't know better, I'd still believe all the talk about you being Scrooge incarnate."

"Do you know what it takes to keep a town financially healthy?" Everett stared down at her through his glasses. It was the icy stare he'd often used on her prior to buying her that hot chocolate. "Much less to make it grow?"

"Nope." She was as immune to icy stares now as she'd been then. "I barely know what it takes to make a business grow."

"I was hired to get the town's finances in order." Each word he uttered was as sharp as a fresh icicle.

She nodded, still immune. "And you're doing a good job."

Everett's gaze thawed. "Did you have retail experience before opening your store?"

They stopped at a corner, waiting for a car to pass before crossing.

"Nope. I worked as a nine-one-one dispatcher before I moved back home." Rosalie slowed for an icy patch of sidewalk. "I worked at the Feed Store at first but Victor Yates treats pets like livestock." It had bothered her. "To me, pets are part of the family."

Ga-rumph.

Remington slid a few inches. Rosalie led him onto the fresh snow on her uncle Mateo's front yard. It was slower going but less slippery.

"Pets are family. Your attitude explains everything wrong with your business." Everett picked up Tinkerbell and fell into step behind Rosalie. "You've got too much heart invested in your store."

Too much heart? Those were too similar to Marty's words.

"Rosalie?" Everett was waiting for her defense.

She shook off the lapse. "You're supposed to be passionate about your business. The things I stock are meant to bring love to pet families and in turn that love overflows into the community."

Remy grumbled, which she took to be agreement.

"What I meant was, your margins are too low because you're too worried about selling to your friends." The ice was building in his tone.

"My margins aren't too low." Were they?

"They are. Lydia bought those same copper bowls for Tink in Denver for over fifty dollars. You had them marked at thirty-five. And don't give me the excuse that this is

Sunshine." He pointed at a Mercedes SUV as it drove past. "Folks have money here. Let them spend it."

"I'm not Scrooge." And she was getting by. She'd used some of Marty's life insurance to get the store started, plus some from a family investor. She was saving money by sleeping on Kimmy's couch. "I don't need to fleece people and fill my home with lots of *things*." Expensive things, like dining room sets.

They crossed another street, continuing south. Walking single file. Not talking.

Bright lights adorned houses. Glittering Christmas trees were featured in front windows. Everywhere she looked there was color and life and holiday spirit. It was just inside her that the colors were a bit muted, life less sparkly, her holiday spirit a bit forced. Maybe she'd been working too hard.

"I've hurt your feelings," Everett said softly. "And you don't believe you should charge more because increasing your margins might remind you of the dining room table you wanted."

Her chest constricted. "I never said that."

"But you thought it." Everett increased his pace until they were walking side by side. "It's okay to make a living, a nice living."

Rosalie pressed her lips together.

He touched her arm, stopping her because the contact was so unexpected. "Let me assure you, you'll never get rich running that store. But someday, you might be able to buy a nice dining room set. And when that day comes, you should feel pride, not guilt. And when you use it, it should make you happy, not sad."

That sentiment seemed as out of reach as his heart.

A gust of wind. A patch of ice. They were swept

against a six-foot-tall cinder block wall, thick and impene-trable, like the imaginary wall made of the differences between them.

"You and your husband were public servants—a cop and an emergency dispatcher." Everett's voice was soft, gentle, understanding. "You've spent your adult life serv-ing others. Maybe it's time to devote a little more time and energy to yourself."

He was giving her permission to put herself first. No one had ever done that, not even Marty.

"I'm not sure..." She hesitated. "I don't think..."

"Rosalie." Everett touched her hand where her mitten had a hole. "Your dog's sweater is new but you won't even buy a new pair of gloves." He was right.

"I don't live to the excess. I don't have a closet full of clothes. My gloves..." She stared at his hand holding hers. And still, she rebelled against the idea of putting herself first. "My gloves are fine. I'll make do."

The wind gusted again, tugging at her knit cap and her resolve to keep her heart on her side of the imag-inary wall.

Everett tucked a shivering Tinkerbell inside his red coat. And then he moved closer, sheltering Rosalie from the mountain gusts. "I understand. Growing up, we made do too. Until the year my dad bought all of life's luxuries— a new car, a big TV, name-brand tennis shoes. And then he left us to pay the bills. After that, Mom was always working. Working at a call center during the day. Scrub-bing corporate toilets at night. And still, we had next to nothing." His expression was grim. Not uncaring, just grim. "Nothing in savings either. Which was bad, because when Mom was out of work for three months because of a car accident..." His grim look turned into a grimace.

"Living paycheck to paycheck...People like you and me know how dangerous that can be."

"I'll be fine. I've got family to fall back on. And besides, there's a need for my store in Sunshine." Rosalie trembled, hoping she wasn't being overly optimistic. "And I want to provide a service that spreads love and happiness in a small way. Your situation, your job, is completely different from mine."

"Is it? Two years ago, I was doing well. After Lydia was arrested and the government took everything for reparations, no one would hire me." He swallowed, inching closer, seemingly without knowing it. He stared deep into her eyes with a gaze that was warm, not icy. "All my adult life, I had six months' salary in savings, but they took that too and left me with nothing." And then he added, almost under his breath, "Just like when I was a kid."

His comments gave meaning to his career, a reason he chose to be Scrooge.

"You should know," he said, "this job...Sunshine...It's just a stepping-stone."

"You want your life back." She'd bet that included fancy cars and leather furniture. A life of excess she didn't believe in and wouldn't aspire to.

"You don't approve." He was very close to her now. Close enough to kiss.

But emotionally, they were worlds apart.

"I don't..." Rosalie stared deep into his gray eyes, wondering why she was attracted to this man, wondering if it was their differences that intrigued her. "I'm not interested in making an impression or earning enough to buy creature comforts. And..." She swallowed as a car drove past. "It doesn't matter to me if you're the city manager of Sunshine or of Denver. It doesn't matter to me if you live on the north side or the south side of town. What matters to me is who you are inside and how you treat others."

The imaginary wall between them had come down.

"We weren't talking about..." He drew back by degrees. "We were discussing your business."

"Were we?" Rosalie's cheeks burned with embarrassment but she wasn't going to back down. They'd been discussing their philosophies toward life. They'd found similarities that bridged their differences. They'd made a connection. She knew it.

Beside her, Remy grumbled in apparent agreement.

"I want nothing more than to kiss you right now." Everett's voice was as gruff as Remy's grumble. "But we want different things in life."

"Yes. Although I can't help but believe that common ground motivates us to do what we do. Which makes us not so different after all." To prove her point, she reached for the placket of his jacket and held on. "After all, you're a public servant. That must mean that, deep down, you care about people the same way that I do."

And then Rosalie did something completely out of character. She stretched up on her toes and kissed him.

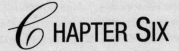

CHAPTER SIX

*T*he weather outside was frightful.

Rosalie offered warmth, the same way she always did—with unexpected determination.

Yes, Everett had wanted to kiss her. Yes, he knew kissing her wasn't good for his career goals. He was supposed to be the impartial man in town, the executor of hard choices to avoid municipal bankruptcy. He wasn't supposed to feel. And because of Lydia, he'd spent the last eighteen months in an emotionless limbo.

But Rosalie's kiss...It made him feel again. A heart-pounding, breath-stealing feeling that he should drop everything and pay attention to the woman nestled in the crook of his arm.

She ended the kiss on a sigh.

"Rosalie." Her name on his lips was little more than a sigh itself.

She blinked, flinched, and drew the Saint Bernard between them. "You don't approve. Well...I started that," she admitted baldly. "It's all on me." She picked her way carefully along the icy, snowy sidewalk and away from him. "No harm, no foul, no commitments. Don't think you have to ask me to dinner or send me flowers."

Despite common sense telling him to turn the other way, Everett followed her. It was dark, after all, and cold. And she seemed more shaken by their kiss than he'd been.

"I may have stopped traffic in my youth but I don't make a habit of leaping out and kissing random dudes." Her laugh sounded forced.

"I'm not a *random dude*." His comment appeared to go unnoticed.

Inside his jacket, Tink squirmed. He drew his zipper down enough that she could poke her head out.

"Jeez. I'm thirty-four. And a widow." Rosalie laced each word with frustration. "Not the kind of woman to go attacking a man on the street."

"Again, not a random dude on the street, and you didn't attack me." Although it was nice that she'd taken the initiative. And since she wasn't looking at him, he allowed himself a smile.

"If Kimmy ever finds out about this, I'll never hear the end of it. She'll be like, *Rosalie, you always reach out and take what you want*. She'll say that whether I'm reaching for a dinner roll or reaching for you." Rosalie gasped. "Never fear. I'm not going to be reaching for you again."

Everett choked out a laugh.

Rosalie drew up short, turning. "What's so funny?"

He was very careful not to smile. "The fact that it was one kiss and you're having a meltdown. It was a kiss, not a marriage proposal."

She made a frustrated sound and turned down a street. "Are you walking me home?"

"I…" Was he? Everett glanced around. "Do you live on this street?"

"Yes. Don't expect a good-night kiss." For being such a short person, she had a brisk, long stride. "I don't do repeat performances, not when I bombed the first time."

"You didn't bomb."

"Right." She turned up a driveway.

The small bungalow had Christmas lights strung from the eaves and a large wreath hanging from the door. Blanketed in snow, there was a charm to it. But there was something about the house that reminded him of his childhood, of upkeep put off and occupants hopeful that ends would meet.

The front door opened. "Rosalie, dinner is ready. Why do you take that dog for such long walks? We're waiting on you." The woman silhouetted in the doorway gasped. "There's a man behind you."

"I know, Mom. He's—"

"You didn't tell me you were bringing a man home. I'll set another plate." Rosalie's mother turned away from them. "Honey, we have company."

"Mom…" Rosalie's shoulders drooped. She didn't turn. "You do not have to come in."

If he'd been asked to a family dinner in the moments before they'd kissed, he'd have refused. But Rosalie's kiss had breached the security system around his hardened heart. It felt good to laugh, to smile, to enjoy being in a woman's company.

He had tomorrow to regroup and return to the status quo—Scrooge. For tonight, he'd act like a man who'd never been played the fool, one who took everyone at face value.

Everett grinned as he took Rosalie's arm. "I'd love to come to dinner."

* * *

"You didn't tell me you were dating Scrooge," Kimmy whispered to Rosalie in the kitchen.

Everett was sitting in the living room next to the Christmas tree with Tinkerbell in his arms and Rosalie's father grilling him as if he were a murder suspect.

"I'm not dating him," Rosalie insisted for what felt like the hundredth time.

I'm just kissing him.

It had been a great kiss too. If only she could keep the memory of that kiss and dump everything that came afterward... except maybe Everett's grin as they'd walked in the door. It was the first time she'd seen a genuine smile on his face. It had transformed him into the man she'd expected him to be when she'd first laid eyes on him.

Aunt Yolanda came into the kitchen. She'd moved into Rosalie's old room last spring after her divorce and planned to stay until she'd regained her financial footing. "What is Scrooge doing in our house?"

"Rosalie's dating him," Kimmy blurted gleefully.

Rosalie hurried to assure Aunt Yolanda this wasn't true.

"You couldn't have warned me?" Mom raced around the kitchen, stirring meat in the frying pan in between filling bowls with condiments. "Why you chose to bring him to the house on Spam taco night..."

"You think he won't like Spam tacos?" Kimmy grinned as she reached for the cluster of garlic on the counter. "I'll add garlic. Garlic makes anything taste better."

"Touch that garlic and you'll be helping me scrub toilets at Prestige Salon." Their mother gave Kimmy the evil eye. She ran her own cleaning service, and when the girls were younger, that particular threat had worked wonders. "These are sriracha tacos. Add more garlic and it'll unbalance the chili."

Kimmy's hand hovered over the garlic just the same.

Rosalie pulled her sister out of garlic range. "We should all just calm down because I'm not dating anyone."

From the dog bed in the corner of the kitchen, Remy grumbled, as if refuting her statement.

"Good." Aunt Yolanda nodded. "Do you know he double-checked my cash box today? I've worked there for over twenty-five years and he doesn't trust me?"

Rosalie decided not to point out Everett's history. With a past like that and a job like his, he wasn't going to trust easily.

"Has anyone seen my phone? I'm expecting a call." In crisis mode over an unexpected guest, Mom flitted about the kitchen, ignoring her sister's complaints. "I don't even have dessert. What will his mother think of me? Spam tacos. No dessert."

"She'd love you," Rosalie reassured her mother, giving her a hug before releasing Mom to swoop around the kitchen some more. "But we're not dating so it's highly unlikely that you'll ever meet her."

"Thank heavens." Aunt Yolanda blew out a breath. "I'd have to rethink my investment in your store, Rosalie. Cash out or something."

Everyone in the kitchen froze.

Rosalie's stomach tumbled to Tinkerbell height. Was this how it was going to be from now on? Her aunt holding her investment over her head?

"Just kidding," Aunt Yolanda mumbled.

"Don't joke about that." Mom darted out of the kitchen on a quest for her phone. "We all pull together in this family."

As if proving Mom's point, Aunt Yolanda followed her out. "Where did you see your phone last?"

Kimmy nudged Rosalie with her hip and whispered, "Everett's staring at you like he's planning his good-night kiss strategy."

Rosalie refused to look. "Stop it." It was bad enough that she'd kissed him but now Kimmy had romance between her teeth and wouldn't let go.

"Let me tell you, Sis." Kimmy's voice dropped even lower, until Rosalie had to strain to hear. "He's thinking hot thoughts right now, despite the fact that Dad is practically asking him for his social security number and date of birth."

"Stop it." Rosalie snatched up a dish towel and swung it in a circle above her head.

"Hot thoughts," Kimmy teased, scooting out of reach.

"Can we eat?" Rosalie demanded. "I need to iron out the details of my Santa Experience after dinner."

"Sit," Mom commanded, charging back into the room, cell phone in hand, Aunt Yolanda still trailing behind her. "Everybody come. Sit. Everett, you take the chair next to Rosalie."

"What is a Santa Experience?" Kimmy asked Rosalie.

"You have experience with Santa, Rosalie?" Everett grinned, carrying Tinkerbell as he approached their kitchen table, which had seen better days. He stared at the scarred surface, and then his gaze sought Rosalie's as if to say, *Do you want to replace this table too?*

Guilty.

But she wouldn't. It was still a sturdy table. Rosalie shook her head slightly and then spoke in a brisk tone. "I'm scheduling an event where people bring their pets for a photo with Santa. I'm calling it the Santa Experience."

Everett sat. Tinkerbell jumped out of his lap and snuggled next to Remington, causing Everett's jaw to drop.

"Pet photos with Santa." Her father passed Everett the warm tortillas. "Our Rosalie is so creative."

"I'm creative." Kimmy frowned. "Everyone raves about my gourmet sandwiches at Emory's Grocery."

Her mother passed Everett the platter of sliced, fried meat. "I hope you like Spam and sriracha sauce. I can always make you something else if you don't." Knowing Mom, if he didn't, she'd race to Emory's Grocery and pick up the ingredients for enchiladas, making Dad promise to keep Everett here until he'd been properly fed.

"I haven't had Spam since college." Everett placed long slices on his tortilla. "I can't remember why I stopped eating it. It's so good."

Rosalie couldn't tell if Everett was joking or not but she appreciated the effort to make her mother feel at ease.

Aunt Yolanda, on the other hand, appreciated nothing about his presence.

"Everett, you're so nice." Mom sprinkled shredded cheese on her tortilla, visibly beginning to relax. "It's hard to believe..."

Everyone at the table stilled. A smile grew on Aunt Yolanda's face but she was the only one smiling. Rosalie's parents exchanged horrified glances. Mom had just brought up the elephant in the room.

"You find it hard to believe that people call me Scrooge?" Everett doused his taco in sriracha sauce. "Honestly? That's my job description—to save Sunshine's pennies." His tone implied he was fine with the nickname but a muscle in his cheek ticked.

Without thinking, Rosalie patted Everett's knee.

Without thinking...she snatched her hand back.

She couldn't afford not to think. That was how she'd ended up kissing him in the first place.

CHAPTER SEVEN

"That's it. I'm done." Yolanda blew into the town hall the next afternoon on a flurry of snow.

Everett got up from his desk and went to lean against the doorframe. "You're quitting?"

If he sounded hopeful, Yolanda didn't seem to pick up on it.

"No. I need a new car." She unwound her purple knit scarf from her neck like a spool of twine attached to a rapidly rising kite. "Kevin forgot his speech, and I drove it over to the retirement home. And then my car wouldn't start. Not so much as a *click-click*."

"Dead battery?" Everett asked.

"Dead car." Yolanda threw her scarf at her feet and stared at it in defeat. "Darnell Tucker says he thinks my block is frozen, maybe cracked." She wrapped her arms across her chest in a self-hug. "I invested what little savings I had into Rosalie's store to protect it from my greedy ex." She paused, possibly realizing Everett understood about greedy ex-spouses. "How am I going to pay for a new car?" She lifted her lost gaze to Everett's. "If I ask Rosalie for my money back, she might go under."

It was all Everett could do not to squirm. As part of his cost-cutting plan, he'd been filling out Yolanda's termination paperwork.

He attempted a smile. "I've found Sunshine to be a very walkable city."

"You drive your car to work every day." She sank into her chair and put her head in her hands. "And your apartment is only three blocks down. I really need you to be a compassionate coworker right now, not Scrooge."

Everett hesitated, and then he came to stand by Yolanda's side and gave her shoulder a sympathetic squeeze. "Everything happens for a reason." That was what his mother said every time something bad happened. She'd told him that when he was a kid and they'd been evicted. She'd told him that when Lydia pled guilty. It was a hollow line, something you said when you didn't know what else to say.

"If you're thinking of telling me what doesn't kill me makes me stronger..." Yolanda sniffed, grabbing two tissues from the box on her desk. "I'm not strong enough to hear that yet." Her shoulders shook.

Everett stared at the ceiling, trying to be both supportive and cognizant of a coworker's personal space. "Why don't you take the rest of the day?"

"I can't." Yolanda wiped at her eyes, not that her action stopped the flow of tears. "The tree-lighting ceremony is at six."

"I insist." As a compassionate coworker. "As your boss."

"It's three thirty." She blew her nose. "I can make it."

All that emotion. All her protests. Yolanda claimed she

didn't want Scrooge but talking to a caring coworker was sending her into a downward spiral.

"Go home, Yolanda," Everett said in what he was coming to believe was his Scrooge voice—low, gruff, firm. "You can make up your hour tomorrow." Everett stepped back and braced himself for her reaction.

Yolanda's shoulders stopped shaking. Head bowed, she scrubbed her face with a tissue and then blew her nose like a trumpet sounding a charge. Her head came up, revealing eyes sparking for a fight. "You'd send me home on one of the most important nights of the year for us? As if I had nothing to do with the coordination of this event?" Yolanda snatched up her purple scarf and wrapped it around her neck. "What? You think I'll trust you to ring the bell for Haywood?" She laughed, a short bark of sound that echoed through town hall. "Not on your life."

"Okay." Everett nodded, weathering her storm. "Why don't you go outside and make sure everything is going according to *your* plan."

"I will." Yolanda pushed past him, past the nearly empty tin of candy canes, past the full toy drive box. She blew out the door, slamming it behind her. She marched across the snow-spackled road and into the town square without looking back.

That's the way she'll walk out when I lay her off.

Everett's stomach turned. He hadn't realized Yolanda's future was tied up with Rosalie's.

I can't let that influence my decisions.

He glanced toward his desk and the termination paperwork, which sat next to the pet bed, where Tink was curled up, watching him.

The front door banged open, and Bitsy scrambled inside,

clinging to a door carried back by the wind. Everett hurried over to help her shut it.

"You're here!" Bitsy clutched his arm. "I need you to come with me right away."

"Why? Is there an emergency?" Everett glanced across the road, gaze searching for prone bodies. "Is anyone hurt?"

"No one's hurt but it's an emergency." Bitsy grabbed his jacket off the rack and thrust it toward his chest. "Grab Tinkerbell and let's go."

Everett didn't budge. "I can't just leave. I'm the only one here. What if someone needs something for the tree-lighting ceremony?" Unless there was arterial blood spurting, there was nothing the older woman could say to get him out of the office right now.

"If anything happens, they'll call Yolanda the same way they always do." Bitsy gave him an impatient look. "Everett Bollinger. Move it. Rosalie needs you."

There was a line out the door of Sunshine Pets.

A line of customers with pets on leashes, in crates, and in boxes, waiting to come inside.

Rosalie should have been ecstatic. The Santa Experience had struck a chord with Sunshine pet owners.

Just her luck. Santa had called in sick.

She'd enlisted the help of Paul Gregory to play Santa. She'd rented a Santa suit, including a lovely white beard, chest padding, and shiny black boots. And then twenty minutes ago, Paul had called to cancel from the emergency room. His service truck had slid into a ditch and he'd hit his head. He was fine but was being kept at the hospital on concussion watch.

The best-laid plans…

She had fifteen minutes to find Santa.

"I found him," Bitsy said breathlessly as she burst into the shop, dragging Everett behind her. "I found Santa."

"Whoa." Everett dug in his heels, despite little Tinkerbell prancing forward toward Remington. "I thought you said it was an emergency, Bitsy." He gave Rosalie a full-body visual inspection. "You look okay. Are you okay?"

"It is an emergency." Bitsy tried to tug Everett farther inside.

"A serious emergency." Rosalie rushed over to hug Everett, relaxing into the circle of his arms. "Paul canceled. Everyone in my family is at work. I need a Santa Claus."

"I'm Scrooge," Everett said gruffly.

"Not always." Rosalie drew back to look him in the eye, to smile as tenderly as that kiss they'd exchanged. "And not today."

He pressed his lips together.

Unwilling to give up, Rosalie turned him toward the windows. "Do you see that line? That's my line. My new customers. People who love their pets enough to brave the weather for a photo of their fur baby with Santa. And I achieved that line playing by your rules, Everett. Please. Say you'll be my Santa."

He heaved a sigh.

Taking that as assent, Rosalie half led, half dragged him to the back room and the Santa costume, pausing only to hand Tinkerbell's leash to Bitsy. "I know what you're thinking," she said as Everett fingered the full white beard.

"You have no idea," he murmured, staring at the costume.

"You're thinking this is a new low." She rubbed his back, which was broad and strong enough to carry the burdens of others. "You're thinking Scrooge is playing against type."

His gaze swung to hers, eyes narrowed.

Santa Claus isn't coming to town.

"But you're not Scrooge," Rosalie said a bit desperately, pointing at the Santa costume with both hands as if that proved her point. And maybe it did. Scrooge would never don Santa's suit. "What you're not seeing is what a great opportunity this is to prove it."

"You're right about the not-seeing-it part," Everett said.

The clock was ticking. Rosalie needed Everett to move, not hesitate.

"This is just like when you charmed my mother last night." Rosalie laid a hand on his arm. She liked touching him. And the good news was that he hadn't walked out. "If you want to be understood, you need to show your true colors."

"Only I'll be wearing a fake beard." And a scowl, if his gruff tone was any indication.

"And a bowlful of jelly." Rosalie held up the chest padding and smiled as brightly as she could.

Ar-ar-ar-ooo. From the store proper, Remington sounded like he was nervous.

Tinkerbell barked once.

"Um, Rosalie?" Bitsy called through the closed door.

"*Please.*" Rosalie put all her desperation into that one word. It was either beg or begin to practice her cancellation speech.

Everett sighed. "Okay."

"Really?" She drew back, countering the urge to throw her arms around him. "Can I use your photos on my website?"

"Don't push it, Rosalie." Everett faced her squarely but his gaze landed on her lips. "Out."

She ran out before she succumbed to the impulse to kiss him.

* * *

"This was such a fun event." Wendy Adams, the elementary school secretary, had her tortoise in a box on the sales counter. She paid for her purchase, a T-shirt decorated with sea creatures that read, *Skip the straw and save the ocean.*

"Your photo will be ready for pickup tomorrow." Rosalie was sending all photographs to be printed at the pharmacy. She'd probably lie awake tonight wondering if all the files would go through. Next year, she needed to print everything in-store.

Wendy stuck her T-shirt in her hobo bag and pulled her knit cap down on her blond hair. "How in the world did you get Scrooge to play Santa?" She sneaked Everett a look over her shoulder.

"Everett is a charming gentleman," Bitsy said. She'd been a godsend, helping customers find items for their pets while Rosalie worked the register. "Just look at him with little Vivvy."

A blond toddler sat in Everett's lap, cradling a big white bunny. Mims Turner had brought the little cherub in with her rabbit and hovered nearby, grinning.

Rosalie experienced an unexpected wave of pride for Everett. "He makes a perfect Santa." She couldn't stop smiling. Not even when she caught Everett's eye. Her heart was full.

With Everett around, she wasn't alone. He had her back. He may claim to be a number-crunching, detached machine, but she knew that wasn't true. Everett had a heart. He just hadn't been given an opportunity in Sunshine to let others see what Rosalie saw. Until today.

"A man like that..." Bitsy came to stand next to Rosalie. "They don't come along often. A man like that fills the lonely corners of a widow's heart."

Rosalie murmured her agreement, ringing up another customer.

A man like Everett had a heart big enough to accept a cast-off, high-strung dog. He had the strength to talk to Rosalie about sensitive topics, like her dead husband. And for as much as folks complained that he was by the book, no one ever said he did anything shady or underhanded. He must have been crushed when his wife's crime was discovered. Everett was honorable. A great addition to the community.

A wonderful addition to my life.

Love—or its early warning system—pulsed in ever-tightening bands around her chest. Love wasn't supposed to feel constrictive and tense. Love for Marty had been a lighthearted, soaring feeling.

Rosalie glanced at Everett once more. He was leaning forward to mug for the camera next to a chocolate Labrador's happy face.

He'd said he wasn't staying in Sunshine. He'd said that once the budget issues were resolved he'd move on. He had bigger dreams than she did, bigger desires when it came to material possessions. Was that the source of her tension?

Rosalie stared across the store. Everett sat alone.

It seemed like, almost in the blink of an eye, everyone had left to go to the tree-lighting ceremony. The store was nearly empty. No one else was in line. Everett disappeared into the stock room, presumably to change.

"He's really nice," Bitsy emphasized again. "One of a kind."

"Has my mother been talking to you?" Rosalie shook her head. Love continued to hug her chest as if afraid to let go. She drew a deep breath.

Don't let me fall for a man who isn't planning to stay in Sunshine.

Bitsy studied her closely. "I've been married and widowed three times. I think it's okay to open up your heart to ideas and possibilities. And love."

"You've definitely been talking to my mother." Rosalie rang up the last of her customers.

Tinkerbell trotted over to the supply room door. Remy joined her. They both sat down, waiting. Bitsy rearranged the remaining ornaments on the Christmas tree while Rosalie straightened up endcaps and displays.

A short time later, Everett appeared, his hair askew. He picked up Tinkerbell and snapped on her leash. "Ladies, we need to hurry, or we're going to miss the tree-lighting ceremony."

"Oh, I almost forgot." Bitsy bundled up and gathered her things. "I've got hot chocolate to sell."

Rosalie couldn't move, not even to hand Everett his dog's booties.

"Aren't you coming?" Bitsy turned, pausing at the door.

"We'll be along," Everett told her, a smile building on his handsome face as he looked at Rosalie.

A smile.

The man had been barked at, shed over, and drooled upon. He wasn't Scrooge. He was Santa on vacation—good-natured and joyful. She'd bet he was determined to hide his softer side. But she'd seen it more than once. And now it was on full display.

The tension around Rosalie's chest dissipated into a flurry of heartbeats.

Everett walked toward her, Tinkerbell in his arms. Remy fell into step beside him.

Two sweet dogs and one lovable man.

We could be a family.

Over the store's speakers, the least romantic carol played: "I Want a Hippopotamus for Christmas."

Rosalie didn't care that there weren't flowers, love songs, or candlelight. Nothing could ruin this moment. She was in love, and the world was full of laughter and sunshine. Finally, finally, finally. The something she was missing was here. The world seemed brighter and in sharper focus.

Everett set Tinkerbell down when he was a few feet away from Rosalie. "Your customers were happy?"

"Yes," she breathed, unable to move when more than anything she wanted to step forward and be loved by him.

Everett came and put his arms around her. "And were you happy?" A question spoken in a low, intimate voice.

"Not as happy as I am now," Rosalie said as his lips lowered to hers and she opened her heart to possibilities.

They didn't make the tree-lighting ceremony on time.

They didn't care.

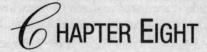

CHAPTER EIGHT

Are those the numbers?" Kevin shut his laptop and sat up in his chair.

Despite it being late and no one else being in the office, Everett closed the door behind him. "Yes." He handed Kevin the budget.

Just a few hours ago, the tree-lighting ceremony had been a success—not that there'd been any doubt. The only thing different this year was the bell-ringing by Yolanda after Haywood's proposal.

When the bell had rung, Rosalie had flung her arms around Everett and kissed him. He'd almost walked over and given Haywood fifty dollars. Because in that moment in her arms, he'd forgotten responsibilities and hard choices ahead. There had only been Rosalie and her outpouring of affection.

Kevin stared at Everett, not at the pages. "How'd we do?"

"It's not enough." Everett had run the numbers backward and forward. He'd reduced seasonal employment and scaled down next year's tree-lighting ceremony. "You know what we need to do."

Kevin's expression hardened. "My father never laid anyone off."

"No offense, but..." Everett leaned forward, hoping his words would sink in. "Your father is the main reason the town is in this mess." Him and that warehouse.

"It was a gamble," Kevin said defensively. "A risk taken in good faith." In his eyes, his father could do no wrong.

Will he feel the same way when I lay off Yolanda?

Will Rosalie?

Everett's stomach clenched. "We could still land some federal money." To refurbish the warehouse. "But only if the budget is balanced by January first." A long shot. "I've pitched the warehouse to development companies across the state." And heard crickets in response. "I've reached out to Greeley." The town closest to them. "If we let go of a fireman, a deputy, and someone at town hall"—they both knew the latter was Yolanda—"they're open to being our backup emergency service." If Sunshine's short-staffed emergency-services crew couldn't handle the workload. "But we'll pay a premium." Still, it'd be less than paying salaries and benefits.

Kevin stared at the proposed budget. "There's got to be another way."

"Besides cutting staff and reducing pensions?" Everett shook his head.

"It's Christmas." Kevin raised his gaze to Everett's, blue eyes haunted. "We can't do this to people at Christmas."

"You could find someone famous to buy the town." And when had that ever worked? Never. "That was a joke." Everett sighed. "It's probably not the right time for jokes."

"No, it's not." Kevin handed the budget back. "I can't

give you the go-ahead right now. I need a few more days."
Kevin was hoping for a Christmas miracle.

Everett was fairly certain that wasn't going to happen. He
let the reality of the situation settle between them. "Look,
Kevin, I know the last thing you want to do is to disappoint
people in this town. But…you hired me to be your gun-
slinger." To take the heat for the tough decisions that needed to
be made. "We have to make more cuts. People who lose their
jobs will rebound. The town will rebound. By the time the next
election rolls around, no one will remember the layoffs."

But Everett wouldn't be around to see it.

No. He'd be working in another town, one with bigger
problems and a bigger salary for its town manager. Someplace where he wouldn't walk his dog next to a pretty
woman. Someplace where he wouldn't be called Scrooge
and think of it as an endearment.

The week after the tree-lighting ceremony was a blur for
Rosalie.

There were walks with Everett before and after work.
Softly exchanged words and long, slow kisses. Rosalie invited
him to her house for dinner. He politely declined, claiming he
had a lot of work to do. She invited him for breakfast at the
bakery. He politely declined, same reason. She invited him to
join her on the dog walk through Sunshine's Christmas Tree
Lane. He hedged. Rosalie refused to be discouraged. It was a
busy time for him. Love could be patient and so could Rosalie.

"Where's Everett?" Kimmy didn't have a dog but she'd
agreed to lead the pack for the evening dog walk with Remy.

"He said he probably wouldn't make it." If not for their
twice daily walks, Rosalie would've thought Everett was
giving her the brush-off.

She couldn't worry about Everett. There were at least

thirty pet owners milling about on Garden Court. It was seven o'clock. Time to organize the group into a line to walk the neighborhood and admire the Christmas displays.

"Okay, everyone stay on the sidewalk and follow the Saint Bernard," Rosalie said when she had some semblance of a line formed.

Yap-yap-yap.

Everyone turned.

"It's Santa!" someone said, inspiring holiday greetings from others for Everett.

He waved, moving to join Rosalie at the end of the line with a small smile.

Rosalie gave Kimmy permission to start before turning to Everett. "Thank you for coming."

There was a furrow in his brow as if he'd had a rough day at work. "Tink needed a walk."

"And you did too, I bet." She linked her arm through his.

Everett slanted her a glance, expression lightening. "And I wanted to see you."

Her heart soared. This is what she'd been waiting for, a sign that she meant something to him. "Most people are here to take in the holiday lights with their fur babies."

"Merry Christmas and all that," Everett said flatly, the crease returning to his brow.

"Merry Christmas and all that," Rosalie repeated. Whatever problem he was facing, she knew he'd find a way to work things through to everyone's satisfaction. Rosalie stretched on her toes to kiss his cheek.

"What was that for?" Everett slowed as they approached the rest of the crowd, who'd bottlenecked to admire a yard with a *Star Wars*–themed holiday display.

"A kiss for luck." Rosalie snuggled closer. "You'll make the right choice. You always do."

He frowned. "The town council approved the parade ending on Sunny Avenue."

"Really? That's wonderful." And just in the nick of time. The parade was in a few days.

Everett walked in silence, accompanied by his frown and his furrow.

"Is there a problem?" Rosalie asked, unable to shake the belief that they'd be closer if Everett would just open up to her about his concerns and his feelings.

"No. I'm just trying to figure out some work stuff." Everett patted her hand, finding the hole in her mitten.

That simple touch. It reassured. There was more here than heated kisses.

But nothing she said for the rest of the walk seemed to change his mood.

The day of the Christmas parade dawned sunny and bright.

Rosalie's holiday inventory was running low. And like any good retailer, she'd restocked with merchandise for the next holiday—Valentine's Day.

Aunt Yolanda had come by, making noises about needing an early dividend to make car repairs but backing off when Rosalie asked her how much she needed. She'd given Rosalie's new merchandise a frown.

Kimmy showed up to help Rosalie, in case there was a rush after the parade. She'd brought her three-legged kitten, Skippy, and immediately purchased a collar decorated with Valentine hearts and a set of Christmas-themed cat toys.

The Widows Club board entered the store with Mims's adorable granddaughter, Vivvy. Bitsy waved, and then the group drifted over to the live pet display, which Eileen had restocked with roly-poly puppies and a pair of brown furry guinea pigs. Vivvy and Mims were singing "Must

Be Santa," flinging lines at each other as if they were in a rap battle.

"I think you and Everett make a cute couple." Kimmy sat on a stool behind the register with Skippy in her lap.

"Are you still blue about Haywood?" It seemed better to change the subject to a man her sister had always been sweet on than to talk about Everett and a future together. He'd kept Rosalie at arm's length all week long.

"Haywood was my childhood crush." Kimmy cuddled Skippy. "And Ariana was his."

"But you dated him—"

"One time," Kimmy said briskly. "Don't make it more than it is. They're engaged. Now about Everett..."

"Don't make it more than it is." Rosalie's heart panged. Nothing seemed right between them, not even their walks.

People were congregating on the sidewalks of Sunny Avenue. The high school band was scheduled to bring up the rear of the parade and perform one last song in front of Rosalie's shop. It was perfect for business but Rosalie couldn't enjoy it.

"I asked Haywood to look for a space for me to open my own sandwich shop." Kimmy stared out the window, gnawing on her lip. "I figured if you could open a store, then I could go out on my own too."

"Oh, Kimmy." Rosalie hugged her sister. "What a fabulous idea."

"You don't think I'll fail?" Kimmy's normal smile was conspicuously absent.

Rosalie was quick to encourage her sister. "I think your gourmet sandwiches are going to be the talk of the town."

"Look, Gammy!" Vivvy pointed out the window. "It's my parade."

"Life is too short." Rosalie hugged Kimmy again. "Don't let the parade pass you by."

CHAPTER NINE

$\mathscr{T}$he Christmas parade was a huge success.

Rerouting the gala to end on Sunny Avenue reduced the amount of congestion on the streets and sidewalks.

Afterward, Everett requested a group of people meet at the town hall. He couldn't put off what had to be done any longer and neither could Kevin.

Sheriff Drew Taylor arrived first. Shortly afterward, the fire chief showed up. And finally, Kevin and Yolanda joined them in the conference room.

Everett left the front office open since many residents had told him they'd be dropping off toys for the toy drive. He took a seat against the wall, intending to let Kevin deliver the bad news.

"First off..." Kevin looked about as comfortable as a chicken trapped in a coop with a fox. "Thank you all for coming. We wanted to use this time to brief you on our progress in balancing the budget in time for federal funding consideration."

Everyone nodded. They all knew about the budget crisis.

"We've come to a point where some hard decisions have to be made." Kevin met the gaze of each person in the room. His smile was the perfect balance of compassion and regret. "We're going to have to cut the budgets for emergency services and—"

"Hang on." Sheriff Taylor's back stiffened. "You want to cut public safety?"

Kevin's expression didn't change. "Yes, and—"

"Is that wise?" the fire chief asked, just as angry as the sheriff. "Shouldn't you be cutting nonessential services?"

Kevin nodded mutely. His gaze came to rest on Yolanda, and he paled.

Silence stretched through the room. Kevin let it linger too long.

Everett stood. "What the mayor is trying to say is that if a miracle doesn't occur by December thirty-first, we will have to lay off someone from the sheriff's office, someone from fire services, and someone from nonessential services here at the town hall."

"You mean me?" Yolanda said in a small voice. She stared at Everett, not Kevin.

"We mean you," Everett said in an equally small voice. "I'm sorry." Despite his best intentions, he'd grown fond of the prickly woman.

Something fell to the floor in the lobby.

Everett stepped out of the conference room, leaving further questions to the mayor.

"I...oh..." Standing next to the Christmas tree, Rosalie picked up the set of toy dishes she'd dropped. "I'm sorry. I didn't mean to eavesdrop." She stared at the dishes and then set them near the overflowing toy drive box.

He'd just let her aunt, her investor, know she might lose

her job. She couldn't brush this off the way she brushed off everything else he'd done in town.

Everett moved closer, waiting to hear Rosalie's opinion of him, prepared for the worst.

"So this is what you've been working on?" She stared at the floor. "What you've been stressing over? A plan to fire people?"

"We've been trying *not* to fire people."

It was as if she didn't hear him. "This kind of thing doesn't happen in Sunshine. We hire our friends and neighbors. We don't let them go, especially not at Christmas." Finally, her gaze came up to meet his. "Your job is done. You're leaving. You came here to do this horrible thing, and now . . . and now it's over and you're leaving."

"Yes." He could stay another six months per his contract. But if Rosalie stopped talking to him, stopped looking at him like he hung the moon, and stopped kissing him . . . he'd just as soon leave.

"But you and I . . ." She gestured back and forth between them. "I've been defending you and your reputation. And all this time . . ." The blood had drained from her face. "You really are Scrooge."

She whirled and rushed out the door.

"Rosalie, wait." Everett grabbed his coat and followed her, leaving Tinkerbell behind.

Rosalie didn't wait. She walked away with a gait just short of a run. "If my aunt can't find a job, I'll have to cash her out. This changes everything. And you knew. You knew it was coming at me head on."

"I couldn't tell you." He reached her side, dodging holiday shoppers.

"I ordered specialty products through Easter." She pulled

her knit cap around her ears as if she didn't want to hear him. "And I'm a horrible person for thinking about myself when my aunt just lost her job."

"Technically, we have ten days to save her job." Snow and salt crunched beneath his feet as they crossed a street.

"I wish...I wish...I wish I could find the words to express how disappointed I am." Her big brown eyes were shadowed with sadness.

"If I've given you the wrong impression..." Everett couldn't finish that thought. He'd given himself the wrong impression. It was time to come clean. "I'm forty. I'm re-building my career. I don't know where I'll be next year."

From down the street, Bitsy wished them a Merry Christmas.

Rosalie returned the greeting. And then she rounded the corner and shifted back into quick-step mode. They had reached the end of the block before she spoke again.

"You never say it to anyone." Rosalie turned and stayed him with a gloved hand on his chest. Her pink skin was apparent through the ever-widening hole in her red mitten. "You never tell people Merry Christmas."

"I'm not feeling very merry," he said in a gruff voice. Truthfully, he hadn't in years. He resisted the urge to draw her into his arms and forget about budgets and layoffs, knowing his touch would be unwelcome.

"Did you ever say Happy Thanksgiving?" Rosalie's hand moved over his heart.

I hope I have a heart when this is over.

"Rosalie..."

"I'm not sure what's been going on between us." She drew back, taking her hand and her warmth with her. "There was...We were..." She raised tear-filled eyes. "I thought I loved you."

Loved. Past tense. If it was…If it had been…His heart seemed to shrivel in his chest.

In the distance, Christmas music played. People's voices and laughter drifted on the air.

"Rosalie…" Everett couldn't seem to string a sentence together. He didn't know how to react. What to say. What to wish for.

When he didn't say anything, she resumed walking, crossing her arms over her chest. "I knew we were different in some ways, but I thought you were the kind of person who'd do anything to protect people and their jobs." She choked on what sounded like a sob. "I was wrong. So don't worry about disappointing me by keeping your feelings to yourself. I don't want to hear them."

Feelings? That was the trouble. When Everett was with Rosalie, he felt too much. He felt happy and hopeful. He felt like he belonged in Sunshine and that could never be the case. He was a hatchet man. People who didn't already hate him were going to hate him as soon as word of the layoffs got out.

"It's okay," Rosalie said softly, walking a few steps ahead. "You may not love me but you gave me something I haven't had since Marty died. I can see my future. I couldn't see it before. Things were in the way. Anger. Grief." She waved her hands as if waving them aside. "The future was all so tenuous and uncertain. And then you bought me a cup of hot chocolate."

Now wasn't the time to admit he hadn't been that generous.

"Rosalie." Panic. It trilled through his veins. He didn't want to lose her. "Rosalie, slow down."

"I can't." She marched ahead. "For the first time in a long time, things are turning around for me. And no matter what happens when I go around that corner toward home..." She stopped suddenly, and her voice turned cold as she faced him. "You won't be with me."

"Rosalie."

"Everett!" Down the block, the front door of Rosalie's childhood home swung open, and her mother leaned out. "We're having tamales tonight. Come inside. You look like you haven't had a good meal since Spam tacos."

The wind gusted, and Everett felt as if he might blow away.

"All your plans. All your numbers." Rosalie backed away. "And you didn't plan for me. You didn't see..."

Rosalie was right. He hadn't figured falling in love in his plans.

"And now..." Rosalie swallowed thickly. "All my plans won't include you."

"Everett is such a jerk." Kimmy sat in the corner of the couch in the apartment they shared above their parents' garage. "Firing Aunt Yolanda? She runs that place. I don't know how you could fall for him."

"Hey, don't judge." Rosalie took a love letter from Marty out of a small cedar chest. She'd found the letter in his bureau after he died. "I didn't question why you fell in love with Skippy."

Kimmy dangled a cat toy over the kitten's belly. "Skippy's never going to mastermind dastardly deeds like Everett did in this town."

"You know it's not like that." Rosalie unfolded the worn paper. It was becoming fragile from being read so frequently. "He was hired to do a job."

On the floor next to her, Remy rolled onto his back with a mild grumble.

"Yeah, well, if you'd been working at the town hall, he'd have fired you."

"Yes."

Kimmy stopped playing with her kitten. "And you're okay with that?"

I am so not okay.

"Don't judge my attempt at adulting." Rosalie smoothed the love letter on her leg. "I'm a business owner trying to see what's good for the town. But you know I hate that he gave Aunt Yolanda the ax." She'd told her aunt she was canceling her spring merchandise orders, which would free up cash in case she was let go. "Am I upset with Everett? Yes."

"That's my girl." Kimmy went back to her cat-toy game. Rosalie turned her attention to Marty's letter.

My darling Rosalie,

If you're reading this, I'm gone. And for that alone, I want to apologize. My job requires me to protect and serve. And if you're reading this, I've had a truly bad day, and I ache for putting you through it.

I can imagine you sitting down and reading this. I can hear your voice in my head, telling me I should have been more careful. I can hear your grief and your anger and your words—you've always been good at tossing words. Kind words. Loving words. And yes, angry words.

It's okay. You can be angry with me. If I'm gone, it's because I was doing something I believe in and because bad stuff sometimes happens to good people. Be angry. It will give you a reason to go on until the anger fades.

I know it may take time, but I want you to remember how much I love you. I want you to remember how important we felt it was to live a life looking outward, helping to spread love and kindness in small and big ways. Take time to grieve, love, but then look around and know that it's okay to reimagine your life. Our jobs take a toll. It's okay to move on, to find another way to touch people's hearts. To live again. To love again, even if you have to fight for it. Even if a good man has to fight for you.

Try new things. Live in new places. Cut that hair you love so much. Take a risk. Reach for a new dream. You won't be alone. I will always have your back. When you look up at the stars, know that I'm the brightest one shining back on you.

I won't be home tonight but I can keep this one vow, the promise I made you on our wedding day. I will love you to the end of time.

All my love, Marty.

"You shouldn't read that letter so much." Kimmy handed Rosalie a tissue.

"I'm going to read this letter until it disintegrates in my hands." Rosalie wiped her eyes. "And do you know why? Because it reminds me that I loved a good man. And that when I fall in love again, it should only be with another good man. Someone Marty would approve of."

And that man wasn't Everett Bollinger.

"How'd it go?" Everett stood in the doorway to Kevin's office.

Kevin was slumped in his chair with Tink in his lap,

his gaze attached to a spot on the wall. "About as well as you'd expect. Rationally, they get it. Emotionally, you and I are the Antichrist."

Everett thrust his hands in his jacket pockets and tried not to remember the look on Rosalie's face when she told him they were through.

"We were so close." Kevin blew out a breath. "You brought the debt down from a couple million to a couple hundred thousand."

"I didn't want it to end like this." Not for Yolanda and the others. Not for the town. Not for Rosalie.

"I know."

"You can blame me." That was what he paid Everett for.

"I know." Kevin swung his head around to look at Everett. "But I won't. The buck stops here."

"If only we could have sold that warehouse." If only they'd had more time. "I can't do anything more for you. Consider this my two weeks' notice."

They both fell silent. Tink stared at Everett as if awaiting a command.

Everett rolled his shoulders, trying to ease the ache that extended throughout his chest, knowing that ache originated in his heart. "If I had the money, I'd have bought the warehouse. Rosalie thought it would make a great set of loft apartments over retail and restaurant space, instead of another small mall."

Kevin sat up. "What a brilliant idea."

"Lofts?" Everett blinked at him.

"No. You. Investing." Kevin put Tink on the floor and reached for a pad of paper. "We contacted developers but we didn't think to organize our own group of investors to—"

"Buy and renovate the warehouse into income-generating space." Everett drew a deep breath as the idea took shape. "We could recruit investors, maybe even offer different levels of financial participation."

"People invest in civic works all the time." Kevin scribbled names on his pad. "We'll need a couple of big investors. But we should let folks buy in at affordable amounts."

"They'll feel good about saving the town and their friends' jobs." Everett picked up his dog and held her close. "But we've only got ten days." Less if you counted the holidays.

Kevin raised his head. "Are you the same guy who worked budget miracles in six months? How hard can forming an investment group be?"

"Hard, not impossible. But hard." Everett latched on to his boss's enthusiasm. "We'll need a renovation budget and projected rents."

"Luckily, we're on good terms with a Realtor by the name of Haywood, who probably knows a few good contractors."

Everett grinned.

"Well?" Kevin asked. "What are you waiting for? The clock is ticking."

"Right." Everett hurried downstairs with Tinkerbell.

If he could work some Christmas budget magic, he could save a few jobs. And it was a long shot, but maybe he could stay in Sunshine and salvage things with Rosalie. Permanently.

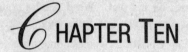

CHAPTER TEN

The emergency meeting of Sunshine's town council was held on the afternoon of Christmas Eve in the high school gym.

They'd needed a venue large enough to fit everyone who wanted to attend. And everyone wanted to attend. Even Rosalie.

Everett had seen her come in with her family. When the meeting started, he sat next to Yolanda in the front row, holding her hand while Kevin explained how important it was to invest in Sunshine and fielded questions. Yolanda had helped pull things together, both for the warehouse and for a special project of Everett's. They were in this together.

Kevin being Kevin, he wore an expensive suit and his professional smile. If he'd chosen to go into car sales instead of politics, he'd probably have owned a chain of dealerships by now. "Before we make contracts available to those interested in investing, I'd like to turn over the floor to our town manager, Everett Bollinger."

The audience booed.

"Pay no attention to the peanut gallery." Yolanda stood with Everett and gave him a hug. "I've spent over half my life working for this town. You, my dear Ebenezer, are one of the good ones. If my job is saved, I have you to thank. May both of our Christmas wishes come true."

"Thanks for helping me prepare for this." Everett kissed her cheek and whispered, "How about I get up on that stage and do something everyone will remember later?"

"Go slay." Yolanda grinned.

Everett climbed the steps to the stage and took the microphone. He straightened his glasses and surveyed the crowd until he found Rosalie sitting between her mother and her sister. They'd come wearing matching scowls.

"Ladies and gentlemen." Everett tugged down the ends of his ugly Christmas sweater. Yolanda had helped him pick it out. It was purple with a Christmas tree strung with flashing lights. "Before we begin, I'd like to wish everyone a very Merry Christmas."

Rosalie's eyes widened, and the crowd quieted.

"When I was hired to help Kevin and his staff get the budget back in line, I'd never heard of Sunshine, Colorado. I came here . . . " He'd toyed with glossing over this part but in for a penny . . . "I came here. Age forty." He ran a hand through his hair. "I earned every one of these gray beauties working in six different cities, doing exactly what you hired me to do here. But all my experience only prepared me for the financial challenges. It didn't prepare me for the challenges of the heart." Everett tapped his chest, sending the star at the top of the tree glittering.

He may have been on stage but he spoke directly to Rosalie. The shadows were back beneath her eyes. He had himself to blame.

"I wasn't prepared for the close-knit community of Sunshine. For the extended families and friends who make up modern-day families." He cleared his throat. He'd considered skipping this next part too. "Most of you know my ex-wife is a convicted felon. Many of you probably know I was the one who uncovered the way she was cooking the books. The day I confronted her...the day I had to turn her in to the police...I thought that was the most heartbreaking day of my life. I loved her. But by abiding by the law, I learned my wife didn't love me as much as she did money. Anyone's money."

The audience shifted, whispering, judging.

Everett didn't care. He still only had eyes for Rosalie. "When I arrived in town, I was still reeling. It was nearly two years later, but I hadn't rediscovered a way to trust my fellow man. So when I showed up in town with my fancy ties and my shiny shoes"—he'd heard people whispering to Yolanda about that—"I didn't care, because I hadn't come here to make friends. Or to find true love."

There was more whispering and perhaps less judging. Nothing pleased a crowd like a teaser. And he'd mentioned the L-word.

"Despite that, a few of you won my respect, like Kevin. And a few of you earned my trust, like Yolanda. And one woman won my jaded, guarded heart." Everett pointed toward that woman. "Rosalie."

The crowd murmur rose to a soft roar. People turned in their seats, looking for the object of his affection.

"She's pretty spectacular," Everett said. "Her store is awesome, and the idea to turn the warehouse into mixed-use space was hers."

This news created a smattering of applause.

"But..." Everett had to raise his voice to be heard, even

with the microphone. "But before our love could even get off the ground, we announced the possibility of layoffs."

And they were back to boos.

"Hang with me on this, folks." Everett caught Rosalie's eye. "Because as much as Rosalie and I are different, as much as we've discussed our careers are on different paths, they're not." He lowered his voice, imagining Rosalie was standing next to him, not sitting half a gymnasium away. "We were both raised to make do but lately that feels more like we're just getting by. Honey, you think I need a big house and a fancy car. I don't. Not as much as I need you. I've put money down on one of the lofts in the warehouse. You think I need the prestige of working for a big city from inside a corporate office? Not as much as I need you, babe. I want to work toward a future with you in Sunshine. And since I've accepted a permanent position as town manager, I'm not going anywhere except on long walks with the woman I love and our two dogs."

Rosalie gave him that warm smile he loved so much. She stood and made her way to the aisle while Everett made his way down the stairs and to her side.

He dropped down on one knee. The crowd was silent now.

"Rosalie." Everett snapped open a blue velvet jewelry box containing a ring Yolanda had helped him pick out. It was big enough to be noticed and small enough to lack ostentation. "I love you. I love the way you saw the good in me and the way you think about the happiness and welfare of others. I love the way you consider pets part of the family. I love that you're brimming with ideas and that you're not shy about telling me what you've come up with. But most of all, I love that you found a place in your heart for me." And by the look of things, despite her words the other night, he still had a place there. "Can you find it in your heart to forgive me?"

"Yes," said her sister, Kimmy, earning a shushing from everyone around them.

Rosalie's warm hands closed around his, closing the ring box. She drew him to his feet. She didn't smile. She didn't speak. She simply stared into his eyes.

Kimmy chuckled.

Nerves had Everett talking. "You know what season it is, don't you, honey?"

"Christmas?" A hint of a smile flashed past her lips before disappearing.

"The season of love and forgiveness." He was in desperate need of both. "I don't want there to be secrets between us. The Widows Club bought you that cup of hot chocolate, not me. But I've regretted not buying it every day since. Can you forgive me? Enough to marry me?"

"Yes," Rosalie said simply, although he'd asked so many questions it wasn't clear what she was agreeing to.

"Yes, you'll marry him?" her father asked before Everett could.

"Or yes, it's the season of love and forgiveness?" her mother asked, hot on her husband's heels.

"She didn't even look at the ring," Kimmy said, laughing. "How can she say yes to anything?"

"I don't need to see the ring." Rosalie hadn't broken Everett's gaze. "Yes. Yes to everything," she said. "As long as my Scrooge says he'll be my Santa too."

"I'll be your anything, love." Everett's arms came around her. His Christmas wish was coming true. "And I'll be your always."

"That's all a girl can ask for." Rosalie kissed him, long and slow.

The meeting went on without them. Two ranchers, Tom Bodine and a man Everett didn't recognize, invested heavily. Enough other residents put up money to make Yolanda's Christmas wish come true.

Later, Kevin announced their financial goals had been met and Sunshine was saved. No layoffs would be made.

All in all, it was a great Christmas. Everett got everything he wanted—love, forgiveness, and a balanced budget.

About the Author

Melinda Curtis is the *USA Today* bestselling author of lighthearted contemporary romance. In addition to her Sunshine Valley series from Forever, she's published independently and with Harlequin Heartwarming, including her book *Dandelion Wishes*, which is currently being made into a TV movie. She lives in California's hot Central Valley with her hot husband—her basketball-playing college sweetheart. While raising three kids, the couple did the soccer thing, the karate thing, the dance thing, the Little League thing, and, of course, the basketball thing. Between books, Melinda spends time with her husband remodeling their home by swinging a hammer, grouting tile, and wielding a paintbrush with other family members.

Learn more at:
  www.melindacurtis.net
  Twitter: @MelCurtisAuthor
  http://facebook.com/MelindaCurtisAuthor